Raine hugged Gavin tightly. "I fear for you. I don't want you hurt. Not anymore. Not by anyone."

Gavin held her, absorbing her compassion for him. Her hope. He needed to give her something in return.

"You waltz, I presume?"

"Not badly. But I've never done it on a beach."

"There must be a first time for everything." He led her toward the shore and took her in his arms. "I used to practice here when I was young. The dancing master forever swore I was born with two left feet. Would you care for a demonstration?" When she agreed, he urged, "Now you are the better singer, so pick a tune, will you?"

"Something Viennese?"

"Is there anything else?"

"I doubt it," she replied and threw back her head to smile at the night sky.

What was a man to do with such an armful of heaven? He knew.

"Kiss me, *cherie,* for inspiration. For courage. And I will kiss you in thanks for all the help you have given me."

THE NIGHTINGALE'S SONG

"Brimming with humor (there is a wonderful scene where the dialogue is all double entendres), passion, brilliant colors, and fascinating history . . . *The Nightingale's Song* is a banquet of medieval tidbits sure to be relished by those who wish to immerse themselves in a rich romance set in this turbulent era. Jo-Ann Power draw[s] readers into a carefully constructed novel that is part mystery, part romance, and all shining brilliance."

—Kathe Robin, *Romantic Times*

"This compassionate page-turner will keep you enchanted right up to the heart-melting conclusion. Jo-Ann Power has gifted us with another winner!"

—*Rendezvous*

"With her marvelous talent, Jo-Ann Power empowers her audience with a sense of seeing firsthand the Middle Ages as few writers are capable of doing. *The Nightingale's Song* is a fast-paced story line that will thrill readers with the dilemma between honor and love. This is a great work that should not be missed."

—Painted Rock Online Reviews

"A great romantic escape!"

—Ann Taylor, CompuServe Romance Reviews

"Ms. Power evokes a stunning love story that is imaginative and unforgettable. Her ability to bring to life a turbulent time in history using original and endearing characters is a joy to behold."

—Tanzey Cutter, *Old Book Barn Gazette*

"Another lyrical masterpiece of beauty, high romance, enchantment, joy, love, and happily ever after. Jo-Ann brings Clare and her Dragon to life with the power, purity and beauty of her words. . . . A book to cherish."

—Kay Bendall, The Book Rack

Books by Jo-Ann Power

You and No Other
Angel of Midnight
Treasures
Gifts
The Nightingale's Song
Never Before
Never Again

Published by POCKET BOOKS

JO-ANN POWER

NEVER AGAIN

POCKET STAR BOOKS

New York   London   Toronto   Sydney   Tokyo   Singapore

This book is a work of fiction. Names, characters, places and
incidents are products of the author's imagination or are used
fictitiously. Any resemblance to actual events or locales or persons
living or dead is entirely coincidental.

An *Original* Publication of POCKET BOOKS

 A Pocket Star Book published by
POCKET BOOKS, a division of Simon & Schuster Inc.
1230 Avenue of the Americas, New York, NY 10020

ISBN: 0-671-00899-4

First Pocket Books printing November 1998

10 9 8 7 6 5 4 3 2 1

POCKET STAR BOOKS and colophon are registered
trademarks of Simon & Schuster Inc.

Printed in the U.S.A.

For the many small inspirations of which one novel comes, I am grateful to many people. Susan King, for her friendship and especially for her suggestion of remote, forbidding Tantallon, Scotland. Terry Oliphant, for her help with creole and Cajun cooking. And my husband, Steve, who—when my time is spare and my intentions greater—always welcomes yet another pasta dinner!

NEVER AGAIN

Prologue

June 15, 1876
London, England

GAVIN GLARED AT SEAN O'MALLEY, COGNIZANT OF THE growing afternoon crowd that watched them. "I won't argue with you in public," he seethed, unwilling to damage his reputation further by yelling at the man. "But I do want to know why you changed your mind."

Louise Stoddard sniffed, blinking as if tears were about to come to her eyes.

Gavin dug out his handkerchief and pressed it into her hand. "Oh, there's no need to cry."

"How can you be so angry with him?"

"Because, Mrs. Stoddard, he changed his vote. That is not done without first telling the sponsor."

"You won't hit him?" She dabbed at her dry eyes and took her lover's arm protectively.

"Hit—? For pity's sake, I haven't said or done anything that wild." Gavin was aware the onlookers gathered closer to eavesdrop.

1

"You did once."

"That's a lie."

"I won't let you hurt Sean." Louise's silly little hat bobbed up and down as she pulled Sean toward the speaker on the stump. "Come along, darling. You needn't stand here and be accosted by this hothead."

Gavin cursed. He'd been careful not to lay a hand on anyone, lest he find himself characterized in the tabloids again as a man who settled disputes by brawling.

Sean straightened his shirt and pulled at his coat, making a show as if Gavin had roughed him up.

Gavin knew Sean was doing what he did so well in the Commons, winning the audience over to his viewpoint with false emotion. "Playing to the crowd again, Sean?"

"It's not hard, Gavin. You cooked your own goose, when you decided to take this matter up with me here in view of all these people."

Gavin shot an arm toward the Member of Parliament who had taken the stump to preach in favor of an Ireland made free from Great Britain by any means, even violence. "There was a day you agreed with me—not him. I'm leaving, but we will talk, O'Malley. Quietly. Privately. And you will tell me why you changed your vote on my bill."

"I'm a free man, Sutherland. Don't threaten me."

"Really," Louise spat, malicious as a cat. "No etiquette at all."

Gavin had been raised to show his best manners. Not many believed he possessed any since John Gaylord had assaulted him last month on the floor of the Commons and the newspapers falsely concluded Gavin had struck the first blow.

Gavin surveyed the milling crowd, some of whom were peering at the two Members of Parliament who seemed about to trade punches. The throng pressed nearer, jostling him. A lovely blond woman and another MP, Ryan Ahearn, moved aside. A few other faces looked familiar. But Gavin was too angry—too concerned that his actions were being misinterpreted again—to register precisely who was watching him.

He knew he had to leave here now.

His own canvassing agent appeared in front of him. "My lord, let's go—"

Gavin shrugged him off. "Reynolds, I told you to go home." He strode a pace, but the man who was paid by his father to get him elected and keep him in office hung on. "Take your hands off me, I am going for a long walk. Alone."

He'd work off his anger with the exertion and recoup his ability to focus on the logical aspects of O'Malley's desertion of him, their party, their plans, and their bills to make the Irish equal citizens of Great Britain and her Empire.

If he stayed here any longer, he would create a public spectacle.

Timothy Butler stepped down from the speaker's stump and caught Gavin by the lapels. "What the hell is the matter with you, Sutherland?"

"I have a few principles, Butler. More than you and your new friends." Gavin nodded toward O'Malley and Ahearn, with Louise Stoddard standing by.

Butler sneered. "I doubt you can persuade these folks of that, Sutherland."

Gavin gave him a to-hell-with-you look and wove his way through the multitude.

He walked on blindly. Anywhere. Endlessly. As the sun set and the crisp breeze off the Thames led him to button his coat and yearn for solitude and a retreat to his family's summer house at Chipswell-by-the-Sea. He felt choked by fear and the need to escape this city where he only encountered people to tear him down, criticize him. Why was that? Up to a month ago, he had been lauded in the press for so many of his positions. Including his attempt to bring about peace in Ireland by making her a free and equal partner with England, Scotland, and Wales.

He wandered on. Through the park. Past the Serpentine and Rotten Row.

Only his instinct led him. His instinct for survival.

How had he gotten into yet another incident which would erode his public image?

He wanted to correct this terrible problem. But how to stop this awful decay?

Blind to everything, he saw only the pain and fury of the last month when he had been ridiculed unfairly in the press. He had desperately tried to rebuild his reputation by giving interviews and issuing clarifying statements.

But he had been unable to stem the tide of destruction that swept over him at every turn.

His public criticism had begun that day a month ago when John Gaylord and he had debated the bill to admit Catholics to the English bar. Gavin had supported the bill. Gaylord stood and called Gavin a "lover of revolutionaries not fit for our courts." Gavin had tried to counter with some logic. Gaylord had scoffed at Gavin and approached him, shaking his fist in Gavin's face. Gavin had stepped forward and Gaylord turned his back to the other members and drove his fist into Gavin's gut. Gavin had reacted—and hit the man on the chin. The two of them locked together like wrestlers and fell, scuffling to the floor.

Gavin, who was bigger and more fit, easily gained the advantage—and just as easily lost the contest in the newspapers the next morning when they blamed him for the fight. What the spectators had seen from the gallery was that John Gaylord had been struck in the face and pushed to his knees.

Each day thereafter for the next few weeks, Gavin could count on the newspapers dragging out old incidents from his youth. His defense of maypole dancing in the Cranborne public park, which resulted in a heated argument with one of the village elders. Or Gavin's insistence that his political party support land tax reform for Irish peasants, which caught so much attention in the papers that he had been labeled the Judas of Commons, to sell the English out to Irish revolutionaries. When he had wanted only peace and justice, equality among all men and women.

It seemed that lately, no matter what he put his mind or hand to, he was misinterpreted.

He had told himself to lay low, do his work, propose his new bill quietly, rationally. He even went about collecting support, talking serenely to his party members and to those of the opposition whom he knew to be sympathetic to his cause. But Sean O'Malley had broken his promise and broken ranks to vote against his bill this morning and his negative vote had sent the bill down to defeat.

Gavin, in his second time out to sponsor a bill, had been defeated.

He felt betrayed, cheated.

By Sean O'Malley, a so-called friend, a prime mover among the Irish MPs.

Why had Sean deserted him?

Sean had a reason. Money or people had spoken louder to Sean than party loyalty or friendship had. But what had been Sean's political motivation?

Gavin had to learn.

He spun on his heel. To hell with brooding over what the cause might be. He would confront Sean O'Malley. He'd find out. Have this out with him.

He looked up, saw the street sign, and realized his wanderings had taken him far from Hyde Park. To Kensington. A few blocks from Louise Stoddard's house.

Eager to get this confrontation over with, Gavin jogged across the street, avoiding a passing hansom, headed for the corner. The sun had set, the street lamps cast flickering shadows upon the sidewalks.

Damned if he hadn't walked over London for God knew how long, cooling off, when Sean O'Malley needed a tongue-lashing. Sean had welshed on his promises twice now. As a result, Gavin's prestige with his voters and the party diminished because he could not get his own bills through the Commons. He had to insure Sean O'Malley understood the costs of depriving him of support at the last minute. Gavin would notify Sean he couldn't do it again without an equal loss of his own power to sway Gavin to his causes.

He marched up the steps of the tidy brick townhouse and rang the bell.

No one came.

"Hurry up." He rang it again. He knew Sean and Louise were here. They flagrantly slept together at her house whenever her husband was away.

Still no one appeared.

Gavin lifted the knocker and when it banged down, the door fell open.

He frowned. Where in God's name was the butler or a maid?

"Hello? *Hello.*"

No one answered.

He stepped inside and shut the door.

Somewhere a floorboard creaked. Elsewhere, all was silent.

Gaslight spilled into the foyer from the front parlor. Gavin strode toward the light.

He walked through the double doors. "There you are—"

He swallowed his words. His stomach lurched.

There sat Sean and Louise.

He gazed down at the two lifeless bodies before him and ran a hand over his eyes.

Was he out of his mind?

No. They were quite real. Very dead.

The man and woman faced each other, sagging, tied by the drapery cords to their chairs, and still bleeding from so many knife wounds that Gavin knew a madman had tortured them.

He felt bile rise in his throat at how he had argued with them in Hyde Park only . . . was it? . . . hours ago.

Who could have murdered them?

Gavin saw no knife, no sign of a struggle—only the stark look of horror on their faces.

He put a hand to Louise's forehead and groaned. Her skin was still warm.

"Oh, God." He had to get out of here.

"Be calm," he warned himself, clenching his fists and circling the bodies, his eyes checking the draperies that no one could see inside, see *him*.

His gaze dropped to the bright white scrap Sean clutched in his hand. Soaked with blood. Sean's blood.

Seeping into Gavin's handkerchief. Over his initials.

Gingerly, Gavin slid it from the dead man's fingers. That was all he needed—to have the police discover that and arrest him. He hurried toward the door.

Turning, he took one more hard look around. Wondered oddly why Sean's trouser pockets were turned out, then left.

He hastened down the empty street, praying no one would be the wiser he had been there. No one would ever know he'd taken his own handkerchief—and saved himself from the hangman's noose.

Chapter 1

"Justice delayed is justice denied."
— WILLIAM GLADSTONE

May 1877
Chipswell-by-the-Sea
Norfolk, England

GAVIN ROSE FROM HIS DESK AT THE FIRST RUMBLE OF THE lorry up the cove road.

His housekeeper had told him two days ago that she'd learned in the village a widow had rented the cottage that stood in his line of vision toward the sea. His first reaction had been, *how dare this stranger intrude upon my solitude*. His next had been, *who dares to break my exile?*

He stuffed his hands into his trouser pockets and glared out his bay window across the cove as Chipswell's lorry driver pulled up before the tiny periwinkle door and reined in his two nags. The man hopped off of his perch and came round to help down the passenger whom he had collected, with her trunk and reticule, from the train station and brought to her new home.

Gavin narrowed his gaze on her. She looked stiff and nervous, jerking her head about from the sight of her new home toward his.

He could not see her face for the shadow cast by the broad brim of her hat. But he could detect she was very tall, extremely trim, with a pile of pale blond hair, and a full sad mouth.

Her sorrow struck him as a duplicate of the one he had witnessed when he stared into his own mirror. She was in mourning for her husband. He was in mourning for his own demise.

He shut his eyes and lifted his face to the sun, which he hoped would burn some warmth into his brain. He hadn't found any for his heart, though. Sometimes, he thought he never would again.

Life had been unjust to him. Taken from him family, friends, career, reputation. Hope.

What was left to him?

Not much—only his undying determination to find a way to live again in dignity. And though he managed to lick his wounds in privacy until now, this widow stepped into his beloved view of the sea and sands, subjecting him to the sight of her own grief.

My God, as if he needed to see more.

Raine Montand waved good-bye to the driver and closed her little Dutch door with a thud. She bit her lip, pleased she was here at last within shouting distance of Gavin Sutherland, but scared as a mouse in a hole that she had probably just made the most stupid move coming to this fishing village to seek out the man she had ruined.

She yanked off her gloves and strode to the window that faced his white mansion. The house hovered over the rocks and sands like a huge white gull. "Too big for you, alone," she murmured to the man she had never met but watched that fateful day almost a year ago when he'd argued with Sean O'Malley in Hyde Park.

"Well, I'm here now. You must deal with me," she told the unsuspecting man to whom she meant to make amends for the awful injustice she'd done him. "I hope you haven't hired anyone yet," she prayed, folding her hands together, restraining herself from marching across the cove and applying this minute to become his secretary. She forced herself to turn away to do her unpacking.

She took in her new home. Not quite her uncle's grand house in Belgravia, but she'd make the little one-room cottage cozy with her own touches. She had enough money to spruce it up a bit with some eyelet and bright swatches of yellow, maybe as curtains. When the lorry had driven up, she had noted the rosebushes out front and a few herbs in the garden. She would weed out the patch, prune the bushes, throw herself into making her little house livable. And after a suitable length of time, so as not to look like her actions were planned, she would walk over to that bigger white house and apply to work for Gavin Sutherland.

She would, she repeated like a mantra from an eastern religion. She sought courage as she hastened to open her trunk. She had instructed the driver to place it near the far wall, closest to her bed. She flipped up the latches and lifted her new black and purple clothes which she'd bought to appear the grieving widow. She hung them on the old clothing bar and returned to extract her petticoats and underclothes and place them in the dresser. She had not brought many possessions with her. She had instructed the Forsythe House maid to pack only the bare essentials for her "holiday by the sea." So she reached the bottom of her clothing pile in minutes. Except for . . .

Mon Dieu. The maid had packed Raine's sketchbooks. The one she'd drawn in most recently and the one she'd kept with all of the cartoons she'd drawn of Gavin Sutherland's argument with Sean O'Malley and Louise Stoddard in Hyde Park. Raine snatched her hand away from the two large pads in the bottom of the trunk.

Beside them lay her pen and pencil case. Why had the servant included them when Raine had specifically told her to leave them at home?

Habit. Just that. The maid—no one—knew that Raine's talent for drawing people was the means by which she had destroyed Lord Gavin Sutherland's political career. The maid did not know that Raine had vowed to never draw again.

She pushed the lid closed. It fell with a thwack. Raine jumped at the sound, and went about cleaning her new home and setting the world aright for herself and for the man whose life she had destroyed with the touch of her pen to paper.

Gavin Sutherland looked remarkably recovered from the public assassination he had suffered at her hand.

"Come in, Mrs. Jennings."

Raine would even conclude he was serene.

"Sit here." He indicated the chair before his colossal desk. His gaze sluiced her body like icy spray from the North Atlantic, then darted up to her eyes with a prick of curiosity. He turned his back on her to his window overlooking the sea, thank God. His swift inspection of her plain plum walking suit made her heart thump. His scrutiny of her face made her palms sweat.

Does he know who I am?

No. He couldn't.

Only her publisher knew her identity and what she had done for a living. Raine had never told anyone the truth.

Her Uncle Skip had seen her leave their fashionable Belgravia home each morning for a year and a half to go to work at *The London Times-Daily.* Although she'd been hired to draw advertisements, within six months her publisher had asked her to substitute for the newspaper's ailing political cartoonist. Secrecy, said her publisher Matthew Healy, was useful for collecting information and protecting herself from harassment.

Raine had followed his order and not even confided in her cousin and best friend Ann Kendall. It had been easy to avoid discussion of her job with Ann, who lived far north of London in Lancashire with her husband, the Duke of Carlton and Dundalk, and their small son. Ann, like her father, Skip, thought Raine worked at the same kind of job she'd had at *The Washington Star* before the three of them had come abroad two and a half years ago with their Aunt Peg and two friends.

Only Healy knew that last June, Raine Montand transformed into Raynard the Fox, the political cartoonist for the city's largest paper. She prayed now that Gavin Sutherland didn't know it, either. Her success here depended on it.

She strode across the length of his library and forced herself to look comfortably seated in the old ruby leather chair which faced the barricade of his desk. Its mahogany expanse gleamed with refracted rays of morning sunlight, causing her to squint as she noted his neatness. He had put one stack of notebooks in the middle, another of correspondence to its side. Between them lay one fountain pen. Raine was not surprised. Many attributed Lord Sutherland's rise to fame in four short years to his passion for order—and his dispassion for patience.

"Thank you for responding so quickly to my application, my lord." She had walked her letter across the cove from her cottage to his house yesterday after breakfast and within the hour, he had sent his summons to an interview via his housekeeper.

When he remained silent, Raine resisted the urge to arrange her skirts and instead, worked at removing her gloves, finger by finger. "My letter was only one page, I realize, but demonstrated my abilities to write well."

He could have been deaf or dead, for all the movement he made. He wished to test her nerves, did he?

"Even without references, I hoped my letter might show that I am qualified to become your secretary."

"I could say it is my pleasure to see you so quickly,

13

Mrs. Jennings." He did not face her, yet she could feel his low bass voice sink into her skin. Whenever she had heard him from the visitors' gallery in the House of Commons, the resonance of his tones had always stirred her blood as much as the spare beauty of his rhetoric soothed her soul. "It is necessity."

"I understand. I know you wish to write your second novel quickly." He needed the money because his family had cut him off not only from their affections, but also from their funds. Since his resignation from his seat in Parliament last September, he had written one novel which still sold well after four months in bookstores. Rumor mills had it he wished to follow that success with another. Rumor also declared his father—as punishment for his son's disgraceful behavior and for resigning his seat in the Commons—had demanded his son reimburse him for his last campaign expenses; hence, Gavin needed the financial windfall a second book might provide to repay the noble Marquess of Cranborne. But Raine had heard from her editor that in truth, Gavin was not indebted to his father for any amount, but he did need money—like any other man—to pay his daily expenses—and he was succeeding in doing *that* very well.

"How convenient you know so much about me." He jammed his hands into his trouser pockets.

The move pulled the navy wool across his hips, and Raine noticed. She frowned that once again she had noted how appealing his huge male body was to her. She didn't usually think of men in any physical way. She was drawn to their mental abilities first and last.

"I do hate idle talk, Mrs. Jennings, but in interviewing applicants for this position, I must make an exception. I am bone-tired of those who have come to twitter at my door, hoping to fly away with a worm to feed to some tabloid."

Raine's stomach lurched. She shut her eyes. No, she had not moved here to this little fishing village four weeks ago to draw him and destroy him further. She had done her damage. Her depiction of him exactly as she had seen him, arguing with another member of Parliament in Hyde Park two hours before that man and his paramour were murdered, had led the Metropolitan Police to question Lord Sutherland about the crime. Her cartoon of his confrontation with Sean O'Malley and Louise Stoddard combined with the previous firestorm over Gavin Sutherland's uncontrollable anger made him the prime suspect in the still unsolved case.

Later, politicians and pundits alike cited her cartoon as evidence that the popular, if inflammatory, Lord Sutherland could be unpredictable and therefore did not deserve to sit in a deliberative body like Parliament. The public cried out in letters and newspapers for the arrest of a suspect in the murders—and when none was named, for lack of evidence, they insisted Gavin Sutherland must be the perpetrator. They began to call for his resignation.

The clamor had taught Raine the power of her pen. She had learned at his expense that she must not use her art to expose people to criticism—nor to ruin them. She had rented the cottage in the cove so that she might meet him and help him—compensate him in some small way for the damage she had wrought. What better way than to apply for the position which after two months was still vacant?

"So you will understand then, Mrs. Jennings, how I must hear what you know about me and my unfortunate past."

She faltered at how to begin.

"Do it quickly," he ordered, sounding put upon and taking her hesitation as fear, "or leave."

"I have heard in the village that you wish to hire an assistant to help you write your next book. You have searched for two months now with no success." She paused, seeking the diplomacy she required to continue and the bare facts he would welcome. In truth, few wanted the position of secretary to this outcast. Her publisher had predicted that fewer still would apply in response to Sutherland's ad. Who wished to work for a man so notorious that no advancement in prestige or salary would ever come their way? "I am here out of necessity, my lord."

"Financial?"

"Yes."

"Political?"

She gave a short laugh. She'd been prepared for his suspicion that she wished to work for him so that she could spy on him. "If you mean to ask if I am collecting information for the opposition party, then I must say no. I agree with many of your own views actually."

"Oh? Which ones?"

"Your attempts to improve public transportation and better lighting and sewage are ones I applaud."

"Ah, you believe that government can be a force for change."

She nodded. "When it is quiet and deliberative."

"How sweet."

"And when its legislators are, too," she persisted, throwing his sarcasm back at him and only too late, wondering if she'd insulted him.

"Bravo."

"Nor," she charged on, barely registering his feigned plaudit, "when those people engage in violence to prove their point. . . ." Oh, *mon Dieu,* she'd killed her chances with him now. "Or when they declare war."

"You state this with such passion that I gather you have suffered from war in your own country?"

"My parents and three brothers died in our War between the States. Our home was burned, our crops destroyed."

"And yet after such loss, you trust that government can serve constructive ends?"

"Yes."

"Can it serve justice?"

"Government must try. I believe that justice must prevail. That criminals should be punished."

His big hands coiled into fists. The move did not frighten her. At twenty-five, Raine told herself she had recovered from her childhood wartime horror—witnessing men becoming savages. Besides, she had often seen Gavin Sutherland show his frustration with this curl of his hands. But she knew he had never hit anyone. Not even John Gaylord in the Commons. Gavin Sutherland preferred to impress people with the force of his words. That was one reason Raine doubted he had committed murder. One reason why others assumed he had. Nonetheless, she had summoned the courage to come here and try to discover more facts about the crime for which no one had been charged.

"I applaud your beliefs," he told her though he did not turn. "I share them. I have worked to make them a reality in government, but I don't seem to have benefited from them. I wrestle with my newfound cynicism and my daily proof that life is not fair." He inhaled, the breath expanding his broad shoulders with a magnificent ripple of muscle.

His movement stirred her memory of another man who was once as mighty as this man had been. Her father had also been brought low by circumstances beyond his control. Raine bristled, forcing herself to listen to Gavin Sutherland.

"Forgive me if I belabor a point, Mrs. Jennings, but tell me more about why an attractive widow applies for a position as secretary to a disgraced politician."

Raine couldn't stop the smile that curved her lips. He was doing with her exactly what he did with his peers in politics. Shocking his opponents first, prodding them with bluntness, and demanding honesty in return. Later, Raine would hope he would continue with her as he did with them and show her great kindness. That way he gained the advantage, controlled the action—and finessed them to his cause.

This morning, Raine would not let him dominate their meeting. She had a duty to herself to discover if he was guilty of the deed many suspected he had committed. She had tried for six months to find evidence of that and failed. Stymied in solving the crime, she was determined to help Gavin Sutherland build a new career.

"I wish to work, Lord Sutherland." That was the truth. "You have interviewed a few applicants. Three, the villagers tell me, each of whom you have rejected. Yes, I would predict that anyone who came in response to your advertisement would have curiosity for the details of the crime for which there seems to be no motive and no perpetrator. But I will speculate that whether the applicants sought titillating information or not, you rejected them because they were unqualified in more important ways. Yes, you value people with ambition. But you revel in intellectual companionship. Even if you could suffer an ordinary mortal day in and out, you work best with those who are articulate, witty, and bold. While I can only demonstrate those qualities daily, I can say I had an excellent education. I write and read English and French. I have traveled in America, Ireland, and here. Last year, I visited the Continent briefly to study painting. I am intelligent, healthy, and eager to help you. To finish your novel quickly," she spoke the words she prayed would not be a lie, "I offer you hope."

He swung around, and she felt as if she should recede into the leather. She didn't. She knew how to hold her ground with strong men.

This one was the opposite of most others she had known.

He was hurt. The agony pooled in his cool gray eyes. She had helped to put it there.

He was impressive. His impossibly broad chest, his towering height as he came around the desk, illustrated graphically why the visitors' gallery in the House bulged with women when word went out that the striking bachelor would speak. He had been powerful, charismatic, revered. She had helped to bring him down.

"Hope?" He snorted. "Hope," he repeated with sad consideration. He sank against his desk, his trousers conforming to thickly muscled legs, his eyes boring into hers. The ivory linen shirt he wore shifted over the contours of his chest as he crossed his arms. In the village, they said the Sutherlands descended from Viking raiders. Gavin looked it, every inch. Raine could render him that way with ink in hard lines, long arcs, not one an exaggeration. Even his straight bronzed hair, slicked back in a blunt cut across his nape, added to the image of might. He needed nothing more—except perhaps the removal of the boyish dimple from his left cheek.

He now used that very asset which had sent women into rhapsodies over him when he had been the talk of the town and unscarred by scandal. "Mrs. Jennings, you are very young and recently bereaved." His gaze dropped to the hair-brooch at her throat and then to the dark purple of her skirt, those indications she had worn to signal her half-mourning for a husband who had never existed. "How can you talk of hope?" His eyes seared her with a languid heat Raine could describe only as hot ice.

"I am old enough, Lord Sutherland, to know that I must look for it each day. I find it when I feel useful. When I work."

"Why work for me?"

"Your situation attracts me. Saddens me. Angers me. My situation compels me to apply to you. I want to be helpful. I can be to you. You need not educate me about English society. I am American, but I have lived in England for two years, and I enjoy the people and their politics. I am energetic, awake with the sun. You need not inspire me to long hours with high pay, because I want to work for you. I understand your need to make a success of your writing career by following your first mystery with another—and soon. Furthermore, I live close to you, less than a two-minute walk across the beach. I fill my days with activity, but I can amuse myself with reading novels and writing letters and cooking for myself for only so long. Then solitude loses its appeal. In assisting you, I would do more than exercise my brain. I would become useful."

He rolled his tongue around his mouth. "You *are* bold."

She suppressed the urge to laugh. "You will not hire me if I am otherwise."

"True. But we have another problem."

"Ah, well, money is not a problem for me."

He assessed her attire in one long sweep of her body—and she felt as if she'd been undressed. "Meaning you don't want a salary or you wish to work for nothing?"

"You cannot pay much, that I know. I have heard from the villagers that you are willing to spend ten pounds a week. That sum will do nicely for me."

"It's less than many a London maid receives."

She nodded. "Yes, but I will not be working as a maid, nor in London."

"I planned to supplement the low wages with room and board. My home is large." He made a sweeping gesture to indicate the twenty-two-room mansion which perched over the rocks and sands. "Too big for me alone. I wished to offer the secretary a suite in the north wing."

Raine shivered at the thought. "I like the sea, but prefer a southern exposure. I'll stay where I am in my cottage, thank you. If you'll hire me, that is."

"You're awfully accommodating. Too much so, perhaps. But the problem I wished to discuss is not money."

She cocked her head. "What then?"

"You are a woman."

This time when she smiled, she did it so broadly that he arched both brows. "You cannot refuse me on that count, can you, my lord? Not when you have given such great voice to the movement for a woman's right to vote.

Equal to a man there, so am I everywhere. So must I be here in your presence. Deny me nothing on grounds of my gender."

"Interesting that you do not fear scandal."

"I will not live here in your house, but work in it, my lord. You employ a housekeeper, who is in residence, and a maid-of-all-work who comes in from Chipswell once a week. Neither of them has been ever linked to you romantically by the local residents or the London papers. You also retain a gardener. To hear Ben Watkins talk, Lord Gavin Sutherland may as well multiply loaves and fishes. He doesn't engage in any excesses, except his work."

"A great deal of that."

She smoothed her gloves across her lap. "I think these people are suitable chaperones."

"Rumor has little regard for facts, Mrs. Jennings. Opportunity need only present itself."

"I am aware of this." Raine knew it too well. Her cousin, Ann Kendall, had suffered a lambasting in the gossip sheets when first she and Raine and their two friends had arrived in England more than two years ago. Ann, who had done nothing worthy of censure, found herself discussed and unfairly characterized in the papers. Only her future husband, the Duke of Carlton and Dundalk, had saved her from more ridicule.

"If you hire me, Lord Sutherland, I take that risk of ridicule by a gossip-hungry society. But no one knows me, values me, depends on me. I have no family and no friends to dissuade me from any course I set for myself." That was half a lie, for her cousin Ann had probed Raine for the reason she wished to retire to this fishing village for the summer. She had told Ann she needed a vacation by the sea to ponder whether she would return to her job at the newspaper. She also told Ann she would assume an identity as a widow to insure that another publisher, who had been extremely aggressive, would not find her and attempt to persuade her to come work for him. Raine already knew she would never again draw cartoons for the fun of it.

"My lord, I wish to work for you more than I fear criticism. But your perspective is different, I realize. If you hire me, you risk public censure."

"Could I possibly have *more,* Mrs. Jennings?"

She cast him a considerate look and charged on. "However, you are in need of help to meet your deadline for publication, and no male has shown up on your doorstep who fulfills your requirements. Besides, who is to say that employing a man would insure your integrity? Lord Chuttlesly didn't find that to be so." Raine referred to a Conservative MP who only last month was caught with his pants down in his bedroom by his wife with his assistant—another man.

"You have thought of all the issues, Mrs. Jennings." His observation held a hint of compliment.

"You're certain?" She couldn't help but tease him.

He chuckled. His head thrown back, he afforded her a view of his strong profile in the sun. He looked so jovial Raine dug her nails into her palms to quell the urge to grab up his pen and sketch him that way. Where had her resolution fled never to draw again? Especially not Gavin Sutherland. Was it because she saw that he could still laugh despite what she had done to him?

But his mirth drained rapidly from his face, and when he turned to her, his eyes were empty. "Now I am intrigued. I think I am even flattered."

Can I make you smile again? "Enough to hire me?"

"Enough to marvel at my good fortune."

His words sounded accepting, but she feared he would soon want to know more and there would be questions she could not avoid. "What else can I tell you about myself?"

"How quickly do you take notes? How good is your memory? Do you tire of reading easily?"

"Let me see. In order, I would say, I am speedy, but I

22

can only improve with practice. I have a steel trap of a mind, recalling conversations verbatim, which can save time and breath." She did not add that she also possessed a vivid memory of scenes, an invaluable aid when she wished to re-create a sight on paper. "I never tire of reading. Fiction is my favorite, followed closely by politics."

"I must count myself fortunate you and I share the same interests. To what do you owe the development of these twin passions for prose and politics?"

"My mother demanded that her four children read the classics. We discussed them in the schoolroom on our plantation with the teachers whom she hired but usually dismissed for their lack of erudition. My father served for two terms as a congressman in the United States House of Representatives before our state seceded from the Union. Politics were discussed at suppertime, and my brothers and I were expected to participate."

Gavin stilled. "How extraordinary. Here it is not so. A child does not eat with his parents and when he—or she—becomes an adult, politics never appears on the menu in finer dining rooms."

"Regrettable, isn't it?"

"Deplorable. Did your husband share your enthusiasm for politics?"

"No," Raine replied truthfully. Winston Jennings had been a nice young man, with a passion for his career. She had met him when he was the military attaché to the British Embassy in Washington four years ago. He had called on her twice, taking her rejection of his attentions very hard. When she had accidentally seen him last year on a street corner near Whitehall, he looked ashen. He'd taken her to a tearoom where he had told her he was diagnosed with tuberculosis—and the disease was incurable. He had died in March. When she considered coming to Norfolk to meet Lord Sutherland and apply as his secretary, she felt she needed a false name—and a good reason why an American woman would be in

England. So she took the name of a man who was dead and added a plausible rationale for her residence in England.

"I read a lot of British newspapers. At home in America, I did, too. When I moved to London, I began to read and learned quite a bit about British politics." She paused and considered her fingers, idle now but once so deft at cutting anyone down to size. She had not lied to this man yet about her motives. She would not do so now. "I understand your predicament in its complexities. Doesn't that make me more qualified than the next applicant?"

Bitterness lined his face. "You mean, of course, if there were another applicant."

She stared into his eyes. "You do not trust me."

"Who would you trust, if you were I?"

"No one," she whispered. Aching for him, she felt her hope absorbed like sand into the tide. In this attempt to help him she had failed. She would need to find another way to live with the cruelty of what she had done to him. Another way to salve her conscience.

He whirled away to his window, toward the sea and the sun.

She rose, sapped of her energy, one hand gripping the leather armrest. How would she right this wrong she had done him if she could not work for him?

She had reached his open door and would have bid him good-bye when he called her name and she paused on the threshold.

"Return tomorrow morning at six, Mrs. Jennings."

Chapter 2

"Duty cannot exist without faith."

—Benjamin Disraeli

WHAT DID SHE REALLY WANT?

Gavin watched Mrs. Jennings as she picked her way across the cove toward his house the next morning. Ten minutes early, but bustling nonetheless, she looked more carefree than when she'd approached here yesterday for her interview. Her stride was easier. Her full mouth relaxed. Of course, she'd been nervous. Who wouldn't be when they knew they would confront a man suspected of murder?

But the widow Jennings was very different from the other applicants for this dubious honor of assisting him. She knew British politics and savored them, even though she was an American. She had conviction and courage. He detected that she was honest, too, when she told him she had compassion for his predicament. Life had treated her unjustly, too.

She also had one more motive to work for him than

she had revealed to him. He knew it. He recognized obsession when he saw it, and Mrs. Jennings possessed it to her elegant fingertips. She wanted to work with him very badly. Curiosity drove her, as it did the other applicants. Yet he did not feel she sought lurid details of the murders. She came for facts.

He hadn't yet decided if he should give them to her.

"Which puts you in one hell of a bind, doesn't it, old man?"

He turned away from his window and contemplated the duties he wished to assign to his new secretary. The first one would be to answer his towering correspondence. But the second would be to give order to his collection of newspaper clippings and personal notes on the murders. That done, he'd begin to give her his handwritten manuscript as he produced it to put on the Remington typewriter he'd bought.

If he told the story the way he wanted, he would create a new scandal with his audacity. If he wrote it, not simply to add to his finances, but also to free himself of the filthy accusations about murdering Sean and Louise, he would become unique. A writer who had exposed a criminal to the world. He would create this new novel as a mirror of the real crime—and in the process, she would soon learn the truth. All of it.

There was nothing for it but to learn more about her, try to trust her. His plan and his very future depended on it.

He heard the knocker at the front door, the footsteps of his housekeeper, the murmur of greetings. He went to the hall and stood examining the svelte figure of his new employee. She was removing her short cape, handing it over to his housekeeper as she shot the cuffs of her blouse beneath her spencer jacket. "I trust Lord Sutherland is up."

"And waiting for you," he answered her.

Unruffled, she walked forward. "Good morning, my lord. Did you see the sunrise?" she drawled in that brown sugar voice.

"I didn't notice." *I was too busy watching you.*

"White gold," she informed him.

The color of your hair.

"Against extraordinary blue sky," she went on nonchalantly, "it was spectacular."

But not as stunning as the sapphire of your eyes.

"I cannot get enough of the variations. That's why I get up early every day."

He choked, surprised at his rare laughter that she was getting him up not only early but also with increasingly red-hot frequency.

"Hard as it may be," he rejoined, silently congratulating her on arousing him when he'd not thought of anything amorous in almost a year. With those dreamy eyes and sinuous body of a siren, her image had called to him repeatedly in the hours since they had met. He saw now that he had not fabricated how abundant her hair was, nor how endless her legs or tiny her waist. How many times last night had he asked himself if he hired her out of desperation to begin work on his next novel—or out of desire to simply look at her?

She certainly did nothing to invite attention from a man. Her serviceable jacket, plain white blouse, and black skirt did even less to complement her china complexion than yesterday's somber purple. She'd become more mouthwatering without her widow's weeds. She'd be irresistible without any clothes.

"You are not ill, are you?" she asked him when he didn't seem hospitable.

"I'm very well." *I'd be better if you were ugly and cranky.* "You are chipper early in the morning, I'm glad to note. I get the bulk of my best work done before noon. Would you like coffee or tea before we begin?"

His housekeeper hovered at the threshold of the dining room, eyeing this invader into her domain.

"Coffee, thank you. If it's not too much trouble, Mrs. McNally," she told his housekeeper as she unbuttoned her spencer. "I don't mean to put you to extra work."

"It's not an inconvenience," Gavin assured her and nodded at the scowling servant, who hastened away.

Gavin stood aside for Mrs. Jennings to pass him and closed his library door behind him.

She walked to the middle of the huge room where he had interviewed her yesterday. Then she had come in and headed for his old leather chair, eyes taking in only his desk and him. Now she scanned the enormous proportions of the room which ran the entire width of the house. The mellow oak-lined library was so large it contained carrels, a second story with ladders for access, a round reading table in the center of the floor, with a globe to one side, a telescope to another. Her eyes roamed toward the five-paneled bay window where Gavin had stood during their meeting. She noticed now with a jolt that from his spot, he had a direct view of the beach—and the quaint periwinkle Dutch door of her cottage.

"You are frowning, Mrs. Jennings." He strolled toward her. "I hope I have not hired myself someone who is moody."

Raine faced him, and he could almost feel her spine stiffen at the knowledge that he could go to his bay window and watch her every move in and out of her cottage. "No. Have I been employed by one who is?"

"I fight my devils daily." *Hourly.*

"Oui. As do most people when adversity comes."

He nodded. "I take it then we will suit each other." *Especially because you are humble enough not to ask if I have been monitoring your activities. But then, of course, how could I fail to notice the ethereal widow who moved into the scope of my humdrum existence four weeks ago?* "Remove your jacket and hat, too. No need to be formal with each other, is there? You will call me Gavin and I shall address you as Raine." He said it in such a way that his words were law. "I'd like to acquaint you with where you'll work and what's to be done."

She didn't argue but placed her belongings on a small square table by the library door.

It was as if for the past four weeks he had been patiently waiting for—no, no, *expecting*—her to cross the sands and apply for the secretarial position.

Gavin had spotted her the day in May when she moved into the cottage across the cove. From his window, he'd observed her as she climbed down from the cab she'd hired at the train station in the village. He'd noted how she directed the elderly hackman to take her luggage inside. How she disappeared into the sturdy flint and whitewashed cottage with the tiny double door. How she had blended into the life of the village and yet remained apart, to emerge and walk the beach at any hour which appealed, but most often at sunrise.

She struck him from the first as a woman to watch.

A willow of a woman, she moved with a purpose that seemed at odds with her idle meanderings. She walked alone at dawn and dusk. Not a peculiar occupation for a widow in a strange place, her solitary walks interested him for other reasons. She took paths along the beach and toward the lake that he normally trod at his own eccentric hours. Plus she talked to herself, spotted birds with her binoculars . . . and brooded. In the village, so said his housekeeper, word had it the glistening blond beauty of Mrs. Jennings was dimmed by the recent passing of her young husband. He'd been an English Army officer assigned to the British embassy in Washington when he met and married the American with the lush mouth that alone merited her a portrait by a famous painter.

Gavin had yearned to cast off his gloom and go out to meet her, but had never taken advantage of his knowledge of her activities. In fact, he had ceased taking his own long walks along the same paths and had taken up riding his new Sharp bicycle instead.

His reluctance to meet her and open a conversation was a sign of his dejection and frustration with his own lot. How could he converse and comfort a woman who was grieving when he suffered so much loss in his own life? Her sorrow over the death of her loved one was of greater magnitude than the loss of his job and reputation. He should have been the one to find the means to go on. Yet, he could not. Instead she had come to him with her smashing good looks and her confidence to buck up his spirit with her presence.

"When you arrive tomorrow morning," he instructed as she fingercombed her stray wisps over her ears, "come in through here." He tilted his head to indicate a set of lead glass doors. "You won't disturb Mrs. McNally this way."

"Merci. I do want to remain in her good graces and not muck up her spotless marquetry floors."

He felt a smile play about his lips. "Mrs. McNally will appreciate your kindness. She is, in fact, quite eager to please. You'll see. She will remember that you prefer coffee and brew a pot especially for you. Tell me how you take it and how often so that I can inform her. She will ask, and I like to stay one step ahead of her. Makes me feel I'm in charge."

"Does she challenge you?"

"Not openly. She is a widow, and her only child joined the 97th Regiment and died in the China wars. So she is alone in the world and trying to support herself. I applaud that in a woman."

"I know." Raine nodded. "I have evidence."

Gavin had received so little praise in the last year that he warmed to this lady's generosity. "Mrs. McNally and I have been together two years. She ran my townhouse in London—and she did it to my rather exacting standards. Even if she is not a charmer or a gourmet cook, she is fast, efficient, and discreet."

"Sterling qualities difficult to find just anywhere," Raine offered.

"Yes, and I do not require her company, so pleasantness was never a characteristic I needed to demand."

A grin played at the corners of her mouth. "I will remember that."

His eyes dropped to her lips. "Do." He folded his arms to stop himself from gathering her close and hugging her.

Especially when her cheeks flushed like cherries at his scrutiny. "What about your coffee then?"

"My . . . oh, yes. Well, I drink it in the mornings only. No cream. No sugar. Very strong."

"A taste developed in your youth, I take it."

"Very young. I come from Louisiana where we like our coffee thick as leather."

"Which accounts for your mutterings in French and your English pronunciation, which is a bit different from the other Americans I've met."

"Really?" She fidgeted with the waistband of her skirt. "Some say we southerners speak exactly like you Englishmen. We just take a longer time to do it." She smiled without humor and began to drift along the shelves of one wall. "You have an impressive collection of books."

She was changing the subject. Why? Because she didn't want to become too friendly with her employer? Commendable of her, surely, to want to maintain a distance. But he needed to know more about her than her brief one-page letter described. He had to feel comfortable sharing details of the murder scene with her which only Scotland Yard and the police knew—as well as some they didn't. He needed to be able to trust her and to do that, he needed her to talk to him more freely. Perhaps to get this from her, he had to give her a basis to trust him.

He watched her stop to read titles and forced a smile. "They are not mine, but my father's collection."

She looked perplexed. "Oh, but I thought that he had disown—that is, that you had bought the house from him." Now she became embarrassed. "The newspapers reported that you did."

Did this woman read everything that had been printed about him? Even if she had, she couldn't know the intimate details of his family's reaction to his disgrace—and he had no reason not to share them with her. He had nothing to hide about how they had deserted him.

"I asked to buy the house. My father refused to sell it to me. In my dire circumstances, as he terms my current

status, he allows me to inhabit the property free of rent."
Gavin jammed his hands in his pockets. "But that is all
the Marquess of Cranborne has deemed fit to grant his
dishonored son." *And that's all I'll ever take from him.*

"Gavin." Raine glided up to him, and when she called
his name again and he did not respond, he felt her hand on
his arm. "I apologize for bringing up a delicate subject."

"Don't. I need to voice my anger. Sorry I do it in front
of you." If he had controlled his anger better the night of
the murders, he might not have been suspected of
committing the crime. He might not have been ridiculed
and forced to resign his duties in the Commons.

He glanced about. "The house is lovely—and I have
adored it since I was a child. My father had it designed as
a summer resort soon after he and my mother married.
We came each August and stayed through September,
while most of his set went to Cowes to sail or to Scotland
to fish. We sailed and fished here. This room was my
favorite even as a child. My brother and sister were never
enamored with the written word as much as I. They
sailed or rode. I read. And wrote."

He turned into the glare of the sun. It could not blot
out his anguish. "'Guilty until proven innocent' is the
rule which my father has applied to my situation. He has
bent the rest of the family to his will, too. Not my older
brother, Derek, or my younger brother, Reggie, or my
sister, Jenna, have ever acknowledged my letters. My
mother does not, either."

If that sweet lady had argued with her husband or
written to her beleaguered son, Gavin might have survived more easily the other slings and arrows of his
outrageous fortune. He might have taken with a grain of
salt rejection by the men who had once been his peers in
Parliament and who now could not quite remember his
name. Gavin wondered if his canvassing agent could
even recall how to spell it. But then, why should he? Tom
Reynolds was in the Marquess of Cranborne's pay, as he
had been for two decades.

His father had influenced so many to shun him, Gavin doubted if he could ever forgive the old man his arrogance. Gavin could still recall the day last June only two weeks after the murders when James Sutherland had wrapped about him his noble cloak of indifference and granted Gavin a few parting words.

"No son of the house of Sutherland has ever brought such shame to it," the eighteenth marquess had proclaimed to Gavin two days after he had resigned his seat for the family borough of Appleby. The seventy-two-year-old man whom Gavin had revered for his sagacity in political issues—but whose personal advice Gavin took with a medicine dropper—had agreed to give an audience to his second son only to promptly ask him to leave Cranborne Manor. "We shall not communicate with you until you have been able to clear your name."

God knew, Gavin had tried. However, telling the truth over and over again to the police and Scotland Yard had earned him only police scrutiny, public accusations, and whispered rumors. He had not been arrested. The authorities had no tangible evidence to charge him with murder and put him in gaol. So he took the second route to restoration—he investigated the circumstances of the deaths himself.

However, he had found few facts and fewer possible suspects. He knew he needed perspective to sort out his thinking on them.

Meanwhile, he had to build a new life for himself. To write fiction was the only aspiration he had ever held, aside from becoming the prime minister of Great Britain. Writing a mystery seemed to be a natural alternative to turn to in time of dire financial need. In fact, the man who became his publisher had suggested Gavin write as a means to earn quick cash. When his first novel *Pound Foolish* became such an overnight best seller, neither Gavin nor his publisher, Ned Hollister, condemned the fact that Gavin's notoriety contributed to his sales. So writing a second mystery seemed a logical step which might result in more financial rewards. This secretary gave him a chance to accomplish it more quickly and provided an appealing end to his solitude.

"So you see, Raine, that we will receive no callers from my family. Almost every person I cared for has forsaken me since the murders of Sean O'Malley and Louise Stoddard."

Gavin could hear Raine swallow. Was she afraid to be alone with him? No, she would never have applied. He turned to smile at her but stopped. Tears lined her lashes.

Only two people had displayed any pain over his plight. One had been Bryce Falconer, a good friend of Gavin's and a major supporter of his political party. The other had been Gavin's fiancée, Belinda Derwenter.

Bryce had broken into a fury over the ineptitude of the police and the Yard—then asked if he might assist Gavin financially. Belinda had burst into a tirade against the viciousness of the newspapers—and then dissolved their engagement. Gavin had refused Bryce's money and accepted Belinda's engagement ring. Both had set Gavin free as he had never been before.

But no one had cried over him—except this woman whom he had hired to help him. He was stunned, but he was also gratified. "Don't feel any remorse for me, will you? It will make it easier to wallow in it—and I can't afford the waste of time or energy."

"No, of course not," she sniffed, trying to find a handkerchief in her skirt pocket.

"Here." He took his own from his trousers and had the urge to wipe away those tears himself.

She did it quickly while he fought this growing impulse to put his hands on her. Damn, what drew him to her? Her strength? Yes, but it was also a facade as fragile as porcelain.

She had returned to the carrel and the subject they had left for his morbid walk down memory lane. "Your books are very old." She extracted a leather-bound book and flipped it open. "An original copy of Dickens?"

"My father's goal was to collect only first editions," Gavin provided. "We have American authors, too."

"Wonderful. Who?"

"In the aisle to your right. Yes," he nodded as she hastened there. "Hawthorne and—"

"Mark Twain." She picked up a volume, flipped it open, and read a few lines. "I love his dialogue. It is so true to life."

"Would you like to be a writer?" She had struck him as an artist. Perhaps that was because her hands seemed so often in flight, smoothing her clothes or her hair.

"No. Once, years ago, I thought I might try to write, but my talents seemed to be in other areas. Helping others." She sounded like she had just made this decision recently and would stick to it come hell or high water. She replaced the book. "I can admire those who do write."

"I hope you'll critique my dialogue. I find it tremendously difficult putting people's speech patterns on paper. That is a key to strong characterization." He leaned back on his desk and smiled at how readily she agreed. "I wonder for example, how I would blend your bits of French with your southern drawl?"

"That should be real easy for an Englishman. Ya'll just slur the endings and put in a bit of puffery and politeness, like, 'Ah surely do like your office and your view of the sea, suh.'"

He chuckled and abruptly stopped. "Is that what Twain does?"

She lifted a brow. "I'm certain he does much more."

"I will have to study how you talk." *How those lips of yours caress a word until it's floated away—and a man could be lured anywhere by the sound.*

"You're being polite. I won't be offended if you speak your mind. I think you English talk funny, you know. Too stiff," she said with tight lips and distinct articulation. "No emotion. So if you mean to say, sir, that you find my speech lazy, you can say so."

His gaze riveted hers. "Not lazy."

Her cheer wilted like a flower, scorched in the sun of his regard. She opened her mouth, but could not find the words to ask him to define his thoughts further.

He did anyway. "Sultry."

Raine tipped her head back to survey his second story of bookshelves. "Foghorns can sound better."

"You don't take a compliment easily, do you?"

"Not from my employers," she said, erecting her own wall between them that his congeniality would not breech.

But she had been too artless in her own conversation for him to let her regress now to the rigid confines of his employee. He was the employer. He had to control how close they became. If and when he wanted a stronger bond than payment for services rendered, he would forge it. Not her. *And what if you need someone you can talk to freely?* "You have worked for hard taskmasters, I suppose."

"Not always. I have had the good fortune to have worked for one sweet soul—and one slave driver."

"Who have you worked for?" When she didn't move, Gavin came closer. "You didn't tell me yesterday that you had been employed before."

"They were unimportant positions. Unrelated to working as a secretary." When he cocked his head in question, she added, "I sold ladies' stockings and garters in Washington City in Warfield's Dry Goods Store on Pennsylvania Avenue."

"From your tone, I gather it was not an enjoyable experience."

"Boring, suh, boring. The best part about it was that it was two blocks east of the White House and I could eat my lunch in Lafayette Park across the street and watch the visitors come and go. Have you ever visited Washington?"

"No, though I'd like to. I do know a few people from there who've told me it's lovely. Darcy Warfield, your former employer's daughter, for one."

"Ah, yes. The Heiress of Buttons and Bows."

36

"You sound like you know her."

Raine bit her lip. "I worked in their store. They don't socialize with the help."

"There is another lady here in England who lived on the Virginia side of the Potomac in Alexandria for many years. Ann Kendall. The Duchess of Carlton and Dundalk. Perhaps you know her."

Raine bent to look at the spines of more books. "I have read a lot about her but only here in the English newspapers. Her father is part-owner of a new cruise line, and she came abroad with him a few years ago."

"She is one of the three American Beauties."

"Yes, of course." Raine looked stiff as a board, skimming the shelves too rapidly to really be reading the titles.

"One of the newspapers dubbed them with nicknames when they first arrived in England," Gavin persisted, intrigued by Raine's jumpiness. "Not all are complimentary, either."

"I seem to have heard some things about them, but I really don't read the gossip sheets." She sounded derisive of that kind of journalism.

"I've given them up myself." Every word and cartoon printed about him was engraved upon his mind. Would to God he never saw another. "No one fares too well in those rags."

"The publishers are trying to sell papers. Sensationalism earns them a fortune."

"Yes, and nothing sells like murder—or love. And those girls made headlines husband-hunting."

Raine paused to blink at him, then resumed her scan of his books.

"Did I say something outlandish?" he asked, perplexed.

"No," she lifted a shoulder, "of course not. I just think that what the papers make of nothing is a practice that destroys so many lives. It's unfair."

"I agree. In the case of the American Beauties, they did do them a bit of justice."

Raine widened those extraordinary eyes of hers. "Oh? When?"

"A society florist has named roses after the three of them. Ann Kendall is known as Grace."

"She's the one who is the white rose," Raine said vaguely as she strolled around the end of a carrel.

"There is a yellow and a red."

"Is that so? I can't remember the other two. . . ."

"One is called Wit. The other, Drama."

Of the three, Gavin knew personally only the latter. He wished he didn't. The woman was the wife of Bryce Falconer, and she was making Bryce's life hell with her antics. She drank to excess, wound up singing in public fountains and racing horses at dawn. Colleen Vander-Horn Falconer had been appropriately dubbed Drama by the papers long before she married or began her current flurry of outlandish behavior. The enterprising florist had cultivated red roses as her emblem. However, as the Countess of Aldersworth, Colleen should have taken her fame and retired to the country with her husband and young son and been content to be renamed Subdued. But to Bryce's horror, he could not dissuade her from her escapades. Instead, he devoted himself to his son, his investments, and the Liberal Party. He traveled constantly to remove himself from the agonies of living with his wife.

Gavin let the subject drop. "Let me show you where you'll work," he said to Raine. He led her back through one carrel toward the south wall with a stained glass casement window facing the garden. He inclined his head toward an oak swivel chair behind a desk which was as large as his. "This will be yours."

"All right," she agreed, looking pleased at the garden but casting an eye back the way they'd come. She was too polite to ask why he had put her so far away from him. How would she react if he told her he didn't want her in his direct line of vision? If he let himself look at her all day, he'd be fantasizing about how to undress her instead of how to plot his novel.

"What is this?" She had a hand atop the black metal carcass of the typewriter.

"My import from America. Sent me deep into my pockets for over three hundred pounds, but I thought I'd try it. I've a penchant for machinery."

"My, my. I had heard you liked gadgetry but that's almost one hundred and fifty American dollars." She was stooping to survey the ugly thing. "Do you know how to work it?"

"Somewhat. I'll show you. The trick is in the fingers. Have to be dextrous, you know."

"And the printing?" She was looking at it upside-down like a flamingo.

"Comes up here on the paper, over the drum. Legible and good, except the letters are all capitals."

"Makes it hard to read, then."

"Yes," he agreed, "but I bought it anyway." He explained his reasoning with an absent air. "I wrote my first book alone. Fast, to earn much-needed money to live on. I tried not to think of hiring anyone to help me with this manuscript, but I must. There is too much to do. Too little time to finish it. This," he patted the contraption, "should speed you along."

"We hope. Well then, where do I begin?"

"With something easy." He walked toward a closet, opened the door, and took out a large paper box filled to the brim with letters, mostly unopened. He returned to the desk with it.

"My correspondence," he declared. "This is the first of three. Daily the postmaster delivers dozens more. I cannot keep up with it, since my announcement came out that I will write my second mystery."

"There are hundreds here," Raine marveled, one hand scooping up envelopes.

"Amazing, isn't it? Some come from my former borough, some from others. Most, in fact, come from London, from people who have read the police reports and inquest descriptions in the newspapers. These are people who wish their views to be heard, people who care enough to take time to write. Some are eloquent. Some are not. Your first task will be to read them and answer them."

"Answer? But why?"

He scowled. Folded his arms. Walked away and then faced her. "Here is your first test as my employee."

Her head tipped to one side. "The test is for—?"

"Loyalty."

"Very well." She nodded. "Go on."

"No one knows this yet. . . ."

"Why tell me that?" Her anger brimmed. "It means I can easily pass the test by saying nothing. Why not tell me something utterly preposterous, issue no warning, and see if I betray you?"

"I suppose I don't want you to."

"Yes," she said with some conviction. "I can see that. Come then, tell me this big secret. The better to have it out now so that you can catch me at my subterfuge tomorrow."

He pursed his mouth, unhappy she could see through his facade to his need. "Some day," he repeated the promise he made himself daily, "I will return to Parliament."

"You're going to run for Parliament again?"

"Shocking, I know, but true."

"How? I mean . . . your father has withdrawn his financial support, and the people in Appleby are reported to be against you ever showing your face there."

"I won't run in Appleby. I'll be newly elected in a borough that's free of patronage. Free of my father. I'll be elected because I have views which are my own, not the Marquess of Cranborne's nor my party's, but these people's." He swept a hand over the box. "I'll go with as much public support as I can muster. So to do that I must keep my support alive while I am out of favor—

and you will help me. Your first task is to sort the mail into three piles. Those against me, those for me, and those who live in Appleby. To those against me, you and I will devise a standard letter to answer them. Polite but to the point, the letter will thank them for writing. To my supporters, wherever they live, we'll create another standard letter and say thank you and create a list of their names and addresses."

"For when you need to ask for their votes."

"We think alike, Raine."

Dubious, she shook her head. "I still don't know how you'll be able to run without overcoming the effects of the scandal."

"People have a short memory," he told her, wondering why a devil in his mind whispered that he'd better know her more intimately before he took her into his confidence. He had learned in his four years in the game of democracy when to be content to hold his cards until he felt comfortable playing them. Each time he ignored his instinct, he paid dearly for it. But he had hired her and he could not have her sitting here, being paid for reading his father's collection of first editions. He wanted her doing his work. "Meanwhile, I am developing the patience of Job."

"A commendable trait," she offered with a small smile but great skepticism.

"Yes, admirable. But not very useful in this circumstance." She had read so much about him, and probably about the murder investigation, that it would be silly not to tell her his plan before he began to give her his drafts to type. Once she read his chapters, she would see how he intended to duplicate the plot and the real crime. Best to be forthright with her.

"What do you mean?" she pressed.

"I must write this book to earn money to support myself."

"Yes." She cocked her head, sensing his tension, perhaps even his need to test her again. "And?"

"It will be another mystery."

"Good ploy. Best to stick to your knitting and build your readership. Somewhat like being a member of Commons. Please your audience over and over again." She smiled.

He didn't. "It will have a different plot from the first book. It's not about embezzlement of funds, nor does it star a hero whose major challenge is his lack of ethics."

Her gaze searched his uneasily as she said, "The mark of a true professional is to write an original piece of fiction every time. With a well-drawn main character with a unique conflict and personal challenges. Tell me," she urged in her quiet southern drawl, "what is the crime committed here?"

The words barely escaped her lips before she knew the answer to her own question. He could see the trepidation loom in her eyes. "Murder."

She did not blink. "Of two people?"

He nodded. "A bachelor and his married lover. In London. Together one rainy night in a townhouse where all the servants have been dismissed for the weekend."

"Why?" she asked, breathless.

"I have no recourse left."

"But the police—"

"Have stopped looking for the person who did it. They'll never find him—or her—unless I keep the issue alive before the public. Make people talk about it and demand the authorities keep the investigation open. They haven't solved the murder in a year when everyone's memory was good and the evidence fresh. They never will unless I do something."

"You can't predict that a mere novel would flush him out of hiding," she countered.

"The same way you cannot predict it won't. But a best-selling novel would keep the subject on people's lips."

"Oh, people will continue to talk about you—and what they'll say will not serve to gain you votes."

"I have no other choice, Raine."

"But to write this is sensationalism."

"Yes," he agreed with a wry twist of his mouth. "If you can't beat them, join them."

"You can't do this," she said rabidly.

"The hell I can't." He'd terminate her employment if he had to, but she would not argue with him about this.

"It's beneath you."

He scowled at her. "What?"

"You are not worthy of this. Suppose you lead the public to think that another innocent man or woman killed Sean O'Malley and Louise Stoddard. What public service have you rendered? Have you served justice? Or committed the same crime that was committed against you?"

He considered the far wall with surprising distaste. "I thought of that."

"Good. You should. You must. If you mean to stand for Parliament, you must retain your integrity."

"My integrity—in case you hadn't seen it lately, Raine—has been rather riddled with insults."

"That's what your critics would like everyone to think, but Gavin, it is not true."

"How can you be certain?" he challenged this stranger who brought him the passion of her conviction and her concern for his public stature.

She slapped her hands on the desktop and darted up from her chair, her chin lifting. "How can you not?"

How could she champion him so fiercely? But she did and he reveled in it. Bathed in it. Drank it in like medicine. "I haven't looked at it lately."

"You need to start then. Now."

He knew she had a point. "I will try."

She crossed her arms. "And the real murderer will be drawn in your novel?"

He dearly wanted to live up to her vision of him as pure and full of honor. "I will not cast aspersions on anyone but the true criminal."

She inclined her head. "There is also the small matter of your own safety."

"Small but manageable."

"Really. At precisely what point when he—or she—reads your book will he come to claim his revenge?"

"That's debatable, I suppose." *As debatable as me telling you the answer to that.*

"You have thought of this—and you persist?" She was aghast at his selflessness, which clearly she interpreted as stupidity.

"Yes."

"My God, *why?*"

"I will have finished the book before it's published, Raine. The secret of who the real murderer is will not come out until the last chapter—and my publisher will know his identity. Hopefully, by that time the police will be shadowing the suspects so that they will not hurt me. Be assured, I intend to live a long and healthy life."

It suddenly hit him that her life would also be in danger. *And I'd let no one harm you, either.* If the culprit took it into his head to hurt Gavin for writing it, the man would hurt Raine for helping him write it. He stared at her, curling and uncurling his fingers with that temptation to drag her near and kiss away her fears for him.

She wasn't thrilled with his answer, but it would do for now.

"Very well. And while you are working on that," she sank to her chair and dug out a fistful of letters from his box, "the sooner I begin to answer these, the sooner you can toss off your sackcloth and ashes and go back out to campaign on the hustings."

Chapter 3

"Three may keep a secret if two of them are dead."

—Benjamin Franklin

MRS. MCNALLY RAPPED ONCE ON THE LIBRARY DOOR BEFORE she pushed it open and rolled in her tea cart. Laden with a freshly made cream cake, florentines, and scones, the housekeeper's desserts always satisfied Raine's sweet tooth. It also signaled the end of the workday for Raine.

"I'd say that you didn't like your job by the way you jump up for afternoon tea," Gavin teased her when she emerged from behind the carrel that hid her from him. "Thank you, Mrs. McNally, we can serve ourselves."

Gavin's servant grumbled and backed out the door. The woman left it ajar for propriety's sake as she had these past two weeks Raine had worked here. The first day of Raine's employ, Mrs. McNally had mumbled about the need to maintain some decorum, and Gavin didn't debate it with her. Nor did Raine. The two of them smiled together over his servant's attention to etiquette.

Raine took her usual spot on the small Empire sofa

and picked up a cup to pour for Gavin. "You could complain, except that you can see what I'm accomplishing." She inclined her head toward her desk. "Go look at that box."

Gavin sank into the leather club chair opposite her. "How many letters do you have left to answer today?"

"Five."

He rubbed his face with the heels of both hands and reached across to take his cup from her. "Thank you. Wonderful."

"What is? The tea or my efficiency?"

He cocked his mouth to one side. His dimple appeared. "What do you think?" He might be weary but he didn't stop his banter. In fact, Raine had watched him become more easy in his skin since the first day of her employ. He still gazed out his window far too often for her taste, but she knew he required the sight and sounds of the sea to soothe his nerves and heal his injured soul. If he could only give her half a smile today, she hoped she could encourage him to give her another tomorrow and the day after. His lighter mood was progress, and, at whatever pace, she took it as her reward for helping him.

"It hasn't been difficult for me to answer them and make the three lists." She busied herself cutting an apple scone in half for him, his regular and only accompaniment to his afternoon tea. "How long did you think it would require?"

"No idea." He closed his eyes, inhaled, and let his head fall back against his chair.

She examined him. Every day since she'd begun work for him, he seemed more frustrated. "You hired me to relieve you of your workload. Yet each afternoon you seem more exhausted than the previous one. Are you . . . healthy?"

He slowly opened his eyes to slits and peered at her. "Very."

She sat back and sipped her tea. "Maybe you need to

give up this pekoe. It's irritating, you realize, and if you are mentally not up to snuff, then you might need a more soothing brew. An herbal. Comfrey or chamomile, maybe. With lots of cream."

His shoulders shook in silent laughter. "Nursery tea."

She was baffled. "Nursery—?"

"Tea for children, Raine. Before they go to bed."

"Well, maybe that's what you need."

"To go to bed?" His eyes shot wide open and landed on her.

"Do you have a better idea? You look pale and you definitely need a little sleep—"

"Sleep," he said the word like it was the last thing on his mind, "is not what I do when I go to bed."

"That's what I thought," she murmured.

He plunked his cup and saucer on the tea table before her and rose. He looked down at her for a long minute, then turned away. "Perhaps what we both need is a little port."

She winced. "Not for me. I hate the stuff."

He paused, one hand to the doorknob. "What do you like?"

"Before supper?"

"Anytime."

"Whatever you'd prefer."

"That," he said with ruefulness, "is not among the selections. I am going to have something strong and neat . . . straight up, that is, to you. Are you joining me?"

She put her own cup down and frowned at him. "Why do you need to drink?"

"Afraid I may be drowning my troubles in liquor?"

"I know what heinous acts a person under the influence of alcohol can perform."

He looked alarmed. "Such as?"

"We are not talking about me, but you. I believe in moderation in the consumption of alcohol."

"Good for you. I do, too, for your information. You can be extremely argumentative, Mrs. Jennings. I would simply like a shot of liquor to relax my nerves."

"Liquor does not relax a body, it stimulates it."

"Raine," he sounded irritated and amused at the same time, "my body is so stimulated that a little relaxation even for a few minutes would be a welcome relief. Now are you drinking with me or not?"

"Do you get drunk?"

"I did when I was very young and paid the price of a bad night and day. But I don't make it a practice now. Do *you?*"

"Never."

"Nor I. Why," he pressed, "do you drink alcohol?"

"I like the flavor."

"Good. You're in it for the flavor. Right at this moment, I'm in it for the lift I get from my worries. What do you say?"

"Only if it's excellent quality," she stipulated. "I don't like to get headaches or a funny buzzing."

"Now really, Raine, do you think that the Marquess of Cranborne could stock penny gin in his liquor cabinet? Come downstairs with me and I'll show you the wine cellar, too, and you can select what you like."

"No. Thank you." She gave him a watery smile. She wasn't going anywhere dark and intimate with him. Wasn't it enough that she thought about him constantly when she was away from him? That she saw his figure in the fragile mists at night when she walked along the water's edge? Wasn't it bad enough that her need to draw him had her returning to her cottage, abandoning her resolution not to sketch anything, grabbing up the newer pad, and filling the void by sketching animals? She would fall into bed at one or two, and arise at five, refreshed, eager as a girl to see her lover. Then she would come here and sit with him. Knowing that as he worked on his manuscript, he tried to eradicate the harm she had done to him. "I'll stay here."

"Shall I bring up what I think you'd like?"

"White wine. A Riesling from the Alsace or—" Why not tell him what she really adored? "champagne."

He whistled. "Your husband must have had a difficult time keeping you in champagne on a lieutenant's allotment."

Briefly, he skimmed her lace collar and linen shirtwaist. Then he headed for his wine cellar.

Raine sat very still. What was it about her that had him constantly glimpsing her body? She was old enough to recognize that his glances were the indications that he found her appealing. Her hand slid up to her throat where she felt her blood pulsing in reaction to his perusal.

Her fingers toyed with the Luccan lace collar. This was what he had examined. Could a lieutenant's wife not afford such a decoration to her clothes?

She lowered her palm to her heart, pounding at the scrutiny of Gavin Sutherland. At the moment, her delight at his interest outweighed her fear. Her fingertips brushed her breast and she groaned. Her nipples hardened again at the thought of him.

Foolishness.

She vaulted from the settee and strode to his bay window.

Think of something else, she demanded of herself. Something as alluring as Gavin Sutherland's dulcet, gray eyes.

The sun was setting in the west, casting a glare atop the crests of the North Sea. Golden sunshine would be streaming in her tiny kitchen window now, waiting to greet her when she returned to her cozy home to cook her supper.

Tonight, she would make herself a special treat. At noontime, the fishmonger had come to Gavin's house with the last of a fresh catch of sea bass. Mrs. McNally had turned the man away, but Raine had bought one for herself and asked Mrs. McNally to ice it for her in the kitchen. Raine savored her evenings and her suppers prepared her own way. Afterward, she would scrub her pots and dishes, take up a wool shawl, and walk along the pebbly beach, away from Gavin. She never came toward his yellow brick house along the cove, lest he see her and think she wished to seek him out. Though she would have enjoyed conversing with him about his experiences in the House and his borough, she knew she must not give in to the urge. There should be a strong barrier between employer and employee—and theirs was a thin wall which became more flimsy each time they did talk. She reveled in their growing camaraderie while warning herself against it, understanding that keeping her identity a secret was a safer bet if she kept her mouth shut.

During the day that was easy to do. Gavin barely spoke to her, except at morning coffee time and luncheon—and afternoon tea. But she was constantly aware of his presence, even though she could not see him from her desk.

He talked to himself. Most of the time he made tremendous sense. He was even funny when he could have been, like most men or women in solitary communion, downright dull. She knew when the writing was going well because he would say, "Yes, *yes!*" and his pen would scratch the paper with rapidity. With increasing frequency, though, he would mumble, pace, and resume his seat, scraping his chair across the floor. Today, she had heard very little from him except expletives. His pen had touched paper briefly. His hands would crush his efforts and throw them away.

She worried about him.

She wanted him as productive as possible. She had no doubt he would write another suspenseful novel. With its publication, she prayed he would flush out the culprit. Exonerate himself. In dark moments of torment on her solitary walks, she worried about his safety. Horrified that the murderer who had so brutally stabbed Sean O'Malley and Louise Stoddard might do the same to

Gavin, Raine would pray that that person would never be so bold.

She pleaded with God, whom she thought had long ago deserted her, to let Gavin Sutherland succeed in publishing his story and revealing the murderer.

She also hoped his vindication would bring her own. She was uncomfortable with her own load of sackcloth and ashes she had donned this past year. Self-ridicule was new to her, even if it inspired a humility which she could say was healthy.

If from her little nook she silently cheered Gavin on, she blocked from her mind what his mystery might require of her in the way of revelation. Gavin gave her no indication whether he meant to duplicate all the circumstances of the crime, its final scene, or if he even could. In fact, he had not told her more than what he had that first morning she'd arrived for work.

What did she know about the murders of Sean O'Malley and his mistress, Louise Stoddard?

Like thousands of others in Britain, Raine knew the sordid details of the murder scene and the causes of death from the newspapers. Reliable and otherwise, the papers had printed police reports, interviews with Gavin's London neighbors and even his postman. They had also reproduced transcripts, whole and partial, of the inquest.

Raine knew more than that. From her two years in England listening not only to Parliamentary debates from the visitors' gallery but also to political discussions at society gatherings, Raine knew Sean O'Malley had been a good friend of Gavin Sutherland's. O'Malley was a young MP elected from an Irish borough, and he belonged to the same political party as Gavin. Louise Stoddard was the wife of Hamilton Stoddard, a man two decades older than she, and an undersecretary in the Home Office.

Other than that, Raine knew firsthand only what she had drawn in her cartoon. That scene in Hyde Park of the argument among Gavin, Sean, and Louise. It began as a confrontation between the men, until the woman interrupted and turned on Gavin.

Hamilton Stoddard had discovered his wife's and her lover's bodies the day after, a Saturday. News of the crime broke in the papers on Sunday morning. Raine had drawn the disagreement she'd witnessed on Monday. She had taken the cartoon into her publisher, strong in her belief that the public needed to know all the facts surrounding the grisly murders. Healy had been startled that she had witnessed the confrontation, but immensely pleased that he could use such a piece of evidence to stir public opinion. He printed it the following day in both the afternoon and evening editions of the *Times-Daily*.

Raine's cartoon raised a hail of questions about why Gavin Sutherland was arguing with his friend in public before O'Malley was brutally killed. The questions became suspicions that Gavin might be to blame for the murders. A storm of demands that Gavin be arrested arose in the newspapers. When the police declared they had no substantive evidence on which to charge him, Gavin was tried in the press. Members of the House called for his resignation. Within three months, Gavin was hounded from office. Rejected by his family and his fiancée.

The crime had occurred almost a full year ago, on June 15, 1876. Gavin had managed to survive the chaos.

Raine wanted Gavin restored to the life and career which she, in her lack of wisdom, had torn from him.

He had to write this book. He would. She would see what he needed and provide it. Objectivity. Encouragement. Prodding. What else?

She spun and took a step toward his desk. Today, his neatness told the tale of hours spent filling his trash bucket. His pen lay in the exact position he left it each night. Perpendicular to the remaining blank sheets of white paper. She retrieved a few sheets. He wrote no words, but drew objects. Triangles and arrows. In thick lines with sharp points. He was angry.

"Here we are. Malted Scotch for me and a Rothschild champagne for you." He had both bottles tucked under his arm and four glasses dangling between his fingers. "Getting a view of the sea at sunset?"

She nodded. "Getting a better picture of what you've accomplished today."

"Nothing to rave about, is it?" He busied himself with opening the champagne, popping the cork with an agility which shook her with a memory so old, so dear, that she paused. Her mind jumped to a time and place she never let go. To a man whom she would never forget, especially how he died.

"Raine?" Gavin was standing in front of her and raising her chin. "Raine, what's the matter?"

"I was remembering my home and my family. Silly of me . . . but of course, you look nothing like my father."

"Why did you think I was?" Gavin whispered, his gray gaze caressing her features.

She took her flute from him and a sip of the fine liquid. She easily recalled what had reminded her of her father. "The way your shoulders moved when you levered the corkscrew must be . . ." she flexed her own body in small imitation, "the way he did. He was an extraordinary man. Hale and hearty. As muscular as you and . . . just as breathtaking."

Something raw appeared in Gavin's eyes. He put his palm to the bottom of her flute and influenced her to lift the crystal. "Have another sip of your champagne, Raine. I am not your father, *ma cherie.*"

"*Oui.* Your visage is broader——" She raised her hand. The urge to trace Gavin's mouth and to test the depth of that dimple stirred the ashes of her vow to never draw him again. "And your coloring is brighter with the red in your hair. Your similarities to him are numerous." Her fingertip brushed Gavin's jaw, his cheek. He did not breathe. The feel of his warm skin ignited embers of her ambition to render him, not in black ink as the caricature she had once portrayed him, but in a palette as diverse as the virile and yet tender man who stood before her.

Gavin licked his lower lip. He knocked back a swallow of Scotch and said, "Why not tell me about him? I'm intrigued now." He walked backward and resumed his seat in the huge leather chair. "Come along. You can't toss down that champagne or you'll experience the buzzing you don't want." He tilted his head, as carefree as if to ask *Why not pass the time with me?*

That, too, reminded her of her father. "Now you look like him when he spoke the patois. He was very droll."

"A characteristic he passed on to his daughter."

She took her seat. "My friends call me a cynic."

"Really?" He rolled the Scotch around his tongue and leaned forward, elbows on his knees.

She nodded and took another satisfying drink. "You must agree," she urged.

"Mmm. I'd say you were prickly."

"I have a few sharp points, eh?"

He smiled and when her eyes lit at his expression, he broadened it to a grin. "Useful ones. Why are you a cynic?"

"If I tell you, will you smile again?"

"Try me and see."

She was feeling no buzz but a distinct lightness of being. She let her head drift back to study his carved plaster ceilings. The first things it brought to her mind were the angels and roses painted all over her cousin Ann's bedchamber ceiling. She giggled. "People think I am cynical because I find little humor in anything."

"Not from what I've witnessed," he said. "You laugh out loud more each day you are here."

She thought on that. "I don't know why."

"Perhaps you feel at home."

"I've never been to Norfolk before. Let alone Chipswell-by-the-Sea."

"Is scenery what makes you happy?" he asked, pointedly looking for another reason.

"Only certain scenery."

"Such as?"

"I like to be near water. We lived between the Mississippi and a large lake when I was young." There it was again, the recollection of her childhood she never encouraged. She rolled a shoulder. "I love my cottage. It is mine. As no home has been since I was twelve." She sat forward and put her glass down.

"What friends did you have who thought you found little humor in things?"

"What—?" Her mind went blank.

"—friends?"

"Those in London." Why couldn't they talk about him?

"Is that where you lived?"

"Before I came here, yes." *The man is invading your past. Destroying your mask.*

"Who were your friends?"

She ran a finger around the edge of her flute, proud of her casual manner. "No one you'd know." *I hope.* "Gavin," she began to chastise him, "we do not come from . . . ." The same circles? She couldn't say that. She had tried not to tell lies, but to word her replies in a truthful way. How many tales could she pile up and remember the details day after day? She had not counted on enjoying his company so much, so quickly. She had not predicted the spontaneity he could arouse in her. How could she lie to him and feel good about herself? Or accomplish her goal?

"Surely you must have known other Army wives?"

"Yes," she said emphatically. Army wives seemed like a safe statement. "A few."

"I understood that many commanders refused to permit their junior officers to marry until they achieved the rank of major."

"Winston was different." She took another sip, madly

searching for an appropriate comment. "Dedicated and ambitious."

"And so much in love with you, he'd break convention."

"Yes, he was . . . his own man in many things."

"Where did you live?"

"London." She set her jaw. She had to change his line of questioning. She certainly could not tell him she had spent the past three years in a Victorian mansion at 15 Belgrave Square with her Uncle Skip who was reputed to be the richest American this side of the Atlantic. "A part of town we could afford. But I liked it. For London. I prefer the grid pattern of streets in American cities, of course, because places are easier to find. Even in Washington, with its circles, there is a logic to the form."

"Not like London's winding roads at all."

"No."

"What part of London did you live in?" He looked as if this were a chat about the weather.

Damn his curiosity. "Seven Dials."

"You lived *there?*"

"Yes." She announced it like gospel. She knew that Seven Dials was a less expensive part of town to live in, but she'd never been there. Not even when she was drawing her cartoons did she ever have cause to go. Her trips took her to Parliament and Whitehall. Even Hyde Park, where one afternoon she had spied Gavin Sutherland arguing with a man and woman.

"Good God, Raine, why there? It's notorious for cutthroats and thieves. . . ."

"I don't know. It seemed a good choice at the time." She left her chair to stand by his bay window again. "I can't talk about these things easily. I have to go home." She drank the last of her champagne and bemoaned the fact she couldn't have another. She put her glass on his desk.

"Forgive me, Raine. I probed too much." His voice, so softly appealing, made her turn.

Gavin stood before her, hoisting the bottle. "Don't go yet. I don't care for champagne as much as you obviously do—and it would be a shame to let it go flat, wouldn't you say?"

"I am afraid . . ." Lord, that was the truth. "I don't drink this much."

Her reluctance to leave gave him time to smile—and pour more champagne into her flute. When his eyes came up, they met hers with an apology. "Stay. I insulted you with my reaction to your living arrangements, and I didn't mean to. I have no company, and you are such a good influence on me."

She snorted. "If you call those empty pages a good influence, then you do need to have another jigger of malt yourself, my lord."

"I meant you influence me in other ways."

She circled his desk and resumed her seat. "How?"

"You brighten my days."

"That's hard to believe." Most people thought her view of people and their foibles rather dark. "I haven't seen you smile but once or twice."

"You make me smile when you hum."

"I hum?"

"You didn't know?"

"Well, no." Why would she? She'd had an office to herself for the last year. Had she made noise when she worked at the *Times-Daily?* She would never be able to say. Unless someone had overheard her or walked in on her. Which no one had ever dared to do—or they'd get the lash of her tongue. "Do I sing—hum—anything in particular?"

"I have no idea what the name of it is." When she raised her brows in question, he offered his rendition of her song.

" 'Camp Town Races,' " she informed him. "A black-face minstrel song."

He frowned. "I don't know what this minstrel is."

She explained.

"Oh, I see. And then, when you are settling in for the afternoon, you switch to this." He gave her a few full-throated bars of a song her nana had sung to her as a child. She admired Gavin's rich bass, but the tune plucked more strings of sorrow in her soul.

"That's a hymn my nursemaid used to sing before she put me and my brothers to bed at night." She took another sip of her champagne and saw visions of humid nights when the house slaves worked the giant feather fans over her bed. Why did she hum that old song now? "Can we talk about you?"

He had been watching her face evidently, because he quietly took his own chair opposite her as he said, "Whatever you want. What would you like to know about me?"

She'd keep him focused on his goals. "Why didn't you write anything today? You've been productive until now."

"You can tell, eh?"

"I hum, you talk. Today you were mute as an alligator, when you weren't burning my ears with your four-letter words."

"I do apologize for that. I am not in the habit of using foul language. I suppose I've become accustomed to your presence. You are easy to be with, Raine."

"The first time I've heard that." She gave him a rueful grin, but would not pursue that line of their discussion. "What about your lack of writing?"

"Ah, well, I have rewritten the first chapter three times. Each version seems better than the last. Or that's so until I review the pages at night."

"My father used to edit his campaign speeches until he was sick to death of the repetition, but proud of the product."

"Revising is usually a profitable activity for me," he admitted, "but I have other decisions to make about the content of the book—and time and money are pressing me to perform. Although I sold my first mystery to Sloan Publishers, I wanted more money in advance than they were willing to give me. So I went elsewhere. I have signed a contract with the publisher of *St. Andrew's Magazine* to print the story in installments before it goes into book form. The editor paid me two thousand pounds at signing and will write a check for six hundred more on delivery of every chapter. The manuscript of the first chapter is due in two weeks. And I have nothing yet to give him."

Raine rejoiced at the news. The serialization of his novel meant that the work would appear in increments, giving the reading public a chance to talk about it and generate more sales. Then, hopefully, the similarities to the real murder would cause such a stir that the police and Scotland Yard would resume their investigations. This time, she prayed, the culprit would say or do something to give himself away and lead the authorities to his doorstep. Then Gavin would be free of scandal, free to stand for office with an officially clean record.

But Raine was also dismayed at Gavin's explanation. She had briefly met the editor of *St. Andrew's* over a year ago at her cousin Ann's. Raine had been visiting, cooing to Ann's and Rhys's new baby boy, when Rhys brought Sir Edward Hollister in to Kendall Great House for afternoon tea. Sir Edward Hollister resembled a chubby burro with huge black eyes encircled by tiny rimless spectacles, long pointy ears, and a razor-sharp mind. His weekly newspaper seemed more like a magazine, consisting mostly of political commentary, but featuring one piece of fiction per issue. When a series was a success in *St. Andrew's,* Hollister could safely bet that publishing the story in book form would be a profitable venture. Raine imagined that the little man had jumped at the chance to carry Gavin's second novel, particularly if Gavin had written a synopsis for him. "Does the editor know the content of your mystery?"

Gavin twirled his empty glass. "No. He bought it based on my—shall we call it—colorful reputation. Literary and otherwise."

"Is it prudent that he has no idea of your intentions?"

"For me, it is. By the time Ned Hollister realizes what he's got in his two hands, I hope the demand for the next installment will outweigh any consideration he might have to cancel it for notoriety's sake."

"I see."

"But you don't agree."

"No, Gavin, I don't. I think you should tell him you plan to duplicate the plot. Honesty," she told him with an ironic reminder of her own lack of it, "is the best policy. However, my view—and my blessing—are not necessary. The accomplishment of your goal is. And my view won't assist you in that." She took a healthy swallow of her champagne. "Why can't you write a first chapter that pleases you?"

"I need drama to open the story."

"You began your first book as the villain began his first embezzlement. You didn't reveal his name or much about his background, only his motivation. You kept the reader guessing about his identity until the last chapter. Why not do the same thing for this book?"

"You read *Pound Foolish?*" Pleasure made his gray eyes shine.

She nodded. "At last count, I was one of thirty thousand British men and women. Why, I repeat, not start this novel the same way?"

"That's easy to do when you are writing pure fiction, which this is not—or when you know who the villain is, which I do not."

She stared at him. "Do you have any suspects?"

He pursed his lips. "A few, yes."

"Any evidence? Oh, well, that was forward of me to ask." She cast her eyes away from him. "I don't need to know that, do I? And if I did, it would be a measure of how you trust me . . . and you don't. Not completely yet." Her thoughts marched across the room to his bookshelves. She cleared her throat. "Why not take a lesson from other authors then? Develop the novel in a different way."

"How?"

"Let the reader hear the tale through the voice of the accused man, then it becomes a suspense plot. The reader becomes the main character. Will he find the criminal? Will he free himself of all suspicion? Will he forever pay for someone else's crime? Don't you see that way, the reader develops sympathy for the hero. He's downtrodden and oppressed by forces he cannot control. When he discovers who really did the deed, the whole work is more vindicating. Our hero has insured that the justice system works. Our readers are satisfied that crime does not pay." She beamed at Gavin. "Yes?"

"No. There's a rub, Raine. What if our hero cannot bring the man to justice? What if the criminal is too crafty or never feels threatened by the novel?"

What was he speaking of? Fact or fiction? It didn't matter, the answer was still the same. "No one is above the law, Gavin."

"In theory."

She shivered. "You are writing fiction. People read mysteries to have it affirmed for them that everyone is equal before the law. You must write it that way."

He rubbed his jaw with two fingers. "I have my doubts."

"I don't like it when you turn sour."

"I don't, either."

"Stop it, then. Please."

"I shall try."

"What can I do to help you?" she persisted.

"Attempt to learn that machine." He indicated the typewriter.

She waggled her fingers at him. "Aside from that."

He considered that for so long she suspected he left out large portions of his answer. "I have read everything printed about me and the murders. Two days after Sean and Louise's bodies were found, I began to clip newspaper stories about it."

Raine's mouth went dry. Did he have a copy of the *Times-Daily* with her cartoon in it?

"As a result, I know many details about how Sean and Louise were killed. But they are a jumble. I hope you can bring some order to them."

"Of course, I can. Where are they?"

"In that cabinet." He toasted her and sipped from his glass. "I'll get the key and give them to you tomorrow." He gazed at the tall oak piece with myriad cubbyholes. "I need you to take them and make a list of facts—and another of the conjectures, where they came from, who said them, printed them. I tell you, Raine, I am damn glad I collected these but I'm muddled by them. I think about the events of that day so often that fact blends with the lies that were printed about me." His handsome face went lax as he turned to her but didn't truly see her. "Who could commit such a deed as that one, Raine? Who could think I did that? That I could so coldheartedly kill like that? I do know that whoever went to that house slaughtered them like animals."

Raine's stomach began to churn.

"Whoever did that to them had the anger of ten devils in him."

Her head began to throb.

"He bound them to their chairs, Raine. Used the knife on them in deliberate little carvings as if . . . as if to torture them for the fun of it or to make them talk. Imagine—" he said as if he had been there that night and witnessed the horror.

Raine ran through her own nightmare, veiled by years of blocking its existence. She put a hand to her brow, reliving her escape from renegade soldiers who had invaded her home and captured her parents. Tied them up and—

"I'm sorry, Gavin." Blindly, she deposited her flute on the table. "You must excuse me. I can't listen to this."

She had reached her white wicket gate before he got to her. "Raine," he tried to stop her from pushing it open by capturing her hand, "Raine, I am so sorry. I think I can tell you anything, and too late I see you quiver like a butterfly. Christ, you're perspiring. You're not going to faint, are you?" He trailed his fingers from her forehead to cup her jaw, then wrapped her in his arms. "You're trembling."

She clenched her teeth. They chattered. "I am fine." *If you just hold me for a long time, I'll be even better.* She pressed her nose to his shirt. He smelled like sandalwood and ink. He felt so staunch. Her arms went around his waist. She'd not been embraced in years and years . . . so long. She refused to whimper.

He raised her face. "Don't cry."

She shook her head. "I never do."

He brushed a tear from her cheek. "Today—and that first day you came to work—you got a tear in your eye."

She gulped. "I don't remember."

"I do. No one has cared a fig about me, but you."

She liked him this close. She could admire the straight line of his jaw and the brightness of his teeth when he grinned at her as he did now. She could memorize his handsomeness so that years from now, when she could no longer see him in the flesh, she might permit herself the pleasure of drawing him. "Does this mean I can ask for an increase in my salary?"

He threw his head back to laugh up at the sky. It was the same pose she had witnessed the day she applied for his position. She loved the way his laughter rumbled in his chest and reverberated in her breasts and thighs. It was the best medicine for both of them and she needed to taste more. "Will two pounds more a week do?"

One kiss would be a fortune. "Three," she said instead.

"Done. If you can wait two weeks until I get paid from *St. Andrew's*. It's the least I can do since you've helped me with the plot."

"You're serious?"

"About money? Always. A person always needs it." His gaze fell to her lips. "And this. I am very serious about needing this, Raine."

She should have asked him what he meant. She needed to put caution or humor between him and her very compliant body. But her brain was no longer connected to any other part of her. She was on fire in Gavin Sutherland's embrace and all else seemed such drivel. So when Gavin ran his fingers into her hair and crushed her closer, she could not suppress a moan.

"I've wanted you, too," she whispered before his mouth took hers.

His lips were hot but gentle as he kissed her in greedy exploration. She opened herself to him, felt plundered, but starved for more. She pulled him closer. He kissed her again in leisure, and she sensed she was drifting away on the tides into uncharted waters.

"Open your eyes," he told her in a gruff and needy voice. When she did, he urged, "Invite me for supper."

She chuckled. "Why?"

He arched a brow playfully. "For one thing, you have a big fish."

She gauged his shoulders. "I think you're right."

He hooted. "I could go get it." He put one hand along her throat. "I need to be with you, Raine. You'd like my company, too . . . if I'm not mistaken?"

How could she deny it after she had responded to him so eagerly? "We won't talk about the murders."

"Not a word," he vowed. "What stops you? Do you, perhaps, keep a disorderly house?" He tilted his head toward her cottage.

"I am very finicky, my lord. Somewhat like you." She put everything in its place. Including her sketchbook of animals. God forbid Gavin recognize her style and remember the hideous cartoon she'd done of him. He'd turn her out. He'd hate her. She shuddered.

He put his lips to her cheek, his sweet words like balm to her fears. "What do you think? We can't continue to stand here and kiss."

"Why not?" She was flirting with him, the first time she'd worked wiles on any man. She nearly preened like a coquette at his smoky-eyed reaction. She was having fun—and she was shocked at her boldness. Astonished, too, that she desired a man, she was not surprised the least little bit that she yearned for Gavin Sutherland.

"Raine, I am certain my gardener is watching. Or Mrs. McNally."

"There's a sobering thought." She tried to pull back.

He wouldn't let her. "We have to eat."

"Ah, would you relish a change from Mrs. McNally's roasted this and boiled that?"

"I'm sure you have a better dish in mind."

Your mouth. She shouldn't crave him. She shouldn't invite him. Shouldn't encourage him. But she did want to be with him and what better way than to sit with a table between them? "What I was going to do with that sea bass you might find intriguing."

"No more than I already am."

He was her employer. He was the man she had ruined. He was the one she needed to help restore. But he was the only man whose mind and body had ever drawn her like a bee to honey.

For the first time in her life, she wanted to enjoy herself with a man. "Fetch me my fish."

Chapter 4

"Do what thy manhood bids thee do . . ."
—SIR RICHARD FRANCIS BURTON

WHY DID SHE FASCINATE HIM?

It was no mystery.

Gavin studied her as she sailed around her kitchen. Since he had entered with her sea bass tucked under one arm and a bottle of Chateau Mouton in the other, she had made a shambles of the alcove's tidiness. Her cheery yellow gingham curtains filtered the sun into a light show of brass and gold, whetting his appetite for more than what she prepared. She moved from her butcher's table to her black cast-iron stove with a practiced ease which belied her aristocratic tastes.

Raine Jennings was a study in contrasts.

"Why won't you tell me what you're putting in that stew of yours?" He sat at her oak block table to which she'd consigned him with a bit of champagne in one of her earthen mugs.

"It's not a stew, but a sauce." She dropped a pinch of some spice into the big pot she had put on top of a burner. Then she made his eyes pop when she put in the head of the sea bass—wrapped in a muslin knapsack. Noticing his reticence, she blithely said it was important not to waste any portion of the fish.

"I can condone the extravagance of throwing it away, if it means eating that."

"The head adds flavor. You won't even know you're tasting it. You eat kidney pie, don't you? And liver and tripe?"

"Not I. I gave my nursemaids hives by refusing such offerings."

"You'll like this. I've never known anyone who didn't enjoy creole cooking. I've used a few different ingredients than what I'm used to, but they won't change the flavor that much. I have had to be inventive in England."

"When I interviewed Mrs. McNally, I specifically requested that she not be innovative with her menus."

"Ah, but you made no such stipulations with me— and you invited yourself to dinner. So you, my lord, are stuck with me."

A delightful jam. "Is the recipe an old family secret?" He had hired Raine out of expediency and asked far too few questions. Now his curiosity about who she was and what kind of life she had lived before she came to Chipswell mounted like his appetite.

She wiped her hands on her huge white apron, clucking her tongue at him. "We don't have recipes. We have techniques. Opportunities to use fresh seafood and vegetables. For instance, tonight we have . . ." She hoisted a bulb of garlic, broke off a portion, and crushed it with the flat of her knife. "About five cloves of this. Mrs. McNally will definitely leave us alone tomorrow."

I'd like to lock the door and throw away the key.

"Onion, for added incentive."

As if I need more.

"Lots of tomatoes. I am eager to have my own tomato plants blossom," she muttered, cradling in her palm one ripe fruit Gavin's gardener had given her from his vegetable plot. "There is no substitute for a fresh one."

Gavin mentally measured the small firm fruit against the slightly larger delicacy her breast would be. "I can imagine."

"I can guarantee—" she brandished her knife gaily as if she knew precisely what he wanted, "that you've never had anything like this."

How true. He'd never hungered for a woman like this. Not even Belinda. That woman's interest in politics had first attracted him to her, and her strong dark looks had doubled the appeal. Raine Jennings's wealth of alluring characteristics could not be listed in any order. Each morning she arrived at his garden doors, he found a new asset he admired as much as the last. Her punctuality and élan invigorated his days, even while her beauty tantalized him. Stymied in writing his mystery, he could have produced dozens of fantasies about how Raine Jennings walked and talked and laughed.

Repeatedly, he told himself he had to concentrate on his novel. He failed. This afternoon as he conversed with her during luncheon, he concluded that he must do one of three things immediately. Sack her and remove himself from temptation. Kiss her and discover his daydreams about her were so much fable. Or find another woman on whom to shower his attentions.

The first solution was impossible. He simply could not bear to send her away. What reason would he give? And what relief would he get if she were merely across the cove within his sight? He'd still watch her, wondering what was beneath her oh-so-serene exterior. He had to have her within reach—and no other woman within a hundred miles appealed. Belinda certainly paled. So his decision to kiss Raine and end his torture had landed him in this fine kettle of fish.

He wanted her again. Her mouth, at the very least. Regardless of propriety and logic. Tonight.

"How long does it take to prepare whatever it is you're

cooking?" He silently damned the increasingly uncomfortable caned chair. Now that he had sampled her lips, he simmered with the urge to trail his tongue around her two perfect breasts. But her nipples were the dish that set him to hard boil. He had no idea how he'd get a taste, and he'd have to learn soon or go jump in the sea for a cold swim.

"Twenty minutes at most." She gave him a congenial smile and stirred something else into her pot. "Will you stop worrying if you'll like this?"

I worry you'll give me nothing—or too much I can't do without. "What is it called?"

"My version of fish *en papier.* I don't have all the spices and herbs I should, either—"

More than enough to make me hot.

"But I'm adept at going by instinct."

No need to tell me that.

She tried so valiantly to maintain her social distance as his employee. But she was not oblivious to his delight in her companionship nor his desire for her. When he kissed her, he had witnessed her pleasure with the sway of her body to his, the clutch of her fist on his shirt. He prayed those were not the actions of a widow substituting any man's affection for the one she'd lost, but Raine Jennings's need to kiss him, only him. He had marveled at the look of enchantment on her face when he'd taken his mouth from hers. He felt the same as she, and he needed to know for his own egotistical reasons if she'd care for a repetition. Meanwhile as she drifted around her kitchen, cooking for him, he'd have to remain content to mentally undress her to her shoes.

"Since I've come to England," she was elaborating, "I haven't found any strong cayenne nor any parsley that's sweet, but here in Norfolk, I do feel a smidgen compensated by using the local saffron. It's wonderful to have it so fresh. The color is superb. A delicate golden pink. . . . You look rather flushed." She took a few steps around her chopping table and looked him over. "Is it too warm in here for you? With the oven fire so high, I know it must be more than what you're used to. Gavin?"

He tried to look nonchalant but his heart wasn't in it. "Perhaps it is more than I can bear."

"I'll let in some air." Raine floated around him, toward her sitting area past her bed. "There," she announced and inhaled the smell of the sea. "Each night the breeze off the water is divine."

Gavin could feel it from here. Cooling his skin, the winds did nothing to dampen the fire beneath.

What was the matter with him? He couldn't be thinking of taking his secretary to bed. He didn't need the distraction. He didn't want the entanglement, delicious as the very thought could be of her legs around his. He had a book to write, money to earn, a reputation to restore—a seat to gain in the Commons. His list of goals sometimes seemed endless. So difficult to accomplish. So uncertain.

He took his mug and began to walk about her little one-room house. "I like the way you have refurbished it. The widow who lived here was an independent soul. She would not take anything from us, though she lived from hand to mouth. Her husband had been my father's gardener. He and she planted those roses you tend in your garden."

Raine searched his expression. Gavin knew she realized he watched her as she pruned the rosebushes. "I suppose she planted the chives and dill, too."

"I'm certain of it, yes. She was—some said in the village—a witch."

"Ah, every village should have one. On our plantation, we had a woman who was our overseer's wife. She was from Jamaica and knew voodoo, but I never saw her practice it. She did know how to treat every malady from the croup to indigestion, though."

"Ours did the same. She mixed a tea for gout which my grandmother swore cured her in a week. The woman's fame spread so that she earned her livelihood in trade by prescribing for anyone who came to her."

"I wondered who she was because I love her little herb garden and her old oak furniture," Raine said with an approving glance around. "I was pleased when the advertisement said the cottage was furnished. I am not rich, and I needed to come here without spending everything I had in savings."

"I like your additions." He inclined his head toward her bed. Trimmed in yards of white eyelet and Irish lace, Raine's coverlet was another indication of her stylish taste and background. "Especially your choice of fabrics."

"Thank you," she said, quite surprised. "I didn't think men liked such frivolities—or noted them."

"They suit you. As if to say one must handle with care." Before she could debate that, he noted her polished silver brush on her dresser top. "Did your husband share your love of fine things?" *And if so, why take an exquisite creature like you to live in Seven Dials?*

Her face acquired that look for which he could find no other description but trapped.

He'd loose her from her bonds, if he could. How? He had to know more about her, and she was so reluctant to speak about her past. Grief stopped her, but his curiosity was going to eat him alive. "You like silver. Lace. Champagne. Expensive saffron."

"Yes, we both enjoyed comforts far beyond our means. It is a trial to grow up accustomed to a certain quality and then to learn that maintaining your standards is not cheap. Food," she said with a brave attempt to inject a spot of levity, "is a basic means to survive any hardship, however."

Gavin lifted his nose into the air and said, "I am about to learn that, firsthand, I think."

She laughed and wended her way past him to her pot. "Thanks to the bounty from the sea."

He followed her. "What else do you know how to cook?"

"I can prepare a gumbo that will fire your innards for a week or make a *boudin* which will make your eyeballs water for a month."

"What is gumbo and . . . ?"

"*Boudin* is a sausage filled with pork and spiced rice. Gumbo is a soup which you fill with anything you have left over from the day before. A base of a roux—" she laughed, "lard and flour mixed on a high heat—almost to a burn, rich and brown, and to that you add onion, green pepper, and celery. 'The holy trinity,' we say. If you have a bit of chicken or shrimp, crawfish, or alligator—"

"Just a minute. Alligator?"

"Very tender. Better than chicken."

"I'm glad I know what I'm getting tonight."

"Do you?"

He could dream, couldn't he? "That was a sea bass I carted over here. Two pounds at least. Are you disguising him in something so I won't recognize him?"

She lifted the fish from the fishmonger's wrapping and set it down into a pile of flour she had salted and peppered. "If you don't taste it, I haven't done my job correctly." She tossed Gavin a tiny smile. "You can terminate my services."

I doubt it. He sipped his champagne. "I am very glad you chose this village."

"So am I," she said, lining a baking dish with a huge piece of brown butcher paper.

"Why didn't you go home to America?"

"I have no family there."

"What made you come to Chipswell?"

"The sea." Her fingers fussed with the paper. "I read the newspaper advertisements, looking for a place I could go for a rest. I needed to think about what I wanted to do with my life now that . . . things have changed for me. I saw a cottage for rent in Deal in Kent, but the owner wanted five pounds a month. The ad for this cottage said two pounds so I thought that affordable."

"I think it's hideous that the army does not give widows any death benefit or a pension. With the empire growing and thousands of our men needed to patrol its borders, we must provide for them and their wives in the event of tragedy."

"A suitable cause to add to your platform for election, don't you think?"

"Consider it done." He raised his mug to her. "When you read the ads for a house to let, did you also see my ad for a secretary?" She seemed so suited to him and his needs, he could not believe simple providence had brought her to him.

She raised her eyes to his. "Yes. I wanted to apply to you from the first day I saw your ad. I knew you'd want a man. Most men in your position do, don't they? Well, anyway," she pushed a lock of hair from her cheek with her shoulder and lifted her fish into the paper. "I decided to come to Chipswell. I needed the rest and the diversion of the sea. Once I was settled in though, I spent my days screwing up my courage to apply to you for the job. When I heard in the village that you hadn't hired any of the applicants, I finally threw caution to the wind and wrote you my letter."

If there was a connection between her choice to come to Chipswell and her desire to work for him, she made it sound more like coincidence than a plan. He thought it might be a bit of luck. His. "I told myself I wasn't going to hire you. Even though I invited you to interview." *But you looked too lovely—and so lonely that I could not ignore you—or reject you.*

"Mmm," she agreed as she worked on, "that's what I thought."

"I wanted to keep my life simple."

She paused for a second at the implication that her presence complicated his existence.

"If any of the three men who did apply had been conversant in the Queen's English, I would have hired him in a heartbeat."

"Idiots, weren't they? Or so I heard from the greengrocer who'd been told by Mrs. McNally."

He shook his head. "She does talk sometimes."

"It's natural. She's proud of you and jealous of her role in your life."

He didn't want to talk about McNally. "You haven't talked to very many people since you came here. You've made no friends."

"I haven't made a project of it, no." She turned her damper to redirect the cooking heat to the oven.

"It must be terribly difficult to deal with the loss of someone you loved dearly. Certainly someone who was young and—"

"Yes," she said and lifted the lid from her pot on the stovetop. "Winston died of tuberculosis. He was a sweet man." She arranged her fish just so within its paper nest. "Kind. Quiet." She ladled her tomato-studded broth over the bass, crimped the paper over her creation, and folded it closed. She unlatched her oven door, donned two mittens, and deposited her fish inside. "Can you set a table?"

"Why is it that women think men are helpless?" He reached for the plates she extended.

"You are the second son of one of the premier noblemen in England. I have few indications of what you can and cannot do living as an ordinary man."

"Ouch. Stung. Is that your American background speaking out against the terrors of nobility or is it engendered by some personal knowledge of our inadequacies?"

She faced him. "That was unkind of me. No, I have no bad experiences with noblemen. It is my American tendency to deprecate them—and my awful manners." She brought utensils to the table and stood beside him to set them about. "I am sorry, Gavin. You've been good to me and I hurt you with my views. I have told myself I must become less judgmental." Her sapphire eyes met his. "I will try to be more positive."

"Oh, but I would not ask you to change, Raine. I like you as you are."

"Caustic." She sniffed and walked away.

"Becoming less so, I venture, in the past two weeks.

Why don't I pour more champagne for you, it might help you smooth over the rough edges?"

She waved a hand in agreement.

He sat down at the table to wait for his supper. She cleaned up the pile of flour and wiped down her butcher block.

"You are very expert in a kitchen. Who taught you how to cook?"

One shoulder lifted. He recognized it now as a defensive gesture. This was a sad memory or one she did not wish to discuss for too long. "My mother, my family's cook, and the overseer's wife."

The aromas of garlic and tomatoes wafted around him. "They trained you well."

"Ah, ah. Don't speak until you have tasted the wares, my lord."

"Do you think you will ever go back to America?"

"Maybe. Someday. But I cannot imagine why. I prefer Europe. It may be the Old World, but for me it is new. Filled with paintings to view, cities to visit. I have no reason to go home to Baton Rouge. It is a place filled with evil memories." She slowly faced him. "One in particular. My parents are dead. Civilian casualties of war. They died horrible deaths, killed by our own troops, Confederates fleeing upriver from the Yankee invasion of New Orleans. I have never come to think idly of those days . . . and I cannot speak casually about them."

"Raine, I am so sorry I brought this up."

"Perhaps we should agree on what we can discuss. Like the weather?" she offered, too chipper to be serious.

He spied her binoculars on her bedside table. "Your bird-watching."

Again that look of amazement at the fact that he had observed her so closely stole across her features. "It's not just birds I watch."

"What else?"

"Deer, squirrels . . . foxes."

"Alligators?" he asked, to find that note of levity they'd struck before.

"I did watch them when I was young. Fascinating creatures. Alligators have great character."

"For what? Being eaten or eating people?"

"No, they are strong, distinctive. They know their purpose in life, they go to it, and so they are easy to draw."

He had noticed long ago that she had the slender fingers perfect for a pianist or an artist. "Do you draw?"

She flexed her jaw. "A little. I have not done it in ages. I'm just teaching myself now how to do animals."

He glanced around and saw no evidence of her endeavors. No pens, no pads. "When do you do it?"

"At night after supper. After my walk on the beach."

"May I see a sketch?"

"No."

"You think I'd be critical?"

"You could be," she allowed. "I'm not that good."

"How do you know?" When she would have backed away from the subject, he would not let her. "Unless you let someone else see your drawings, you will never know what quality they are."

"I've only just begun to sketch animals in the last week or so. I can't show you." She sounded more resolute with each word.

"All right," he relented because she seemed frightened. Terrified, really, of criticism. "I am not that harsh a judge, Raine."

"Probably, but I still can't show you."

"I can remember a time when I didn't want anyone to see my writing. I thought it mundane or much too melodramatic, and I feared people would laugh."

"I know you wouldn't be so unkind as to laugh at my work, Gavin. But I am sensitive."

How well he knew that. "Show me when you're ready, Raine."

"I will try."

Gavin knew that was a concession she made but had

no intention of keeping. She finished tidying her kitchen, her actions creating a greater chasm between them. He remained silent, confident their natural camaraderie would return.

It came when she served her fish. Transferring it from the baking dish to a steaming platter, she had left the fish in the paper. Charred to a crisp, the casing was puffed like a balloon. Raine brought it to the table, poked it with a fork, and steam whooshed through the holes.

"I may not have to eat," he closed his eyes and inhaled, "I've already gone to heaven."

"Oh, good. More for me." She was silently laughing as she served the fish to his plate.

When she had taken her chair across from him, he lifted his mug. "To you, your drawings, your dinner."

"Thank you. To you, your book, and your seat in Commons." She sipped her champagne but sat, waiting for him to take a bite of the fish. From the glee on her face she was not disappointed by his reaction. "I haven't lost my touch, I guess."

He smiled. "Ah, but you must cook like this for yourself or you wouldn't have bought the fish."

"I do," she said and took her first taste. Her mouth moved in a slow motion that churned up his need to put his lips on hers once more. "But it's not as wonderful as when you can watch someone else enjoy it."

How well he knew that, too. He tried to divert himself from his erotic thoughts of her by taking another mouthful. "Perhaps you'll invite me again."

She toyed with her fork. "Maybe I will."

"What can I do to insure it?"

"Clean your plate."

"That won't be a problem."

She tipped her head to one side. "Help me wash the dishes."

"I think that sounds like a dare."

"No. Division of labor. I cooked, you wash," she chuckled and tucked into her food with more gusto.

"Oh, my. Here we are at the issue of aristocratic privilege again."

"Don't most men in your class have servants to do everything? Even when you're very young?"

"Yes, but that doesn't mean we take advantage of the situation."

"Didn't you?"

"At first, yes. One does not know any differently. My older brother Derek was my model. He enjoys his station. Heir to the power and the glory, that he is." Gavin picked up the bottle of champagne. "But I am not the heir to anything. I had to learn to make my own way. Carve a future for myself."

"You did a very fine job of it, too," she declared.

"Until one evening, everything I had worked for was taken from me by circumstances beyond my control." He poured more champagne for both of them. "Do you know what they call that in fiction?"

She leaned toward him, ready to object, and he wouldn't let her.

"Tragedy."

"At the risk of sounding like a preacher, I'd say you're becoming morose again. Gavin, your story is not finished yet," she came to his defense. "I mean the one you live, not the one you intend to write. You must cast off this negativity. You won't write anything worthwhile that way. I can't sketch if I'm dwelling on the things I cannot change."

He was grateful for her words—and her insight. How did she acquire it, though, if she'd been drawing for only a week or so? Such reflections on the emotional balances of an artist come to one who has engaged in his or her art for years. "What do you do to free yourself of such thoughts?"

"I have had to build a wall against reality. Live only in my fortress with my characters. Never let another thought come into my head until I cannot render any more onto the paper that day."

"I will try that. Anything."

"Others may have better means to accomplish the same detachment. Experiment. Perhaps you know other writers who would have better suggestions."

He looked askance. "I am acquainted with only two writers who earn their living from their novels. Believe me, their solutions are not ones I'd use."

"Who do you know?"

"Milton Attenborough and Wilkie Collins."

"So," she licked her lips, "Mr. Attenborough does find inspiration in a bottle?"

"Hourly."

"And the rumors about Collins are also true?"

"Cocaine is served with after-dinner drinks."

"It's no wonder he produces so few novels. How can he find time to write if he boggles his mind with hallucinogens *and* bobs around among two mistresses and one wife?"

Gavin shook his head. "Words escape me."

"Let alone Mr. Collins." Chuckling, Raine raised her glass. "A salute to Mr. Collins. His inventiveness—and his stamina."

"Hmmm, yes," Gavin agreed with a click of his mug on hers. "May I emulate his sterling qualities."

But in order to do that, he had to begin to write something quickly. His mood, so easily lightened by Raine's company, sank again.

It was becoming increasingly easy to chastise himself. From there it was a small step downward to dwell on all the negative aspects in his life. His resignation, his exile. He became adept at reliving the night of the murder, the argument in Hyde Park—and his subsequent visit to Stoddard House in Kensington. He scoured his memory of the murder scene, looking for clues, something he'd missed to indicate who had done the deed for which most thought him responsible. The crime for which he had unjustly paid in so many ways.

"You are lost again," Raine intruded on his reverie, her frustration evident in the firm set of her mouth.

Why waste precious minutes with Raine on a memory which yielded nothing useful? Why couldn't he learn to enjoy the moment? And this scintillating woman? "I have had so little company in the past year that I am rusty at making polite conversation."

"Part of that is my fault, too. I know I have not been easy to talk to. I don't make a habit of sharing my past with just anyone. The alternative to prattle on about nothing does not thrill me. Not with you. We are far better acquainted than that."

Her honesty and her admission of their friendship dissolved his sadness. "Most dinner discussions are such a bore."

"Turning the tables when you'd much rather let the discussion flow. Avoiding important topics like politics in favor of gossip. Separating the men and women afterward for coffee and brandy." She grimaced. "I would much rather stay with the men to drink and smoke."

He chuckled. "I can oblige you there."

"Is that so?" She eyed his plate. "Eat up."

"Do you like any particular type of cigar? I have Cuban and Brazilian or—"

She wrinkled her nose. "I prefer a pipe."

"And a brandy?"

"Cognac or absinthe."

"I can accommodate you there, too."

Her eyes lit up like fireworks. "I may not report for work so early."

"A small price to pay for a little joy in life."

She laughed. *"After* we do the dishes."

"Did I say otherwise?"

"No, but—"

"You don't trust me."

"You? Of course I do. Could I work for you if I didn't?"

He sat back, fingered his mug, then asked her in a hushed tone, "Why do you trust me, Raine?" Her mouth slowly parted. "Don't you ever wonder if I killed them?"

No. There was no sound to her reply.

"Why?"

She went still as the air around them. "I did question if you could have done it days afterward when all the stories began to appear in the newspapers. But I had to ask myself if a man of your background and caliber could murder another human being. I decided that you couldn't."

"How could you deduce that from—" his waved a hand, at a loss, "what you had heard or read about me?"

"I had heard you speak in the Commons. And I have good instincts." She looked him square in the eye. "I get into a passel of trouble when I don't use them. In your case, my first thought was that you might have killed them. You see, I . . . knew about that argument you had in Hyde Park with O'Malley and Louise Stoddard."

"I must thank the famous cartoon in the *Times-Daily.*"

"Yes," she said and took a drink of her champagne. "But as I began to think about the possibility that you may have hurt those two people, I realized what my eyes had seen . . . must have another interpretation." She fell back to her chair. "You are not the usual professional politician. You don't take up causes to gain more votes, but support specific ones in which you believe. You don't insult others to gain attention or the upper hand. You don't purposely misstate facts to win a point. Finally, your anger is honest. The man I saw in the Commons becomes impassioned about causes he considers just, not causes he thinks are beneficial solely to his career."

He sat back, overwhelmed with the variety and depth of her observations. "If you can see this, why can't others? Why do people suspect me of that hideous crime?"

"They believe what they read. Or they take the answer that's offered them. They don't have time to investigate or assess. That's what they have police and courts for. And justice is supposed to be blind. Weighing only the facts. There are very few in this case."

He bit his lip, resigned. "Thank you."

"You're welcome." She examined him as if she was committing his features to some treasure box, then grinned. "In reality, you resemble an alligator."

He snorted. "This is what you call a compliment, I gather?"

"You are strong. You know your purpose here on Earth. If I were to draw you . . . ."

Feeling naked to her probing gaze, he found he loved the scrutiny. "What would you make of me?"

"No more or less than what you are. An honorable man. A wounded one. But determined."

"I would like to see such a portrait, if only to reinforce the hope that this man exists."

"Take it from me, he does. You need not see a sketch to prove he is alive and well."

"Alive." *Especially near you.* "Not so well. Not yet."

"As you start the book and gain momentum, you'll feel better. I'll organize those clippings of yours, too— and that should help to clear your thinking."

"I hope you are right."

"I know I am. Another serving?" She nodded toward his plate.

"Yes, thank you."

They left the subject which belabored him for the more delectable act of finishing their meal and their champagne.

As he rolled down his sleeves and took the dishpan from her dry sink, he asked her if she'd care to have her brandy and pipe now or later. Immediately he saw that the idea of later accosted her sense of propriety. "I thought you might like a walk along the beach first. It is what you usually do, now that your mornings are spent with me."

Something about that bothered her, but she didn't voice it. Instead, she began to clean up and he helped.

When he had dashed the dishwater along the rocks and returned to her kitchen, she hung the pan on the little hook near her window, took a shawl from the chair near her front door, and went out with him along the flat stepping-stones down toward the edge of the sea.

"I noticed you used to go out in the mornings and take your binoculars," he observed to break their silence.

"I'm studying the birds to draw them more accurately."

The sun had set to their left, and the sea on their right was turning to slate. The breeze that had floated into her cottage before picked up, taking her hair from its pins. One escaping lock astonished him for its length. It reached past her thighs.

He turned his face away from the temptation of her to the sea.

"Why do you watch me?" Her voice reached out at last to caress him with a silken curiosity.

"You fascinate me," he told the wind, but faced her with the explanation she sought. "From the day you moved into the cottage, I found myself spellbound by your looks, the way you walk, the way you talk to yourself. You brood," he affirmed when she shot him a look. "You did it a lot or rather you did when you first moved in. Now you do it less. Yes, I have seen you walk the beach at dusk. I watch you because you have so many traits similar to my own. I told myself your sadness was grief at the loss of your husband. Mrs. McNally told me about you and his death the first day she met you at the butcher's. Then I saw you with your binoculars and I wondered who you were, what you did."

Raine narrowed her gaze on the water. "Now you know."

Do I? "Not enough."

She shivered and stepped away.

He stopped her as she teetered on the edge of a rock, his hand to her elbow. "I'd like to know if I could kiss you again."

She smiled winsomely. "It's not a good idea."

"Afraid you might not like it as much as the first time?"

"Afraid I'd want to do it too often."

"Well, then." He gathered her in his arms.

She put both palms flat to his chest, her elbows digging a barrier. "This is not in my list of duties."

"I had no idea I'd want to kiss my secretary or I'd have put it first."

She swallowed. "It could become a habit."

Please, let that be true. "We could agree on a time and place."

"No." She yanked away from him and in her haste on the wet rocks, she slipped.

He caught her. "Only at night, here, when no one can see except the man in the moon."

She laughed. "You are a persistent man."

"You are not a cooperative woman."

"I don't have to be."

He felt like a child denied a treat—and hated to be petulant. Had he misinterpreted the depth of her interest in him? "Don't you want to kiss me?"

"You are not fair to ask me that."

"I'll be more unfair." He gripped her a little harshly. "Why not, Raine?"

"You were the most sought-after bachelor in the Commons. The man women call the Man with the Quicksilver Voice. How could a woman ignore that you are handsome and desirable and considered quite a catch?"

He must have looked like *Alice in Wonderland*'s Cheshire Cat the way he grinned. Even in the dwindling light of day, he could see Raine's cheeks blushing. "What then is your objection to a kiss?"

"This." She grabbed his shirt and went up on her tiptoes. Her mouth to his was a cool surprise, but her urgency was a warm solace.

"Raine," he murmured as he brought her nearer, and his mouth sought hers out again and again. Her lips were an invitation to sweet hours of exploration.

"Gavin—"

"Hmmm?" His brain was concocting ways to take her into his house, his bed.

"You see what happens when we do this?"

See? He was blind with the need to hold her and not let her go until he'd tasted every delicate inch of her. "Tell me you want to stop, and I'll say you are a liar."

That made her still. "I won't lie to you. But I am not a woman who does this freely with a man."

"We'll have an agreement. We'll ration them."

Dismay dashed across her features. Mischief emerged. "All right," she said slowly. "One kiss . . ." She tossed her curls, a glint in her eye. "For each chapter."

"You're serious!" He was incredulous, but she waited for his hilarity to subside.

She strained away from him. "You have some fast writing to do."

"What do you mean?"

"You're already in debt. There is this kiss—"

"Raine. There were three."

She blinked hard, remembering. "You were counting?"

"Couldn't you?" He drove one hand up into her heavy hair, said "Lucky me," and took another leisurely sample of her lips.

After this one, her lashes fluttered open. Her words sounded smooth, but had an edge. "Before supper there were . . . three more."

"Which adds up to seven."

She pulled away and tucked her shawl up around her throat. "Time for me to go inside. See you in the morning."

He watched her leave, a silly grin on his face. "But what about your pipe and absinthe?"

"Not tonight, Gavin." She climbed up a dune. "I've had enough."

He hadn't.

"Damn," he told himself as he strolled across the beach toward home, "if this won't be the longest book a man has ever written."

Chapter 5

"Give the lady what she wants!"

—MARSHALL FIELD

"WE'RE GOING TO HAVE A VISITOR." GAVIN APPEARED BE-
fore her desk five days later with a stack of papers in one
hand and a letter in the other. "This came in the
morning post."

"From your frown, I'd guess that whoever it is, he's
not welcome." Raine's thoughts sprang to the other
possibility that Gavin's guest could be a woman. His
mother. His sister. Or, if the lady came with a chaperone
and a hope to make amends to him, Gavin's former
fiancée. She had broken their engagement—and she did
not deserve him back because she wouldn't stand by
him. Suddenly, like the evil weed it was, jealousy
bloomed before Raine's eyes.

"Now you're frowning. Don't. I do like him," Gavin
affirmed. "He is very amiable. It's my publisher."

"Sir Edward Hollister?"

"Yes."

Raine put down the pages of Gavin's manuscript

which he had given her to read this morning. Would Sir Edward remember her? They had spoken for two minutes, at the most, as Raine left Ann's home on the Strand over a year ago. That day she had taken her luncheon with Ann, soon after the birth of her son. If Raine's memory served her well, she could say she had worn her usual business attire, one of her severely tailored walking suits. She'd also worn a hat and her veil was already in place when Rhys and his guest walked into Kendall Great House. She and Sir Edward had never met again. But how many Americans did an Englishman meet? In Rhys Kendall's magnificent mansion on the Thames? And what had he and she discussed? Was it any topic which might make her stand out in his memory?

Gavin arched a speculative brow. "What shall I say about my progress on the book?" His gaze rose from her hands to her lips.

Gavin had not kissed her since that night she had cooked for him and they had shared so much more than supper. He wrote from the moment she arrived each morning until—she guessed—well after she left at dusk. He would break for luncheon and tea, but immediately afterward, he would return to his scribblings, mumbling to himself and refusing to let her see a word until he felt comfortable with the results. Finally, this morning as she stepped through his garden doors, he had handed a stack of paper over to her with a wink. She had read the pages with surprise and pride at how very exciting the plot was.

"You've been very slow writing these." *To my sorrow and relief.* "But it has been worth it."

He grinned wolfishly. "I certainly hope so."

She cast him a withering glance, but acceded, "Your story is superb. Fast, gripping."

"I'm thrilled you approve. I'll be more delighted when I can begin to collect what's owed to me."

"Collect?" There was no mistaking his implication. Raine's skin burned at the expectation of more of his kisses. Truth to tell, she was wild to have his mouth on hers again. It was silly, a schoolgirl's crush, an obsession she had never known and wished she didn't now. She held up his manuscript nonchalantly. "I see only five chapters here."

"Ah," he flourished the sheaf of paper he held, "but I just finished the sixth."

"Which means you have to write one more to even the score."

"But I have almost completed two more."

She could imagine how two more would fan the flames of her weakness for him, undo her resolve to stay away from him and never to kiss him again. "That's impressive."

Amusement brought out his dimple. "I hope so. I've been fantasizing for so long about them that I want to make them the best you've ever known."

"Writers," she couldn't suppress her urge to chuckle, "and your double entendres." Her sense of propriety took hold. Now that he had finished these new chapters, he was becoming charming and much too familiar. He must not pursue her with words and looks which verged on the improper. Acknowledging such emotion was simply not done. Not by men and women in polite society. Not in Baton Rouge. Definitely never in Norfolk, England.

But she had brought Gavin's attentions on herself by inviting him to supper and suggesting they share a kiss for each completed chapter. "Your tendency to confuse your story with reality can get you in trouble some day soon."

He rolled his eyes and would have replied, had Mrs. McNally not cleared her throat, long and loud. The woman had recognized the attraction between her employer and his secretary from the first. She also had no compunction about showing her disapproval whenever the opportunity presented itself—which was at least once a day. "Pardon my intrusion, milord, but luncheon is served."

"Yes, thank you, Mrs. McNally. We'll be along in a minute." The woman's footsteps resounded down the center hall. "I'll let you finish reading these chapters, Raine. I'm editing the other two now. Expect them later today."

She ignored his innuendo that at the end of this day, he might be kissing her again. "All the better for when Sir Edward arrives. Which is when?"

"On this afternoon's train."

"Good God, so soon." She had to find an excuse to leave Gavin's office early and remain out of Ned Hollister's sight. Her plan to help Gavin write his novel would be dashed if Hollister recognized her as Raine Montand, Ann Brighton Kendall's cousin. How would Raine explain to Gavin that she was not an English lieutenant's widow in need of a salary, but the American Beauty whom many dubbed Wit? Witless would become her name if Gavin turned her out. To come so far and help him, only to be thwarted, made her hands clench. Her will to succeed coupled with her fear that she could fail. "How long does he stay?"

"Only a night or two. Says he doesn't want to interrupt my flow, so to speak, but he's coming to look in on his investment."

"Naturally."

"He will want to read what I have and take back the first chapter." Gavin sat on the edge of her desk. "Do you think it's good enough to let him print it?"

"Absolutely. Better than the first chapter of *Pound Foolish.*"

"Really? Why?"

"I adore the hero. He is——" She paused when desire streaked across Gavin's features, "admirable. Troubled by those who fear he has acted rashly. Conflicted by taking money from his father——"

"And his influence, too."

"Especially that. If I didn't know you were British by the way the dialogue sounds so veddy uppah crust, milord, I'd say some of the sentiments you express are utterly American."

"How so?"

"This man," she brushed her palm over the manuscript, "will become his own person. Self-made, beholden only to himself for the success he enjoys."

Gavin closed his eyes a moment, his expression one of silent gratitude. "I am so glad you see it."

"You've made the character intriguing. The reader can tell from the opening lines. 'He wanted more than life had granted him. He'd known since he was in knee breeches he'd have to give more than many a man to get what he desired, too.' That's a man who will mature during the actions of the novel into one who is a true hero."

"Not a tragic one, Raine. I don't want him to be pitied."

"Yes, I know. I can see he has a fault, an Achilles' heel."

"His impatience."

"It gets him into many a tight spot," she agreed. "But you give the reader inklings that he recognizes his weakness and will attempt to change. That will not only make him triumph over evil, but over those ills which would lay him low. He possesses another quality which will make him memorable, too."

"What is that?"

"He is like his creator. Persistent."

"An alligator?"

"A rather big one." Raine beamed at him. "I am very proud to be associated with you on this project . . . but I have a problem. I am perplexed."

"How so?"

"I've been working to catalog all the newspaper clippings, but I haven't seen you use them."

"When I began these chapters last Thursday, I had great motivation to get to work. I found I didn't need the clippings. Not yet."

She crossed her arms. "You have gone at it like——" she assessed him a second, "——a beaver."

He chuckled at the comparison. "Nonetheless, I was still skeptical of how good the chapters were, until I reread them last night. Your assessment now confirms my belief that they're worthy of publication."

"Gavin, with or without your . . . motivating factor, you have written these in a flurry——"

"I was terrified last week that I couldn't write at all. I needed to prove to myself that I could at least begin the story. I had been so fearful for so long that I couldn't accomplish my goal." His expression became mellow as his words. "Raine, you didn't have to do much else but sit here and inspire me."

Her nerves jumped at his nearness, his smile, his words. She was his inspiration? He was her own brand of it. Pure torture. How much longer could she work this close to him and not try her skill at duplicating the perfection of his face and form? "I must do something useful. The daily correspondence takes less than an hour each morning now. The catalog will take me a day more at most."

"Begin to learn that thing." He meant the Remington. She groaned.

"Your services are expensive." Humor turned his eyes a smoky hue. "Read these, and if you approve of them as is, type them."

She muttered about being careful what she asked for.

"Hungry?"

She got to her feet.

"Milord?" Mrs. McNally stuck her head in the door. Her urgent tone had Raine biting her lower lip to keep from laughing.

Gavin fought a smile. "We're right behind you, Mrs. McNally."

"My potatoes are getting cold," the woman accused him.

"Come along, Raine." Gavin extended his hand toward the dining room when his housekeeper had stalked away to her duties. "We must not dally, lest we be so unfortunate to learn what else is chilling."

When Raine's smile had faded and Gavin was pulling out her chair for her next to his, he told her that he wanted her to go home after lunch.

"What?"

"And take a nap."

She noted his smirk and became more suspicious of his reasoning. "Why?"

"I would like you to be rested and pampered and do all those wonderfully frilly things women do before a supper party." When she froze, he continued, "Now, Raine, that's not such a frightening prospect, is it?"

If you only knew. "I don't want to come," she blurted. The truth, discourteous as it was, was the best way to deal with this possibility of dining in the lion's den.

"Hmm." He looked nonplused as he cut into his lamb chop. "Easy to see."

She waited and he munched. "But you want me to come anyway?"

"I planned to open a grand *cru* of Estate Martin champagne."

Raine's fingers twitched in her lap, and she was immensely thankful he could not see them. "Gavin, it's kind of you to think of me."

"I was thinking of me, too. Selfish, I know, but I'd like you here."

She shook her head. "I can't imagine why."

"I can. I want your company. Then, too, the champagne deserves someone to fully appreciate it. Perhaps I can lure you with another possibility to please me. Why not give the champagne as good an accompaniment? Could I persuade you to tutor Mrs. McNally to create something memorable with scallops or shrimp? Would that fill your rabid need to work for me so diligently?"

Fear nibbled at the edges of Raine's control. "I would be happy to do that, but I can't dine with you."

"Why not?" For the first time in three weeks that Raine had known him, his eyes turned hard as granite.

"I'm not very personable in public."

"Of course you are. You don't engage in banter. You discuss viable matters. That makes you exciting company."

"It makes me odd, Gavin. A bold and very controversial woman."

"I know."

He was being too stubborn for his own good. "I tend to raise men's hackles."

She remembered just such an incident last Christmastime at her Aunt Peg and Uncle Gordon's in Grosvenor Park. Her aunt and uncle had invited a handful of guests for one of their regular Thursday evening at-homes. Gordon Worminster was an inventor, and he had friends and acquaintances who included scientists from many disciplines. Ordinarily, Raine enjoyed meeting these people, some of whom were dons at universities like Cambridge, Paris, and Turin.

That night, a renowned anthropologist held forth on recent discoveries of fossils of prehistoric man. A birdlike little man with a paunch, he chirped about his theory that no matter the age or type of the remains, the females' skeletal structure was always smaller than the males'. Then he blithely proclaimed that because their brains were also smaller, this proved they were the more inferior of the species. Raine could sit still for none of it and told him so in blunt terms. He had flown from the table and the house in a tizzy. Raine had remained to the bitter end, determined not to be intimidated by his rudeness and committed to proclaiming by her actions that she could not be dissuaded from her stance.

Comforted by her aunt's cooing and her uncle's ridicule of the anthropologist's arrogance, Raine had gone home to Belgrave Square with her Uncle Skip and vowed to him that she would never appear in anyone's drawing room again. But of course, she had returned. It was the best way for her to hear in-depth discussions of those subjects she cared about. Working class wages and living conditions. Public transportation. The Irish Home Rule Question. How certain MPs voted on that controversy. Including Sean O'Malley and Gavin Sutherland. So if she felt in her heart that she had done the right thing to take the stuffing out of the self-impressed professor, she knew that to most people—especially men—she posed a threat to their peace of mind.

"You don't affect me that way, Raine."

Clearly.

Gavin leaned toward her. "Ned is only one man, Raine, not a horde. Besides, I think you'd find Ned likes a lively conversation, particularly with a lovely woman. He is very well-connected in the City and socially. He is trusted with confidences by many from Whitehall to Dublin Castle. Justifiably so, too, because he never betrays his sources. I wrote and told him about you, and he's eager to meet you."

"What have you told him?" *My name?* How many women had the same Christian name of Raine? She had met only two in her lifetime. If Hollister connected the Raine he'd met ever so briefly to her, she'd be foiled, unable to rectify the wrong she'd done Gavin. Ever so much worse, she'd never see him again. But then that was foolish hope, too. She had never meant to stay with him after he completed his book.

And oh, how she wished she could. Sorrow at leaving him washed through her like a tide. She rebelled at the prospect, forcing her mind to the issue at hand.

What could she say to deter Gavin from this ludicrous idea? She had to soften the blow of her rude rejection, too, or she could be minus a position for her boldness. "Please, Gavin, I am still in mourning, and I do not wish to have to explain who I am or what I am doing here. Mrs. McNally finds it odd that you employ a female secretary, and she doesn't approve. If Sir Edward is of the same opinion—"

"Ned is a very practical man. He will not judge you."

She stared at Gavin. He could not be oblivious to the fact that the two of them got along like a pair of old shoes. Ned would see it, note it. Like Raine, the man would wonder where such a relationship was headed. "I prefer not to leave him with false impressions."

Gavin put down his fork and put his hand on his hip. "What precisely is false, Raine? You and I get on splendidly. Better as days roll on. I can't conceal it. I won't try. You shouldn't, either."

He was right. But she couldn't say that. If she did, she'd encourage his attentions even more. "You are obstinate."

He surveyed her eyes and her lips, then took up his fork. "I think for your own good, Raine. I want you to meet Ned. You'd like him. Despite your mourning period, you deserve to enjoy an evening which stimulates you with ideas and gossip about the city you left to come here." He waved a hand. "And I repeat, I want you with me, Raine. I need your company more than I want you to have Ned's. Even when I stayed up till God knew what hours this week to write, I did it so that I could enjoy your company fully when the manuscript was well-along." His eyes grew soft with concern, even as his jaw set with determination. "You must come."

She stared at her plate. "Will you sack me if I refuse?"

"No." His voice was gruff with frustration, but his next words were ones of regret. "I'd never force you to do anything against your will."

"I didn't think so," she whispered. "I am sorry, Gavin. Under other circumstances, I might truly enjoy Sir Edward, but I just can't tonight. Not . . . anytime soon. Forgive me." Her gaze traveled to his. "I would like to go home now. Do you mind?"

"Yes, I do, Raine."

She knew he would not pressure her, and she threw him a winsome smile. "I'll walk down to the village and buy some scallops and shrimp, if Jamie has any today."

He was contemplating her stubbornness and allowing her to escape him. She grinned. "Then if Mrs. McNally will let me, I'll advise her on a way to steam them in white wine with peppercorns and mustard seed."

"Do that. Take the phaeton if you like—or ride my bicycle, if you wish." He smiled. "I've seen you look at it and consider giving it a go."

"I'll try it one day soon, but not today. Besides, I don't have any bloomers to wear when I ride." She had left her only pair of the avant-garde underclothes at Forsythe House, never thinking she'd use them here.

"I could offer you a pair of my trousers."

She snorted. "They'd be so large, they'd fall down around my knees."

"Not a good idea. You'd never get home, what with all the men coming to your rescue."

"Phooey," she chided. "I'm so sharp-tongued, most of them would never even look my way."

"I would," Gavin proclaimed. When she didn't quite know how to reply to that, he offered an explanation. "It is a terror to employ a cheeky secretary."

"And a woman at that."

"With the prettiest cheeks I've ever seen."

She considered the friezes on the ceiling. "Gavin—"

"Raine, don't you see it's the devil's own misery not to tease you and laugh with you?"

She bit her lip.

"I've given up trying to be formal with you. I consider it a bloody bad waste of time."

She nodded. "Fruitless."

"Precisely. Go buy the fish, Raine. I'll bring my next two chapters over when I finish them tonight."

When her eyes rounded, he sighed. "Don't worry, my dear. I won't make you do anything you don't want to do. Including kiss me."

Little did he know that kissing him was becoming the

one act she thought of before she fell asleep at night—
and she had invented a thousand exotic ways to do it.

Raine's joy at escaping into the village died at the sight
of Mrs. McNally in Jamie the fishmonger's shack. "I
didn't know you were coming here," she said to the
woman as she collapsed her parasol and waved hello to
the young man who was so eager to show her his catch.
"I would have walked in with you."

Mrs. McNally didn't sniff, but she looked like she had.
"Lord Sutherland says 'e wants fish for 'is guest tonight."

Raine wondered if the woman eavesdropped on her
conversations with Gavin. But Raine was certain Gavin
would have been forthright with her. And Raine was
interested in making the housekeeper more of a friend,
so she smiled and said, "Yes. He likes fresh seafood."

Mrs. McNally lifted her nose so high, she was going to
strangle herself in her tightly-laced little straw hat. "And
other fresh things, too, since you came to work for 'im
and cooked 'im 'is supper."

Raine sucked in a sharp breath. "Mrs. McNally, I
hardly think that—"

"Turned 'is 'ead, for fair, is what you've done, Mrs.
High and Mighty."

"No, I—"

"'O do you think you are? Coming 'ere, worming your
way into 'is life? 'E doesn't need you and your kind."

Jamie appeared in his back doorway and handed over
whatever the woman's purchase had been, wrapped in
old foolscap and a bit of twine. He must have heard her
last words because his jaw went lax as a coon dog's,
before he tried to smile. "There ye go, ma'am. I took 'em
from the sea this dawn, I did. You simmer 'em no more'n
ten minutes and his lordship'll like 'em, I wager."

"Thank you, Jamie. I'll do me lordship right, I will.
Good day," she said to him, but marched around Raine.

"Wait just a minute, Mrs. McNally." Raine would not
allow the woman to mistreat her. In front of Jamie or

Gavin, Raine had had enough of her insolence. "I think you owe me an apology."

"Don't be daft, woman. I've not a thing to be sorry for. You're the one 'o—"

Raine stepped near and maneuvered the woman near the wall. "I am the one Lord Sutherland hired to help him. It's apparent that you think our relationship is too informal."

Mrs. McNally fairly blustered with outrage. "A polite way to put it, I'd say. But it's also a lie." She clutched her fish to her chest like a shield. "Now if you'll excuse me."

"But I won't. Mrs. McNally, I see you have his lordship's welfare at heart. I want you to know so do I."

"If you 'ad, madam, you would'na even 'ave applied for this position. Why, the very idea of a woman working day in and out for a man like Lord Sutherland. If 'is parents ever knew, they'd be off their 'eads with worry."

"They aren't concerned about him. If they cared for him," Raine paused to consider a sad fact, "they would have known he couldn't commit that dreadful crime and regardless of the gossip, they would have stood by him. They didn't."

"'E has no one, poor man."

"Precisely."

"That's why I disapprove of you, Mrs. Jennings."

Raine's brow furrowed. "Pardon me, you must explain that to me."

"'E does not need you to fill the void left by 'is family *or* 'is fiancée."

"I assure you that I certainly have no intention of becoming . . ." *Enamored* was the only word which sprang to Raine's mind—and she told herself it was the wrong word.

"I see the writing on the wall, Mrs. Jennings. 'Is lordship is lonely and you are very appealing. You are also to 'and."

"Because I am nearby does not mean I'm available for . . . dear God, whatever you're suggesting."

"No? Lord Sutherland is kind. Too much so to a beautiful woman."

"What do you mean?" Raine searched her memory for any rumor that Gavin Sutherland had a way with women. She could not recall any hint that he had ever had an *affaire de coeur*. He had only been romantically linked to one woman, Belinda Derwenter.

" 'Is bride-to-be planned to snare him. I watched 'er do it. For months before 'e asked for 'er 'and, and after she 'ad his ring and his promise, she would come to 'is 'ouse at late hours, uninvited. Oh, do not doubt that to add to the show, she'd tote along 'er maid for chaperone. I prayed to God no one would spy 'er comings and goings, and put it in the papers. They didn't. But Lady Belinda was discreet—and yer not."

Raine stood, shocked speechless as McNally drew herself up, her voice screeching as she protected her employer like a cat whose tail had been stepped on.

"I saw you kissing 'is lordship by yer garden gate last week. I 'ear you laughin' together at mealtimes and tea. I *know*, Mrs. Jennings, that a woman o' your kind cannot be good for my dear Lord Sutherland."

"I have no intentions of being other than what I am, Mrs. McNally. His secretary."

" 'O knows what you are? You're one of those American gels. Flibbertigibbets, with no breeding, like that Jennie Churchill who takes to the Prince of Wales more 'an her own 'usband. An' then there's that other one—"

Raine's heart sank. She predicted who McNally would name.

"—that ghastly wife of the earl of Aldersworth."

Colleen VanderHorn Falconer. The American Beauty the British called Drama.

Colleen, her sister Augusta, Ann Brighton Kendall, and Raine had been friends for almost ten years, since they had enrolled at Mrs. Drummond's Finishing School for Young Ladies in New York City. Colleen had married Bryce Falconer, the twelfth earl of Aldersworth, a few months after Raine's cousin Ann had married Rhys Kendall, the sixteenth duke of Carlton and Dundalk. While Ann had wed her husband in a formal public ceremony in Kendall High Keep Castle, Colleen and Bryce had hurriedly married in the American embassy in London. The Falconers' nuptials were hastened along by the impending arrival of Bryce's heir, now a charming toddler, Bradford. But Colleen had not been content. Only God knew why. Her husband was attentive to her and their son. Bryce seemed to love Colleen, even if she had enticed him to marry her by offering him the benefit of union before it was blessed by church and state. Why Colleen drank too much and flirted too often with other men was inexcusable. Her actions tarnished so many. Raine cared for Colleen despite her indiscretions, but found herself disclaiming her friend's actions. "No, Mrs. McNally, I—I'm not like—"

"I 'ave *seen* her," McNally sneered. "She used to come to visit my Lord Sutherland with 'er 'usband. She'd laugh and joke about, lounging over the furniture like she was the Queen of Sheba. Maybe they allow that sort of doings in America, but 'ere young ladies are quietlike, even after they're married."

Raine ignored the insult, needing information more. "Lord Sutherland knows Bryce Falconer?"

The housekeeper scrutinized Raine's features. "Of course 'e does. The earl contributes to 'is party's campaign funds. They're friends."

"I see."

McNally harrumphed and taking that as the end of their discourse, she worked her way around Raine.

But Raine stopped her with an outstretched hand. "Please, Mrs. McNally, don't jump to conclusions. I can't help it if Lord Sutherland and I have a congenial relationship. I can only be thankful for it. There are so few of those one is given in a lifetime. And because of what he has been through in the past year, Lord Sutherland needs all the friends he can get. Wouldn't you agree?"

McNally took her time considering it.

Raine knew she lied when she said, "I am trying to survive the death of my husband, Mrs. McNally, not involve myself in another relationship—and certainly not with my employer. I am not rich." Wasn't that the truth. "I want to earn my keep—and no one fit his lordship's requirements for a secretary. Please, Mrs. McNally, be fair to me—and to Lord Sutherland."

The woman squinted at Raine. "I'll not like it if you 'urt him, mind you. He's a sweet soul."

For Gavin's housekeeper to conclude that Raine interested him enough to do that was a startling discovery. One she'd deal with in the privacy of her own home later. "I would not harm a hair on his head."

"I 'ope there'll be no more kissing."

"I assure you there won't be."

"I shall hold you to it."

"You may."

"If you thought I was rude before, Mrs. Jennings, you'd see I'd waste no time, none at all, to go to 'im and object to your behavior."

Raine lifted both brows, saying nothing about how Gavin's behavior might well be involved, too.

"I'd risk 'is lordship giving me my notice to see you put in your place."

"I am forewarned." Raine put out her hand. "Can we call a truce?"

Mrs. McNally's head wobbled. So did her resolve. "Lord Sutherland wants me to allow you in my kitchen."

"It's your domain. I promise to be courteous—and help you wash up, too."

McNally twitched her nose. " 'E says there will be only two for supper."

Raine cocked her head. "Did he also tell you that I refused to come?"

Reluctantly, the woman said, "That 'e did."

"Well, then, aren't my intentions clear?"

A ghost of a smile crossed the woman's face. "I must go to the greengrocer and choose two vegetables. Then the confectioner's."

"I do adore your talent with pastry."

Mrs. McNally's pudgy faced turned upward. "Would you like to come with me?"

This was a concession Raine would not refuse. "I want to drop this letter into the post next door. Then I'll join you."

"Good enough."

Raine watched her duck to leave the shack. McNally's head was held high, as if she'd won the battle of Waterloo. McNally probably considered Gavin family and therefore worth defending and protecting. An alliance between McNally and her was the best way to go on.

Content, Raine asked Jamie what the housekeeper had bought and smiled when she learned it was shrimp, scallops, and mussels. "Good afternoon, Jamie."

Raine walked out into the sunshine intent on turning toward the post office to mail her latest letter to Ann. But she halted in her tracks.

Across the street, two men emerged from the front doors of the train station. Gavin's gardener, Ben Watkins, strode forward to meet them and indicated the pony cart he'd brought instead of the small phaeton. The cart, Raine knew, would hold more luggage. And they needed it for two visitors.

Ned Hollister—Raine recognized him by his resemblance to an old donkey her father's overseer at *Belle Chenier* had owned.

But the other man who joked with Hollister struck Raine like a bolt of bright light. She had seen him often in the past two and a half years. She could spot him across a ballroom or a dusty village lane by his wheat-blond hair and the striking black eye patch. Lately, his demeanor was distinguished more by the sadness over his wife's behavior. He wore his gaiety like chain mail. It hid his melancholy from those who did not know him well.

Raine shrank to the wall, pulling down the veil on her straw bonnet and pushing up her parasol.

What was Bryce Falconer doing in Chipswell-by-the-Sea?

As he climbed into the pony cart with his baggage, Raine knew only one fact. Bryce had come with his friend Ned Hollister to visit his other friend, Gavin Sutherland.

Thank heaven she had excused herself for tonight. But what would she do to avoid meeting them tomorrow?

Chapter 6

"Is the country not overridden by aristocracy when Lord Lambswool not only possesses his own hereditary seat in the House of Lords, but also has a seat for his eldest son in the House of Commons?"

—ANTHONY TROLLOPE

"FINE MEAL, GAVIN." NED HOLLISTER GRINNED OVER HIS rimless spectacles and put a bejeweled hand to his stomach. He waited for Mrs. McNally to remove the remains of the main course before he spoke again. "Haven't had such a delicacy since I was in Paris last autumn. Most English women believe the only fish dead or alive is haddock. To whip it to death, they cream it, stew it—or fry it with chips."

Bryce Falconer chuckled. "Has Mrs. McNally gotten adventurous in her advancing years and rebelled against your edict for plain fare?"

"Actually, my friends, we have my new secretary to thank for this unique dining experience."

"This *is* news." Ned guffawed. "Your secretary cooks?"

Gavin nodded. "And teaches my housekeeper a trick or two."

Bryce added, "He does it well, too. Might we hope his talents extend to the dessert course?"

"No. That she cheerfully leaves to Mrs. McNally."

"She?" Ned gaped, so stunned his glasses slid down the beak of his nose. "When you wrote that your secretary was educated and American, I thought that explained your other term of 'extraordinary.'"

"Gavin," Bryce's aquiline features drifted from shock to amusement, "wherever did you acquire a woman?"

"Here in the village. She rented the cottage in the cove. I have reaped many benefits from her proximity."

Mrs. McNally reappeared, this time with the dessert of a compote of pears and chocolate soufflé, onto whose excellence the conversation switched. The three men quickly dispatched with the sweets, and Gavin knew the way was now cleared for a more substantive topic. He was eager to get to it. He knew Ned was here to preview the novel. Bryce accompanied Ned, perhaps for that reason as well, but probably for others more vital. Friendship could be one, loneliness another, diversion a poor but necessary third. Gavin surveyed his sated guests and asked, "Shall we retire to my library for our brandy and coffee?"

"Good," Ned agreed and pushed back his chair.

"Anything in particular?" Gavin asked. He knew his publisher had cultivated a taste for blended Irish whiskey. "I've a choice of Tullamore Dew or John Power and Son."

"The first. My mother's favorite, too. She came from Cork, did you know?"

"No, I didn't."

"Gavin," Bryce persisted when they had wended their way from the dining room down the hall and through to Gavin's office, "I'd like to know more about a woman who qualifies to be your secretary and happens to live close by. I'd say the probability of that coincidence is slim and none." He settled his long frame into the leather chair opposite Ned.

"Ordinarily so would I, Bryce. But she is a widow of an English Army lieutenant—and badly in need of employment." He went to his desk and pulled open the deepest drawer to extract his humidor.

"An American without money." Bryce's brows knit. "Unusual."

"To men of our status, yes, very." Gavin strode over to Bryce and opened the rosewood and cedar box to offer him a cigar.

"I should know firsthand, shouldn't I, that not every young woman who crosses the Atlantic arrives with a doting mama, a rich father, and a mad ambition to marry a man and his castle. When Skip Brighton came abroad with his American Beauties, I was not struck by their urge to marry at all costs." He pursed his lips, and Gavin wondered if Bryce would amend that statement, making his wife Colleen the exception. "In the past two years, however, I think we have seen a tidal wave of American heiresses with few scruples coming ashore."

Ned cast a surreptitious glance at Gavin who allowed Bryce to survey the selections in the cigar box before he found diplomatic words. "We inhabit the upper reaches of society where American girls' fortunes make them visible."

Bryce took a fat Havana. "And desirable."

Though Gavin well understood that Bryce Falconer had married his American heiress because he cared for her, not for her wealth, their marriage was foundering on other rocks. Gavin had no idea what these were, and he feared Bryce didn't either. Whatever the causes of the Falconers' discord, Gavin would not broach such a delicate subject. He could only accept Bryce's increasingly frequent visits and give the man what he required in diversion and friendship.

Gavin handed Bryce the cigar cutter. "At this point in my life, I cannot afford to ignore such windfalls of good fortune. Certainly, no man worth his salt was applying for the job. Only three pitiful excuses came to my door."

"What, I ask you," Ned wondered, "is an American girl doing in Norfolk's byways, alone and working?"

"She is in mourning for her husband and wants a little solitude to recover."

"How did she meet him?" Bryce wanted to know.

"In Washington when he was posted to our embassy there. She came abroad with him when his tour was up. They'd been here for two years or so when the poor man developed tuberculosis. He died a few months ago. She came to Chipswell in May to get away from London and sort out her thinking for her future."

"Understandable," remarked Bryce.

"Hmmm," Ned mused, "have to make it on her own, what? Especially since we grant no widow's pension. What we have is Royal Cambridge Asylum. Ever seen it? No? I have. Wrote a story about it a few years ago. Dastardly, I tell you. We give them a cubby hole of a room, tuppence for coal, and seven shillings a week for food and whatever else the pittance can buy. The building accommodates only sixty women, and is not only fragile as parchment, but infested with a horde of vermin."

"I read a general staff report about it which stated the army could not afford to house any women with children either," Gavin said with distaste.

"Does your secretary have children?" Bryce asked.

"No." Gavin extended the humidor to Ned. "But still, she'd find the place intolerable because she has a taste for the finer things."

Ned unbuttoned his waistcoat. "As I can well attest."

Gavin returned to his desk and looked out his bay window upon the soft black summer night. "She must work, and she had no taste for London. Lived in Seven Dials, if you can imagine that. I'd want to leave myself. When she had heard in the village that my post was going begging, she applied."

"Gutsy of you to take her," Ned stated.

"Necessary, too." *Because standing here watching her*

for so many days, I had to find a way to learn everything I could about her. Gavin studied the void which was the cove. Above it, a light flickered in Raine's window. She had probably finished her own supper and was cleaning up. Gavin wished she had relented and come to dine with them. "She has been a godsend to me."

"How's that?" Ned wondered.

"She's helped me with motivation."

Ned struck a match. "Whose?" he asked between puffs. "Yours or your characters'?"

"Both."

"Good. When might I see the product of this relationship?"

"I'll give it to you tonight, Ned. Your bedtime reading."

"Keep me awake, will it?"

"If it doesn't, I need to rewrite it."

"Why not give me a summary now?"

Gavin shook his head. "I'd rather not."

"Impertinent bloke, you are." Ned widened his eyes at Bryce. "Why do we still tolerate him?"

Bryce exhaled a long stream of smoke. "Because we know he's tough . . . and sensitive. The perfect politician. We need to talk about the party, Gavin."

"That's why you've traveled up here together, I presume."

Bryce gave a rueful smile and rubbed a finger beneath his eye patch. "Among other reasons, yes."

Gavin waited.

It was Ned who introduced the subject which Gavin presumed he and Bryce had discussed on the train this afternoon. "Gladstone continues his so-called town meetings around Lancashire. He's bringing out tens of thousands in Birmingham and Manchester. He speaks so forcefully against Disraeli extending the empire, and he has struck a spark among the working class."

"Once again," Bryce examined the end of his cigar,

"the Grand Old Man resurrects his popularity. Rhys Kendall declares his duchy hasn't been the site of such support for any government figure since Charles the Second made his last royal progress."

Ned chuckled. "If you listen to Rhys's wife, Ann, talk of Gladstone, she'll tell you no populist American president was ever so well-received as Gladstone is now. Over there, they call it barnstorming."

"I have never met her," Gavin put in, "but many say that Rhys's duchess is one of his best assets."

"Her perspective," Bryce interjected, "—to say nothing of her ability to pick sound investments—make her invaluable."

Gavin nodded. "She has become—some say—his adviser in business and finance."

"Ah, but Her Grace, the Duchess of Carlton and Dundalk, has another observation of Gladstone which I think has her husband reconsidering his disinterest in politics."

"What's that?" Gavin wanted to know.

"Gladstone's wife, Catherine, is becoming more active in his campaigning."

"Interesting," Gavin concluded.

"Helpful," Ned told him. "She has determined that Gladstone made a mistake when he retired two years back, making way for Dizzy and his so-called empire. Catherine feels that she can aid him in increasing his popularity so that even the Queen will love him."

"Catherine would have to pull rabbits out of hats to do that." Gavin laughed. "Gladstone speaks too loudly against the rights and privileges of the Upper Ten Thousand aristocrats for the Queen to give him the time of day. If we want him back as prime minister, we must persuade him to a softer tone on that issue."

"Ah, but—" Ned raised a finger, "Catherine Gladstone does that for him. She smiles and waves and invites the hordes into her home for little afternoon receptions. There is a lot a woman can do for a man. It is the wave of future campaigning, I warrant. Mrs. Gladstone is pioneering it."

Silence fell among them.

"What is it?" Gavin asked them both. "Out with it. You came to tell me this news or whatever you call it. I know you did not travel so far simply for my sparkling company."

"We came for your cuisine," Ned teased.

"Twaddle. You expected my housekeeper's usual porridge. So. Bryce?"

"Not me." Bryce tilted his head in Ned's direction. "I vow never to discuss how a woman can disrupt a man's career or his business."

Gavin dare not respond to that, lest he acknowledge how Bryce's wife was fast ruining her own reputation as well as her husband's. While Gavin had no idea how such shenanigans as Colleen's were viewed in America, he knew they did little here to enhance a man's standing among his peers. Bryce, who was so heavily involved in numerous ventures from omnibus manufacturing and cruise liners to Liberal Party politics, could only be adversely affected by his wife's lack of decorum. Who would respect a man who could never count on his wife's proper behavior?

Gavin sank into his own chair. "Now you two do intrigue me." He was smiling, but he concluded it probably was not for long. He was right.

"What do you hear from the Derwenters?" Ned asked.

Gavin gave him an answer with raised brows.

"That's what I thought," Ned replied. "Sidney Derwenter retired to his estate in County Mayo for the summer season, but before he left London, sent word around among his colleagues that he wishes his daughter had not broken with you."

"Sidney," Gavin announced, "always did possess astonishing gall."

Bryce agreed. "Yet, he did pass it round that he put Belinda up to breaking your engagement."

"He *and* his wife," Gavin clarified.

Ned grimaced. "Ooh, there's a woman to make your liver shiver. I'd say you are well out of that family, my friend. Sidney married that lady for her money, and must have suffered temporary blindness to ignore her mudpie face. How'd you like to wake up to that sad puss each dawn, eh?"

Gavin recalled how Belinda fortunately looked exactly like her father. Over the months since Gavin had been away from her and her influence, he realized too that he had admired her striking gypsy looks, but he didn't miss them. He liked her grace on a dance floor, her conversation during at-homes and her pluck to appear at his townhouse at odd hours to share kisses. Her charm had however failed to steal his heart. He knew it the minute she had departed, leaving her ring cold and useless in his hand.

"To the devil with all the Derwenters," Bryce condemned them. "Dear Sid has made his bed now, coming out against the Irish Home Rulers. Few people like him waste their breath arguing against the Irish wanting their own representatives to make their laws for them."

"It never ceases to amaze me why he does it then."

"Yes, well." Ned cleared his throat. "He now says it is for reasons of national security. There've been home-burnings by British guards, turning out slackers who haven't paid their rents. Two weeks ago, a group of homeless attacked the village constable after midnight. Killed him, his wife, and two children. Outright slaughter, it was."

"I read about it in the *Times*," Gavin said. "Sad business. I knew it would come to this. I wish I had more information—or better that I had my seat and a say about it all."

"Ned and I thought you'd want to read more about

this so we brought with us as many of the newspapers as we could carry in our suitcases."

"Thank you. I appreciate what I can get. What will Sidney do though about the rioters?"

"He claims in the *Times* that the villagers were supported by someone," Ned told him.

"But what he really thinks is that they are supported by some *thing.*"

"Meaning what?" Gavin asked.

"Sidney is determined to find evidence about who instigated the murders."

"If it doesn't exist," Gavin said, thinking of his own similar situation, "he can't manufacture it."

"He thinks it is the Fenians."

Gavin frowned. The Fenians were dedicated to creating a free Irish state—and using revolutionary means to obtain it, if they must. They consisted of small bands, armed with whatever weapons their members could afford to buy out of their own pockets. Their biggest weapons—and their most effective to date—were their words. Inciting the Irish to act against their English rulers and refuse to pay land rents to their English-ascendancy landlords, the Fenians were gaining popularity. They were also affecting how the sixty Irish members of the Commons voted on many issues. These representatives were becoming more vocal and demanding more consideration for Irishmen's rights. Some of them declared themselves Fenians outright. Most were MPs who stood for the Home Rule League, a group of moderates who wanted more equal rights for Irishmen within the realm of the British government.

Gavin's position, when he'd been an MP, was to promote the Home Rulers in their peaceful quest. Sean O'Malley had sided with him. After Gavin resigned from Parliament, the Home Rulers had lost their most influential voice among the English representatives to the legislature. Gavin's disgrace had not just detracted from their numbers, but left a vacuum of leadership across the spectrum from Fenians, to Home Rulers and English sympathizers. Meanwhile, the rivalries between the Home Rulers and the Fenians were becoming more ticklish by the day. This latest incident would only irritate matters.

Gavin itched to be involved. "Nonetheless, Ned, Sidney will have to be very careful here and not accuse them of anything he cannot prove."

"He is trying," Ned replied. "He won't have to look too deeply, he thinks. It is well known in Mayo and Dublin, and many a village from the Causeway to Derry, that the Fenians are now supported by a great amount of money."

"From whom?" Gavin asked. "The average Irish peasant hasn't the coin to contribute."

"The donations come from the Irish Famine Relief Societies."

"From America?" Gavin was momentarily stunned, but then asked the more important question. "How are they spending it?"

Ned pursed his lips. "Buying supplies."

"What kind of supplies?"

"Pistols. Rifles. Dynamite." Ned examined the end of his cigar. "We have traced three shipments recently to two steamers which unloaded their cargo bays in March in the dead of night off the shores of County Waterford. The goods were smuggled into coves and dispersed among fishermen headed for Dublin and other northern ports along the Irish Sea. The ones we've recaptured were manufactured and shipped from Germany."

Gavin stared at Ned, then Bryce. "I always warned that this would begin to happen. If a people feel they are mistreated, if justice cannot be theirs, they will rebel."

Ned continued, "In the past, the Irish could never find the means. The past thirty years they had no will to fight. No strength. The Great Hunger killed more than a third of the Irish. But that has passed. The Irish peasant is once more healthy enough that he no longer needs to think about food or emigrating to Boston or New York. Instead, he gets his brother or his son to send him money for guns—and now he can buy himself a revolution."

Gavin cursed. "How many people know this?"

"Too many to keep it a government secret much longer. A private memorandum goes from our Viceroy in Dublin Castle to the Prime Minister and the Cabinet next week," Bryce said with a sigh. "The opposition will want to send more police and perhaps the army. That will only make the Irish more angry."

Gavin ran a weary hand across his eyes. "I gather then that you are here to ponder the connection between what happened in Mayo and Sidney Derwenter's renewed interest in my relationship with his daughter." When neither man responded, Gavin continued. "Sidney would spread such a rumor about Belinda and me only to see if I will nibble at the bait and write her or some such silliness. Of course, Sid and Belinda can wait for that until hell freezes over."

"You don't want her back then?" Bryce asked.

"Never." Why would he want a woman who turned away from him in a desperate hour?

"For desertion," Bryce pursed his mouth in thought, "I think a man must sever all ties forevermore."

Gavin wondered if they spoke of him or Bryce.

"So," Ned pondered, "back to Sidney Derwenter's ploy."

"I see," Gavin nodded at each man in turn, "that you want me to say the obvious. Sidney is interested in maintaining his own seat in the Commons. To do that and appease those voters in his own borough who are Home Rulers, he'd like to realign himself with me— through intended marriage to his only daughter. That way he can appear to be sympathetic to the Irish Home Rulers, as I always was. Ride my coattails, tattered and muddied as they are."

"Nonetheless, by befriending you, Sid appears to serve Irish justice and freedom," Ned said.

"Sid serves only himself," Bryce scoffed.

"He wants to rid his borough of the Fenians," Gavin rejoined. "Show how reason and accord can bring peace. But none of this does him any good, because I am disgraced, still, until we discover who killed Louise Stoddard and Sean O'Malley."

"Ah, you may be out of power," Bryce pointed out, "but not out of mind."

"Whose minds?" Gavin asked him.

"Those who wish to precipitate a peaceful solution to the Irish question."

"Such as?"

"Gladstone, Her Majesty, and a few of your friends from Ireland."

"Those MPs who are in favor of Home Rule."

"Yes," Bryce said. "I have it from a good source that this motley band are pressing to reopen the investigation into the murders of Louise and Sean to find the culprit and clear your name. They feel you are the best spokesperson for peace and they need you to take your seat again."

"Why couldn't they help me before I lost my seat?" Gavin asked, almost rhetorically.

"The public censure was too high. Your anger—that incident in the Commons when you lost control of yourself and you scuffled with Gaylord—branded you a hothead. It takes time for people to forget that."

"The way they conveniently forgot that it was Gaylord who attacked *me* physically."

"Yes," Bryce said sadly, "but you provoked him verbally."

"I did. I have learned a little patience and more diplomacy, finally. Hell, when can a man leave his mistakes behind him?"

"Now," Bryce shot back. "Particularly when a few of our party members wonder if all that criticism of you wasn't a conspiracy by a few Irish MPs to discredit you and, therefore, your very vocal support of an equal and free Ireland to be admitted to the fold."

That his friends might voice that possibility and help him now struck Gavin as vindication. But it was a fortune he would never collect. "I am pleased at this new insight some have. I am also honored—hell, I'm ecstatic at this offer. But I will not stand again for Appleby."

Bryce and Ned gaped at him as if he'd lost his mind.

"I won't."

Ned rallied first. "Your father will come round once he—"

"I won't talk to him."

Bryce frowned. "Money is not an issue, either. I have persuaded two friends to donate sizable sums to the party purse lately. They also favor an end to the violence in Ireland."

"In addition," Ned's features spread with glee, "you can always ask me for more advance money for the new book."

"Thank you, but money doesn't stop me, either. Choice does." He paused to think of Raine's words. "Integrity, more. You must hear me when I tell you that *if* I ever run again I will do it on my own, in a free district."

"Leave Appleby to that . . . that boy, Royce?" Ned was aghast.

"I shall leave Appleby to the imperious Marquess of Cranborne, who replaced me in my borough with William Royce the day after I resigned. I want no part of Appleby."

Bryce toyed with a grin. "I like your attitude."

Ned agreed. "I am pleased, even if it means I shall eventually lose an author who could make me and himself rich."

"That remains to be seen," Gavin pointed out. "My biggest hurdle is one over which I have little control—

and neither do you or your little band, as you call them."
He put his brandy aside and made his way back to his
desk. "I must be cleared of all suspicion in the murders
of Sean and Louise, else I can stand for nothing. Not a
seat in the Commons, and not democracy in Ireland."

Ned objected. "If there were evidence the Yard could
go on, they would have it by now. I think you must
accept the things you cannot change, Gavin, and change
the things you can. Come back to London when you
finish this book. Prepare a campaign plan with us. We'll
find an independent borough for you, if that's what you
want."

"No. I would never run for government with half the
people in Britain thinking I might be a murderer. How
can I promise to make the law of the land when people
question if I broke it?"

"People have short memories," Ned insisted.

"I don't." Gavin pulled open his second drawer and
took out his manuscript. "Forgive me my insistence, but
it must be this way. I will not run again without a sterling
reputation. And tonight I am weary. I've been writing
eighteen and twenty hours a day this past week and I'm
strung tight as a noose. Pardon me, I must take a walk.
Help yourself to more brandy, please. You can find your
way up to your bedrooms, can't you?"

"Not a problem, except," said Ned as he eyed the pile
of paper in Gavin's hands, "I need my bedtime story."

"I doubt it's worthy of a snore, but I will be interested
in your assessment." *If once you read it, you see how it
will cause a national sensation—and flush out the man
who ruined me and killed two innocent people.* "Perhaps,
I can be reelected for my way with words."

"Tomorrow at breakfast," Ned promised, "I'll let you
know." He tucked the stack under his arm and ambled
away.

Bryce stood. "Not a happy business in County Mayo."

"Sidney is just one of many who refuse to see that

people have changed. Democracy is a disease everyone likes to acquire. The Irish need self-rule—and self-respect."

"Don't we all," Bryce lamented. Then he downed his brandy. "I'm off early in the morning to catch a train to Peterborough and then up to Edinburgh. Take care of yourself. Finish this book quickly. Think about what we're offering."

"My position won't change. But perhaps you'll consider returning for a longer stay. We can sail and fish like we used to when we both went regularly to Cowes for August."

"Thank you, but no, Gavin. I'm awfully bad company." He knocked back the remainder of his liquor and put his snifter down on the deal table.

From the moment Gavin saw Bryce step down from Ben Watkins's pony cart this afternoon, Gavin suspected that Bryce was here not only for political but also personal reasons. Escaping his wife—or rather the shame she cast by her behavior—was becoming a habit Bryce covered with a veneer of indifference. Gavin knew, however, that Bryce had married her for love.

"What are you doing up in Edinburgh?" Gavin did not recall that Bryce had a house there.

"I'm taking a cottage by the sea in Tantallon."

"Alone?"

"Yes."

Gavin balked that such a gregarious man would seek such utter solitude. "Why?" Bryce Falconer was once considered one of the beacons of English society. He'd inherited his earldom at age eight after his parents died in a typhoid epidemic. Raised by his uncle and aunt, Alaistair and Letitia Houghton, Bryce had received their kind, if indifferent, attention. By the time Gavin had met Bryce, a few years ago, Bryce had been dubbed one of the famed Ten Bachelors To Be Sought. Debonair, and educated at Cambridge and Heidelberg, Bryce was rich as Croesus from his investments in American silver mines, railroads, cattle, and sheep, plus British mining in Africa. The twelfth earl of Aldersworth had charmed his way through the available English girls whose blood was verified as blue by Debrett's, and fought duels over two of them. He then proceeded to shock society when he married a red-blooded American heiress whose parents seemed thrilled to be rid of her.

Colleen VanderHorn descended from a Dutch patroon's family that settled Manhattan and the Hudson River. Her grandfather had made a killing, so to speak, in the fur trade. Her father doubled the fortune from government contracting during the American Civil War. Colleen displayed her paternal lineage by her rambunctious behavior. Some whispered that the real jewel of the family had to be Colleen's younger sister, Augusta. Gavin thought they were right in that assessment. He had met Gussie, as Colleen called her, and even now at eighteen, the girl was the polished gem Colleen could never be. She was spirited, just like her older sibling, but she was effervescent, polite, and without airs. To Gavin's knowledge, Gussie still resided in London with her own duenna, Ellen Newton. In fact, Gussie would debut this coming spring season.

"Christ, Gavin, I cannot bear to stay in the same city with her any longer."

"What has she done?"

"Or *not* done yet?"

Gavin recoiled at Bryce's uncharacteristic sarcasm.

Bryce looked over Gavin's shoulder toward the sea. "Last week, she went to the theater. I let her go alone. It is the custom, but it is a damn bad one, I tell you. She must have had a snoot full of whatever the hell the St. Jermains were serving in their box, because my darling wife took it into her head after the play to climb not into our brougham but into the fountain outside. She regaled quite a few theater patrons with a rendition of 'Yankee Doodle.' You can imagine what she looked like when she got home. She was virtually nude in the wet gown. She apologized to me, of course. She always does. But I can feel the probing eyes of every man upon her now——and the looks I endure from women would turn your stomach. I must escape. Have time to think."

"Is it wise to go alone?" The gossip created by Bryce leaving London without his wife in tow would billow into a scandal of unparalleled proportions.

"I cannot breathe any longer when I am in her presence. And her parents arrive in September for a holiday here. They'll reside at The Langham, thank God, but I must, of course, for appearances' sake, return to Park Lane for the duration of their stay. I'll gird myself. I like Colleen's father, we get on well. Thurston's an adventurer, but like Ann Kendall's father, Skip Brighton, he is a cautious one. It's the mother Veronica I cannot abide. Neither can Colleen. Even sweet-hearted Gussie merely tolerates the witch."

"What about Bradford? Where is he?"

"I have sent him with his nurse to Aldersworth. I have set Colleen packing. She goes with them."

"That's wonderful." Vital to keep the scandal down.

"She refused at first. Didn't want to retire from the field, as she so aptly put it. She hates the quiet in Aldersworth. Always has. But I couldn't have her gallivanting around singing and dancing in the altogether, could I? I told her I'd cut her allowance if she defied me. I'd close Park Lane, by God. Turn out the staff, if I had to, to make her leave."

The desperation Gavin heard in his friend's voice gutted him. "Bryce, why not go to Aldersworth, too? You and she might need some time alone to——"

"Talk? No. No." Bryce's expression became bleak. "I can't do it. I know what will happen. She'll get under my skin again, and we'll wind up in bed. It's where she gives her best performances. I must find a way to control her. She's becoming a drunk and . . ." Bryce's lips moved. *A whore.*

"Colleen's young yet. Perhaps she has——"

"She's twenty-two years old, Gavin. The same age as her friend, Ann Kendall. You don't see Ann running about naked in fountains. You don't see her in London at all without Rhys by her side. Perhaps, that's what I did wrong—I allowed Colleen to follow the English conventions, when I should have refused her the opportunity to live her own social life. . . ."

"Bryce, why not stay here? You like the sun and the sea. I must work most of the time to get this book done, but—"

"No, thank you, Gavin. I could not impose. And I must have a few weeks of solitude to sort out my thinking. When I return to London to welcome the VanderHorns, I'll collect Bradford and Colleen from Aldersworth first. But I will also know what I will do after the VanderHorns leave for New York. You see, I care for Colleen, but after this incident, I wonder how much."

Was Bryce actually considering divorcing his wife? Many might think of it, but few ever followed through. The effects were disastrous for both partners, ostracizing the wife and branding the husband as unfit. "I wish you well, Bryce."

"I know you do. I'll take my breakfast early and alone, if you and your housekeeper don't mind."

"Of course not. I'll tell her."

Chapter 7

"In the happy little village of Portarlington, two hundred constituents choose a member among them or have one chosen for them by their careful lord—whereas in the great city of London something like twenty-five thousand registered electors only send four to Parliament."

—ANTHONY TROLLOPE

LESS THAN TEN MINUTES LATER, GAVIN KNOCKED ON RAINE'S little Dutch door. She called through it. "Yes? Who's there?"

"Gavin. I've come with a few items you need."

He heard a rustle as she padded away and returned to open the top half of her door a crack. Her champagne-colored hair cascaded over her shoulders as she clutched her robe to her throat. The garment was no more than a pale cotton affair, rouged in the light from an oil lamp lit somewhere behind her. The rays cast shadows across her delicate face, but Gavin could see her eyes dance as he hoisted his presents.

"Absinthe and two pipes?" She was incredulous and gave a full-throated laugh. The intoxicating sound of it brushed his senses and stirred a deeper need than merely to talk with her. Her joy reinforced his instinct to come at such an hour and ask to see her.

"Won't you invite me in to share them?"

"It's late."

"But you weren't in bed. I saw your light through your window." He leaned against the jamb.

Her gaze darted to his hands. "No chapters?"

"None. Relieved, aren't you? Hmm. Yes, well, I didn't have a chance to write. Once they arrived, I was caught up in conversation. My two guests adored your supper."

"Mrs. McNally's," Raine corrected.

He gave her an agreeable nod. "As you wish. They noted the difference from the usual fare. How could they not? They dearly wanted to compliment the chef."

"Thank you. But . . ." Her fingers fiddled with the eyelet-edged collar of her wrap. He noticed how dark smudges from her hands were marring the cloth.

"You were drawing," he concluded.

"Yes. How . . . ?" She thrust her hands out in front of her to examine her fingers in consternation. "Oh! It's charcoal. When you knocked, I forgot myself." Her robe parted at the neckline to reveal a matching nightdress. He could see now the elegant line of her throat, for the first time unobstructed by cloth or lace. The hollow deserved the homage of his lips.

He looked away a moment, smiling. "Won't you ask me inside?"

"No. I shouldn't."

"Not proper, yes, we know," he complained. "Come walk with me out here then." When she balked, he brooked no argument. "It's a tad brusque, but the absinthe should warm you up. What do you say? Want to please your employer, don't you? It's a wise idea for job security."

"Slave driver," she muttered. "I'll get my coat." When she emerged and closed her doors behind her, she had a blanket flung over her arm. "Do you mind," she wondered, "if we walk toward the north?"

"Not at all," he said but asked why.

"Mrs. McNally would not approve of us being together. I'd prefer she not see us."

"Ah. You two have made an *entente cordiale,* have you?"

"Something like that." Raine smiled briefly.

"In that vein, is it also useless to ask you to come sailing with me and Ned Hollister tomorrow? Ah, yes, why did I try?" He sighed. "Very well," and followed her as she took her first steps northward along the beach.

She had donned a plain dark walking coat which reached to midthigh. Gavin had seen her wear it before when it rained severely one morning. Tonight, her layers of nightdress and robe flapped against her legs in the offshore breeze. "I brought a blanket, too, for you, just in case you get cold."

"Thank you. What else have you got there?" He could discern she dangled two long objects from between her fingers.

"Ta-da!" she said with a flourish and produced two stemmed glasses. "Not crystal, but they can do for your absinthe."

"Good. Let's go this way." He took her arm to lead her up among the rocks which at this point became more numerous. They also became taller as they headed north. Raine strolled along the beach with him, their silence comfortable as they picked their way through pebbles and darted over errant shallows cast by the late tide.

"Up here," he directed and took her hand to help her climb over a rise along the shore. This brought them to a semicircle rock formation almost as high as Raine's shoulder. "Have you seen this before?"

"I haven't ever ventured this far. I usually take the tributary and go to the lake. To see the grebes and their latest flock of chicks." She was running her hands over the smooth boulders, polished by the sea in its endless ebb and flow along the shore.

"Do you draw them?"

"Absolutely. They're very comical with their brood upon their backs. Did you know that each parent takes half of the brood and shepherds his or her portion of the flock?"

"My, my. Interesting concept, division of parental duties. Did you know that the Great Crested Grebe is nearly extinct? Only fifty pairs left, all of them here in Norfolk, it seems. Most have been slaughtered to get their magnificent feathers for ladies' hats."

"No! How do you know that?" she asked and sat down on a huge flat rock in the center of the formation.

"I was petitioned last year by the Society for the Preservation of Fowl." He stood in front of her and put one foot upon the edge of the rock to lean over her. "Want to smoke? No? Me, neither. Too windy. Another time, we'll have a go." He tucked the pipes in the back pocket of his dinner jacket. "The society is headed by a husband and wife. Both of them—who put me in mind of ducks themselves, if I may be so bold to say—came to me to persuade me to introduce a Plumage Bill. They accused the millinery industry of secretly raising and then killing birds *en masse* to fill the orders for feathered hats."

"I often wondered how the hatters got their supply."

"The milliners' guilds claim they buy only plumes which birds have shed upon the floors in rookeries."

"From your tone," she stated, "I gather you doubt that."

"It does seem extraordinary that birds could possibly shed the amount of feathers needed to keep the milliners in business."

"Explain that to me."

He smiled. Most women would have thought this issue worth a snore. Even Belinda would have been interested in this subject up to the point at which he said it was to be a bill in Commons. They'd find little empathy for a bird, compared to their own need to be in the latest fashion. "After Mr. and Mrs. . . ."

"Fowler?" Raine supplied.

"But of course," he grinned, *"Fowler* left my office, I looked into the matter. I learned from the London Commercial Sales Group in the City that in '75 alone, they sold wholesale to milliners one thousand six hundred and five packages of herons' plumes."

"They didn't have figures for grebes?"

"Unfortunately not, but parallels exist." She nodded and he went on. "Each package weighs thirty ounces. This totals somewhere in the number of forty-five thousand ounces. Hardly a weight which anyone can imagine scooping from the floor of birdhouses."

"If that were so, the poor creatures would be naked."

"Right you are. Furthermore, Mr. and Mrs. Fowler contend that the current demand for heron, egret, peacock, ostrich, and grebe aigrettes is detrimental to them. If we do not halt the exploitation of these birds, we could see the extinction of more than sixty species of them in the British Isles within the next twenty years."

Raine was shocked, but said, "A wonderful cause to espouse, protection of the species."

"Yes. I shall, when I am returned to the fold."

"Or the flock, so to speak." She chuckled, but became serious. "It won't be a popular issue."

"Not much of what I've stood for has ever met with great public support. But I march on."

"Ever true to yourself," she announced. "That's why you will triumph."

"I take risks few others do. Some think that makes me foolish, Raine." He rubbed one hand across his mouth. He had taken a risk the night that Louise and Sean were killed. A risk that had backfired on him. He had told no one about how or why he had gone to Louise Stoddard's house after the three of them argued. Yet, his actions might still come to light and ruin him, put him in gaol, send him to the gallows.

Should he tell Raine now? She would know immediately what he'd done when she read the next two chapters of his manuscript. Then, if Ned decided to publish the book, the world would know. Including the murderer. To tell everyone all the facts surrounding the murder was what Gavin had intended. But now that he was at the point of revelation in print, he pondered the wisdom of his plan. Particularly since Ned and Bryce had come to offer him restitution without benefit of a cleared name and restored reputation. Did he have to continue with his original intention to write everything he knew about that night and the murders?

His sense of honor told him he must. There was no other way to live with himself—and flush out the person who had murdered those two people so brutally. He would shock Ned, his family, and the world with his audacity. But he did not want to shock Raine. She had reacted so violently to his previous description of their stabbings. He had to prepare her. He had to tell her the whole truth before she read it.

She was contemplating him with the patience of the artist she was. What did she see? That he had hidden facts from her? He wouldn't any longer. He needed to be completely honest with one person. He had carried the burden of his actions for too long. He needed perspective. Advice. Hers.

"You are worried, Gavin. Why?"

"Obvious, am I?"

"Maybe only to me," she ventured. When he searched for the words to begin, she inhaled the sea air, closed her eyes, and said, "Do you ever come here on your walks?"

"Before you arrived in Chipswell, I think I would come at least once a day. It's a favorite haunt of mine. I used to come here to play as a child. When I was shorter, the rocks seemed like giants to me. I often pretended this was my castle. Without a roof or doors, I knew no one could value it as much as I." He extended an arm to define the semicircle of large rocks. "This was my great hall and this—" he indicated the flat square rock in the center, "—is where my retainers and I sat to deliberate war and peace."

"I bet you dubbed them the Knights of the Square Table."

"Very funny. Actually, I did name them. They were Knights of the Wind and the Rain." He put the chubby liqueur bottle down on the flat rock and worked at the stopper.

"And what was your name?" she asked as she extended the two glasses for him to decant the absinthe.

"Oh, I was the Lord of the Sun."

"Very appropriate."

"How so?" He tried to ask in a disinterested fashion, but he was fast becoming addicted to Raine's compliments, and he needed them like air and food.

"Your hair, your demeanor, your personality. You are a man of light and possibilities. It's no wonder you are— were, and will be again—a man who leads others." She raised her glass and clicked it against his. She drank.

He didn't.

"What did I say?" she asked him as he turned toward the sound of the sea surging up across the sand and rocks.

"You think a person looks like what they will become."

"To an extent, yes. Why? Have you looked in the mirror tonight and questioned if you were meant to lead people? You shouldn't."

"You have great faith in me."

"I believe you will do as you say."

"What if I can't?" His voice was a rasp.

As the clouds scudded across the moon, he turned to see her expression. She knit her brows. "Why," she stepped near and put a hand to his arm, "do you suddenly have doubts? You mustn't. What has happened? Did your friends say something to make you wonder if you can be elected?" She sounded like a distressed mother hen. "If they did—"

"No." He took a long draw on the sweet drink. "On the contrary. Both Ned and Bryce want me to stand for election without benefit of clearing my name of murder."

"But *why?* That's political suicide."

He smiled wanly. "Exactly my thought."

"Has Ned read your chapters? Doesn't he want to publish them? Is he afraid of scandal? Is that why he encourages you to run without finding the murderer?"

"No. Nothing like that. Ned, in fact, is reading my masterpiece only now. In his room." Gavin lifted the glass in the direction of his house and toasted his publisher with another long pull on the liqueur.

"I don't understand. Tell me why Ned and Bryce want this of you."

The fact that Raine called the two men by their first names rang an odd note in his head. But he had called them that, and Raine and he were standing here on a beach, near his table in his great hall, at the bewitching hour of midnight. He could find other more luscious facts to ponder, couldn't he? Like how alabaster Raine's hair became in moonlight. How silver her sapphire eyes. How irresistible her lips.

He shook himself from his desires to the necessities of the moment. "Some terrible events have occurred in Ireland. Riots."

"The ones a few weeks ago in County Mayo?"

"You read it, too?" He knew she devoured the newspaper after he did each afternoon. "There is more ugliness than what's been printed. A few murders. Some people in government have evidence that these kinds of crimes will continue, because now many people donate their money to revolutionary societies. Ireland has always been rife with them, but lately we have one group gaining favor."

"The Fenians," she said beneath her breath.

"Yes."

She shivered and crossed her arms. "So Ned and Bryce want you to return to Parliament because you favored a peaceful solution to the Irish demand for self-rule."

"Yes, but I told them I would not run in Appleby again. They were prepared to go to my father and ask him to oust the chap who's warmed the bench for me."

"Royce?"

"Yes. But I told them both no. They were stunned, said they'd find me a free borough. Quickly." He took another swallow, discarding the other news about Sidney Derwenter wanting to renew the engagement of his daughter Belinda to Gavin.

"No wonder they came here to tell you this."

"I want to stand. I am so tempted, Raine. But I must not. I will lose that integrity you urged on me weeks ago."

She smiled, pleased at her and him. "You'll be happier in the long run."

He lifted a hand to her hair. One curling lock trailed along her neck over the curve of her shoulder to her breast and down her crossed arms. He skimmed its length from her ear to her throat. It felt like cool spun gold. "I know you're right. I have you to thank."

"Oh, not me. Yourself, Gavin. That's who you must—"

He put a finger to her lips. God, they were soft. Softer than he'd expected—and more compelling than any other woman's. Suddenly he felt light as air, free of Belinda, his father, and the party which he served. He felt suffused with the power of his own convictions. It was heady, inspiring greater courage.

"Do you tell secrets?" he whispered, the need to feel her close gnawing at him.

"Never."

"You won't tell mine, then." He knew it was no question.

"Oh, Gavin." She was trembling, her eyes pools of pain. "You may trust me."

He lifted the glass from her fingers, put his and hers on the table rock, then he gathered her near. She fit him, contour for curve. He swallowed, desperate to share his agony with her, if only for a little while.

"The night Louise and Sean were murdered, I argued with them both in Hyde Park."

Her throat convulsed. "Yes, I know."

"That cartoon in the *Times-Daily* told the world, didn't it?" he asked ruefully. "That's not all that happened that night."

"No," she agreed, "of course not."

"Sean and Louise had returned to her house in Kensington when they were stabbed by an intruder. An intruder who left no evidence of who he was." Gavin checked Raine's eyes. "You said before that you didn't think I could have killed them." She nodded. "I didn't. But I was there, immediately after they were killed."

Raine stiffened in his embrace.

"I arrived minutes after they died. Their bodies were still warm."

Her mouth moved, but no sound came out.

"It's true, Raine. No one knows. I could not tell the police or the detective from the Yard. But I was there. I rang the bell. No one came. I let myself in. The door was unlocked. I found that strange and I thought to myself, where the hell is the butler or a maid? I called down the hall. No one answered. I went in. The place was deserted. The glow from gas lamps spilled into the foyer from the drawing room. I walked toward the light. Who wouldn't? It was the only sign of life. But then, I had only to walk through the doors and there they were, the two of them, sagging in their chairs, facing each other, witnesses to the other's torture . . . tied by the drapery cords to their chairs . . . still bleeding from the knife wounds . . . the starkest look of horror on their faces. Unnerving to see someone you know so well dead of such brutality. It guts you."

Raine's knees were buckling under her. He caught her, pressed her close, his lips to her ear. "I've upset you. I didn't want to. I should not have told you, I suppose, but I needed to confide in you and—"

"I'm fine. I am. I'm glad you're telling me." She ran a hand along his temple. "There is more you want to tell me, isn't there?"

He'd come this far, he'd go the rest of the way. "Sean's trouser pockets were turned out. A diversion perhaps to make police suspect it was a robbery."

She examined him and in her eyes shone a sympathy he neither desired nor refused. "The police never told that to the newspaper reporters or in the inquest."

"No. But it eats at me. The turned-out pockets mean something significant. It's a sign or a signal of some sort. If I only knew what, I might learn the cause or the perpetrator of the crime."

"Oh, Gavin, how you must have suffered." She put her lips to his cheek as she whispered, "You were right not to tell anyone you'd gone there."

Her approval brought him more solace than he had had in over a year. He clung to the warmth of her. "It doesn't excuse me from my failure to tell them the truth."

She swallowed hard. "If they'd known, the police would have looked no further. You would have paid for a crime you didn't commit."

"I have anyway."

"But not for long." Her eyes widened, a question rising in their depths. "Will you make your hero go there in your novel?"

"I must. How else am I to describe the scene?"

"Won't the police conclude you were there and didn't tell them? Won't they then want to arrest you?"

"I'll be careful. Change a few elements, use your catalog of newspaper clippings to find some description of the scene and say I reproduced the reporter's account."

"Which means you cannot write that Sean's pockets were turned out."

He paused, knowing she was right. "I must do something to flush the murderer from his sanctuary. What better way to do it than to make the account factual? Lead him to believe I know who he is?"

"But you must do it in such a way that the police do not become suspicious of *you*. Make up some small fact. Think. Surely there must be something you saw that night which you could elaborate on. Something to make the murderer question if he covered all his tracks."

Gavin agreed. He had to find a way to write his mystery so that the killer would become frightened enough to ask questions or say a few indiscreet words. A bit of conversation to a friend. Better yet, a few unguarded words said to a colleague, a peer. Among government circles, any hint of impropriety became grounds for dismissal. Any rumor of misuse of office became reason for investigation by the police. Gavin was fairly certain that Sean and Louise had been killed because Sean had information which someone wanted badly. Enough to torture them to reveal it.

"According to police inquiries in the Stoddards' neighborhood," Raine recounted, "two men came into the square that night. One came in a hired cab. How he left, no one could say. The second man arrived later on foot. I gather this was you?"

"Yes."

"Who else have you told?"

"That I was there? No one but you, Raine."

"The police could not determine which of the two visitors to Stoddard House was the murderer. I suppose that was because they were not notified of the deaths until the next day when Sean and Louise's bodies were . . . cold."

"But I know the murderer was there minutes before me. If only I knew his identity. . . ."

"That will come," Raine said with certainty. "Think of other facts you could use to scare him."

"There are a few things I saw which I could turn to my

advantage." But he had to be careful. He wanted to startle the murderer into an indiscretion. Not unnerve him so badly he would come here, attempt to silence Gavin . . . and Raine.

"What?" Raine persisted when Gavin stared at her, horrified at the possibility of her being harmed.

He shook his head. "Only I will know that. It's better if I keep my own counsel."

She hugged him tightly. "I fear for you. I don't want you hurt. Not anymore. Not by anyone."

He held her tenderly—her courage and belief in him was a sustenance he couldn't bear to let go of. He needed to give her something in return.

What could he give a grieving widow who had brought him hope?

"I feel stronger, freer than I have been, Raine. Thanks to you." He took hold of her hands and asked with a smile, "Do you dance, Mrs. Jennings?"

Concern and humor warred with each other in her eyes. But laughter won. "Yes, why?"

"Then you waltz, I presume?"

"Not badly. But I've never done it on a beach."

"There must be a first time for everything." He led her from his hall toward the wider expanse of the shore. He stopped them both at a clearing. "I used to practice here when I was young. My mother would send in the dancing master for us at three every Saturday in the summer, you see, and I was the one whom he had sworn was born with two left feet. Would you care to have a demonstration?" He lifted one hand and wrapped his other arm around her waist. She was chortling when he urged, "Now you are the better singer of us two, so pick a tune, will you?"

"Something Viennese?"

"Is there anything else?" he asked wickedly.

"I doubt it," she replied and threw back her head to smile at the night sky. He had the mad urge to kiss her throat then, perhaps never stop, but she brought her face down and grinned at him as she began to hum a Strauss waltz. He had no trouble stepping into the rhythm she created, and soon they were twirling harmoniously upon the sands and pebbles.

"Well," she exclaimed as he led her into a reverse round, "you have outgrown your malady, milord."

"You think so, eh?" Gavin said and picked up the tune with her when she began again.

"Absolutely. It should be the devil's own challenge to waltz over rocks. Two left feet, my foot."

He slowed their pace and brought her closer. Her body heat sank into his waistcoat and shirt to sear his skin. Her legs underneath the two thin layers of cotton slid against his. He needed more than the proximity of dancing. "Anything with you is better."

"Better than—" She snapped her mouth shut. In the ebony cloak of night, he watched her face flame with embarrassment.

"Better than whoever you wanted to ask about."

She averted her face, strained back, but he caught her chin and brought her around. "Not Belinda Derwenter, if that's who you meant."

She bit her lower lip.

"Not anyone." He bound her closer. "Raine." He felt her stiffen. "Don't," he begged and gave into the temptation to bury his face in that cloud of star-kissed hair. The minute he did, he heard her groan and predicted she'd try to break away. He clamped her more tightly. "Just stand here for a minute, will you, Raine? I . . ." He swallowed, dying to tell her how he had to kiss her, denying himself the pleasure lest he scare her away. "I won't hurt you. You feel wonderful. Warm and strong, Raine."

She was shuddering in his embrace, but not pulling away. He understood, in his rapidly heating mind, that was a victory he could not throw away. Patience would win him more.

Her face turned into his chest and like a trusting creature, she nestled her nose into his shirt. He ran one hand, fingers splayed and greedy, up into her hair. A handful of silk, an armful of heaven, what was a man to do with all that wealth?

He tugged her head back.

Her eyes were limpid and full of raw despair.

"Oh, Raine, don't. This is not the end of the world." He couldn't let her look like that. Not for long. Not this close. He needed to make her happy. And himself. "To kiss you wouldn't be a crime, darling." He wrapped her so close, he could feel her heart beat, her breath race. He felt her suppress a cry of protest.

"I am supposed to help you," she moaned.

"You do. You will. Kiss me for inspiration. For courage. And I—" he smiled to comfort her, his fingers fisting in the glorious mane of curls, "I will kiss you in thanks for all the succor you have given me."

She laughed, rueful through the tears that welled in her eyes. "How can I refuse you that?"

He grinned. "Call it necessary to my election."

"For that, most men get a haircut and a few new shirts and suits. That would help you among the voters more than this." Her eyes dropped to his mouth.

"The outer trappings of a man, that's all those are, Raine. While kisses . . . ," he brushed his lips across hers, "feed the soul."

She had stopped breathing when his mouth touched hers, but now she wound her arms around him and bound him close. "Gavin," she beseeched him, "I need you, too."

He kissed her hard the first time. His hunger had built to famine. She gasped at his eagerness, and when he took his mouth away, she objected. Twining her fingers into his hair, she urged his head down while she stood on her toes. He kissed her a second time until she swayed. He cursed to himself, scooped her up, and felt her grab for his coat as he carried her to his flat rock. There he sat down and spread her across his lap. His hands were in her hair and around her back, pressing her as close as he could be. "You taste divine," he said and then a thousand other things he had never considered saying to Belinda. Each one was punctuated by a kiss of such depth or intensity or sweetness that he marveled at the variations he could produce. His hand edged up inside the back of her coat to cushion her from the rock, while his other hand stroked her hair, her cheek, her throat.

Aware that somehow Raine was now on her back and he above her, he tried to be gentle. "I don't want to crush you."

She shook her head, the equivalent of "no, you can't," he supposed, as his lips caressed hers and his tongue delved inside her moist mouth for the first time. She nearly vaulted into his arms. She grasped his shoulders, and arched up.

"What is it?" he asked, afraid he'd frightened her by his crazed need to take her so erotically.

"The way you kiss me," she marveled. "Do it again."

"And again," he promised and took her down, exploring the lush recesses of her mouth. She responded as if she had never kissed another man, making little urgent cries. He knew a way to make her feel even better, and he brought his hand from her back to settle between her breasts. Under the coat he felt her heart pounding, her skin burning. Her fingers undid the few buttons. He locked his eyes on hers. His fingers went to her breast and with only two cotton layers between his body and hers, he knew by the hard nubbin of her nipple, she wanted him badly. His thumb circled and his lips followed. He couldn't taste her, but oh, God, he gave a damn good go at trying.

He opened her robe and then his mouth found only one layer between himself and paradise. She groaned, and his fingers had to have more of her. He found the pearl buttons of her nightgown—and soon in the sheen of moonlight, the white perfection of her skin. "God, darling, you're beautiful." His palm skimmed her from throat to waist, from heartbeat to beautiful firm breast with rosy hard nipple. "Let me see the rest of you." He pulled away and spread the yoke wide. She bit her lip as he lifted her other breast, weighed it, kissed it, suckled one, and then the other.

He was between her thighs now, her legs cradling his hips, her fingers clenching his coat as he lavished her with the praise only his mouth could adequately give. He wanted more, all of her, the rest of her, and he knew he could not do it here. Nor could he take her home. Not to his bed, not yet. They had more to learn about each other, and he understood in the marrow of his bones that he could not hasten her into his bed to become one body before they were more of one mind. She had a husband to forget—and Gavin wished the man godspeed. He would have no other man in her thoughts. Not when he wanted to be the only man in her heart.

He groaned, astounded at the depth of his feelings for her. He rested his head between her lovely breasts and rose on his elbows. "Sweetheart," he whispered, "much as I want to go on, I know we shouldn't."

She clamped her eyes shut and tried to drape her arm across her breasts. He captured her wrist and kissed it, then put it at her side while he laved each hot little nipple to a diamond point. "Don't cover them. Not from me."

She bucked against him, an effort to get up.

He drew the yoke of her gown together and began to button the little pearls. For a woman who had been married, she seemed as modest as a bride. Hadn't her husband ever showered her with such attentions? Gavin ran a hand into her curls at her temple and asked in a hushed voice, "Didn't your husband ever kiss you there?"

She shook her head no.

The fool. He did not die a happy man. "Most husbands do, *ma cherie*. I'm sorry if I embarrassed you." Was the man an oaf? Or one of those prudes who never took the time to remove his wife's clothes? Or to caress her till she wore nothing but her hot desire on her skin? Damn, but he would never make love to Raine Jennings with anything less than the passion of his bare heart.

"No. Don't apologize. It's my fault, too."

She was being her ever valiant self. "Fault? Oh, Raine. There is no fault here. I wanted you. You wanted me. We kissed each other." He helped her sit up. "Raine," he lifted her chin with a finger, "there will be no more talk of chapters."

"It was only a ploy to buy time," she admitted, though clearly from the torment on her face she hated her honesty.

"Forthright Raine." He admired her as he straightened her coat and buttoned it up to its prim collar. "I know you need time to get over your husband's death, and understand me well, Raine, when I say that I do not want him in your mind when we kiss again."

"Oh, Gavin," she objected, "he never was."

"Well, then," he tried damnably hard not to preen and caught her close to begin again, "what is the problem?"

"I couldn't think of anything but you." Her voice dropped to an inaudible level. It was all breath when it came out, but he understood anyway. "I didn't want you to stop."

His mouth fell open in surprise, but she saw, and angry at herself, she stood, rearranged her coat, and trod off.

He watched her go, pleased, delighted, inspired, hopeful.

He was awake the rest of the night, having given up plotting his novel in favor of planning when and how to woo Raine Jennings out of her widow's weeds and into his bed.

Chapter 8

*"It is natural for man to indulge in the illusions of
hope . . . and listen to the song of the siren. . . ."*

—PATRICK HENRY

"COR!" MRS. MCNALLY BENT OVER THE STEW POT. "WOT
are ye puttin' in there, girl?" Her nose wrinkled like a
dried banana.

Raine chuckled. "Trust me, Mrs. McNally, Jamie
knows how to catch big Dover sole, but I know how to
cook it." She dropped the shells of yesterday's shrimp
and Dungeness crab into the broth of white wine and
currants. "We'll boil this down and add a pinch of
peppercorns later, not too much to kill the delicacy of
the sole though. Then, we put in some rice and a bit
of onion—"

"Ooh," the housekeeper complained. "We don't want
to make a poorman's hash."

"Not a chance we can, I promise."

"Smells wonderful." Gavin stuck his head in the
kitchen door and beckoned Raine. "Come talk to me a
minute, will you?"

Raine washed her hands at the dry sink, wiped them

on a towel, and then walked down the hall toward their office. She slipped inside the door. Gavin crooked a finger at her, and her heart skipped a beat. She recognized his madcap air which signaled the arrival of the high point of her day. Purposely—for Mrs. McNally's continuing sense of propriety and her own need of it with this debonair man—Raine left the door ajar as she faced him.

"What do you need?" she asked him as she pushed a stray tendril behind her ear.

Gavin had made his way back behind his desk, and he stood, fingering his mail when he lifted his eyes to her. Humor and approval of her disheveled appearance twinkled in his gray gaze. "Whatever you're preparing," his voice was a croon, long and low, "I'm eager to sample."

"You're an outlaw, Gavin Sutherland." She stood her ground with him. She had to. Over the past three weeks, since they'd waltzed by the sea, the man had turned into a satyr. A delicious temptation to her night and day. "Why did you bring me away from my cooking?"

"I want your advice."

She cocked a brow. "I've heard that before."

The man used any excuse he could find to be with her, near her, beside her. She hadn't been so pursued, so consumed by a man in her life. She reveled in his attentions. She craved them. She knew she trod down a path that would end in his arms. Again.

As she was every day, just once. She never could predict quite when. Only he, devious man that he was, knew that. He would wait for the moment, the silent second that bound them, irrevocably, and drew them together. It could be at dawn, when early light lined his handsome face and he emerged from his French doors to meet her as she marched across the cove into his garden. It could be midmorning when Mrs. McNally brought her coffee and his tea, and he reached across to take her cup from her fingers and let her taste his cream and sugar from his lips. It might be later, as he came to watch her peck over the Remington keyboard and curse, then he'd bend over her shoulder, press his mouth to her ear, lift her hand, pull her up, and kiss her lips. Morning, noon, mealtime, midnight, he appeared when he wanted, lured her to him with any rationale, and then gave her what they both enjoyed with a passion that left them gasping.

He kissed her freely, leisurely, but rationed the goods—the schemer—to one kiss a day. She began to wage bets with herself when he'd make today's move. She usually lost. Unpredictable in his timing, Gavin Sutherland was ever inventive in his method. Each kiss was like no other. Not even any she'd imagined in her cold and lonely bed. Languid and lush were the only two qualities which marked his repertoire. Moist, hot, fervent, tremulous—his kisses had infinite variety. She tried to think of new ways he might approach the art of the kiss and found she had not the experience to adequately predict him. Much less avoid him.

Nor did she want to.

To her dismay and delight, she knew each morning when she arose, she would live for the second his mouth would meet hers. She would welcome him. Why hide her joy in him? From the first day she had applied to him, she had felt the power of their accord.

Now, after two months with him, that ease which had burst into friendship so readily shimmered with the promise of a deeper emotion. Day in and out—here in his office or in her rose garden or at a picnic by the lake to watch the grebes—they worked and found small joys together. She typed his manuscript on the infernal typewriter he had bought and worried about the content of his story. He was creating an interesting mystery, and she wondered how much of it was fact—and what was fiction. When she asked him, he would smile and say she did not need to know that. She understood he did it to protect her. And she cared for him all the more. His protectiveness drew her closer to him, not that she required more reasons to admire him. His delight in her matched her own in him. Each evening, as they walked or waltzed along the beach, they shared stories of their childhood, their aspirations and their disappointments.

He asked nothing about her life beyond Baton Rouge. She asked nothing about his beyond last June. Their silent resolution not to cross those chasms in their lives made their relationship a surprise and a staple of her days. It created a magic respite, a golden cocoon in which they spent their hours in each other's company. And Mrs. McNally, Ben the gardener, and even the maid-of-all-work who came in once a week to do the laundry and dust the furniture, would pause to watch Gavin Sutherland laugh—and Raine overheard them talking one morning over tea, crediting her with his transformation.

She praised him for her own. She was drawing him in her one little sketchbook, and she felt as though she had been released from a dungeon into the light. Late at night, each night, she gave into the itch to portray him as she now saw him. Jovial, thoughtful, industrious, and tempting. She rendered him not in ink, as she had before in her fateful cartoon of him, but in charcoal. She yearned to try her hand at painting him in color. Not in water. But in bright oils. Her Gavin. The way she viewed him—and she wished the world would—in fact, knew it would, quite soon. Bronzed hair; soft, considerate gray eyes. Sweet dimple. Alluring mouth. Strong jaw. Confident air. Head thrown back, laughing at the sky, daring the elements of the universe to deny him his rightful place in it.

With his renewed exuberance, she told herself she was satisfied. She had accomplished a portion of her goal. Not quite what she had set out to do, of course, but making Gavin Sutherland happy in any way at all was balm to her tortured soul. She owed him whatever happiness she might bring him.

If in the process she brought herself a similar joy, she was thankful. But she warned herself that this side benefit was one she should not invest any hopes in. Gavin Sutherland might like to work with her, laugh with her, seek advice from her, but there she must let her expectations end. She had ruined his life and there was no way to compensate him for it—and certainly no way she would ever be able to admit it or explain it to him. To do so would equate her with the unfeeling monsters who had killed her parents, with all others who committed senseless crimes—and escaped punishment.

Yes, with his one kiss a day, she told herself she was more than satisfied. She was enjoying more than she deserved. She would not ask for more.

But, oh, how she wished she could.

She pushed away from the door, took her apron off over her head, and threw it over one shoulder as she rolled down her sleeves.

He rounded his desk to stand before her, run his big warm fingers up her wrists along her arms, and wind them around her waist.

Her breathing became shallow.

His lips curved. His dimple appeared. "Want to kiss me now?" He lured her with a whisk of his mouth along her cheek. "Or should we save it for later?"

"What good does it do me to wait?" she murmured, as she arched her head back and felt his breath heat her skin.

"What good would you like it to do, *ma cherie?*" he asked against the curve of her chin.

"Some reward would be in order."

He kneaded her spine and cupped her bottom, bringing her close to his hard, hot length. "More than one kiss? Would that help?"

His mouth was trailing down her bodice now, territory he had not claimed since that first night upon the shore. She clutched the muscles of his back, let him brace her as he put his mouth over the point of one breast. "You never know until you try."

He groaned. "Raine, Raine, my pretty Raine. You're driving me crazy with longing." He swept her off her feet and walked with her, smiling at her, nipping at her lips. "You smell like fish." He chuckled and sat down in his desk chair with her legs over his. He held her cheek. "Let me see for once how many ways I can kiss you, Raine."

The imp in her nature emerged. "You'd better."

A rogue in his own came forth. "It's two o'clock."

"How long do you have to devote to this?"

"How long do you want, Raine?" He was waiting for a serious answer.

She swallowed. "Gavin," she examined the lure of his eyes, "don't even try to make this logical."

"I have to hang on to some sanity," he proclaimed and flicked open the top button of her blouse. "I think of nothing but this spot here." He illustrated by placing his mouth into the base of her throat. "I wonder what other places are as soft—" He nuzzled behind her ear. "As untouched." He spoke against her temple. "I think there must be a thousand points of delight on your body and I map them in the hours when I don't have you in my arms. Someday soon . . ." he trailed his fingers into her chignon and held tight, "I'm going to explore."

"Then what work would get done?"

His fingertip traced the outline of her mouth, and suddenly she held it between her teeth and flicked the end of her tongue against the pad. He stilled.

She pushed backward, and he let her get up and walk to the window. "We can't continue like this. As much as I'd like to, I have to find the willpower not to succumb to this. You must stop trying to seduce me, and I must stop allowing you to do it."

"We have a relationship, Raine. Built on shared interests and values. Let's be blunt, shall we? You are not interested in having a physical relationship with me—and I don't blame you. I don't want one with you, either."

She spun on him, her mouth dropping open.

He put up a hand. "Not until we have a few issues settled."

"Well then, for the sake of my—" dear God, she'd almost said *virginity,* "virtue, you'd better spell them out."

"Precisely my thought." He rose, shot his cuffs, winked at her like a cavalier, and hitched a hip onto his desktop. "Tell me," he cocked his head, "did you get along with your husband better than with me?"

"No."

Pleasure, molten and fierce, narrowed his eyes. But his words were cool. "Did you spar with him? Verbally?"

"Yes," she said, because that was true. She engaged most people in a strong repartee or left them quickly to their own bland devices.

"What attracted you to him? Initially."

"I . . . can't remember."

"His looks? No? His intellect? What then?"

"His humor."

"He was funny. Well, that's a help."

"For what?" She waved a hand. "What are you after?"

Gavin chastised her with a look. "Isn't that obvious?"

"No."

"I need you to talk about him."

"Why?"

"I must hear what you thought about him when you met him, loved him, married him. I must know how you felt when you buried him."

Sorrow, that was all she'd felt for a young man gone before his time. But she knew Gavin expected her to say more, and if she did, she'd be lying. The very thing she avoided like the plague.

"I have not asked you, Raine, because I wanted to give you time to recover, to forget him, to enjoy me as I so fully enjoy you."

"I thought we had an agreement that we wouldn't talk about such things."

"I never agreed to anything like that. You must grieve for him, talk about him, and I must hear how you do it."

"I do very well." *If I forget about him any more, I'll find myself in quite a pickle.*

"So how did he kiss you?"

"I don't see how that's important."

"To me, it's vital. Did he or did he not kiss you like I do?"

She rummaged her brain for a description, but since she'd never been kissed so often nor so thoroughly by any man, how could she talk about the lack?

"Did you like his kisses? Did you melt like butter in *his* hands? No? Good, very good. Did you like making love to him?"

Her throat went dry.

"What does that look mean? *Yes,* too much, or *no,* not at all?"

"I—he—didn't—" She was trying to be honest, but for the life of her, she couldn't think of a reason that a man would not make love to his wife. "He didn't give me a chance to learn to like it."

"I see," he said, stunned.

"I doubt it," she murmured and crossed her arms. "Are you satisfied now?" Her nerves twitched. Being cornered always scrambled her brain.

"Do *not* turn away from me, Raine."

"I don't know what you're trying to prove here, but—"

"Clearly."

"I don't want to ignore your questions. I swear."

"And I don't want you to freeze up on me when I ask for details about your husband and your relationship."

"I am trying, Gavin, to be honest with you. Can't you see that?"

"Plain as day. So let me be as open. Raine, what I am trying to do here is save myself another endless day of wondering when and another sleepless night of dreaming how I'm going to make love to you. And I want to be different for you because, darling, you are different for me."

"Oh, Gavin, how are you so sweet?"

"You've been courted before. You must recognize what is happening between us is extraordinary."

Courting her. Was that his objective? Well, she would stop him. "Extraordinary, yes. But that's all it will ever be."

His complexion went beet red. His eyes became steel. His hands flexed in frustration.

An anger that hot had her stepping backward. "Don't—" She put a hand out, blind to everything but her own fear of a man's rage. "Please, don't—"

He took a step forward, ire transforming into shock.

She wanted to escape, but encountered the window. "If you're going to yell at me, I must leave."

"I'd like to take you over my knee—" his fingers combed into her curls and at his gentleness, her eyes fluttered closed, "—and kiss you till we are both old and gray. Raine," he nestled his lips into her hair, "I would never hurt you." His arms wrapped around her. "How can I prove it to you?"

"Just hold me like this. I don't like arguments." She inhaled the comfort of his scent and embraced him. "I avoid them."

"Yes. I know." He tipped up her chin. "With your sharp tongue . . . and your exciting mouth." He blessed each corner of it with a quick kiss and then gave her the full benediction of his ardor. He urged her lips apart and then invaded her mouth and her senses with the homage of his tongue. She welcomed him, bathed in the wealth of his fervor, drowning in her own desire to taste every bit of paradise he offered. He left her panting, yearning, reeling, as he whispered against her ear, "I like you when you are here in my arms, Raine. I want you nowhere else. In fact, I just want you, night and day." She would have responded to that, but he slanted a fingertip across her mouth. "I'm a different man than when I incited John Gaylord to attack me in the Commons. I swear it to you, darling. It kills me to think that you'd believe I'd hurt you just now."

"The memory of angry men is one I'd like to forget."

"I know. I saw it in your eyes, sweetheart. They were black with fear."

She lifted a shoulder. "It's silliness."

"No, it's very real to you."

"They are such old memories. A child's."

"But they are powerful."

She agreed. "I do not like anger. Because I saw much of it during the war. Men who were drunk with fear of capture and death. Men who abused the power of their weapons to . . . threaten others and survive by any means."

Gavin sighed and cradled her closer. "Are you referring to those men who killed your parents?"

She nodded.

"At last we arrive at the moment when you can tell me about that."

"Why would you want to know?"

He led her forward and sat in his chair, then patted his knee. "Because I want to know everything about you, Raine. Because you must learn anything you want about me."

"That's not . . ." She looked away. *Wise.*

"Necessary is what it is." He tugged her down to his lap. "Isn't there something you would like to ask me? Some fact which you dare not ask because it seems too personal?" He challenged her with a lift of his brows.

She burned to know how he felt about Belinda Derwenter. Her eyes went to today's mail delivery of the London newspapers on his desk.

His gaze followed hers. "What? I'll trade you intimacies. You ask me your question and then you will give me what I need to know."

Raine clutched a paper. "The gossips say Belinda

Derwenter and her parents 'would welcome a resumption of your relationship.'"

"You're protective," he said, smug.

I'm jealous. "I'm furious," she corrected with a spin of the tabloid over his desk.

"Sidney Derwenter has put that rumor about for political reasons."

Raine burst with sarcasm. "How sweet of him to hail you now that the first four chapters of your new book are out. The letters to the editor are all about you and how good it is."

"Not all. Three of them in the *Gazetter* don't like the novel at all. 'Too provocative,' says one. 'Too akin to a real-life incident in the author's life,' declares another."

"Two in the *Times-Daily,*" she added, "and one more in the *Illustrated News* praise it. And think of all those others who have read the installments—and *haven't* written in to comment. Oh, Gavin, this is wonderful. Few people are in London the first of August, but they're hearing about your novel. Reading it. Exactly what you wanted. Everybody who is anybody may be in the country for the salmon fishing and foxhunting, but you are being acclaimed for writing the best mystery since *The Woman in White.* The first two installments in Ned's magazine sold out. Ned's thrilled with the profits—and the expectation that you are on to a way to vindicate yourself of suspicion. People have your name on their lips." She ground her teeth. "Even Derwenter, I would conclude."

"People have begun to talk about the murders, too. A coup."

"Derwenter," she said his name like a curse, "is a shrewd politician."

"He thinks he is, Raine. But only to a certain extent."

"A man will do a lot for his daughter," she murmured.

"Sid does this for his own benefit, Raine. He wants to realign himself with me because I support a peaceful debate over how Ireland will be governed. He is worried about retaining his seat if there is a by-election in the fall. The Fenians are gaining support in his borough—and he may not have enough votes to win against a Fenian candidate." Gavin smiled sweetly at her. "But even if Sid and his daughter had just a personal reason in mind to put that rumor out, it would not matter a fig to me. Belinda withdrew from our engagement last June. Like my father and most of my so-called friends—even some of my colleagues—Belinda deserted me. Do you think I would want a woman who had hurt me so?"

Raine saw in his eyes the answer to his question. "No. Of course not." *But do you still love her?*

"What else bothers you?"

"People make mistakes, Gavin. She may have when she parted from you and she may be sorry for her error."

"If that were true, why isn't she here telling me?"

"She might be constricted by rules that say a woman cannot come to a man—"

"Rubbish. She was never constricted before. She came to my townhouse whenever the spirit moved her. I had a devil of a time keeping both our reputations spotless."

"Yes, I know. Mrs. McNally told me," Raine offered. "She was aghast."

"Poor Mrs. McNally. My watchdog. My conscience."

"She adores you."

"Poor woman treated Belinda to a few glares of her beady eyes. Belinda never seemed to take heed." Gavin touched the end of Raine's nose. "You have brought Mrs. McNally to heel."

"She accepts me *and* my cooking now. She understands I wouldn't harm a hair on your head."

Gavin put a finger to each button on her blouse down to the waistband of her skirt. "A body would have to be blind not to notice that, Raine." He took both her hands in his. "Tell me about your dislike of conflict."

She suddenly began to laugh.

"What's funny?"

"My parents always said you have to learn how to talk

really well. Sweet talkin' is the best way out of any swamp, 'cause the gators are big and mean—and the reeds'll tangle up your legs and won't let you go."

"Trapped by one," he ran a hand down her thigh to pull her close, "and about to be gobbled by the other. Start talking, Raine."

She toyed with his watch fob. "There is not much that I remember clearly."

"Give me your impressions then. They are the stuff of our perspective."

A sad resignation made her smile. "How did you get so smart?"

He took her hand, turned it over, and kissed her palm. "I have you to tell me I am."

She warned herself to tell him generalities. Few specifics. Too many of them and he'd feel sorry for her. She couldn't bear that. Not from anyone, but especially not him.

"We had four hundred and fifty acres. We grew corn and cotton, and to pick it, we owned more than four hundred slaves. My *grandpère* had bought the land sixty years before, and many of our field hands had grandparents who had belonged to us from the day they were born. The land was rich, cool in the shade of cypress trees dripping with Spanish moss. The days were long, humid, and when the rains came they were downpours. Sometimes we got flooded by the Mississippi rising over its banks. But nothing was so devastating to us as the war."

She looked Gavin in the eye. "My father was a representative from our state of Louisiana to the Congress in Washington. He didn't support secession from the Union, and he was not popular in our parish for it. My mother was not trusted, either."

"Why not?"

"She was born in Baltimore, a city north of Washington, in Maryland, a state in which a man could own slaves if he wished. She never did, nor did her family, but when the war started, tempers ran high. There were parish meetings at the church, and many of the voters who had elected my father ridiculed him for his desire to stay in the Union. But soon, none of it meant much. The Union put a blockade around the Confederacy—and to stop trade in New Orleans. Even though we were about forty miles upstream, almost as soon as the war started, we felt the effects of the Yankee attacks. We couldn't ship our cotton out and couldn't get supplies in."

"How old were you when the war started?"

"Nine. By the time the Yankees took New Orleans, I was nearly eleven."

"Awfully young to endure such hardship."

"My brothers and I didn't think much about what we lacked. Children don't, do they? We were proud we were rebels, even if our father wasn't. My oldest brother joined the confederate army. He was seventeen and eager to fight. My next oldest brother soon ran away to do the same thing. He joined a ragtag unit who wore the funniest red and blue uniforms. I can still see them lined up like skinny marionettes on the wharf in New Orleans. They took a ship north to the Carolinas and from there went on a train to Virginia. They walked to a little town called Bull Run and met the enemy. Gervaise died with them."

"And your oldest brother?"

"Etienne's name appeared on a list of wounded in a Yankee hospital. But after my parents died, and I left Louisiana, we had no idea what happened to him."

"Why not?" Gavin was horrified at the idea of such loss.

"So many . . ." she cleared her throat, "so many simply disappeared." After Lee surrendered to Grant at Appomattox, her Uncle Skip had called upon his friends in the War Department to try to track Etienne. If she told this to Gavin, he would ask about her uncle, and one fact would lead to another so that she would be revealing more than was safe. "The cannon fire, you see, was . . . devastating."

Gavin took her hands in his. "And your youngest brother?"

"Died with my parents." She squirmed. "Francis was twelve, one year older than I. He and I had gone to the lake to watch the herons one afternoon. We were later than usual getting home. It was dusk when we came along the front lane. But we should have noticed something was wrong when we saw no candles burning from the parlor window."

"You had gone out alone to the lake and came home alone?"

"Yes. Many of our slaves had left us. New Orleans had fallen to the Yankees the month before, and my father thought it best to give them the right to leave before the army reached us. They fled upriver into the forests. We should have, too." She brushed her cheek with the point of her shoulder. "Francis noticed there was no lamp lit in the parlor. I told him I had to go pick some greens from the kitchen garden. My mother always liked fresh herbs to cook with, and our meals were smaller all the time because we lived off our crops. Anyway," Raine left Gavin to stand by the window, "Francis went in. The door closed behind him. I went around the house to the side plot that was mine to tend, and it was then I first heard the sound that made me shudder. Someone was crying, keening really. I thought it was one of the house cats. But I picked my leaves of parsley and sage, then followed the sound to the dining room window. My mother and father—and Francis, too—were tied to their chairs." She turned slowly to face Gavin. "Like Sean and Louise, they were tied with the drapery cords. Thick, ugly ropes of gold. I always did hate those green velvet drapes. That day, I loathed the trimmings more."

"Raine." Gavin got up from his chair and stepped toward her. "What a thing to witness."

Her gaze went toward her rose garden. There where she nurtured the old English moss roses, her mother's favorite, planted in their formal gardens at home in *Belle Chenier*. Red ones and white ones and a delicate few, the yellow of the sun at dawn. "There were three men in the dining room, Yankees. Dirty and ragged. Drinking *Papere's* brandy and asking him to tell them where his money was, and using Mama and Francis as the means to get their information. They used . . ." she could remember the flash of the steel, "our cook's biggest kitchen knife."

Raine felt Gavin's arms around her then, warm bands of comfort.

She would not cry. "They died. I ran. I ran, Gavin."

"Darling," he whispered against her cheek, "you were eleven years old, alone and defenseless."

"I could have done something, though. I should have."

"No." He turned her around and took her face in both his hands. "You would have died, too."

"I fled upriver, into the woods."

"Where did you go?"

"Our overseer had a house in the pines. I had been there often. Every Sunday when I was six and seven for catechism lessons which his wife taught in French."

"And how long did you stay there?"

"For almost a year."

"And then where did you go?"

She looked at Gavin. *What can you say, Raine?* "My uncle came to find me. When he saw the plantation deserted and the three graves in the backyard, he looked for me. He took me back to Baltimore to live. He lost a lot of his family in the war." Raine did not add that she remained there in his house on Charles Street for a year and lived with their Great Aunt Peg. When the war ended, Uncle Skip took Raine to Alexandria to live with his wife and daughter, Ann.

Gavin was puzzled. "When did you move to Washington?"

So many questions. Too many. Her thoughts raced—and tripped in the muck she'd made with her own lies. "Two years ago." She hoped that was right. "That's when I met Winston."

"And your uncle? He's the one you write to, I suppose."

"Write to?"

Gavin paused, a moment too long for Raine's comfort. Her mind raced. *Mon Dieu,* what had she said about writing letters to people? "You told me the first day you came here that one of your pastimes is to write letters. I would assume your uncle would be one of those."

"Yes." *But I write rarely to him—and only through Ann.* "He is such a busy man. He corresponds infrequently."

"I see," Gavin said and Raine knew he wished he could see more than he did. "Where is he now?"

"In Marseilles."

"Oh?" That shocked Gavin. "He's not in America, but Europe? Interesting. What does he do there?"

"He goes at least once each year on business, but he primarily goes to take the sun at a spa. He has consumption, and if he's careful and doesn't expose himself to too much damp and chilly weather, he'll live a long time." Raine anticipated Gavin's next question about how her uncle could afford to take the waters at a spa. "He owns—" she said, scolding herself for lack of planning on this topic, "a shipping company." *And is a director of the largest Anglo-American cruise line crossing the Atlantic.* "That's what he did during the war." *As a blockade runner.* "That's what he still does. He is," she said with rueful honesty, "ruthless in business but a dear to those he loves. He rescued me from a very sad existence and gave me a home. He has been generous to me. Far too generous, sometimes." She smiled with little mirth. "To his chagrin, I have insisted on working."

"Hence, your stint as a saleslady at Warfield's Dry Goods Store," Gavin added with a flash of humor.

"Precisely," she said and walked toward the door. She had to get away from Gavin and his quest for details. "I must return to my bouillon or we will have gruel for supper." *The exact consistency of my brains, as we speak.*

He put his hands on his hips and narrowed his eyes at her. "That wasn't so terrible to tell me, was it?"

"Not at all," she gave him blithely and left him with that false impression.

Throughout supper, Gavin picked at his food. He wanted something he wasn't getting, an element necessary to his well-being—and he couldn't figure out what it was. Raine asked if her cuisine were to blame for his silence. It was not.

Neither did their walk along the shore improve his disposition. He apologized for his mood, dropped a kiss on her forehead, and left her at her door. In her eyes, a wariness grew. He had no explanation to give her.

He returned to his office and sat in the dark. From his desk chair, he could see Raine's cottage and the moonlight dancing on the water in a restless silver plane.

When he had been a child, he often imagined himself as Neptune, god of the sea. He would grow fins and a long tail and swim beneath the waves to view the wonders of the world hidden from his human sight.

He wanted to know more about Raine Jennings. He needed to dive beneath her cool surface. He had glimpsed some of her depths today. She loved her family. Missed the serenity of her childhood existence. Had been brutally torn from its idyll by war and savagery. She had survived. By her own instinct for self-preservation. And she had learned how to retreat into herself to nurture that child.

He needed to learn more about the woman. Today, he had discovered so little. He had heard enough from her to reaffirm his decision to keep secret what was fact and what was fiction in his mystery. If she knew that, not only would he tap memories which might rise like ghosts to send her away from him, but she would ask too many questions about what had happened the night of the murder. He would have to give her answers which might also put her in danger. He would not risk that. From the day she had first come to him, he had known Raine Jennings was unique. Now he knew she was more rare. She was essential to his existence.

He wanted to become necessary to hers. He congratulated himself that he had been so calm today. So ready to act serene. He let her recount the crisis of her youth. However, she had recited facts, not emotional fathoms. In some ways, Gavin decided he did not require the detailed account of her existence since the day her parents and brother died. He had the woman before him to give evidence to that. She was energetic, ambitious, and so damn determined to be independent.

But he wanted her. Not just in his bed. But in his life. Despite his lack of a regular income, a sterling reputation, or a vast array of friends and family to welcome her to his world. Those he would acquire. He told himself he was progressing with his restoration. And if he had motive before to attain them, the impetus had never been so great as having Raine in his life permanently.

He wanted to marry her. And he would settle for no less than the whole person. Child, woman, orphan, artist, whatever she'd been, whatever she wanted to become, he had to possess all of her.

Which meant, of course, he had to explore the recesses she kept hidden from him. Perhaps, too, from herself.

Why did she do that? Had she been so frightened by the murders of her parents and brother that she trusted no one? Surely, this uncle who had saved her had reestablished some belief in the power of love. If the uncle hadn't, surely the husband had.

Hadn't he?

Gavin ran a hand over his mouth. He should have asked the uncle's name. Found out where he lived. Washington or Baltimore, he supposed. What sort of man was he that he could travel easily after a war ended?

A man with money, certainly. One with connections, probably. A man who loved his sister and her family enough to seek them out no matter the cost in money, time, or danger.

The next question made Gavin sit up straighter. He peered at Raine's cottage. "Why did your uncle allow you to marry Winston Jennings?" A foreigner. English, but nonetheless, a soldier who would return home—or be posted to any godforsaken black hole in a far-flung empire. Leaving Raine alone. And penniless.

No uncle—who could afford to take the cure at a spa in the south of France and who went to great lengths to save a niece from a war-torn land—would smile on her marriage to a man with slim prospects for a sound financial future. Unless there had been some conflict between this uncle and Raine. Or he had hurt her.

That seemed impossible. She spoke of her uncle with a fondness lacking in her words about her husband.

That realization, more than the others, brought Gavin up short.

Did she love her husband or didn't she? Did she long for him or was she relieved that he'd gone? Did she miss the man's affections? Her reluctance to discuss their nature might have been a young woman's natural shyness to discuss such things. But Gavin suspected her reticence was based on her husband's inability to be kind or patient with her in bed.

He would ask. Again and in detail.

He told himself he had a right to know. If her husband had shown her no courtesy of kisses and caresses, she would continue to be shy. Gavin wanted her bold in his arms, the way she was out of them.

If her husband had taken her to bed and acted brutish, she would have no idea of the beauty which intercourse could bring to a relationship. Gavin wanted to teach her what he knew of such delights. He licked his lips at the possibility of showing Raine the effects of spontaneity—and the uses of generosity.

And what if her husband had not taken her to bed? There was that possible interpretation of her words.

Gavin swallowed hard on the hope that he could be the first to show her what ecstasies a man and woman could find together in a bed of mutual pleasure.

Her reluctance to share her past barred her from sharing her future. He would tear down that wall. Discover why she thought she could work for him, cook for him, joke with him, waltz into his life, and then think she could dance out the door when he was restored to his good name.

"Oh, Raine," he sighed, "you make me angry and impatient." Two characteristics he'd vowed to tame. He would now.

He had shown her kindness and patience, and she had drawn closer to him. Despite her desire to maintain her independence. And her need to keep secrets.

Now he wondered what she'd do when he showed her the newest aspect of his nature. How much he loved her.

Chapter 9

"A picture is something which requires as much knavery, trickery, and deceit as the perpetration of a crime. Paint falsely and then add the accent of nature."

—EDGAR DEGAS

TEN DAYS LATER, THE FEARS RAINE HAD HARBORED ABOUT Gavin's novel bloomed like a plant full of poison. She reread the latest installment of *The Accused* which had been released two days ago to ground herself firmly in what it did say—just to make sure she knew what it did not say.

This was the sixth chapter which described the hero Samuel Grant recalling details of the murder scene.

Gavin had rewritten it since he had given it to her to type. He had added one element which had not been described in any of the newspaper accounts. In Gavin's version, his hero found his own embroidered handkerchief in the hand of the murdered man—and he had taken it with him when he left the scene of the crime.

Raine startled. Was this fact or fiction?

Yes, she had encouraged Gavin to use his imagination to change the circumstances, to frighten the real murderer into making some false move. Was this the alteration that would bring the criminal to the fore?

Whether true or false, this would create an even greater stir in England than the book had so far.

The letters to the editors in the past few weeks' publications were only a shower of distemper compared to the storm of controversy which raged in the tabloids this week. Now other MPs were issuing statements to the press, supporting or castigating Gavin for his novel. Editorials also appeared in seven of the eight major dailies.

Most praised Gavin—and his alter ego, his fictional hero Samuel Grant—for the man's courage to delve into the unsolved mystery. Three ridiculed Gavin, declared him the most likely suspect in the O'Malley-Stoddard murders, and criticized Gavin and his publisher for printing what each called "such trash." "Prurient . . ." declared one. Another said, ". . . disconcerting that fiction could be fashioned so closely to fact that we are given pause to question the wisdom and procedures of experts at Scotland Yard and the police." A third asked, "Merely by its revelations, are we not led to believe that the author knows as much as the perpetrator?"

Only her former publisher, Matthew Healy, abstained from the brouhaha and printed an editorial about the odor of the Thames. He ranted and raved how the city must deal with this issue of sanitation, especially because members of Parliament were to reconvene in five weeks—and should not ". . . bear the stink of the river wafting into the windows of Parliament." To accompany the editorial, Raine's successor as political cartoonist drew a man, who resembled Gavin actually, with a pincer on his nose, grimacing as he overlooked the river on Westminster Bridge. She thought the cartoon was a double entendre, one of Matthew's delicate barbs meant to prick the sanitation issue—and wound Gavin as he resurrected public discussion of the murders.

She rose from her desk when she'd finished, knowing

what she wanted to ask Gavin when she heard a knock at the front door. The postman usually wended his way by on his new bicycle at this hour of the afternoon. Unlike London, mail service here on the coast of Norfolk came only once a day, in the early afternoon. Today the postman was late, and Raine knew Mrs. McNally would be cleaning up from luncheon service and would be deep into her supper preparations. So Raine would let him in. On her way to the hall, she passed Gavin at his desk, rubbing his chin and scowling at what he'd written this morning.

"Good afternoon, Mrs. Jennings. How are ye? 'Is lordship 'as lots o' mail today." The skinny postman handed over an unusually tall stack of mail.

Raine wondered if the increase in letters was indicative of interest in *The Accused.*

"I've put yer mail here too, Missus Jennings. Two letters from—"

"Thank you, Peter," she cut him off, scanning the wealth Peter was putting in her arms. Her letters could be only from her cousin Ann who was at High Keep Castle in Lancashire for the summer months. Raine did not want Gavin to overhear and ask questions about who she knew in northwest England, hundreds of miles from London.

The postman winked at her. "Why not just leave 'em 'ere with you, I thought, eh? Your little mail slot in yer door wouldn't take those fat letters. An' yer always 'ere anyway, ain't ye?"

"No," Raine objected, "there is so much for his lordship," the letters were overflowing her arms, "I would prefer you leave mine at my door, Peter."

"Well, hello, Peter, how are you?" Raine jumped at Gavin's approach. He took a handful of the letters from the man. Raine prayed none of them was hers. "I can take some of those from you, Raine."

She stepped backward. "I'll sort and open them for

you." Those were her ordinary tasks. She could do them and ferret out her two letters. Away from Gavin's gaze.

He scooped up more mail. "Thank you, Peter. See you tomorrow." He smiled and closed the door on the fellow. "Your uncle must have become inspired to write," he said as he examined the envelopes he'd taken—and he'd taken most of them.

Raine's heart pounded in her ears. "What?"

"I overheard Peter say you have two letters today," Gavin said by way of explanation. "Wish I could get inspired like your uncle."

"Are you stuck?" she asked, glad to lead Gavin off the subject of her correspondence and on to his writing.

He hitched up one side of his mouth. "Got any ideas?"

"Lots of questions."

"I hope I've got answers." He strolled to the library table, dropped some of his pile as he proceeded to his desk. "One from Ned. One from Bryce—and judging by the postmark, he's gone back to London from Tantallon." The third made Gavin hoot. "Derwenter."

What could he want? "Interesting assortment," she offered, pushing curiosity aside in favor of her relief that she had in hand her own two letters. Each of them bore the distinctive white wax seal of the duchess of Carlton and Dundalk. But there was another, too. From London. This could only be from Matthew Healy, who was the other person who knew she was here—under the name Mrs. Jennings.

But Gavin had stopped in his tracks. "Damn, what does he want?"

"Who?"

"My father."

He rounded his desk, anger stiffening his muscles.

Raine tucked her letters beneath others so that Gavin might not see hers if he came to stand beside her. Considering his scowl, the chances of that were small, but nevertheless, Raine prayed he would remain where he was. Her letters would surely raise his eyebrows—and his suspicions. The one from Matthew seemed to be of normal size. However, the two from Ann Kendall were fairly bursting their envelopes, an indication of much news from a woman who was usually brief in her correspondence.

Gavin was consumed with his own mail. He took his father's vellum and placed it squarely in the center of his desk. As if it were a sacrificial offering or a snake, Gavin focused on it for long minutes. He tore himself away and chose to read Ned Hollister's letter first.

"Ned has had to double the print run of *St. Andrew's* for a fourth time," Gavin informed her when he looked up and he tried for levity. "Good news, eh?"

"Superb. I wish I could be a fly on the wall in a few London drawing rooms to hear what's being said."

"Do you know that old Irish saying, 'Be careful what you wish for'? You might not like what you hear, Raine."

She didn't answer. She knew the proverb. It was one her cousin Ann's husband, Rhys Kendall, often quoted. But of course, Raine didn't respond. She didn't have to. Gavin was tearing open another letter.

At last, he said, "Well, well, Bryce has outdone himself."

"Oh, how?" Raine wondered when Bryce had returned to London and what he had decided about his marriage. Not only had Gavin confided in her about his friend's quandary, but Ann had written her days later to say that Colleen was frantic because she did not know where her husband was. Raine had written Ann, asking for news about Colleen and Gus as she always did, but disclosing nothing about Bryce's visit or what Gavin had told her. To do so would have meant that Raine would have to tell Ann how she had become acquainted with Gavin Sutherland—and become friendly enough that he would share his distressful news about another friend. Ann might ask questions about Gavin and Raine's relationship that Raine would not wish to answer.

"Soon after Bryce left here, I wrote to him in Tantallon and asked him to do me a favor. He got my letter before he left, and he has included a list of free boroughs which will become vacant in the next election or two. Among them is Chipswell."

Raine was shocked. "You're moving ahead with their suggestion to run? I thought you decided not to do that until the novel was finished and the crime solved? What happened after he left to change your mind?"

Raine could not think of any extraordinary occurrence since Bryce had gone, except for that afternoon Gavin had kissed her senseless, and she'd told her story of her parents' deaths. Since then, certainly, Gavin had changed in two ways. He was a very happy man. But that she credited to the growing popularity of his novel. He was also very free with his kisses. That Raine attributed to her increasing responsiveness to them.

"I thought it best to move quickly on that matter. I become more eager daily to settle my future," he said and stirred her curiosity as to why he'd do that. "Besides, you never know when someone will decide to step down." He hoisted Bryce's letter. "And here is an opportunity in familiar territory."

"Yes. I didn't know that the current MP was interested in retiring." What was his name? Had she ever met him? Heard him speak?

"Neither did I. I haven't taken the time to visit him in months. Shows you how out of kilter I've become. Writing makes one a hermit." Gavin read on.

"Who is he?" She couldn't remember anything distinctive about him.

"William Pumphrey. He's sat for—good god—for more than twenty years, I think."

Pumphrey. Yes, she had heard him speak when she had visited the gallery. But he had never held forth for long on any issue. He was a politician who preferred to work his will among his friends behind closed doors. Raine knew it was always best to meet a man on his own terms—and then bring him to yours. "Perhaps, you should have Mr. Pumphrey to supper."

Gavin winked at her. "I think so. Next week. You will preside, of course, as my hostess."

"I will cook. I will not dine."

"Raine—"

"Secretaries do not partake of meals with their employers in public. Especially female secretaries."

"Disraeli once entertained the idea of a female secretary," Gavin informed her with a teasing tone.

"But he didn't employ her, did he?"

"No. He learned that she applied to him because she wanted to insinuate herself into his life—and his heart. She told him bluntly that she wanted to marry him."

"What happened? Dizzy is supposed to be a ladies' man. Was she uncouth? Ugly?"

"On the contrary, she was a countess, a lady of breeding and beauty."

"Well, then?" Raine asked, the matter still puzzling.

"Dizzy has loved only one woman. That was his wife and now that she's gone, he could never think of putting another in her place. Besides, he told me personally, a man should never mix romance and politics."

"And why is that?"

"Politics requires alternatives. Romance excludes them. Confuse the two and you fail at both."

"So a man in politics should never take his concerns home to his wife?"

"Mmm, that seems to be Dizzy's moral here."

"Unless he does not love his wife," she quipped, got Gavin to laugh, and then let him resume his reading.

Until at length, he said, "My God," weary as she had ever heard him.

"What's wrong?"

"Bryce Falconer has decided to divorce his wife."

Letters drifted from Raine's fingers. *"No."* She couldn't believe it. "That's never done." Was that why she had two letters from Ann? Ann was shocked. Gus must be, too. And Colleen? Colleen, despite her reck-lessness—ah, *mais oui,* her irresponsibility—would be devastated. For once in her life. Because whatever Col-leen had done to anger Bryce and shame him, Colleen loved him. As much as she could.

Raine's instinct was to run to London.

Ann, Colleen, Gus, and Raine had always been togeth-er at the turning points of their lives. Ever since the four of them had entered Mrs. Drummond's Finishing School for Young Ladies in Manhattan in '67, they had weathered so many tribulations—Gus's monthlong coma after a fall from her horse at the age of twelve; Colleen's fever from an infection caused by her mother's use of a whip to make her comply with the woman's wishes; the death of Ann's mother; Ann's decision to come abroad with her father and her request to bring the other three with them.

Raine put a hand through her hair. What could she do? She had been present when Ann had fallen in love with Rhys Kendall. When Colleen had notified them she intended to make the elusive Bryce Falconer marry her. When Gus had gathered her courage and refused to return home to New York with her parents after Col-leen's wedding. But today Raine was here, miles away from London and unable to offer support or advice, unable to leave Norfolk. Unwilling to leave Gavin.

She swayed with the sudden knowledge. *None of them matters as much to me as Gavin.* And she groped the table for support.

Gavin flipped to the second page of Bryce's letter.

Raine stared at him. This man whom she had met two and a half months ago—and yet knew intricately. How had he come to mean so much to her that she would choose him above those who had shown her friendship, love, and compassion for ten years?

No, she would not answer that. Her instinct, which served her so well in so many ways, told her she would not like the answer. She avoided it in favor of the topic of

Bryce and Colleen's marriage. And she had to think clearly here, lest she give away more than she should about her understanding of the Falconers' discord.

Over a month ago after Bryce had left Chipswell, Gavin had summarized for Raine his friend's decision to spend some time in Scotland in seclusion. She had had the devilish job of keeping her responses objective as Gavin related the tale Raine knew firsthand. Afterward, Raine had written to Ann, hoping for a response which would give a greater explanation about why Bryce had gone to Tantallon alone. But Ann was in Lancashire at her home in High Keep Castle for the summer months, far from Gus and Colleen, who were in London. Her reply briefly recounted Colleen's latest incident in the London fountain and Colleen's fear that Bryce may have left her for good.

She put a hand to her chest. This attempt to help Gavin was becoming more and more of a vise around her heart. Attempting to avoid lying to Gavin and Ann, she was nonetheless committing sins of omission.

Did the end justify the means? She had never believed that.

How much longer could she condone her behavior to right a wrong she had done him? She couldn't.

She must leave him soon for her own peace of mind. But how could she go when she had not completed her goal?

Gavin's voice seeped into her misery. "Bryce says he can no longer stand by and allow her to ruin his good name. He won't permit her to shape Bradford's life, either."

Bradford was only one and a half years old. What would Bryce do? "He can't mean to take her child from her," Raine whispered.

Gavin frowned at Raine. Blinked. "Yes. Yes, he does. He will sue for sole custody."

"Is that done? May fathers do that here in England?"

"More men have in the last thirty years or so. A

Parliamentary divorce permits it. The procedure is a long process and expensive."

Raine could not imagine a worse scenario than for Colleen to be denied her baby. Coll did love the little boy. She doted on him, when she was not recuperating from her excesses of too many parties and too much alcohol. She played with him, sang to him, conducted one-sided but nonetheless copious conversations with him. Poor Ford. "What are the chances under English law that Bryce will win his suit?"

Gavin was looking at her oddly. "I should think very great. His wife is American, and she may want to return home and, perhaps, take the boy with her. Bradford is Bryce's heir, so I doubt he'd permit her to do that. But I also believe her public behavior will weigh heavily in the judge's decision to allow Bryce to keep the boy."

Raine knew from discussions before Ann's marriage to Rhys that American women who married Englishmen automatically became English citizens. Colleen might bring her own custody suit, but Raine doubted she could win. Not in England against a peer of the realm. Not with such a disastrous reputation as she had. Even if Colleen decided to bring a suit in an American court, she would not win because of her behavior.

Raine bit her lip. She was stepping more into a mire each day with Gavin. What had she said, in her shock, even now? Anything to make him wary of her identity?

She itched to rip open her own letters. Read her cousin's description of this scandalous event. Oh, poor Coll. Her mother would rise like ten devils at her daughter's fate. Voracious Veronica would take the next ship to England, shanghai the captain if she must, to get here earlier than they planned. Veronica would try to browbeat Bryce into reversing his decision.

"That's a terrible tragedy," Raine finally said, realizing Gavin was watching her, waiting for some comment.

"Yes," he agreed after a long moment, and reached for another of his letters. This one was not his father's either. It was from Derwenter . . . and it had Gavin laughing and sinking into his chair. "I'll be damned."

She looked at him blankly, not wishing to appear too eager to hear more news. She had already said too much. Her emotions had been too apparent to him. What would she say was the cause when he asked? Because knowing Gavin, he would ask.

"I am invited to join Derwenter at his club for supper. What do you think of that?"

She had the queasy feeling the only reason Gavin asked was because he knew she wouldn't volunteer the information. "That depends on what he wants. And you won't know unless you go."

"Interesting that he wants to make a public show of it when I am becoming controversial again."

"Maybe he likes standing in your shadow," Raine ventured. *Or maybe he wants his daughter to.* "I think you should accept."

That caused one brow to rise. "You approve?"

"Of learning all you can? Yes. From anyone. Derwenter was a friend of Sean O'Malley as well as a colleague to both of you in the Commons."

"You're right again. I must look at all contacts now for their potential to give me information about the murders." His gaze dropped to his father's letter. With measured movements, he took his letter opener and sliced it.

Raine had never seen Gavin become so furious, so fast. Her breath caught in her throat at his transformation.

In the two and a half months she had worked for him, she had seen a spectrum of emotions from him. That first day, he was placid—and beneath those still waters, sad and apprehensive. Since then, he had regained his joie de vivre, learned to laugh, and aroused Raine to do the same.

Now he was a hurricane. He cursed, crushed the pages of his father's letter and hurled them across his desk. He stalked through the garden doors and left them banging against the walls. The room filled with a chill wind from the sea.

She had to run to catch up to him. He was well beyond his favorite spot among the rocks before she reached him. He was wild, hurling stones into the surf that churned with the coming storm.

She did not have to ask him, he told her what his father had written.

"I am to cease and desist." Gavin picked up another, bigger rock. This time he walked toward the raging tide to throw it out to sea. "My illustrious father is distressed. Disappointed, to be exact. Well, I am disappointed in him. What man deserts his son without even a thought, a question, of his innocence?"

Raine hadn't meant to say anything until Gavin had vented all his animosity. But she could not let this pass. "You don't need him."

He spun on her, gripped her arms, and kissed her deeply, quickly. Then he wrapped her so close, he nearly hugged the breath from her. "How right you are, sweetheart. Never again." He dropped a kiss into her hair. "Help me do that, will you?"

She pulled back, nodding. "Of course. You know I will."

He ran his hand back into her hair. "You are the one person I can count on, Raine. Come with me into Chipswell tomorrow. I want to call on William Pumphrey, say hello, and see if he'll give me any information about his stepping down. I will introduce you as my secretary who has come to take notes."

"Gavin—"

"Raine, please don't say no. In the village, they know you work for me. What harm is it to Pumphrey know, too? Perhaps he has already heard about you from his neighbors. I need you to impress him. He's a wily old goat, but he knows this borough like the veins in his hands. And he's ill. You'll cheer him, darling. If I'm to stand for Chipswell, I will need his knowledge and his support. Come and we'll have a wonderful afternoon filled with all those things you love. Politics and important conversation. And on the way home, I want to ask your opinion on a purchase I hope I can soon make."

His mood was lighter now, and she meant to encourage him to keep it that way. "Spending your millions before you have it, my lord?"

"Think I'm impatient, do you?"

The light in his eyes told her he was eager for more than money. It was the look he got before he would kiss her till her bones turned to porridge. "Don't count your chickens," she had to warn him.

He lifted her chin and took her lips in the sweetest, softest caress. "Planning my future, darling. What's wrong with that?"

"Nothing," she told him with a smile—and lied through her teeth.

The rain began then. Huge hard drops that pelted them and made them run for cover in her cottage.

Later as they dined at his house on a saddle of lamb and roasted parsley potatoes, they listened to the storm batter the roof. Gavin seemed oblivious to the turbulence outside. Raine hid her own turmoil from him well, she thought. Otherwise, how could he sit there and speak so nonchalantly of issues that mattered to Chipswell voters? Shipping and fishing regulations. Monies for canal building to better local transportation.

Her mind drifted to other matters. The way Gavin spoke as if she would help him form his own approaches to those issues. The way she would charm the pants off ol' Will Pumphrey tomorrow.

She didn't have the heart to stop him. She didn't have the nerve to tell him he was planning too much of his future—and including her was not a wise idea.

Chapter 10

"An honest politician is one who when he's bought, stays bought."

—SIMON CAMERON

"I APPLAUD YOU, GAVIN, FOR GREAT TASTE. DOES HE TREAT you well, my dear?" William Pumphrey adjusted his gnarled body in his drawing room chair. All the while, his beady blue eyes ate her for teatime snack. He really did resemble an old goat.

"He pays me well," she told him honestly.

Pumphrey stroked his pointed white beard. "Works you long hours?"

She removed her gloves, finger by finger. "If I ever learn how to use the American typewriter he bought me, I'll have more time free." She smiled radiantly, as if she saw no innuendo in his leading questions.

"You give her time off?" he tsked at Gavin. "Bad form, my boy. Secretaries need to be loaded down, else they have time to ponder and feel free to burden you with advice."

"She has already done that, Mr. Pumphrey. The day

she began work. I cannot call it back now. I am stuck."
Gavin threw up his hands in mock resignation.

"And beautifully so, I see." He licked his lips. "Any
problems with your housekeeper over her working for
you?"

"None that I know of." Gavin checked Raine's gaze.

"There were a few in the beginning, but Mrs. McNally
soon saw I meant his lordship no harm."

"Wise woman," Pumphrey acknowledged.

Gavin pursued the issue further. "Any rumors among
the villagers about Mrs. Jennings that you've heard?"

"What one can expect. Great speculation. Who is she.
Why she's come here. What's her motive. Seduction and
marriage or spying on you."

Raine felt her spine stiffen more with each word.

Gavin shook his head. "Why not employment?"

"That's what we have all concluded." Pumphrey
smiled at Raine. "Mrs. McNally sends out the word that
you have made a great improvement in Lord Sutherland's attitude. You have won a great battle there, Mrs.
Jennings. Bravo. But you must also know, my dear, that
people in Chipswell have known your employer since he
was in dresses. Once he was breeched, he became the
village terror. Took a pie from Mrs. Arnold's bakery
once. Sailed Jamie's father's fishing boat out to sea one
night. Alone. Got lost. Found some sense of direction."

"The stars," Gavin explained.

"And didn't come home till dawn."

Gavin snorted and informed Raine, "That cost me my
month's allowance to pay for the hole in the hull I
caused. My father also made me publicly apologize to
him and give a discourse on the sanctity of private
property." He grinned. "That gave me my first taste of
public speaking."

"An appetite which you have not lost, thank God.
Ever heard him speak, my dear?"

The speed and shock of the question left Raine no

chance to lie. "Yes. I have," she admitted, and felt the bore of Gavin's gaze. She smiled at Pumphrey. "He's inspiring."

"He's bloody hell-on-wheels. Could lead me to a revolution, I tell you." He tilted his head. "But the means you always advocate are peaceful ones. A shame what happened to you."

Pumphrey's butler knocked briefly, then entered with their tea. While the man served, Pumphrey led them in a conversation of banalities. The weather. The opening of Parliament in a few weeks. The return of society from the country. When the butler closed the door upon them, Gavin and Pumphrey looked at each other for a moment.

"You'd like to know why I've come."

"No time like the present to tell me, Gavin."

"I need your advice."

"You shall have it. You were helpful to me last year when I needed the Maritime Fishing Bill amended. It was not the first time you came to my side in a matter. I have always liked you. As a child, a man, a politician."

Gavin looked grateful. "I presume you know about the stir my novel is creating?"

Pumphrey extended a hand toward the hall. "In my library, I have all four copies of *St. Andrew's* with your series. Very well-written, Gavin. Intriguing, too."

"Thank you. I wanted it to capture people's imaginations."

"The Yard's, too, I would guess." Pumphrey shot a glance at Raine. "What do you think of the letters to the editor?"

"They are precisely the reaction we wanted."

Pumphrey's narrow face broadened with his grin. "A gem you are, Mrs. Jennings. Understands the implications of the public outcry, doesn't she, Gavin?"

"I am very fortunate," Gavin replied.

Raine shifted in her chair, put her teacup down. "I

would appreciate it if you two would not speak about me as if I were invisible."

Pumphrey chuckled. "My dear, you are so visible, you blind a man. To find a woman so intelligent—and precocious about politics as well—can be . . . a stunning blow. Most women," he leaned over to pat her hand, "would not have the vaguest clue about what Gavin is doing. Where *did* you come from, Mrs. Jennings?"

She nearly choked on her smile. She let it appear she took his question as rhetorical—and did not answer.

Gavin left his cup on the tea table and sat forward, elbows on his thighs. "My publisher has written to me just yesterday to tell me this serialization will make him rich—and me as well. He is increasing the percentage of my advance payments."

Raine stared at Gavin. He had not told her that. But then, the increase in the print run of *St. Andrew's* was becoming a weekly occurrence and was perhaps the same as saying that.

"I rely solely on my writing for my income," Gavin continued.

Pumphrey was not surprised. "Your father is renowned for his rigidity. Rumors flew he cut you off. I am damned astounded he let you have the house."

"That magnanimity was, I think, forced upon him by my mother. As for his rejection of me in all other ways, I have learned to live with that. My father will never change. I do not want his help—nor do I need it."

"The marquess will wear his stubbornness as his shroud, I'm afraid. Hangs on to his power, wherever he can, like a medieval lord."

"I was always surprised he did not try to wrest it from you here in Chipswell, Mr. Pumphrey."

"Bah! The only reason he ever let this borough remain free of his influence was because *his* father told him Chipswell had been free land since King John's time. Your grandfather warned him not to try to change that or he'd have rebellion on his hands. Your father stuck to Appleby to get his way in the Commons. I kept my seat all these years because your father kept his hands out of my pie."

"You kept your seat, Mr. Pumphrey, because you are a man who speaks with the voice of the people he represents."

"I take that as high praise from a man I respect," Pumphrey said with no small measure of sorrow. "I wonder if you have heard that I think of resigning my seat?"

"I have."

Pumphrey picked at the antimacassar atop the arm of his chair. "I am ill, Gavin." He pursed his lips, turned blankly toward his window. "I cannot keep up the pace." He collected himself and spun his head toward Gavin. "The questions remaining are when will I go—and who will replace me."

Gavin nodded. "Have you any candidates in mind?"

"Two." Pumphrey wrinkled his long nose. "I don't care much for either of them. But then, there are poor pickings in my party in this section of the country."

"I know," Gavin allowed. "How well do you think the Chipswell voters would receive a candidate from the other party?"

"Chipswell votes for the man, for his stance, not his backers." Pumphrey narrowed his eyes on Gavin. "You have such a candidate in mind, do you?" When Gavin simply stared at him, he whispered, "Wonderful."

"You approve?" Gavin was clearly shocked and pleased.

"Of you? Your ethics, yes. Not your anger, which is your Achilles' heel and you found out you had to cure the fault or lose your soul, didn't you? Yes, well . . . I do approve of you, Gavin. You have integrity. Of that, I could approve wholeheartedly. Of your position on issues? I find many similarities with my own voting record. Your interests are very similar to those of Chipswell."

"Well, then, Mr. Pumphrey," Raine's words slipped out before she knew they were hers, "you could endorse him."

Gavin gaped.

Pumphrey did the same, then he began to shake with laughter. "Damned right, I could!" He slapped his knee and winced. "Aw, hell. The gout is killing me along with the cancer." He rose and limped a bit toward the bellpull. "We'll drink on that, what do you say?"

Gavin had the wild look of a man who'd been caught in a whirlwind.

Raine was fairly bursting at the seams with happiness. "I think we should."

Pumphrey blinked at her forwardness and then endorsed it by asking, "What do you like?"

Gavin supplied the laughing answer. "Champagne."

Raine reproved him with a glance.

"Now, now, my dear," Pumphrey came forward to put a hand up, "don't be mad at him. He's just struck a political deal he didn't know he could make. Cut him a bit of slack."

The butler appeared and was sent away with a request for champagne.

Pumphrey waited until the man closed the door. "I will endorse you gladly, Gavin."

"I am overwhelmed with gratitude."

"My dear boy, you will need to be overwhelmed with money. Your party can donate all of your campaign funds. But if you are elected, how will you support yourself? Can you say this novel will be so profitable as to support you all the rest of your days?"

"If I am prudent with my expenses and invest wisely in a few growing businesses, perhaps I can get along."

"Most men in Parliament live well because they are supported by benefactors like your father. Many of them supplement that income by marrying rich girls."

Gavin waved a hand as if he had quit with that approach.

While Raine was thrilled Gavin had dismissed that means, she wondered if Sidney Derwenter and his daughter had other plans. If Gavin would accept the invitation to dine with Sid. If Belinda would work her way back into Gavin's life once he were restored to his rightful place in Parliament and his reputation.

"By going it in a free borough, my boy," Pumphrey continued, "you live a much more perilous financial existence. We are decades from any bill which grants a salary to a member of Parliament. Living in London is costly. Even a modest home requires ten to fifteen thousand pounds a year to run. As an MP, you'll need a house big enough to entertain for supper parties at the very least. That means a butler, housekeeper, cook, and . . ." his eyes went to Raine and back, "you'll need to pay a secretary."

Gavin agreed. "I have known for a long time that if and when I stood for Parliament again—and if I won, I would need to provide my own financial means. I would have it no other way."

"So then you decided to create a ruckus and send people to the kiosks for the next installment of your book." Pumphrey glowed with pride.

"I did."

"Determined to scare out the murderer, too."

"Yes."

"Planned this well, didn't he, Mrs. Jennings?"

"Brilliantly," she agreed with a lightheartedness she had not felt since the mail arrived yesterday and brought so much bad news. The Falconers' pending divorce, Ann's appeal to come to London, Derwenter's invitation to Gavin to lunch with him ran through Raine's mind. What supplanted them all was the more frightening matter of Gavin's alteration of his manuscript. She had been so taken with those other catastrophes yesterday, she had not asked him if the presence of the handkerchief was a fact—or fiction.

Nor had she time to write a reply to Matthew Healy—and she didn't want to, either. The man had been forward, asking about her relationship with Gavin, how the work was coming, and praising her for the wonderful novel they were producing together. As if she had contributed more than her presence to Gavin's superb work of fiction. As if she wished to share a relationship so essential to her well-being with a man who had been no more than her employer, albeit a kind one.

"I hope Gavin finds a way to retain your services once he goes to London, Mrs. Jennings. Mrs. Jennings?"

She forced herself from the matter of the handkerchief to Pumphrey's words. She lowered her gaze to the floor. "That would be difficult, Mr. Pumphrey. For many reasons."

"Dizzy once thought of hiring a woman as his secretary," Pumphrey offered. "Times are changing, you know."

"Not quickly enough," Gavin rejoined. "I already tried to sell her that bill of goods, Mr. Pumphrey. I did not make a sale. Raine is of the opinion that people will think it scandalous."

The butler knocked again and made his way past them to set down the champagne and glasses.

Raine did not wish to discuss this further. She rose and walked toward the window.

"They will continue to think whatever they will," Pumphrey persisted when his servant was gone, "no matter that word here is you two are friends. No matter that in London, you, Mrs. Jennings, would live not quite so close as you do now to your employer."

Embarrassed, Raine was unable to respond to this delicate issue.

Pumphrey awaited a response.

Gavin frowned. Sadness thinned his mouth.

Raine turned and found herself facing a long console on which numerous pictures stood. Every one was of Mr. Pumphrey with some government figure. Dizzy. Lord Randolph Churchill—with his American wife, Jennie. Gavin. Sean O'Malley. She spun.

"You knew Sean O'Malley, Mr. Pumphrey?" Relief sang through her bloodstream at the ability to change the subject—and to one so pertinent to Gavin's situation.

"Yes, of course, I did, Mrs. Jennings." He was working at the cork. "Interesting man. Good republican. A pity he's gone. He would have voted with Gavin and me and others to get a peaceful solution to the Irish troubles. Without him, we have one less voice for reason in the Commons."

He poured champagne into the three glasses. "I thought it foolish of him to tarnish his career by carrying on with Louise Stoddard. I told him so." He handed Raine her glass. "A man who wishes to persuade others to his views must maintain the respect of others. Never is that more true than in his relationships with women." His eyes locked on hers. "I am pleased to see you understand this, as well as all the other intricacies, my dear."

What could she say to him—"I am here to help Lord Sutherland, not have a relationship with him"? *But you do,* whispered a voice. *You do.* "A woman must look to her own reputation, Mr. Pumphrey."

He nodded. "Gavin? Your glass. A toast is in order. To the next MP from Chipswell-by-the-Sea." One eye closed in a long wink. "Even if he will come from the opposite party, he will be hailed—and endorsed by his predecessor."

Gavin drank with a smile on his face, but Raine knew him well enough now to predict he would seek answers to the questions that lurked beneath the surface. There was a certain curve to his mouth when he mulled an issue. He returned to his seat now, and she noted the lines that told her to beware his probes later. Because they would come, and she had better have strong answers.

Sweet God, but she had to leave him before she was eaten alive by her own aversion to lying. But just like yesterday when she had learned about Bryce divorcing Colleen, the very thought of leaving Gavin made her knees wobbly. She had tangled with this issue again last night when she read Ann's letters and her appeal to Raine to return to London. Gus needed Raine's support dealing with a distraught Colleen. Ann was preparing to go down to London herself. Rhys and their son would travel with her. Ann's father, Raine's Uncle Skip, was returning from *Maison d'Etoile* next week to be moral support for Colleen. But still Ann said they needed Raine's levelheadedness in this matter. Ann hoped Raine would cut short her vacation to help them.

How could she? She couldn't come up with any excuse to leave Gavin. Certainly, she could not say she had to go to London for a few days to help a friend. Not when she'd told him she had so few friends. Nor could she abandon him when he was getting closer each day to the achievement of his goals. She considered his strong profile and asked herself how she could ever summon the will to leave him.

Gavin was speaking gravely. "I will be frank with you, Mr. Pumphrey. I might not ever be free of this stain to my reputation. My novel may not flush out the murderer."

"A possibility, yes," Pumphrey said as he sank to his chair again.

"How would you feel knowing that your seat went to a man who had such a blemish on him?"

"The police and the Yard have proven nothing, Gavin. No evidence exists to connect you to the murder. Even the motivation most ascribe to you—that of anger at the failure of your bills—does not hold up. The newspapers took a hatchet to your character, my boy. *That* is the only mark against you. Until the police find some better motivation or solid evidence that you stabbed those two, you are presumed innocent."

"Before the law, that's true."

"Are you not also innocent before God?"

The question surprised Gavin but did not stop him from proclaiming, "Yes. I am."

"Well, then. Go forth, I say, and fight this battle. You have my blessing." He lifted his glass and drank liberally. Raine and Gavin did, too, then listened as Pumphrey reflected, "Sean O'Malley's activities are the ones the authorities should examine. He was in love with a woman who had a string of lovers to her name. But she tended to favor Irish MPs. Don't you find that odd?" He focused on Gavin.

"I never looked at her in that way. I don't make a habit of remembering who is sleeping with whom."

"No, of course, you don't. It is usually such silly stuff. But Louise had a taste for them. Ryan Ahearn. Timothy Butler."

Butler. Raine knew him. He was the MP who represented Rhys Kendall's borough in Dundalk. Rhys did not meddle in the borough's politics, though he was the primary aristocrat who could have—if he wished—been its patron. He chose not to interfere. For all purposes, the borough was as free of patronage as Chipswell.

Raine had met Butler three times briefly. Once at an informal supper, again in her publisher's office on Fleet Street, and finally in a cafe where he dined with Ryan Ahearn. She heard Butler speak in the Commons and thoroughly disliked him and his policies. He had once been a moderate, a man who favored Ireland as a part of the British empire, but about two years ago he had turned firebrand. He was the one who had been speaking in Hyde Park the day of Gavin's argument with Sean and Louise. "He joined the Fenian Society," she said.

"In '75," Gavin added. "He is now a hothead, more radical by the hour."

"I don't like him personally," Pumphrey said. "Never have. A hedonist, through and through. While he kept company with the very married Louise Stoddard, he also kept a mistress in lodgings in Marylebone."

Raine remembered Butler. The man had what many called the black Irish looks. He was a man to make many women swoon with his dash and swagger. The way he spoke so soft and low could charm the bark off trees, but his eyes, his green eyes, glittered in such a way that always made Raine shiver. When had she first noticed he had that effect on her?

She closed her eyes and remembered it was in Matthew Healy's office.

"Butler is an opportunist, as well," Gavin said. "He once attempted to court Belinda Derwenter, but she turned him away."

Pumphrey laughed lightly. "Sidney and his wife would have encouraged her to reject him. Butler needs money and Belinda has some. I would guess that Butler gets his living now from the Fenian donations."

Gavin looked Pumphrey in the eye. "You think the Fenians are growing stronger?"

"And wealthier. A lot of Irishmen are contributing their pennies. Our English rule has never been benevolent—from the Irish point of view."

The conversation centered on the state of Irish affairs while Raine focused on those times she had seen Timothy Butler. His green gaze obsessed her, and she began to feel the chill of a stark recollection.

Butler had been in Hyde Park the day that Louise, Sean, and Gavin argued. Standing upon a small platform similar to that which many orators used, Butler had regaled the crowd with a speech about crimes against the Irish. "Injustices for which the English must pay!" he had shouted. Bobbies had had to come and break up a free-for-all that broke out as a result. Gavin, Sean, and Louise began their disagreement minutes after witnessing it.

Timothy Butler was a rabble-rouser, in the truest sense.

"What bothers you, Raine?" Gavin asked minutes later, after they climbed into the phaeton Gavin had his gardener drag out of the carriagehouse for the occasion of visiting William Pumphrey.

She had tried to beg off.

Gavin flicked the reins and told the horse to walk on. "Don't shut me out, Raine. Something is wrong. Surely you are not upset about me running for Chipswell?"

"Oh, I'm overjoyed."

"I wanted to be sure."

"Your decision to stand for Chipswell is a perfect one. Nothing could be more appropriate."

"I pray I find other solutions as easy," he said with some dismay. "So what's wrong?"

"The discussion about Louise and Sean—and Timothy Butler . . ."

"What about it?"

She lifted her shoulders. "You'll think me odd."

"You know I won't."

"When Mr. Pumphrey talked about Louise Stoddard's tendency to have affairs with Irish MPs, it didn't sit well with me."

"I know what you mean. It seemed strange to me, too. And yet, for some reason I cannot define, I am not surprised. Butler is ruthless. He would sleep with anyone to get what he wanted."

"But what did Louise Stoddard want?" Raine asked.

Gavin frowned and turned the horse down a lane Raine had not traveled before. It was one that ran north not south toward his house and her cottage. "I'm not certain what you mean, Raine."

Neither was she. "I got the queasiest feeling when Mr. Pumphrey said that about her. Why would she," Raine knew she was blushing, but she had to say this, get it over with, "have affairs only with MPs from Irish districts?"

Gavin tilted his head. "Irish men are supposed to be charming as the devil."

"Or Louise is."

Gavin scowled at the road. "Her husband always looked the other way when she took up with another man."

"Why would he? Why would any man?"

"I have no idea. My friend Bryce cannot. I couldn't."

"Maybe," Raine speculated, "Hamilton Stoddard was having an affair of his own and he allowed his wife her amour."

"Not Hamilton. He is a staunch Anglican, goes to church every Sunday, and contributes to the coffers more than his tithe. He would never conduct such a relationship."

"The newspapers said he was the one to discover the bodies of his wife and O'Malley the next morning. Do you think the police did a thorough investigation of his whereabouts the night before?"

"I do. He even has substantiation by his host and hostess. He had spent the week with the Baron and Baroness Dunwitty outside Edinburgh."

"It's unusual, don't you think, to go north during the week and arrive home on the weekend?"

"Odd, yes," Gavin agreed. "But Hamilton claimed he had a report due to the Home Secretary on Monday and he had to complete it. He returned to London early Saturday to do it and that is that."

"Still and all," she said, "something is not right there. I'll go through the clippings when we get home." She had to find the reason why Timothy Butler's green eyes bored into her brain. If she could not pick it out with her memory, she would refresh it until she had an answer.

She would also take the occasion to ask Gavin about the handkerchief. It would seem a natural one—or she hoped it would. And she needed it to seem that way, because she had the feeling that Gavin was committing his own sin of omission by telling her only what he wished her to know. His sense of protectiveness was gratifying, but she needed to know the truth about the murders if she were to be of use to him in ferreting the criminal out of hiding.

"Where are you going?" she asked Gavin, noting the smell of salt in the air. They were nearing the northern edge of the village, not the southern coast near his house.

"I told you yesterday I wanted you to see something."

"Your writing is seeping into your daily life." She chuckled. "Now you are acting mysteriously."

"Mmm. It's a surprise."

He drove the carriage up to a small promontory overlooking the sea. Here stood an old abandoned house, weeds and ivy climbing its muted gray, flint walls and cluttering the front walk so badly that it nearly obscured it.

"This is the former home of the Parker family. The last of them, a spinster of eighty-two, recently died, and the family solicitor has put the house up for sale."

"How long ago did she die?"

"Two months ago."

"But it looks like it hasn't been tended in years."

"She was a hermit, her brothers and sisters dead even from the time I remember the place as a boy. Miss Ruth was unable to do much for herself, she relied on the kindness of the local church members to come and cook and clean for her. They did what they could, but keeping up the outside of the house was not a priority. Would you like to go in?"

She knew he wanted her to. But she didn't. She had the sweetest feeling growing in the region of her heart—and the worst sinking sensation in her stomach. "What harm could it do?" she asked with a smile she didn't put much heart into.

Gavin brought the horse to a stop and came around to help her down. "Watch your step. This stone path is badly torn up and perhaps . . ." he swept her up into his arms, "this is a better way to take you inside."

Raine didn't argue. She knew it would be useless. Gavin was not only filled with resolution to have her see the house, he had an edge to his demeanor that cautioned her to beware his anger. Though he had always controlled it with her, this time she had an inkling that he would not hold back. She took a handful of his frockcoat and circled her arm around his back, just hanging on until he put the key in the lock, swung open the door, and set her to her feet.

"Oh, Gavin." She got her balance and her breath. "It's beautiful." The foyer was ablaze with sunlight streaming down from the glass cupola of the roof. The columns were of pink and cream Italian marble, such as she had not seen since Florence two years ago when she visited with Gus, Ellen Newton, and her Uncle Skip.

Gavin put his hand out as he studied her. "Come, I'll show you the rest if you like."

And she did like the house. The rooms were numerous. Drawing room, morning room, library, master suite, nursery of three bedrooms, and a servants' quarters on the top floor. The house was spotless, wooden floors polished to a gleam so hard Raine could see her face reflected in them. What Raine liked most was that the rooms were spacious, sunlit by windows that were terribly unfashionable they were so large. She and Gavin stood in the drawing room on the first floor when she walked to the window and told him, "It would be a shame to put draperies up to hide the view to the sea." She surveyed the horizon as waves danced in sun-drenched rays.

"Why put them up then?"

"Fashion. Necessity. It might be cold. The drafts could chill the whole house. I have a cousin who says . . ." Raine froze.

"Says what?" Gavin was standing behind her, his hands cupping her shoulders.

That English houses are holey as swiss cheese. "That a house should be a haven of warmth not a wind tunnel." Ann did say that. Her very words. Often.

"He's right."

Raine did not correct Gavin's assumption that her cousin was a man. She was trying not to shake as Gavin put his arms around her. "What do you think? Should I buy it?"

She was melting, the same way she always did when they stood so close to each other. "You have decided not to stay in your father's house, then?"

"With the financial success of the novel, I won't have to. It has galled me to have to take his charity. First chance I got, I promised myself I would vacate the house. Standing for Chipswell doesn't change those feelings or that goal, it just means I should look for another house. I had known for months that this one would go up for sale. But I haven't thought about buying it until last week. I wrote to the solicitor, and they said I could get the key from the rector. Mrs. McNally fetched it for me yesterday."

"Did you decide this before or after you got your father's letter?" Raine thought it forward of her to ask, but it was true she had not seen Mrs. McNally much yesterday. That was odd—and if Raine had not been preoccupied with her own concerns, she would have known that Mrs. McNally had gone on an errand to the rector's.

"Before," Gavin whispered, pressing his body to hers and dropping a kiss to her ear.

She let her head fall back against his shoulder as he trailed his lips down her throat. Why couldn't she ever pull away from his caresses with any speed or ease? *Because you want him,* came the soundless reply. *You need him.*

He turned her in his arms and undid the top button of her spencer and canezou. Kissing the hollow of her throat, he was making her skin burn to be free of all her clothes. "Do you think it's a good idea?" he urged.

"What?"

She could feel him smile against her skin and undo another button. "To live in Chipswell?"

"Oh, *yes,*" she gasped when his hot lips branded her between her breasts, "absolutely wonderful."

"To give me access," his words fanned her skin as he dipped a finger inside her corset, pushed down the lace of her camisole and brushed her nipple with his fingers, "to . . . ."

"Your voters." Her brain worked well, she just could barely talk or stand. "They would . . . would love having you . . ." he took her in his mouth and swirled his tongue, "around."

He made some guttural sound, and his hands were tugging on her camisole above the other breast. "Of course, this all assumes that I win." He suckled her lavishly.

Raine got dizzy. "But you will. How could anybody not want you?" *I do.*

"Not all the local residents want me, Raine." He backed her to the wall, taking down her chignon, and drinking in hot kisses as if he were dying of thirst. "They can't find it in their hearts to vote for a man who is suspected of murder. Can you?"

"They're fools," she whispered, her arms bringing him close so that she could sample his mouth in her own way in her own time. At last, she breathed, "I'd vote for you."

"Really? Why?" He was running his hands down her bare back and kneading her muscles.

"You are . . ." she sighed as he pressed both of her breasts together and leaned over to kiss one nipple and the other in rapid succession, "so . . . God, Gavin, I wanted to say you were . . . ummm . . . fair."

He laughed, he muttered, he broke away, and said, "What you do to me is not fair."

"No?" She was enjoying herself, her fingers twining in that thick bronze mane of his and tugging him close for more kisses.

He cupped her face and rubbed the tip of her nose with his. They were both gasping for air. "It's all happening in a bit of a muddle, isn't it?"

Again, she had lost his train of logic. "What is?" she asked as she undid his stock and the top button of his collar. She longed to kiss him the way he had her. Along his throat. In the hollow. There . . .

He had arched his neck, closed his eyes, moaned her name. "Raine, why can't I ever control this?"

"What?"

"How badly I want you." He kissed her deeply, savoring every portion of her mouth. "But we've got to stop."

"Why?" She felt her breasts bare to the cool dark air, but afire where his fingers touched her, shaped her. She wanted him naked for her. Would he groan like she had, if she kissed his nipples?

"Because I want this to be right for you—and not much is happening in an orderly way."

This was a topic she could relate to. She smiled as she put her lips above his heart. "Or rational."

"Raine." He caught her to him with such force she thought he had squeezed the stuffing out of her. "Look at me, sweetheart. Good. Now listen to me. Are you?"

Dieu, what had she done with him? Why did he make her forget everything? Propriety, decorum, yesterday, her need to save him from the harm she'd done him. "Yes."

"Tell me if you like the house."

She looked around. House. Yes. "I like it."

"Tell me if you think it could be cozy."

"Sugar, it's awfully big to ever be cozy."

His eyes lit like fireworks when she called him sugar, and now they rolled. "All right then. Could it be warm, free of draughts? A home."

"A home. A lovely home."

He let her body slide down against his. She knew without a doubt that Gavin had firm intentions then to make love to her. She wrapped her arms around him. *I love you,* she wanted to shout—and couldn't.

Stunned at her knowledge, she stared at him.

How could she tell him that she loved him? If she did, she would have to tell him the total truth. Admit her failure. Her shortsightedness. Her lies. He would think her no better than any of the others who had crucified him without proof he committed murder. She could never bear to see that disappointment in his eyes.

His eyes that swam with compassion now. "That's all I wanted to know. I'll put a deposit on the house then. We will cross our fingers and hope the series continues to sell well." His eyes dropped to her breasts. "I wish I could make time go faster. I want you, Raine. More of you. Not just your body, but your mind, your trust, too. And soon, *ma cherie.*" He wrapped her close. "I want you to trust me enough to tell me all your secrets, Raine." He put a hand to her heart. "Share them with me, won't you?"

She drew him close. "I do want to do that, Gavin. But I need time."

"How much, Raine? I'm chafing sorely in my new-found patience."

"I can't say," she whispered, her body pleading with her to have him, to make love with him, her mind screaming at her to finish her work with him and leave, quickly. "For now, we must go home and look at the clippings."

He snorted. "You are the slave driver, lady."

She smiled as she rearranged her clothes and buttoned her canezou. "Let's go see if we can find anything odd about the Stoddards."

Chapter 11

"Justice is the only worship. Love is the only priest."

—Robert Green Ingersoll

"THERE IS NOTHING IN HERE ABOUT LOUISE OR HER HUSBAND which strikes me as new or different from when I last reviewed them," Gavin told Raine hours later. He put down the last batch of newspaper clippings he'd examined. His desk overflowed with the mass of material which she'd categorized for him—the reporters' accounts of the police investigations, the depositions by Hamilton Stoddard, the autopsy reports, the inquest notes, the maps of the neighborhood, the layout of the interior of Stoddard house. She knew them word for word. Not one mentioned a handkerchief.

Gavin jammed his hands in his trouser pockets and stepped toward his window. "I have read them all so many times, I could recite them word for word."

Raine noticed the corner of one cutting. Her cartoon.

She shut her eyes. She did not need to see it to remember what she had drawn. How she had shown

Gavin as a caricature of the man she had come to know in these past few months. The man she had come to love . . .

She forced herself to look once more on how she had destroyed him.

She slid it toward her.

She could recollect how she felt that night when she had picked up her pad—the one that lay now in the bottom of her trunk. She remembered all the passion she had poured into her rendering of him. Filling pages of the pad until she had a dozen or more scenes and finally, one that captured the essence of what she had witnessed in Hyde Park. As she drew the scenes, her admiration for Gavin had been drained by the anger she had seen him unleash on Sean.

Yet, she had drawn Gavin so that others would recognize him. In profile as she herself had witnessed him. Distinguished. Tall and terribly handsome. With strong jaw and straight nose. Keen eyes. The hand out, his finger pointing at Sean in an aggressive gesture no well-bred man ever used unless he was outraged. Louise had looked on, disdainful, her toque hat bobbing up and down over that doll-like face, while she liberally argued with Gavin.

"How can you be angry with him?" Louise had defended Sean to Gavin. Her voice was clear, carrying easily to Raine who stood paces away.

Gavin had glared at Louise. "Because he changed his vote, Mrs. Stoddard. That is not done without telling the sponsor."

Raine had forgotten she had overheard those words.

She squinted at the drawing she had come to loathe. She had depicted the woman as she felt her to be, not as she saw her. Petulant and pampered were the descriptions which sprang to Raine's mind.

And Sean? What of him?

Raine crossed her arms and rubbed away at the chill which crept up her body.

"I am a free man, Sutherland." That was what Sean

had said. "I . . ." Whatever had followed was lost in the mist of Raine's mind, or had it simply been swallowed by the air?

Would Gavin remember?

Would he tell her?

"What did you and Sean argue about that day at Hyde Park?"

Gavin turned slowly, saw what she had been looking at, and shook his head. "Sean changed his vote on a bill I was trying to pass. It was a bill supporting an expansion of docks in Dublin. It would have meant more jobs for longshoremen, greater trade. He rejected it at the last minute. I knew he would be there in the park to hear Butler speak against it. I was furious Sean had abandoned me, and I went to corner him and give him a piece of my mind. Not two months before, I had supported a bill Sean sponsored for admitting Catholics to Trinity University in Dublin. I felt as if I had been used."

"How did Butler speak against a bill which would mean more work for his countrymen?"

"Butler says the English only wish to exploit the Irish. To him anything English is the equivalent of anything heathen."

"Before Butler joined the Fenian Society, how did he support himself?" Raine asked, some fact nibbling at her, irritating her.

"There's the irony. He was a poor boy, much like Sean O'Malley had been. In fact, the two of them had gone to Queen's University in Cork on money donated by their local parishes. They knew each other while in school, but as for Butler's living? He ran in a borough which is free of patronage. The Duke of Dundalk—an Englishman named Rhys Kendall—does not use his power there. So anyone who runs in that borough obtains his living by independent means. Butler got his from trade associations of carpenters and masons, grocers, and the like."

"And Sean?" she asked.

"Similar means."

"Had they always supported him from the beginning of his term?"

Gavin reflected before he answered. "As far as I know, yes."

"Did they toward the end of his life?" She pulled away, a thought blossoming.

"Sean had conflicts with his supporters."

"Arguments?"

"Yes." Gavin turned toward her. "Why?"

"Did they continue to give him money?"

"I heard rumors they cut his funds, but I have no proof." Gavin explored her features. "You're trying to understand why his pockets were turned out."

Raine nodded. "Suggesting not only that he may have been searched—as a robber would search his victim— but to create some sign to the world—a symbol that Sean is poor or bankrupt—"

"Financially or morally or politically."

"By his supporters?" Raine asked, incredulous.

"Sean had abandoned my bill that afternoon, but he had shifted his support lately on other bills."

"Why would he do that?"

"I asked him minutes after the tally that day. He shrugged me off, said he had a right to support what he chose, the party be damned. The party did not like his attitude or his voting. Leaders were after him to per- form, but he refused."

"Gavin, are you suggesting that someone in your party may have . . . murdered him because he would not fall in line?"

"I am as appalled as you, darling, but what else can I conclude? One of the reasons I was as furious as I was that afternoon in Hyde Park was because a month before, I had been sent to have supper with him. The leaders of the party asked that I dine with him and persuade him to return to the fold. I was also to subtly suggest that his relationship with Louise Stoddard was considered inappropriate."

"Why did they send you to do that? Was Sean so important?"

"Party leaders thought that Sean had a good future ahead of him, perhaps a place in the Exchequer or Colonial Office, if he wished. A salaried position with prestige and some power. They wanted him to marry, and to succeed in politics he needed to choose a woman who would enhance his career."

"Someone with money and a family with lineage and connections. A woman with a solid reputation." *Like Belinda Derwenter for you.* Raine blocked the fury that brought. "What did Sean say?"

"He refused. Told me he would never give her up. Had no intention to marry anyone, if he could not have Louise."

"He must have known that was impossible. She was married. Her husband is older, but in good health. To boot, Louise was such . . ." There was no polite phrase for it, so Raine said it, ". . . used goods. Sean got good press coverage. Many thought he had a solid future. A man who had read for the English bar with a barrister in Middle Temple."

Gavin looked at her with awe. "You never cease to amaze me with what you know about British politics. Where did you find the time to learn all of this? And in only a few years?"

"Interest does much to spur the mind. I read and I remember it, that's all I can tell you."

"You also must have attended quite a few open sessions to have heard me speak and have such an analysis of my skill. I did not do it often."

Raine knew this had been a question brewing since she had admitted this afternoon at William Pumphrey's that she liked Gavin's oratory. "I did go, and I was fortunate enough to hear you. You were exhilarating."

"You are complimentary, darling." He faced the sea

again. "Sometimes, I wonder if I shall ever speak there again."

"You will." It was the most natural act in the world to go and wrap her arms around him, lay her head against his back and sigh. "You will stand for Chipswell and return to Parliament. You'll earn a goodly amount of money and be able to support yourself. You must believe that. Believe in yourself. I do."

He put his hands atop hers. "Why do you?"

She placed her lips to his shoulder. "Because you are the most awe-inspiring man. Because you are genuine— in your support of issues, even in your rejection of other ones. So few politicians are."

"Genuine, even in my outbursts, eh?"

"Of course. I'm certain that many of the registered voters in Appleby must have seen beyond the bouts of temper to value the fire of your passion. Your sincerity will serve you well with the people in Chipswell, people who already have the privilege of knowing you—and loving you." *As I do.*

"What if I am never cleared of this suspicion?" His words were hoarse. "Do you think I can be as loved for my writing?"

"Yes, you will. You mustn't get down about this. Everything is going your way."

"Not everything." He turned in her embrace and his eyes held hers. "You are not cooperating with my endeavor to sweep you off your feet. Why not, Raine?"

She dropped her arms.

He caught her hands. "I need an answer, Raine."

"I am not for you, Gavin."

He flexed his jaw. "Why not?"

"I'm your secretary. Your employee. An American." She heard her tone rising in desperation.

"All irrelevant."

"No." She took a step backward.

He followed. "To me they are and I'm the man who wants you, Raine."

"You must not say these things, Gavin." She wrenched to be free of him.

He did not let her go, but stepped closer and bound her against him. "I will. What's more, I can change some of them. You're relieved of your duties, Mrs. Jennings. There. Now I can tell you that it doesn't matter to me that you are American. I find it very beneficial. You bring a new democratic outlook to my thinking." He sank a hand into her hair to scatter pins and whisper against her lips, "I know you bring a new perspective to my future."

She would not cry. She would appeal to his reason. "You have just sacked me. There is no future."

She sparked his anger.

He went rigid as steel. His hands were gentle though as he cupped her face and captured her mouth with his. He kissed her until her lips parted and his tongue invaded, until her head swam with the need to clasp him nearer, and her body began the melting his merest touch inspired. "Walk away from me," he rasped when he gave them both a whiff of air and sanity. "Say you don't want me."

"I can't," she moaned and pressed a kiss to his cheek. "You know I can't."

"Raine, I wanted to wait to say this until I could offer you everything, but I will do it now. I lo—"

"No." She put two fingers to his lips. "I have nothing you need, Gavin. Don't talk of this or the Parker house. Think."

"I have, until I realize that thinking is not what I require. There is nothing rational about how I feel about you, Raine."

"Oh, God, Gavin. I am not a woman for a man of your ambitions. I can't help you in your career. I don't have any of those qualities the wife of a Member of Parliament needs. I have no money, no suitable English family with prestige and connections. I'm not a debutante. Not an American heiress. I have no wealth to help you in your career. I am almost twenty-six years old, and I know there is more to life than gowns and balls and snaring a man who wants a pretty doll to decorate his house."

"What do you want, my darling?" He kissed her again until she was melting, and he had to hold her up.

"Nothing," she whispered as she trailed kisses across his jaw. "No one means more to me than you."

He bent and scooped her high into his arms. "I'm going to do my damnedest to make sure you don't forget that." He began to walk toward the hall.

"No," Raine said in horror before he opened the door. "Mrs. McNally. We can't. Your reputation——"

"If you think I'm going to let anything stop me after what you just said to me, Raine, you're wrong." He illustrated with a kiss that drugged her with its power.

"Come home with me," she pleaded, knowing full well she was taking him across the lane into her cottage and into her bed. Into her heart. But if she had to leave him, if she could never have him day in and day out as a husband, she would have him now, in her arms, while she could.

He halted. "No reservations?"

Only her fear of what he'd think when he learned she was a virgin.

She would not tell him another lie. She must reveal now that she was inexperienced or deal with the issue in a few minutes after he and she were in bed, when he'd discover her secret. He was not an insensitive man and he had experience with women and maybe not any of them had been virgins, but he would be able to see that she was and . . .

She set her jaw, putting a firm rein on her ramblings. Maybe, as Colleen had once said, not every woman bleeds when her maidenhead is lost. Maybe, as Coll also noted, not every man takes time to notice or care if the woman in his arms is a novice.

But Gavin would know. With her, he seemed to know so much instinctively—and if he didn't, he asked. Would he care that she was a virgin? Yes, of course. But he would care that he was her first and only lover. Later, if he pressed her for reasons, she would find words to sidestep telling him another lie.

But she wanted him and she meant to enjoy him in all honesty.

"Raine, don't frown so. If you are changing your mind, I don't think I can stand it now."

"Allow me a few nerves, will you, for modesty—and lack of experience."

He hugged her.

"Oh, Gavin, you see, I am not . . . Winston wasn't . . ."

"As sweet with you as he should have been," Gavin finished for her, and her courage to tell him she was a virgin nearly died with his misinterpretation.

"You don't understand. He and I never did go to bed—"

He looked like a house of bricks had fallen on him. But he recovered with a hard blink of his eyes, then brushed his lips on hers. "I am thankful he never initiated you, darling." His voice cracked. "I get to show you the pleasures love can bring."

"You have shown me so much about that already." She smiled, tremulous and joyous.

He let her slide against him, but he did not relinquish his hold of her. Instead, he tenderly took her hand and led her toward the garden doors.

Raine hesitated. "Gavin, Mrs. McNally will be preparing supper. Tell her we're leaving or she'll come looking for us and that could be disaster."

He took a tendril of her hair and curled it around her ear. "You won't leave." It was as much a question as a statement—and a measure of his insecurity.

"I promise."

He was gone and back before she had time to catch her breath or do more than reassess the basic logic of her plan to go to bed with him. She was in love with Gavin, and she had a right to give him what she could for as long as she could.

He led her outside and as they picked their way across the rocks, he told her that Mrs. McNally was grateful for the rest from cooking tonight.

"What excuse did you give her?" Raine asked him.

"That we had so much to eat at Mr. Pumphrey's, we weren't hungry."

Raine laughed abruptly.

When they got to her little Dutch door, Gavin stood aside. He wanted her to let him in.

She pushed it open, wondering if she could show him how she loved him, welcome him into her heart and then shut him out when it came time for her to go—when it was time for her to move on with her life, having saved his.

He followed her inside, closed the door softly. Only a few rays of light remained now that the sun had set and Raine went to light two candles on her fireplace mantel. To turn up the gas lamps would seem brazen, giving too much light for her first time in bed with a man. But, oh, how she wanted to remember every move, every word with this dear man—and there was so little she knew how to do to make these minutes perfect. She stood, staring at her candles, wondering frantically what else she was supposed to do, and came up lacking any answer.

Gavin embraced her, his words soothing, taking away her maidenly fears with his sweet confession. "I've wanted you for so long," he said against her ear, his lips nuzzling her. "From the day you moved in here, I watched you from my window. I couldn't stop." His words fanned her skin, becoming hotter with desire with each sentiment. "I thought you were a siren."

He turned her around, his dimple appearing in his cheek as his fingers went to the buttons of her canezou. "I must have known instinctively I needed you. And I learned—" he pulled the garment from her waistband and took it off her shoulders, "in my youth to always follow my instincts."

She went willingly, gleefully into his care. He was so

gentle, so very careful of her buttons and her laces and her tapes, folding each garment as he took it away, admiring what he revealed with a touch or a kiss, and draping each article of clothing over a piece of furniture as he walked her backward toward her bed. How he managed it, she didn't know and really didn't care, but when she stood with the backs of her legs to the tester bed, she wore only her camisole and her drawers with her gartered stockings beneath. Her hair had long since tumbled from its chignon completely, its wealth hiding some of her skin—and a lot of her trepidation.

"I'll be so careful, Raine, I won't hurt you," Gavin vowed, coiling a tress around his finger. He captured her gaze. "I want to bring you only pleasure."

She swallowed. "I know you will. You give it to me each time we speak."

He ran two fingers across her collarbones. "You are exquisite. Meant for the best a man can give you."

His words made every cell in her body vibrate with expectation. "I will try to make you happy."

"Oh, you will, I have no doubts. Will I shock you if I take off my clothes?"

She inched one brow high. "Aren't you supposed to? I mean, I am almost naked. . . ." She blushed. "Am I expected to . . . umm . . . help you? Can I?" The idea struck her as delicious.

Gavin spread out his arms. "I am yours." He made her chuckle.

She worked on his buttons, his hands going to her waist. Beneath his shirt, he wore no underclothes, and the sight of him, broad and muscular and more bare than she had ever seen him, made her hum as she took the sleeves down his arms. She dropped his shirt to the rug and gave in to the urge to drive her hands through the dark blond hair that tapered to his trousers.

"Whenever I heard you speak in the House," she said, her fingers defining the strength in his ribs and his back,

"I marveled at your voice. I have never heard anyone I—" she faltered on the word *love* that she would not use, "admired so much as you." She found the first button of his trousers and began to undo them. And as she worked to free him, she felt the hard outlines of how much he desired her. He watched her as she let his trousers fall, then took one hand and pressed her palm to him. He was hot, long, and hard.

"I need more than your admiration, Raine. I want everything you are." He stepped out of his clothes.

She struggled for air. He was magnificent. Trim waist and lean hips. Prominent hip bones and so much man, all hers to enjoy and satisfy. She leaned against him, her nose to his throat. "I want all of you, too."

He lifted away her camisole and pulled at the drawstring of her drawers. They drifted to the floor and he pressed her body to him, his warm skin heating hers and making her head fall back. He trailed his lips down her throat, between her breasts, and went to his knees. He was groaning as he worked at the garter belt, then peeled her stockings down her legs.

He laid her back across her bed. Removing her hose and tossing them aside, he ran his palms from her toes up her ankles to her knees and inner thighs. "My God, my God," he touched her waist and ribs and throat, "you are more beautiful than I imagined. Champagne." He spread her hair reverently into a fan upon the eyelet. "And strawberries." He took a nipple into his mouth and made her moan for more.

Then he straddled her, his eyes engulfing her with an appreciation that had her lifting her hands to her breasts. "No. Don't hide from me. You are like one of your delectable meals."

She giggled and rolled her eyes. "So complimentary. What a lover."

He laughed heartily, his gray eyes twinkling in the candles' glow. "I'll prove it." His lips blessed her brows.

"Ahh. Cinnamon. And—" he ran his nose around her cheek, "apple." He weighed her breasts. "Pomegranates." Skimmed her ribs and belly and hips. "Pastry."

She lifted a leg straight up in the air.

He licked his lips. "Celery stalks."

She cuffed him.

He wrapped her legs around his hips and settled against her, his eyes sultry. He was wiggling her toes. "Prunes." His fingers traced the inside of her leg up to her center. With his gaze holding hers, he swirled two fingers against her and hotly whispered, "Cream."

She gasped.

He was inserting a finger into her needy body. "Put them together and do you know what that makes, *cherie?*"

She groaned and lolled her head against the pillows.

"My favorite dish," he told her and crushed her closer.

"You are mine," she whispered.

"Now and always." He caught the tip of a breast in his mouth and inserted another finger deep inside her to make her arch. He suckled her, the swirl of his tongue a velvet eddy, his hand imitating the whorl of his ministration and spinning her up into a cyclone of desire.

She had wanted to stroke him, caress him, kiss him, but oh, she had not known her own need to absorb him into her body could be more important than drawing air. "Come inside me," she pleaded. "I don't think I can breathe without you."

"Ah, Raine . . ." Her name became a litany he used as he spread kisses down her body, soft whispers of his devotion that made her writhe and buck. "Shhh, feel how wonderful," he soothed her, as he parted her thighs and stretched her wide. His mouth brushed her hipbone and sank into her curls. He rolled her nether lips apart. She gulped for sanity as he murmured, "I need to taste you like this, Raine, make you mine. Say you want me this way, too."

"I need you in all ways." Even this scandalous way.

She forced her brain to record the sensations his erotic acts aroused.

Gentle shadows mingled with soft rays in the flickering candlelight, casting a glow on the beams of her simple cottage. How many times had she lain awake, dreaming of him, yearning for him to take her, have her? Oh, but none of those delights matched this savage bliss.

He sent his tongue along her folds.

She dug her nails into his shoulders. Cool air swirled around her hot flesh as he stretched her infinitely wider and put his lips to a secret place that had her thrusting upward off the mattress. He groaned and she was sinking, but he slid one hand beneath her derriere and pressed her starving body to him. She found no air in this rare atmosphere. He did not let her go, but forced her to the bed while he sampled and savored her until her whole world tilted and spun out of control. She vibrated as he slid up to wrap her in his arms once more.

He smoothed her hair, stroked her cheek. "Kiss me now, Raine. Taste how good you are." He gave her a lavish banquet of his mouth and tongue until she was reeling. "More," she beseeched him, and he chuckled. "My thought precisely."

His hand lifted a breast, squeezed her waist, drove through the curls he had kissed. Two fingers slid inside her, filling her with an ecstasy and a rebirth of her frantic need. "You are almost ready, darling," he crooned.

She brought his head down. "Kiss me." This delight he brought her made her frantic with the sudden knowledge that passion was fleeting and one day soon she would be gone from him. She'd had so little love that this man's made her greedy. "Please," she said and tasted him, darting her own tongue into his mouth.

"Raine, wait, let me show you how your body can respond."

"Not without you inside me."

He groaned. "Darling, you're a man's fantasy. But I want to make certain you're able to—"

Shifting, she wrapped her hand around him.

He sucked in his breath. "Aw, Raine—"

She gulped, hid her face in his throat, desire beating down all reason. "I need you now. Why should I have to pretend to be indifferent to you when you are everything I ever wanted in a man?"

"Don't ever be indifferent to me, sugar, just be mine." He cupped her nape and brought her up to meet his lips.

If she thought he meant to absorb her mind with the claim of his ardor, he gave her more than she bargained for. She was panting, clutching at him, consumed with the need to have him fill her, a desire that had no beginning, no end. Not until he began to give her what she craved. "Oh, Gavin," she heard herself praise him as his girth satisfied her, "this is heaven."

"Raine, you feel so small." He was speaking against her lips and moving higher slowly, so tenderly that she wanted to shout with her impatience.

And then he paused.

"Don't stop." She was plucking at the covers and rubbing herself against him. "Don't."

He captured her mouth in a mind-numbing kiss and slid inside her so sweetly she could hear her liquid delight in his claiming. And then he could go no further. She felt a rending, but no pain. She sighed, a hint of smile on her lips.

"There's more, Raine. Do you want it?"

"More of you, yes, anytime, anywhere."

"You could make a man die to have you, darling," he rasped and began to pull away.

"Don't leave." She caught him back.

"I'm not going anywhere. I'm trying to show you how to move with me."

"Oh, yes, yes," she agreed over and over as he taught her a rhythm that had her rushing, reaching for another bursting ecstasy that shook her to her soul. His own was just as fast and high and hard, a force that made him curve up like a god from the sea, and drop to take her in his arms and roll with her to his side.

Minutes later, his lips were still in her hair. His hands were on her derriere. "I think the room has turned golden. I feel like Midas, forgiven," he was chuckling, "with the wealth of the world in my arms."

Emotion burned her throat. "Gavin, no wonder you're doing well as a writer." She took a brief taste of his mouth. "You ought to try your hand at writing romances."

He squeezed her buttocks. "I prefer to live one."

"You are," she told him when she met his gaze, and her breath stilled at the depth of emotion she saw in his eyes.

"Are you?" he asked so softly that she could have thought he spoke with his heart.

Her mouth trembled. "Oh, Gavin, how could I imagine a more noble lover?"

"Don't imagine," he rasped and spread her on her back. "Don't look. Say you won't."

His desperation was a wound she could hear in his voice. "Never." She drew him down and gave him a kiss she hoped would prove that to him. "Come inside me again. I'll show you it's true."

He complied with speed and a desire as fierce as their first coupling was sweet.

In exhaustion she slept, and when she woke he had her body spooned against his. She rolled around to kiss his chest. His skin was still slick with perspiration. "That was wonderful. I have to tell you—" she cleared her throat so she wouldn't chuckle, "—I like the way you cook."

He snorted and tickled her ribs. His despair had disappeared. She rejoiced that she could help him in this sensual way as well as all the others. He joined them together once more, and her eyes popped wide.

"You are the stuff of legends, my lord."

"Only to you, my lady," he growled.

"Hardly," she squirmed.

"That is your doing, too, mam'selle."

She guffawed. "How many times can I do this to you?"

He stopped midthrust to arch a wicked brow. "Are you testing my mettle?"

She walked her fingers down his stomach to his groin. "Sugar, your metal astonishes me."

He tickled her again, sending her into gales of laughter. "Unfair," she cried, but he hooked a leg around her and told her with a few long thrusts, she wouldn't leave him anytime soon.

When she was snatching at air once more from the fury of their passion, she sighed against her pillows and let him kiss his way down her torso. "Aren't you tired?" she asked as he took renewed interest in her breasts.

"No."

"Hungry?" She felt him inside her growing larger, firmer. She certainly was developing a renewed appetite.

"I used to be. Right now, I'm enjoying dessert." He nipped her shoulder.

She chortled.

"Want a bath?"

She rubbed the sole of her foot against one of his calves. "You're all I need."

He grunted. "You should run for Parliament, *cherie*. You know the right things to say."

"Mmmm," she agreed as he slid his hands under her bottom and let her feel his rigid intention. "And you don't need to talk at all, sugar."

He didn't. There was no time, no space, no need for words in this bright universe of pounding rhythm and pulsing consummation. She thought she'd never breathe normally again.

But she noted that her heartbeat had settled when Gavin rose and picked up a corner of her counterpane to spread it over her. "Stay warm."

"Where are you going?"

"Just here." He strode to her cistern chain, positioned above her tub in the far corner. "I'll heat some of this so you don't catch cold. August rainwater should be warm to begin with."

Now that he had left her, the reality of what she had done with him seeped into her system. She rubbed her legs together and realized he had been so very tender with her, she didn't feel torn. Only empty. She wanted him back, so close, so far inside her that she wouldn't have to deal with the questions he would ask about why she had been a virgin.

Her eyes darted to him. He was scooping water from her tub into a big pot to heat on her fire. He had stirred the ashes and swung out the hook to hitch the handle and wedge it over the growing flames.

Gavin stood by the fire, his body in silhouette. Naked, broad-shouldered, and lean, he had his hands on his hips as he watched the water heat. His expression was shuttered.

She closed her eyes. God, how she wanted him back. She needed him, and soon.

"There," Gavin said and poured the water into the large copper tub. He smiled at her and she could have sworn he had done it valiantly. "Ready to take a dip?" He was beside her, tossing off the cover and taking her high up into his arms.

She sought his eyes and worked at words.

He did not ignore her gaze. His own was gentle. "Whatever the reason that you and Winston were never intimate, I won't ask." He kissed her forehead. "You don't have to tell me anything. Not until you want to, do you understand me, Raine?"

She looked away. If she let them, tears—so long averted—could easily dribble down her cheeks.

"Don't cry. Please, Raine. When a man and woman become this close, sadness is not supposed to be the result."

She caught back a sob. She had taught him to avoid the word *love*—and he would do it now so well that she knew it was a hollow victory.

He put her feet into the water.

She stood, appalled at her success.

He raised her chin. "Do young ladies now tell gentlemen that they are virgins?"

"No, but—"

"Do proper gentlemen take young women to bed without a clergyman and a license?" When she bit her lip and would not answer, he said, "So you see, my darling, I am not without blemish."

She hooked an arm around his neck. "Kiss me. Tell me it doesn't matter that I—that I hadn't ever done that before."

"Oh, but it does, Raine." He crushed her close and savored every portion of her mouth. "It means you've had no man but me. I am possessive enough of you to roar with delight over that." He spiked a hand into her hair and anchored her while he sampled her throat and her breasts. "I am also insane enough about you to keep you for myself."

Her fingers tangled in the rough silk of his hair. Relief mingled with fresh desire. "You don't think me odd?"

"You? On the contrary, I wonder about Winston."

"You won't think ill of me to make love to you and hate me for being forward and . . . and cast me off?" That she would lose him as others she had loved loomed like a ghost. She pushed the ghoulish thought away, eager to revel in what love she could for as long as she could.

"Darling." He put one foot into the tub with her. "Why would I let you go now that you are mine?"

He would keep her, too.

He looked down at her hours later as she slept. She lay sprawled across his chest, one of her long legs draping his. He smoothed her long pale hair from her angelic face and pressed his lips to her crown.

You're mine.

By right of first claim. Like some medieval lord, he should declare her his. God knew, he wished he could ride off with her. Take her to a church. Make her take his name as she had taken his heart.

But he couldn't. She was no woman to win with force. She was, always had been, a woman to win with words and wit.

What had been the nature of her marriage? Why did she marry a man she did not care for enough to unite with him in body? Even before she married this Winston Jennings, she must have known he did not take her over the moon with his kisses. A woman—this woman—was too smart not to recognize that. But then, she had not met Gavin yet. Not discovered that a special man's kisses could melt her bones.

And she was intelligent, his Raine. She might not have experienced the art of making love, but she had desired it with him. Craved it so much that her virginity—and the strong dose of maidenly modesty which came with that— offered no barrier to her need of him. Because when the time had come and she had known full well he meant to take her to bed, she never once thought of denying him on the basis of her innocence. She didn't balk. She had trusted her own instinct that he cared for her.

He pulled her closer. *Why don't you trust me enough to tell me your other secrets?*

She had them. All of them had to do with this husband and the last decade or so of her life. Had something happened to her that was so awful she would not reveal it? Or had she done something so terrible she could not admit it? Was she so intent on punishing herself for some deed that she robbed herself of joy and love? Why would she not permit him to say the words he'd never said to any other woman?

He yearned to tell her he loved her. But she would run from him, and he couldn't bear to lose her. Instead, he would remain silent and continue to show her instead. Woo her with the patience he had always lacked. With time and his persistence, she would realize that whatever kept her from him was insignificant to how he adored her.

He refused to consider that she might not love him. How could a woman kiss as Raine did and offer her body freely as she did, if she did not care for him?

She had told him the truth about her lack of sexual experience. Brave, prudent choice.

But she had avoided lying to him. He had witnessed her sidestep issues. Make statements carefully.

Raine, who are you?

Who was this uncle that took the waters of a French spa? Was it he who wrote long letters to her? And who was the cousin she spoke about just this afternoon?

There were other questions Gavin had shelved. Things he had refrained from asking her over the months. How had she afforded to go abroad to study painting? Why did she show such sorrow over Bryce Falconer's divorce and custody battle? Did she know Bryce? How could she?

Yet for a woman who had limited financial means, she knew so much else. Politics. Gossip. As if she had nothing else to do but read newspapers and grace the visitors' gallery of the Commons.

In spite of all those mysteries, he knew her. Her goodness, her humor, her unerring devotion to the restoration of his reputation and his political career. For all the times she had failed to share information about her past, she had always encouraged him, promoted him, and bolstered his efforts in literary or political arenas. Thinking of new ways to write his story. Digging in to organize his clippings, his notes. Proposing that Pumphrey, who came from the opposition party, should endorse him in Chipswell. After all of that, how could a man not love a woman?

And she him?

He crept from the bed to walk the floor.

A candle flickered and rays fell across her kitchen table. There, in an open sketchpad, he saw a likeness of himself staring up at him.

She had drawn his picture. He had never seen a portrait of himself in charcoal. He'd seen himself in the family portrait of the Sutherlands that hung in the ballroom at Cranborne Manor. He'd seen a thousand cartoons of himself, like the ones the papers had printed of him all the years he'd been in Parliament. None had portrayed him like this.

Gentle, thoughtful, with eyes like deep pools of desire. "What do you think of it?"

He raised his head and she stood there, alabaster beauty in the moonlight. His elegant siren with the body and voice of a bewitching angel. His Raine.

She bit her lower lip, full of trepidation that he would hate her rendering of him.

"You've captured me well, darling." It was a portrait of a man in love. "I didn't know you were so talented." He rounded the table and took her in his arms. "Perhaps I should commission a painting of me."

"Maybe you should. But I warn you, my services are expensive."

"Bah, lady. That I know. What's your price for painting?"

She flung back her hair and laughed at him. "Two hundred pounds."

"I cannot afford you." He was instantly hard and hurting to bury himself inside her again.

"'Course you can." She giggled when he tossed her over his shoulder and bit her firm fanny.

He dumped her on the bed. Loomed over her. "How?"

"Because if I remember correctly, you fired your secretary tonight. You now have quite a bit of extra money."

He explored her mouth leisurely. "I need her badly. What do you think I should do to lure her back?"

"Oh, sugar, just keep talkin'."

Until he left her before dawn, he ensured neither of them uttered an intelligible word.

Chapter 12

*"What's in a name? That which we call a rose
By any other name would smell as sweet."*

—WILLIAM SHAKESPEARE

"YOU MUST GO TO LONDON," RAINE URGED GAVIN AS SHE
put the latest editions of the London newspapers on the
reading table. The news they carried today meant Gavin
was most likely the talk of the town, maybe the entire
countryside. "Soon."

"I am pleased, of course, that Scotland Yard and the
police have reopened their investigations of the murders
of Sean and Louise."

"It is what we hoped for. . . . You hesitate. Why?" She
went to him when he turned toward his window and the
sea. She knew now this was the scene that engendered a
new perspective in his thinking.

"I wish I could take you with me."

"That's not necessary. Is it?" She took this route to
discuss the news and what he must do now to capitalize
on the reopening of the investigation. Since Gavin and
she had first made love two weeks ago, she had seen the
speculation in his features whenever he thought she

wasn't observing him. He examined her often and at length, for clues to who she was and why she was so secretive about her past.

Caught in a box of her own making, Raine knew the only way out was to encourage him in his efforts to find the culprit, finish his novel, get elected again—and then she would leave him. "You need to see the police and the inspector—what was his name?—you don't need me for that. I'd be in the way. They wouldn't want to talk to me. Wouldn't even want me in the room. So, that's that."

Gavin set his jaw. He didn't like her reasoning, but she knew he thought her right. "I go Monday. Tuesday the next installment in the series comes out, and I want to see the reactions of everyone to that."

Next Tuesday *The Accused* would reveal how the hero, Samuel Grant, considered various clues to who had killed his two friends. He would review his notes, all the newspaper stories, editorials, and cartoons. He would make long lists of possibilities and come up with four suspects. Gavin would leave the reader at the end without any clues as to who those suspects were.

"I'll stay at a small hotel and attempt to go about my business with some anonymity."

She hoped that could happen. The authorities would want to interview Gavin again. Go over the events of that day, that night. He would have to separate what he had known that day from what had been discovered and printed by others later. He would have to keep a straight head about what he himself had written in *The Accused*.

What's more, she would miss him.

Miss his company, in and out of her bed. He had come to her each night for two weeks now, even the past four when the only thing he did was kiss her and embrace her with her long cotton nightdress primly between them. She had her monthly flow. Although their eyes had met when she told him and she saw relief in his gaze, she also recognized a glint of sadness.

"I'm pleased and not, Raine."

She had nodded and would have walked farther down the beach after she'd told him they could not sleep together that evening.

He had seized her wrist. "If I were to get you with child, darling, I'd be the happiest man alive. I would whisk you off in a moment to the nearest church." He tilted up her chin. "You'd marry me because there'd be no alternative for you. But I need you to come to me because you want to do it, Raine, with your whole heart."

She flung her arms around him and whispered into his ear, "I don't deserve you."

"That belief is one of the barriers between us. Won't you tell me why you feel that way?"

She left him with no explanation.

He caught up to her. "Very well. I shall continue to wait."

He had made good on his word. Daily, hourly, he showed her he could throw himself into enjoying each moment in its simple fullness—and cherishing her company for all its unvarnished delight.

She noted his transformation into a patient man and commended him, rejoicing that the benefits were hers. Cursing herself when she saw that the torment was his.

Now that would end, and he would leave. But soon, she would too. His novel was nearly complete. She had finished typing the final draft of the fourteenth chapter this morning. She would proof it for spelling and punctuation, then wrap and send it off tomorrow morning to Ned Hollister. In that chapter, Gavin had led the accused man, his alter ego Samuel Grant, to a crisis. He left the reader wondering what would happen next. The hero, Samuel Grant was walking into a meeting which would reveal the identity of the murderer. She knew all of London and much of England waited with bated breath for the revelation.

In real life, so did Raine.

Alas, so did Gavin.

She had asked what he had expected in the way of enlightenment. He told her he had hoped for some new piece of evidence to come to light. Perhaps that would happen now that the Queen and government and party officials had influenced the police and the Yard to resume their inquiry. Gavin confided to her that he wished for a divine intervention. None was forthcoming.

Meanwhile, Gavin had not explained the matter of the handkerchief. Every time she brought up the subject, he found a way to avoid a substantive answer. Yesterday, he had told her not to ask again, the handkerchief was immaterial. She knew better.

Her instinct alone told her that Gavin had found a handkerchief at the scene of the crime, too. That it was not a bit of spice thrown in to amuse readers, as she had once suggested to him. It was, she was fairly certain, a fact revealed to taunt the murderer into some kind of intimidating gesture. It was more, too.

The handkerchief was not only evidence that might contribute to the discovery of the murderer, but also by having it in his possession, it showed Gavin was obstructing justice.

Producing it—at the very least—was tantamount to admitting he had been at the house, taken it, and perhaps done so because he wished to conceal his act of murder. The handkerchief could put Gavin in jail.

Her torment that this could happen had Raine alternately worrying herself into a frenzy over Gavin's future and arguing with herself to end her masquerade now, tell him who she was and how she had ruined him—how she adored him and hoped he could still love her enough to share what happiness they might before Gavin was taken from her, formally charged, and imprisoned, never to return.

As if it were a book of prayers or spells to ward off coming evil, his novel became a reference Raine consulted to ease her fears. Gavin saw her rereading it at odd hours.

"Put that away," he'd say and lure her into a walk along the beach to see the gulls or the lake to watch the grebes or swallowtail butterflies. He understood, as well as she, that if his plan went awry, these days, these precious minutes, would be all they'd ever have.

The impending tragedy which she in her blasted naiveté had set in motion by drawing that infernal cartoon of him sent her back to *The Accused* with an insanity of desperation. She replayed the facts until she could picture Gavin's actions herself. Step by step, horror for horror.

In the novel, the hero Samuel enters the townhouse, just as Gavin had. Into a dark and eerie atmosphere, the hero lets himself in the front door. He follows the only gaslight to its source and finds the bodies. Both dead. Both still warm. But in the male victim's hand, he discovers a handkerchief. His. Unmistakably his with his initials embroidered on it. Covered in the victim's blood.

Afraid to be accused, Samuel extracts the linen from the fist of the dead man and takes the handkerchief home with him. Never once in the book does Gavin state where Samuel has hidden it.

But the newspapers were alive with the subject for the past two weeks. "Did He Hide It?" screamed the headline on the front page of *The Gazetter*. "Does SG *Still* Have It?" cried the editor in his column at the *Illustrated Weekly*. "Can We Forgive Him?" shouted Raine's former editor, Matthew Healy, in parody of one of Anthony Trollope's most famous novels.

Raine scanned today's collection of newspapers, their front pages and editorials. Their outcry that Gavin may have actually sequestered evidence was amplified today by their delight that the police and Scotland Yard had done their duty by society. Among them, only the *Times-Daily* continued to carry a cross. Matthew Healy demanded Gavin come to London from his sanctuary in

Chipswell-by-the-Sea and bring with him the notorious handkerchief.

From the day Raine had gone to Matthew with her cartoon, he made no bones about what he thought personally. He had thought Gavin guilty of murder. But his private belief, he told her and his reporters, must not imbue the *Times-Daily*'s coverage.

This new hue and cry by him struck an odd note with Raine. This was the first time he had stepped into the fray and taken sides since he had printed her cartoon. Matthew displayed singular impartiality in politics, save for a few issues for which he pecked away at all opponents with the diligence of a buzzard. Maritime rights and the Irish question. He had supported Home Rulers.

"Not pretty, is it?" asked Gavin. "Even Healy moves to one side of the debate now."

"Unusual for him. He does try to remain unbiased."

"Yes. Ever since he ran that first cartoon of me in the park," Gavin reflected while Raine cursed her drawing once more. "Only his support of expanded fishing rights and home rule for Ireland have led him to speak out. I don't like his change of heart to a more Fenian position. I wonder what causes it?"

"Healy is influential," Raine said. "His impartiality in most matters makes him so." This was true. Healy saw himself as a reporter of the news, that was all. When she had told him she had seen Gavin and the other two arguing in Hyde Park, Matthew wanted to report it immediately. Then when she had shown him her cartoon, he wanted to print it in the interest of printing facts the public needed to know.

"I don't like leaving you," Gavin declared in a pivot of subjects that surprised her.

"I hate the idea, too, but I think you must go." She brightened. "A good politician maneuvers for himself and does not allow events to sweep him off course."

Gavin was watching her. "I want your word you won't leave while I'm gone."

She was affronted. "What makes you think I would do that?" she asked, but knew he had not only a right to ask, but reason to.

"I know you too well, Raine. If I were a little more along in my discussions with Mr. Pumphrey about standing for Chipswell, I do believe you would have already disappeared from my life."

That was true. It unnerved her that Gavin could perceive her need to go. She could not love him and stay. She had put him in this terrible mess. She would stand by and help dig him out. "I came to work for you to see you make a success of yourself." She smiled at him, attempting to give him the help which she had promised. "What can I do to help you with your plans for London? Write the hotel? Healy? A few friends?" *Who will you see and why?*

"I'll go to Brown's in Albermarle Street. Ask for a small suite. I'd like to have a few people in to dine. The inspector on the case from the Yard. Charles Washburn. Ask him for Tuesday evening. And Bryce. I don't know if he'll be able to see me at all. He's tangled up in his own sorrows, but I could meet him at his club or anywhere he has in mind, if only for a few minutes. I need to tell him privately about the meetings I've had with Mr. Pumphrey. Ask Bryce if he has any time available Wednesday, day or evening. Thursday, too, if he prefers." He stopped, in obvious contemplation. "I'll write the other letters."

She felt as if he'd gutted her. How could he love her, treat her like spun glass, take her into his arms, and not want her to know everything? She wound her arms around her stomach. Yes, that was what she had done to him, in kind. Now she knew what a hollow feeling it produced. She sank into the chair she'd sat in that first morning she had come to him here and applied.

The front door chimes rang.

Raine heard them but ignored them.

In the hall, Mrs. McNally was scuttling to answer the

bell, muttering, "Now 'ho's that? Peter knows to drop the mail in the slot one by one. 'E'll weary me out, 'e will."

Gavin had come around his desk and was lifting Raine's chin. "What is it?" He ran a thumb over her cheek. "You are pale as a sheet. What did I say?"

She couldn't tell him. If she did, she would admit to herself and him that their love could never be whole or perfect unless she gave him the truth he so justly deserved. Not who she was. The name of Raine Montand meant little. Raynard the Fox was the culprit here. The Fox's greatest cross to bear was what she'd done.

Gavin went to one knee. "Look at me. Oh, Raine. You cannot believe that I am being secretive because I don't trust you?" Her mouth trembled so badly, he placed two fingers there. "I don't want to put you in harm's way, my darling. The less you know about where I go and who I see, the better for you. The safer you are. Whoever killed Louise and Sean knows no mercy. They stabbed two people, repeatedly. They are animals, sweetheart, with little regard for human frailty. You may be my secretary and you are my helpmate in so many ways, but I will not allow you to become an accomplice. You will know only what it is safe for you to know. Do you understand my motive? Say you do."

"Gavin." She kissed him. "How you do amaze me with your generosity and your tenderness."

"You inspire me to those qualities, Raine. You have brought sunshine into my dreary life." He smiled winsomely. "Darling, when I come back and this crime is solved, as I predict it will be, when the wreckage of my life is repaired, you and I will talk about this at length. You won't evade me any longer and I won't allow you to." He gripped her shoulders. "I need sunshine in my life permanently—and I think you not only need it, but you can find it only with me. Is that arrogance, Raine?"

"You haven't an arrogant bone in your body."

He kissed her as if he'd never stop.

Until someone said, "Pardon me, but I had no idea——"

"Milord, I——I *am* sorry, but yer mother insisted——"

Raine sat, dazed at the sight of an embarrassed and apologetic Mrs. McNally dwarfed by a tall handsome woman with a wealth of amber hair edged in soft gray that matched her eyes. She looked anywhere but at Gavin and Raine, as unnerved as Mrs. McNally by the sight before them.

Gavin got to his feet. His surprise faded, mellowing into a wariness. Yet, his good manners saved the others in their dismay.

"Hello," he said with some warmth as he stepped forward to take his mother briefly in his arms. "A complete shock to see you here," he told her with a growing indifference that made the elegant woman in somber blue bombazine blanch an even whiter shade.

"A trial for me to come, too," she admitted and brought forth a skeptical brow from her son.

"Thank you, Mrs. McNally, we'll muddle on. Perhaps you could bring us some tea. A few of your scones and a cake."

"Yes, milord, I can." She curtsied, casting a concerned look toward Raine.

"Mother, my secretary. Mrs. Winston Jennings, known to me as Raine. You might use her name as well because one day soon she will merit the equality you grant her by the fact that she will bear my name as well. Raine, the Marchioness of Cranborne."

Raine could not say who was more shaken by Gavin's introduction, she or his mother. Raine put out her hand and murmured the expected pleasantries.

Gavin's mother recovered quickly, her curiosity rising about this young woman whom she did not know and who commanded a place in her son's heart and future. The marchioness's large gray eyes which were so remarkably like her son's appraised Raine and found her acceptable. Raine also thought the marchioness bowed to her son's fait accompli in the matter of choice of a bride. "I see. How do you do, Mrs. Jennings?" She drew herself up, reclaiming whatever dignity she'd lost in surprise. "I am Frances Sutherland. Since we are to have a continuing relationship and I am to call you by your first name, you must do the same with me."

Gavin was astonished at her offer, but not put off by her largess. "Why are you here, Mama? What is it you want? I must say you've picked an infernally bad time to visit. I have a lot of work to do, and very little time to entertain."

"Gavin." She put a gloved finger to her lips, her words watery. "Please let me have a few minutes of your time. Then I promise to leave you both quickly. I had to see you. Had to . . . tell you . . . how I feel."

Gavin spun away.

Raine could see him in profile. Torn between his ire and his love, he searched his gardens blindly for some middling attitude.

Raine came forward. "Lady Cranborne, please sit down. You must be weary from your journey."

"Thank you, yes. The train ride from Cranborne here does take the starch out of one's endurance. Always did." She took a seat in one of the leather chairs and removed her gloves, then laid aside her reticule. "The house looks lovely. Does Gavin have you to thank for that, Raine?"

"No, my lady. His housekeeper. I am only his secretary."

The marchioness arched a long gray brow. "Clearly, Raine, you are more than that."

"What is it you came for, Mama? Surely not to run your finger along the furniture for dust motes."

She stared at her son, sorrow warring with her pride. "I realize how we . . . I have hurt you."

Gavin could only remain silent.

She cleared her throat. "It took me a long time."

"More than a year," Gavin added with a nod. "What prompts you to this recognition now?"

"Courage. Cowardice."

"Opposing forces."

"Excuse me, Gavin," Raine interrupted, "I will——"

"There is no need for you to leave, Raine," he insisted she stay.

His mother echoed his sentiment. "I have come here, Raine, to take full responsibility for a wrong I have done my son. I care not if you witness it. That Gavin cares for you means he trusts you and your judgment."

Raine almost laughed at the irony of the marchioness's statement. Raine's lack of judgment was the very reason she had come to Chipswell to offer him recompense.

"Stay, Raine," the lady told her, and set her sights on Gavin. She gathered steam for her discourse. "I see no reason for you to leave. I am resigned to eating my share of humble pie for what I've done. I would like to hope that after I have said this, I will not only feel immensely better, but deal with my husband, my children, and any of my friends and acquaintances in a different manner. To send you out now only means you'll have to be let in on what happens here anyway. I'd much rather you witness it than hear it secondhand, even if it is from Gavin." She faced her perplexed son.

"Your father told me last week that he had ordered you to cease writing your novel and that you had replied."

Gavin became intrigued. Raine could see the spark of it as he uncrossed his arms and gripped the back of his desk chair. "I refused."

"Yes," she said, a smile wreathing her face, "I know. I am ecstatic that you did."

Gavin was not enchanted. "I am baffled."

"I expected you to be. I have never taken a position opposite your father's in thirty-seven years, have I? Your brothers and sister find it astonishing, and I am equally certain you feel the same."

"You told him you supported my decision to continue writing?"

"I did," she said with a toss of her wide-brimmed hat. "In truth, I am surprised at myself. But," her jaw stiffened, "I like myself better. I shall stand taller for my newfound spine, especially once I leave here."

Mrs. McNally came in, her distress nearly palpable as she fixed Raine with a desperate look.

"Over on the deal table, Mrs. McNally, thank you," Raine told her softly. She went to pour as the housekeeper let herself out.

The marchioness watched Mrs. McNally depart before she fixed on Gavin again. "I have left your father."

Gavin blinked as if she'd told him the Queen was dead.

"It is quite true, I assure you, dearling. Should have done it long ago. Would have woken him up. Insufferable man. But then, I cannot blame him entirely, can I? I allowed him to maneuver me into my powerless state. Well, no more. I have my integrity to consider."

"I don't understand," Gavin said, hushed. "How can this be? You and he have been married for too many years, and you love him. How can you leave him?"

"Because he acted unjustly. Assumed you had some complicity in this terrible crime. I never believed it and yet, I never raised my voice, never told him. I should have. I have not slept an entire night through since the day you left. I knew it was wrong of him to send you off without a hope or a prayer. For him to offer you this house rent-free was a sop. A gesture to make certain *he* slept at night. But I was so used to letting him do as he wished. In most cases, he was right. He does possess good judgment, except when it comes to his children."

"He wants us perfect," Gavin murmured with resignation.

"On his terms. Well, I am convinced that Lord Acton was right when he said power corrupts and absolute power corrupts absolutely. Your father has gotten a taste of that with what he did to you and now that his wind is up, he has badgered Derek into an engagement with an American heiress. He justifies it by saying we could do with the young woman's dowry to invest in structural improvement in our mines in Wales."

"Good grief, Mama, Derek's engaged? To whom? It hasn't been announced in the papers."

"Not yet. Your father is still negotiating with Mr. Warfield's lawyers."

Raine balked. Darcy Warfield was considering marrying a future marquess? Gavin's older brother? Ann had no idea of it, either, or she would have written. But then Ann was so chewed up about Colleen's and Bryce's divorce, how would she think to write about a woman who had been their friend in Washington years ago?

Gavin shook his head. "I thought Derek was interested in Lord Hanover's daughter."

"He was. He still is. But Sarah is old Hanover's youngest, and she comes with less than her two sisters did. Your father says that's not sufficient for a gel who'll become a marchioness. Your father forgets I came with the clothes on my back."

"Bearing a string of titles older than any of his."

"No money, dearling," his mother pointed out, then grinned. "But we were so in love, nothing else mattered at the time."

"He loved you, too, Mama. Still does. I am certain he is wild with grief to be without you."

"He shall have to learn to live that way, too, Gavin. Unless he changes, I'm not going back."

"Where *are* you going?"

A shimmer of delight radiated her handsome face into a more delicate beauty. "A secret place I have yearned to go. You haven't the vaguest notion, dearling, where it is, but if your father wants to find me—truly desires it—he can. Of course, he must come with a few other requirements under his arm."

Gavin was fascinated. "Such as?"

Her features became stark. "An apology to you. Restitution. An apology to me. A change of heart as to how we shall help our children realize their innermost yearnings. You see he has also alienated Jenna. He has now refused your sister the right to go to Paris to study painting."

It was bad enough that Raine's curiosity roused at the idea that an American woman was being courted by a man who did not love her but her dollars. Raine also felt the rub of a fellow artist, denied an opportunity to pursue her art. Raine poured a cup of tea for Gavin and one for herself, and bit her lip to keep quiet.

Gavin took his cup and did not drink, but stirred his spoon in the brew. "I must say I am startled by your action to leave Papa—and all these revelations. But I require no apology from him. I neither want nor need it, Mama. I am building my life and my career without him this time."

"I could see it, dearling." She filled with a gratification that Raine recognized as universal to parents. Ann over her little boy. Coll over hers. Even Gussie could acquire this look when she gazed at her nephew, Ford.

And you?

The thought—its hope and rejection—had her reeling in her chair. Mother of God, she wanted children. Gavin's.

The marchioness was examining her. "I conclude you have had something to do with this new attitude."

"Gavin had set his goals before I came here to work for him, my lady."

"Frances."

"Frances. Your son needed no help from an American who—" *had ruined him,* "—understood little about English politics and society."

"Mama, do not listen to her. Raine knows buckets more about English politics than she lets on."

Frances Sutherland lowered her lashes so far it was impossible for Raine to read the emotion behind them.

"You must have brought Gavin something more." She faced her son with a quizzical brow. "What?"

"Raine is a hard taskmaster. I burnt candles at both ends and broke my hand scribbling."

Raine was laughing. "Or mine *typing* all in an effort to gain—"

"What?" Frances was anticipating something wonderful.

"Go on, tell her," Gavin challenged, folding his arms, "now that you've opened your kettle of fish."

Raine knew if she didn't, Gavin would. "Kisses."

"You wrote your book for kisses?" Frances did not seem surprised.

"One per installment, Mama."

"Well, well, Raine, I see you have discovered how to make a man do what you want. Did you always know this or is it a new talent?"

Raine's cheeks burned. "Unintentional, Frances, I assure you."

"But instinctive and productive. So, then." She lowered her hands into her lap. "Never change. My second son is a rare prize, Raine. He was spoiled—the cause of his temper tantrums. He can be obsessive in his devotion to a cause—and I always thought, to the right woman. He is impatient to have the rewards of his quests, but he is also a man who never changes his mind. Trust me when I say Gavin needs order in his life. I urge you to continue to give it to him. Likewise, you are fortunate, and I would say that even if he were not my boy."

With that she put her own cup and saucer down, then began to draw on her gloves.

"Where are you going?" Gavin was out of his chair and coming toward his mother and Raine.

"I must catch the next train to London."

"You've only just arrived."

"I never planned to stay, Gavin. I told you, dearling, I am off to my own bit of seclusion."

"You're actually happy about this, aren't you?"

Frances beamed. "Never doubt it. In many ways, I am, yes. I needed to show my assertiveness to your father for years. I made noises constantly. When Derek wanted to go to Sandhurst instead of Cambridge. When Jenna wanted to continue her fencing lessons and your father thought she needed to devote herself more to dressage. Only Reggie has never challenged your father—but that day may come yet. I want to be ready, if it does. You see, I never went into a real tear about any of my feelings. I should have. Now with you and this hideous murder case, your father sent you from us in the most unjust manner. I was a fool to wait so long to tell him he was a blasted old simpleton to do it. But I did wait, and it has cost me my pride and my integrity. No more. Now I am ready to stand on my own and let him discover his own mistakes. Pay his own prices."

"But how will you afford it? Papa has always controlled the money with an iron fist."

"Mmm. Yes. That is something else that will change about the way he and I live. Having come to him with no fortune, I never spent a pound that he didn't know about in advance. That has changed. I have taken the household money for this month. Oh, do not look so aghast, dearling. I assure you Cranborne Manor can survive without it."

"My first thought was that you may need more." Gavin returned to his desk, opened a drawer, and extracted his large cheque book. "If you are going abroad, I don't want you to suffer for any necessity."

"Sweetheart," Frances went to stand before her son and put her hand to his ledger, "I did not come here to ask you for anything except your forgiveness."

"That you have," he offered solemnly.

"Then I am fulfilled."

"I have more than enough, Mama, and I'd like to give you whatever you might need."

"You are generous, but no. I would not take from you.

After I allowed your father to cut you off? I'd not sleep tonight again. Can't do it. I have enough wrinkles and baggage under my eyes. Cannot afford more. Keep your money, dearling."

"What good is money if you cannot share the wealth?"

"I have a need for what you or no one can purchase for me, Gavin. Let me go. Let me do this. What money I took from the Manor's accounts I think are mine to take. I robbed no one. Your father can afford to replenish the pot. I have been frugal for thirty-seven years. That kind of gratitude for loving a penniless girl and marrying her bankrupted *me*. Now is the time for him to show me he can endow me with the currency of equality."

"I think you are right."

"Good." She pushed up her gloves and opened her arms. "Come round this desk and give me a hug and a kiss." They embraced, and tears began to make Frances tremble. "I must go before I ruin my powder and your coat. Good-bye, Raine. When we meet again, I hope we have a longer discourse about something more pleasant."

"I'll have the phaeton brought round. I will drive you to the station. Do not argue with me, Mama. I will do this."

When he returned home, Raine was no longer there. The surprise of his mother's visit and her words lingered, and he longed to talk with Raine.

She was not in her cottage, either.

He closed her little door behind him and stood gazing out to the sea. The sun was bright today, not a cloud on the horizon. He yearned to share such glory with Raine and wondered where she could have gone.

He trudged over to the garden shed and took out his bicycle. Within minutes, he had pedaled to the lake. Raine sat by a log, sheltered by a copse of oaks. She was feeding the grebes bits of bread she'd taken from the kitchen. Her sketchpad and a stick of charcoal lay beside her on the grass. He saw she had been drawing him—as an alligator. It tickled him that she could see such perspectives in people and draw them so astutely as animals. Raine had an inherent skill few others could even cultivate.

"Your mother got off all right?" Raine asked, shielding her eyes from the sun with a hand to her forehead.

"Yes, she's like a child, going on a new adventure." He propped the bicycle against a tree trunk. "Yet, I know she must be leery to travel alone. She and my father have not been apart since the day he eloped with her. My father will panic that she's left. He has no idea how integral she is to his days. Meanwhile, *you* forgot your hat. Don't want you to burn," he said as he sat down beside her. "Come sit in the shade." He patted the spot beside him, then took a piece of bread from her little sack. A fat mama bird waddled up to him and snatched the offering from his fingers. "My mother pelted me with questions about you."

Where does Raine come from? Who are her parents? Why do you love her? Only to the last did Gavin supply a satisfactory answer.

Are you certain you know her well enough to say you will marry her? To that, Gavin compared the three months he'd known Raine to the three weeks his father had known his mother before he whisked her off to Gretna Green.

"I was shocked by how you introduced us."

"I will do it again, Raine, with others. Best to get used to it."

"How can I convince you that you mustn't count on that?"

"Why? Where are you going, Raine?"

She stared at him.

"You keep too many secrets." He tossed another crumb out.

"So do you."

"What do you need to know?" He'd damn well prove

to her how much she meant to him, if he had to yell it from London Bridge. "How many women I have wanted? Dozens. Had in bed? Four, five. I can't remember. Forgettable, each one. How many I have wanted to marry? One. She failed the test of loyalty. Her reputation was more important to her than her so-called affection for me. And then there is you. You, who uphold me at every turn. You, who thwart me in my quest to make you fully mine. What else can I tell you?"

She was growing furious, but still logical. "I want to know if the handkerchief is real or not."

"Why?" He'd push her to the brink of revelations. "Simple curiosity? You advised me to make up some aspect that would draw attention."

"But this puts your life in jeopardy."

"There was no other way to move events in my direction."

"You are a stubborn man. I want to see you as famous as Dickens or as successful as Gladstone. Whatever you want, I do, too. But I also want you alive—not dead."

"And I simply want you. Forever."

"That can never be." She scrambled to rise.

He snaked out his hand. Seized her wrist. Brought her back. Into his arms. His hands in her hair, he pushed her gently to the grass and the sweet scent of it filled his nostrils. Raine filled his senses of sight and touch.

She shuddered in his embrace, her eyes closing, her mouth seeking his. As ever when she was this near to him, she forgot herself, logic, pride, whatever kept her from vanishing. "Kiss me."

"No."

Her lashes flew wide. Injured, she froze.

"You want kisses?"

She bit her lip.

"Earn them."

"Like you did?"

"No chapters. Kisses. For each one, you tell me what I need to know."

She swallowed. "I want to."

He captured her mouth with his in a fierce claim that made her grab his hair and moan. *"Mon coeur,"* he caressed her with his heartache in his voice, "what's your maiden name?"

"Raine Montand."

He gave her a kiss that could set all of England on fire. "And your home?"

"Belle Chenier." She ran her tongue along the seam of his lips.

"Why are you here?" He meant in England.

She took it to mean something different. "Because I care what happens to you."

That was the truth that resonated in her every act. The fact that brought her here and would drive her away. "God, sweetheart—" He sent a greedy hand down her torso. "I need you. Constantly."

She began to undo his buttons and placed her mouth against his throat. "You are not alone."

He slipped into her honeyed passage minutes later, vowing to give her proof that she was no longer alone, either.

By Sunday night before he left for London, he had held her in his arms in her bed, and they had made love enough since that day by the lake for Gavin to hope he'd given her his child. Heaven knew, she had welcomed him each succeeding time with the delight of a woman who could not reject her passion. He felt a desperation to take her often and prove to himself her existence. He thought he had to store up memories because he had a premonition that once he left for London, he would not see her again. He had no idea why he dreaded his departure, he merely knew it to be true.

He told himself not to be foolish. It was childish, he repeated, *childish,* to believe in the idea. But he could not shake his foreboding.

As a result, he reexamined his rationale to go to

London. He had to see these people—and the sooner he
did, the better for his future, the more secure his
finances, and the more easily he could marry her. He
could also more easily persuade her to it—so intent, so
insistent was she that he be restored to all that had been
taken from him.

When he gave her a parting kiss before dawn, he knew
that no matter what he had lost, it was insignificant to
what he had gained the day she had walked into his life.

Strangely, he also understood that he couldn't tell her
that—or she'd leave him in a heartbeat.

Raine bid Gavin good-bye at his house, not wishing to
watch him go, knowing that most likely when he returned she would have no reason to stay much longer.

Her job would be nigh unto finished. Her goal complete. But she loved him—and she felt, saw, reveled in
the love he gave her like a woman who had starved for it.
The banquet of love Gavin set before her daily was a
powerful lure.

But she had committed a crime against him. And
while he might forgive her for her injustice to him, she
could never forgive herself.

Chapter 13

"When you have eliminated the impossible, whatever remains, however improbable, must be the truth."

—Sir Arthur Conan Doyle

Charles Washburn put Gavin in mind of a ferret. One with manners.

"I am grateful you invited me to see you, Lord Sutherland. Sorry I could not see you until today." The short fellow took a chair opposite Gavin in his small drawing room at Brown's. The inspector's pinched face broadened in a hint of a smile when Gavin offered tea. "I don't care for any, thank you. Just finished my breakfast and came here straightaway. I wish to conduct this new investigation speedily. In fact, I had a letter composed to you to ask if I might visit Chipswell when your letter reached me. I would have seen you yesterday as you asked, but there is a new development in this case. I had to pursue it before I came to see you."

Gavin knew better than to ask Washburn leading questions. He would wait for what the man would willingly offer him about the course of the investigation.

"I knew you would want to talk with me, Inspector. My series in *St. Andrew's* has attracted so much attention."

The man sat, stiff as a board. "Quite. It is the reason we have decided to give it another go. Plus the pressure which government and party sources have put to bear on us. But then, I suspect you knew that would happen when you began to write your novel."

"Let us say, I hoped."

"At first blush, not the action of a man who is guilty."

"Precisely. Why resurrect a matter one wishes to bury?" Gavin asked with a great deal of satisfaction.

"Unless he wants to foil the authorities."

Gavin nodded. "You mean, throw people off by acting as if one is innocent."

"Ingenious way to do it, I'd say, my lord."

"You would see through the ploy." Gavin told himself he needed this fellow as his ally, not his enemy. He had treated Washburn with all due respect before whenever the inspector had come to interview him. He'd do it now, too. "My interest was aboveboard."

"I'd like to believe that, my lord. Shall you and I proceed with that agreement between us?"

"I will go forward continuing to protect my own best interests, Inspector. I am not interested in being charged for a crime I did not commit."

"Waste of everyone's time." Washburn folded his hands in his lap. "This case has created quite a stir from the start. The fact that we could never find any evidence or a suspect plagued us at the Yard. The cartoon in the newspaper about your argument proved you were angry at O'Malley, but it gave us no great reason to arrest you. I want you to know that on very few occasions do we fail to produce a suspect. Even before your book began to appear in that paper, at the Yard we wished for some act, some event that might precipitate a new angle to this case that we hadn't seen before. Your series gave us that."

Gavin heard the praise, but detected the lure. "How so?"

"You thought we reopened the case because your story created a ruckus? Hardly. On the contrary, I sit before you because your story inspired someone else to write to us."

Gavin wished Raine could hear this. He could imagine her gasp, her grin. Washburn had already told Gavin more than he should, which in itself indicated the man's tendency to gamble on Gavin's innocence. "Should I ask who?"

"You may ask, my lord. I will not tell. Cannot, but you could predict that. Wish I could, but then your story is not finished, and my words might become the stuff of your next installment, am I right?"

"I don't think it is in my best interests to irritate you that way."

"That, too, is smart, my lord. But," he winced, "on with it, eh? I have a letter. Anonymous. On one of those new typewriters. All capital letters and deuced difficult to read, if you ask me. These things will make our efforts in detecting criminals a nightmare. No handwriting to give away a person's identity. Anyway, it is true that we decided to reopen this case because of this note."

Gavin let the man sit without urging him on. Washburn was formulating his thoughts for prudence and diplomacy.

"Lord Sutherland, the day of the murders, after you spoke with O'Malley and Mrs. Stoddard, where did you go? What did you do?"

"I told you that before, Inspector."

"Refresh my memory," Washburn insisted though Gavin knew the man must have reread Gavin's deposition before he came to visit him this morning.

"I walked around Hyde Park until well past dusk. I was angry, upset. I need to walk or ride or do something physically draining when I am working off anger or frustration."

"And after dusk?"

"I went home."

"Your housekeeper could not corroborate that for us."

"She was out."

"Where was she?"

"Didn't you ask her that?" Gavin could not remember where Mrs. McNally had gone. The grocer's? Wherever it was, she had told the police. Washburn was playing games with him.

"We did, my lord. She said she had taken the air in the park across the street. One of your neighbors thought he might have seen her. It was the best we could do to substantiate her claim."

"So there you have it."

"You never left the house again?"

"No."

"Not until when?"

"The next day. Saturday. At approximately one o'clock I went to eat at my club. Dined with a friend of mine. Lord Falconer. You have that in my deposition, too."

"You will not change this account of your activities?"

Gavin told him he would not.

"You know nothing about the two men who were reported to have entered the Stoddard house that evening?"

"I know there were two men," Gavin admitted and knew he must choose his next words carefully to stay within the bounds of truth. "The newspapers reported that neighbors saw two men go into the square that night. One on foot. The other arrived in a cab."

"We could find no evidence to identify anyone having been in the house."

"Yes. That is your challenge in this case. No physical evidence. Not even the murder weapon."

"Now we have a note which says that one of those men to go inside was you."

Gavin reared back, stunned. "How could that be?" he asked of Washburn and himself.

"That is what I must learn."

"Do you believe the note-writer and if so, why?"

"He says he saw you through the window."

Ridiculous. The window had been swaddled in yards of velvets and tassels. That must mean this person had been inside the house when Gavin had arrived. "What was I doing? Tormenting a man who had been my colleague and my friend? Hurting a woman in a most inhumane way, carving at her like a bloodthirsty beast? Absurd."

"I thought the same. You never did strike me as a man who could do that to another one, let alone a woman."

"Despite the scuffle I had with John Gaylord?" Gavin asked, shocked that this example of his hotheadedness was the reason so many presumed him guilty.

"Gaylord was known as a man who provokes others. As for you, I did not think you had the perversity required to kill with a knife. These murders were planned and carefully executed by someone with more than anger on their minds."

"Thank you," Gavin bit off, his outrage at the brutality of the murderer making him clench his hands. Where was Raine with her calming influence? Blast it, if he'd go anywhere without her again. "You didn't answer me about what the writer says I was doing."

"Removing an object from Sean O'Malley's hand."

"A handkerchief."

"Yes, Lord Sutherland. And then removing something from his trouser pocket."

Dear God. What did his face reflect? Horror? Knowledge? Whoever wrote the note must have still been in the house when Gavin arrived. His blood drummed in his ears. No one knew about the turned-out trouser pockets except the police, the Yard—Gavin—and the murderer. "What do you suppose it was?" he asked the stoic man before him.

"Money, a note. An item given to O'Malley by the murderer. I have no idea, but I think it an interesting tidbit."

To hell with this pussyfooting. "Why are you telling me this, Inspector? You've no need to."

"I thought if I were helpful to you, you would return the kindness."

"If I can. What would you like?"

"To read the next few installments in your book before half of Britain does."

"The seventh chapter appeared this morning. I have finished another seven."

"And when will your Samuel Grant confront the murderer?"

"Chapter Fifteen."

"Do you have a name for this character?"

"Like you, Inspector, I am sad to say I do not."

"You have begun to name a few suspects in your book."

"The murdered man's colleagues and his mistress's husband, yes." *Ahearn and Butler, plus Hamilton Stoddard.*

"Based on any facts?"

"Based on logic, Inspector. I would assume you have looked at those possibilities as well as I."

"I have. Ryan Ahearn and Timothy Butler interest me. Know them, don't you?"

"I do." Gavin sat quietly, realizing he'd learned patience well.

"And I don't seem to have the resources available to me to find what I need to know. Secrets and lies among family and friends are not considered proper territory for men of my ilk to come tramping about. Perhaps you may go where I may not, Lord Sutherland."

Gavin resisted the temptation to look gleeful. If Washburn wanted his help, the man could not believe Gavin guilty. "Perhaps I can. Where should I look, Inspector?"

"I would like to know if Ahearn and Butler are entirely loyal to the Crown, my lord. Could you say?"

"Not with any certainty," Gavin admitted. "I could ask."

"Please do. Then, what do you know about Hamilton Stoddard?"

"Professionally, he has a sterling reputation. Admired for his diligence. Has served in the Home Office for more than twenty years."

"Louise Stoddard was his second wife—and more than twenty years his junior. Within the past five years of her marriage, she was known to receive quite a few gentlemen alone for tea. Most have been MPs who represent boroughs in Ireland. I find that intriguing. She was also seen going without her husband to dinner parties and balls. Lately, she would dance and flirt mostly with Sean O'Malley."

"Many married women go to social functions alone. It is the custom among the upper classes. It is the means by which many marriages survive the conditions under which they were conceived."

"Ah, yes, my lord. For money."

"Or titles, land, or the confluence of blue blood."

"Why did the Stoddards marry?"

Gavin shrugged. "I have no idea."

"I need to know."

"I will look into it." Gavin detected something else Washburn wanted. He waited.

"When do you return to Chipswell, Lord Sutherland?"

"If I accomplish all I need to, Friday afternoon, Inspector."

"Does your agenda include learning the name of the person responsible for the murders?"

"I do hope so."

"If you discover it before I do, I hope you'll come and whisper it in my ear, Lord Sutherland."

Gavin knew it was not a suggestion but an order. "I will."

"Cheeky bugger," Bryce muttered Thursday evening in the library of Brooks's in St. James. The two of them were alone, the door closed. "Wants you to solve his case for him."

Gavin had revealed that the inspector had asked Gavin to divulge the name of the fictitious murderer, but told Bryce nothing about the note or how it stated that Sean's trouser pockets had been turned out. The less Bryce knew, the less Gavin would have to explain—and he didn't want to reveal to anyone how he'd been at the Stoddards' that night. "I'm willing to do whatever I can, if I can. I want this laid to rest so that I can get on with my life." Gavin capsulized the offer of William Pumphrey to support him if he stood for Chipswell.

Bryce leaned forward. "Snap at the opportunity, Gavin. Not that you couldn't win there without old Will's support, but it will help. We have money in the coffers, too, to aid you."

"The series is selling so well, perhaps I won't have to ask you for a penny."

"I think we should give it to you anyway. It's there to assist candidates who have no backing. Plus you may have need of it sooner than your publisher can make you rich. When does Will want to resign?"

"Next spring. Why?"

Bryce swirled his brandy. "Many in the cabinet are talking of calling for a general election. This book of yours raises so many questions of improper investigation—and improper treatment of you—that much of the blame goes to the government for allowing it. Confidence is shaken. Badly." Bryce was relishing the idea of a contest. He had led the last fight for their party and loved every minute of debate, counterattack, and challenge to the opposition. Their party had gained twelve seats, too.

"I'll be damned," Gavin murmured. "A general election. I never thought to precipitate that with my book."

"Best laid plans of mice and men do go awry, don't they? Take our money. It'll be well spent."

"To have party financial support would mean I could afford to do a few more things I planned," Gavin conceded.

"Care to share them with me?"

"I want to get married."

Bryce was shocked—and yet came round quickly. "Who? A girl from Norfolk?"

"My secretary."

"You're serious?"

"Never more so." Gavin knew he trod on perilous ground to suggest he might marry a girl without a dowry and without an English pedigree. "She'll be an asset. I think I told you I have never known a woman who understands so much about politics. It is a passion of hers."

"As long as you are a passion of hers, too, I will be among the first and the few, unfortunately, to say it could work."

"She has a few other delights. She is an artist, wonderful with charcoal. Educated, speaks French, very sharp mind. I must have told you she is a widow."

"Mmmm. American, too." Bryce frowned into his brandy. "They have different views of the world, you realize. The Americans and we may speak the same language but we don't mean the same things. I have firsthand experience with the misinterpretations."

Gavin was silent until he found diplomatic words to broach the subject of Bryce and his American wife. "How are you? Really?" Gavin had noticed new lines around Bryce's eyes.

"Bearing up well, under the circumstances. Colleen was aghast when I told her I intended to sue her for divorce on grounds of criminal conversation. Such polite words for adultery, don't you think? Ah, well, yes, I am bitter. But poor Coll is utterly incomprehensible. She threatened me with castration and poverty, in that order. She told me she would see me in hell before I'd win the custody of Ford but I assured her I had already lived in hell with her—and I planned to leave her in it."

Bryce downed the remainder of his liquor. "Coll made a row when I sent Ford back to Aldersworth with his nanny. I did not want him here when I break the news to Colleen's parents. Poor boy needs a loving hand. I shall bring him back the minute I get Colleen out of my Park Lane house. I expect her to return to New York with her parents when they sail in October. At least in her own country, she won't be the focus of so much notoriety in the papers."

"A hideous mess for you to endure." It seemed like a better sentiment for Gavin to convey than the evil premonition that Colleen would remain in England to make Bryce's life a continuing misery.

"Yes." Bryce rose to go to the decanter on the console. "Another?"

Gavin refused and watched Bryce pour a double for himself. "This meeting with your mother and father-in-law is going to be difficult. I hope you bear up under the strain."

Bryce saluted him with his brandy. "You and me both."

"If I can do anything to help you . . ."

"Thank you. There is nothing. I am desolate with the fact that I must pursue this hideous course." Bryce cleared his throat. "I should never have married her."

"You cared for her."

"That was not enough."

"No," Gavin admitted with dejection.

"Some problems love cannot cure."

Gavin could not accept that. Not for himself and Raine. They hadn't even had a chance yet. But he would move heaven and earth to make one for them. "I need to ask you a few questions, Bryce. They may not even seem rational but I must do this."

"Fire away." Bryce resumed his seat.

"Among the Americans you have met through Colleen, are there any among them who come from Washington?"

Bryce chuckled. "Well, my first thought is an obvious one. Colleen's best friends, next to her sister Gus, are Ann Kendall and her cousin."

"Cousin?" Gavin put his glass down.

Bryce nodded. "They call her Wit."

The one of the three American Beauties about whom he knew nothing. What irony. What coincidence. If Wit were Raine, she personified the name. It gave Gavin reason to ask, "Do you perchance know someone named Raine Montand?"

Bryce smiled easily. "Of course. Ann's cousin. Like the back of my hand. Why?"

"You do?"

"Yes. Raine is Ann's cousin on her father's side of the family. Skip Brighton. Ever met him? No? Well, I know you must have heard of him. Major owner of the Guardian Shipping Line."

Gavin murmured, "The uncle at the French spa."

"Yes, he's got tuberculosis and goes as often as he can to take the cure. It seems to be helping."

Gavin picked up his snifter and drained it.

Bryce narrowed his gaze, spoke slowly. "Skip has lived years longer than his doctors predicted. That's largely because Ann and Raine badger him to go to the Mediterranean often. Now that Ann is married to Rhys Kendall and has had their little boy, it is Raine who ensures Skip goes at least twice a year. She makes him take her abroad to museums, the Vatican, and the Acropolis. She is an artist . . . she sketches like your . . . Do you know Raine?" The way Bryce asked the question, he knew the answer. "Your American secretary?"

Gavin nodded. "Was Raine ever married?"

"Married?" Bryce sounded as if he had just heard the Queen had bedded Gladstone. "God, no. Why would you think . . . ?" He drew in a huge breath, recognizing he'd get no response, then plunged onward. "Raine finds most men a bore. Hates the social whirl. Tried a few balls and supper parties, refused to let her uncle bring her out as a full-fledged debutante. She says the whole idea of such endeavors is vacuous. Demeaning."

Gavin laughed wryly. "Sounds like her."

"She preferred to work. Drove Skip mad for years with her independence. She insisted on earning her own pin money, though she wanted to be with family so much she came with Ann and her father here a few years ago. Great backbone, Raine's got. Humor that can be very cynical, though we have all known she has a heart of gold. Their civil war, I think, must have been a holocaust. Mass murder, chaos like that, does things to people. Builds character, if they're lucky. Destroys hope, if they're not."

I offer you hope. That was what Raine had said to him the day she applied. That was what she had given him every day thereafter. "What did it do to Raine?"

"Gutted her. Every member of her family died. I don't know how. She never talked about it. Hurt too much, I think, to make it part of everyday conversation. But she's strong. You must know this by now if you and she have become friends."

Lovers. "Thank you. I am astonished, as you can see."

"What can I do to help you?"

"Have you ever met a man named Winston Jennings?"

Bryce replied he hadn't.

"I didn't think so."

"What will you do?" Bryce wondered.

"Insist Raine marry me. As soon as possible."

"You'll have to get Skip Brighton's permission to do that. The old man is a bear when it comes to protecting those girls. Making up, he says, for what he couldn't do during the war to make their lives happier."

"Do you know when he returns to London?"

"No idea."

"What if I call on Ann Kendall?"

"She and Rhys are at High Keep in Lancashire. Should arrive in London soon though, especially because Colleen would want her friends around her when her parents arrive. Colleen's mother is not known for her congenial nature in the best of times, let alone at the news of impending divorce."

"I cannot thank you enough for your information."

"My pleasure. I don't know what your conflicts are with Raine, but I wish you well in overcoming them. I see how much you care for her. You both deserve great happiness."

Gavin understood his challenge was to make Raine accept that.

Gavin decided not to take a hansom back to Brown's. The day's events seeped into him as surely as the chill of a mist. Just like the night he had walked after he had argued with Sean and Louise, he needed air to clear his head. But it went round and round today's events instead. He ambled about until he decided to hail a cab and go to Kensington. He stepped out of the cab, paid the driver, and stood on the street corner facing the Stoddard house.

How well he remembered his rage that night. His need to speak to Sean. Knowing he was there with Louise, Gavin had gone and knocked. Of course, he was too late to save them from their deaths. God, that broke him into little pieces each time he thought of it.

He turned, walked a few blocks, and came upon a pub.

"Beer," he ordered from the bartender even before he had his coat unbuttoned. The man drew a draught and slapped a pint down before Gavin.

He sipped at it, thinking of Raine. Wit. He recalled the

first day she had come to work for him and how she had evaded him and their discussion of the three American Beauties. How nervous she had been. How carefully chosen her words were. How lucky she'd been that he never checked up on her marriage to an army man by going to Whitehall's record office. She had lied to him about being married.

He took another drink of his beer. Had she lied to him about anything else?

Not her inexperience in bed. Thank God.

Not her feelings for him. He knew to the marrow of his bones she cared for him. Her body declared eloquently what she had not yet told him in words.

He suddenly understood as deeply why she had not let him say he loved her. She felt unworthy because of her lies.

Plural. Lies.

Because there was a reason she had lied to him about being married. A reason she had come to him. Because she had come to him. Planned to apply to become his secretary.

Why?

Curiosity that a man whom she had seen speak in Parliament would be suspected of murder?

That seemed so weak a motive to flaunt rigid social rules, leave her home and her family whom she adored to work for a man she did not even know.

Yet what other reason could Raine have had?

He itched to be home. To ask her. To kiss her and tell her that whatever her motive had been to come to him, he simply wanted to know. Then he could put the matter to rest and get on with marrying her.

Soon. He praised his foresight to have made love to her often. She had never refused him, a measure of her need for him. And he had done it out of need for her, physically as well as emotionally. Because he had known in his bones that if she carried his child, she would not hesitate to marry him. She was a moral creature, his Raine, his Wit. And her lies had kept her from him long enough.

"Too long," he muttered to himself, then lifted his glass. *To you, my dear, and the end of your single status.*

A group of men in the corner were playing darts. Gavin took his beer and went over to watch. Soon he was a competitor, and conversation turned so that they asked him who he was and what he did. He saw no reason not to be honest.

They regarded him silently for a bit.

"We been readin'," said one elderly man, whose clothes and demeanor led Gavin to think he might be a clerk or accountant, educated enough to read and want to know the end of Gavin's novel. "That's quite a book you got there. 'Ow do you think o' things like that? Must be 'ard."

"Not terribly, no."

"I like the twist you got in there," said another of *The Accused.*

"Which?"

"The 'anky. Why take it, ye know wot I mean, unless ye meant to use it later? In the story."

"'Is 'anky don't mean a thing, Dick. I tell ye it's the woman's 'usband wot did the deed." He made a slice across his neck with his finger. "Ain't I right, milord?"

"I haven't the foggiest," Gavin replied in truth.

"I does. I say it was ol' Stoddard who did it. Didn't like 'is wife stepping into another man's bed."

"Bollocks," huffed a man who'd been silent until now. "Ah know a man 'ho's the 'ackney driver who stands round the corner from the Stoddard 'ouse. 'E says the lady there had many a visitor. 'E even took a few home on occasion."

Gavin straightened. "Is that right? Do you know where I could find this driver?"

"'Course ah do. 'E's me friend, ain't 'e? Want me to go

with you, milord? 'E lives in Whitechapel, and ye don't want ta go in there by yerself, not in the dark o' night nor e'en the light o' day."

"I'd like your company, yes. What is your name?"

"'Arry, milord. Harry Sykes."

Harry's friend was Christopher Pitt.

"Mr. Pitt." Gavin had introduced himself after Harry had told them why they interrupted Chris's late-night supper in the filthy tenement. "I wish to know about anyone who may have left the Stoddard house. Anyone you picked up who didn't live there."

Pitt scratched his bald head, leaving long red nail marks on his pate. "Lots o' men. Lately, two. Looked the same ta me, they did. Don't know their names."

"No, I didn't expect that, but their looks. I'll take that." *Anything I can get.*

"Oh, 'er men looked all the same ta me, I say. You the one writin' that book everybody's blatherin' about? They think you it was carved 'em two open? Why you want to know anything from me, eh?"

Gavin thought a cretin could understand why he wanted that information. His hackles rose.

Harry Sykes vouchsafed for Gavin. "'Ere now, Chris, 'is lordship don't look like a murderer, do 'e?"

"Well, mebbe not. Aw right, aw right, I ken see you gettin' itchy. They was tall and dark complected, like Spaniards."

"Did they speak English?"

"Course! 'ho don't?"

Half the world.

"Polite, they was, 'ad soft voices and I thought to meself, they was too nice, what slimy turds callin' on a lady tagether like they did, for unnatural acts, if ya get my meanin'."

"They would come together?" Gavin asked.

"Odd, ain't it?" Pitt shuddered. "Can't know what them Micks are up to."

"They were Irish?" Christ above. Could Sean have been murdered by one of his own countrymen? Or two? Over a woman's favors?

"Would 'ave bet my 'orse on it."

Gavin thanked Pitt by filling his hand with a ten-pound note, then gave another to Harry. "Thank you. If you think of anything else," he extracted his calling card case from his vest pocket and wrote his address on the back, "please come to see me. I am at Brown's Hotel until Friday morning. If you wish to contact me after that," he scribbled some more, "write to me here."

"Well, yer lordship," Pitt fingered the card, "I don't write, sir."

"Ah do," Harry assured him, "I'll help."

Gavin was about to leave when he faced them both again. "Two more questions."

"Yes sir?" Pitt was more willing to be cooperative with money in his hand.

"When did you last see these two visit?"

Pitt rolled out his lower lip. "Dunno. Mebbe just before that laidy was killed."

Gavin nodded. "And where would you take these men? Where was home?"

"No idea o' that."

"Why not?" Gavin would not tolerate obfuscation now that he was so close.

"I took 'em to two places. One'd ask to go to The Atheneum."

"The men's club in Pall Mall?" Gavin was flabbergasted.

"Right you are."

"And the other man? Where would he go?"

"Fleet Street."

Gavin considered that. Fleet Street was a very short one. One long block, that was all. Lined on both sides with ten to twelve large buildings housing as many publications, their owners, editors, reporters, presses. And typewriters? "These men would go to Fleet Street late at night?"

"They were no fools, 'em two. They would 'ave their fun with the lady and then come back whispering. They had things to do after seeing her—creepy they were. Snickering and crowing about theirselves to other men."

Other men in a club. Other men in the newspaper business.

"You have been invaluable," Gavin told them and asked Pitt to drive Harry back to Kensington and himself to the corner of Fleet Street and Chancery Lane.

Gavin, regardless of the hour, felt compelled to search out the only man he knew who possessed an office, a typewriter, and a membership in The Atheneum.

As he peered up at the offices of the newspaper, he saw a few lights on. Including the main one.

When he knocked, one of the typesetters let him in. The man recognized Gavin and smiled when he asked where the publisher was. "O course, 'e'd like ta see ya, milord. Got company but that's no matter. Go right on up." He indicated the wide stone stairs with the ornate carved balustrade.

As Gavin reached the top, he saw his host rise from his desk chair and shake hands with a tall well-dressed gentleman. Raine would have drawn the visitor as a sleek, keen-eyed crow. "Good to have had this talk with you," he was saying to his guest. "You understand my position, I hope?"

"Certainly, though I don't agree with it. Bad form for a democracy. Well, look who is here to see you?" The man who was vaguely familiar to Gavin smiled slowly and put out his hand. "We have not seen each other in years, Lord Sutherland."

"No, Mr. Healy, we have not crossed paths except in print." Gavin had no need to be cordial to a man who took glee in printing any speculation he could about political figures or their private doings. In the cartoon which had been one of many to criticize him. And in supporting violence in Ireland.

Healy bid them both good-bye and took his hat and gloves before he made for the stairs.

"Well, my, my, hello. Wonderful to see you, Gavin. What are you doing here at this time of night?"

"I have a few questions I need to ask you," Gavin said, the startling findings of the day exhausting him.

"Come then, my boy, and sit. You look drained. Let me pour you a whiskey."

"Thank you, Ned."

"What is on your mind?"

"How many men in Fleet Street do you know who own a typewriter?"

"Two."

"You and who else?" Gavin asked.

Ned nodded toward the door. "Healy."

Chapter 14

"The Assassins are desperate. . . . We must expec[t]
more deeds of blood, and of perhaps a more
serious kind than the last which have occurred."
—John Poyntz Spencer, 5th Earl Spencer, Viceroy of Ireland

"No, ma'am," Ben Watkins circled his hat in his hands
as he stood before Raine on Friday afternoon, "he
weren't on that train. I waited for more'n half an hour
But he just weren't on it."

When she'd seen Ben drive up to the house without
Gavin in the pony cart, panic flashed through her. Call it
intuition, call it insane, Raine knew something was
wrong. Very wrong.

What if Gavin had been arrested? What if he had
gotten angry when he had the interview with the inspector from Scotland Yard? What if Gavin had blurted how
he had been to the Stoddard house the night of the
murders?

What if the murderer had become enraged and learned
Gavin was in London? Invited him to tea or to climb
into a cab with him and then dispatched—

No.

Gavin would protect himself from that. He was a

smart man. A careful man. He would not walk into danger with his eyes wide open.

So where was he?

"I thought per'aps," Ben went on with hope in his eyes, "Lord Sutherland'll just catch the night train."

"Yes, that's a possibility, Ben. You're right."

The possibilities abounded. Normal ones. Gavin could have run a few minutes late and not gotten through the horrific London traffic to the station. He could have been invited to supper by someone whom he thought important enough that he change his plans and come home tomorrow. Certainly, he *could* take a later train that left at six tonight, but he would have to change in Peterborough, and he'd not arrive until after ten o'clock on that one.

Many things could have delayed him. Not just traffic.

His father could have returned to London as did half of England this time of year. The marquess could have called on Gavin—if he had learned that his son had taken rooms at Brown's. That was possible, but not probable.

So where was he?

With the Derwenters? That thought thickened her throat. No. He might call on Sidney, but Gavin would not take up with a woman who had treated him so cruelly. He had said so himself.

Gavin might be with Bryce. That idea sat less lightly. Gavin had learned her real name—and armed with that, he could ask a few questions of the man who had married an American. Gavin could so easily learn that she was a cousin to Ann Kendall, the niece of Skip Brighton, the friend of Colleen Falconer and Gus VanderHorn. Gavin would then discover that she had never married Winston Jennings. And Gavin would wonder why she would lie about her marriage, why she would have to. That no one could tell him but she herself. And she could never admit how she'd hurt him with her cartoon.

"Thank you, Ben. I'll tell Mrs. McNally not to rush supper."

When Raine informed her, the woman put down her spoon. "I don't like it one bit. Why ain't 'e on the train?"

Raine had to know why the housekeeper was as upset as she was. "What bothers you that Lord Sutherland is late?"

"He's always on time. When he says he'll be somewhere he is. He's organized, that man. You can set your watch by him. Even that Lady Derwenter knew when to come to see him 'cause he had a routine that never varied unless . . ."

"Unless what?" Raine asked and didn't like the answer.

"Unless 'e gets angry or sumpthin 'appens unexpected like." She looked sheepish and went back to scrubbing her pots. "I suppose we'll have a quiet supper."

"I'm not very hungry, Mrs. McNally. I'll wait for my supper to eat with Lord Sutherland."

Raine walked down the hall toward the office and found herself standing at the window as Gavin often did. "Where are you?" she whispered to the dying sun. She stood there for a long time watching the iron-colored clouds surrender their pinks and mauves to the end of day.

"I brought you some chowder," Mrs. McNally came in with a tray, "and I want you to eat it. You cannot wait for his lordship to come on the next train just to eat. 'E'll be along, mark my words."

Raine smiled, resigned to the housekeeper's kindness. "Thank you," she told her and watched her set the tray down on the end of the desk. "You have been wonderful to me over the past few months. I don't know how to tell you my gratitude."

"Nor me ta you. When you first came 'ere, I was not kind."

"You were honest. You had Lord Sutherland's best interests at heart." And the servant had had a big change of it, too, toward Raine. "I shall remember that for many years."

"'Ere now! You sound like you're going away. Are you?"

Confronted like that with a question she could not avoid, Raine conceded. "I never intended to stay beyond a few months. The summer, you know. This was my vacation or my holiday, as you say. I wanted to help Gav—Lord Sutherland. I knew what a bind he was in and I—what's the matter?"

Mrs. McNally had tears in her eyes. "Don't you love 'im?"

"Oh, yes, yes. You can't imagine how I care for him, Mrs. McNally."

"Then what is the problem? Why leave him? You've been so good for 'im. So good. He works well, he thinks sharply. He laughs again. You did that for him, Raine. Mrs. Jennings. Why would you go now that you and he . . . ?"

"Mrs. McNally, please. You've been with his lordship for what? Two years? You understand, as well as I, that Lord Sutherland needs to establish a relationship with a lady who can help him in his career. A woman who has prestige and family connections. A lady—"

"Not that Belinda Derwenter woman."

"No. Lord Sutherland would never take her back. But there are many others—"

"'E won't have 'em, is my guess. Only you."

"I will see him finish this book and then I'll go back to—" God, where? London? Why? No place on earth would seem as right as someplace close to Gavin.

But I'll go. To see Uncle Skip and Gus. Or go to Lancashire. She could visit Ann and Rhys, maybe escape the autumn social season altogether. Only a few more weeks until Gavin's book was finished. On Tuesday the next installment would appear, and the world would know who had killed Sean and Louise. Or Raine hoped they would.

Then Gavin would be free of this albatross of suspicion. He would stand here some day soon in Chipswel and win, with Mr. Pumphrey's support. He'd buy the Parker house and move into it. Without her.

"Well I tell you, Mrs. Jennings, that woman'll come back to haunt him. I know she will; if you don't stay here, she'll come to roost."

"Who will?" His mother? Raine was lost.

"Belinda Derwenter."

Were they back to her again? "I don't think so, Mrs McNally."

"I do. She wanted this man very badly. Coming around at all hours of the night, asking me to let her in. I'd put her in the drawing room, proper like, but she would roam. Trying to get in his bed too, waltzing around the house when he wasn't here, into his papers and such."

"She did what?"

"Brazen hussy. She'd gallivant anywhere she pleased. One night I found her in his study, going through his desk, and another night she took herself up to his dressing room. Well, I got her out, I did. Even the night of the murder, she was in his house, snooping around. I caught her coming in in the dark. She didn't think I was there, but I was." Mrs. McNally chuckled. "Cooked her goose."

"Belinda came into Lord Sutherland's house the night of the murders?"

The housekeeper backed off now. "Yes."

"Did you tell him?"

"No."

"Why not?"

The woman was kneading her hands. "I didn't think it was important."

"Mrs. McNally," Raine came around the desk to draw near to the lady, "when did you see Belinda Derwenter? What time that evening?"

"Half seven or eight o'clock."

"But you told the police you were out that night. Didn't you? *Why?*"

"I lied."

"Yes. *Why?*"

The woman began to snivel. "Because I knew he didn't come back when he said he did. If I told them I never heard him come in until eight or more, they'd arrest him, wouldn't they? Wouldn't they? Couldn't have that. He's a good man, he is. Anyway," she rubbed her nose and rummaged in her apron pocket for a handkerchief, "that Derwenter woman never said she'd come to the house. Never told the police she came and he wasn't there. She wouldn't dare. Got her precious reputation to protect, eh? I tell you she would watch her step on that, wouldn't she?"

Raine sought out one of the leather chairs. So there were four people who knew Gavin had not been at home that night when he claimed he had. Gavin. His housekeeper. His fiancée. And Raine.

"Why do you think Lady Derwenter was looking for something?" Raine glanced up at a stern-faced McNally.

"She was a spy for her father, I wager. That old coot never did like his lordship much. Just gave him lip service in the Commons. He let his daughter pretend to love Lord Sutherland just to learn what he could about him."

"Mrs. McNally, political infighting goes on often. You know it as well as I."

"Whatever it was, Mrs. Jennings, I tell you straight and true that that Belinda woman did not care for our Lord Sutherland as much as you do—*and* her daddy put her up to it, fer fair." She gathered her skirts. "I've got water on boiling," she excused herself and left Raine.

Raine's chowder was cold when she went to eat it. She sat instead, stirring it round and round.

The urge to draw zipped through her.

She took up Gavin's pen from his desk and a few pieces of his manuscript paper. She'd not used ink in ages, but the impulse to draw Belinda Derwenter, whom she had seen once in the visitors' gallery of the Commons, bloomed into a caricature of the woman. Tall and dark, a beauty with a serious gaze, a venomous glare, a sultry aspect most men would allow to overrule all other thoughts of her.

Without knowing it, Raine ceased the sketch to render another Derwenter. Sidney, this time. Healy next. Then Butler.

Why had she put them together on the same page?

She had put them on another page. She was certain. And . . . she knew where the drawing was, too.

She opened the French doors and darted across the lawn to her cottage. She went to her truck, snapped back the latches, lifted the lid, and swallowed at the sight of the sketchpad she avoided touching, the one she had used to draw Gavin arguing in Hyde Park.

Courage had never failed her. Even to look at her own mistakes. Hurting Gavin was her biggest one—and she flipped up the cover of her pad with no more thought before the pain of her actions hit her.

She paused. Ran her hand over the first pencil sketch of the man she had seen in the park a year ago and now loved with all her heart.

She recognized the sharp angles and harsh lines as her old cartoon style. But she didn't pause to criticize it or ridicule herself for it. She let her fingers turn the pages.

And memories flowed back like waves to the shore.

The first drawings in the book were of various subjects and scenes. Most were scenes she had witnessed from the visitors' gallery in Parliament. The place where she observed the world of politics which she enjoyed, and which became her venue to launch a sterling career as Raynard the Fox, the cartoonist for the *Times-Daily*.

Two others were conversations she'd witnessed among three MPs. One was of Sidney Derwenter, Ryan Ahearn, and Timothy Butler. It was a discussion which she, in her Raynard mode, rendered as a circle of hounds, conferring on the scent of the prey.

The next scene was in a drawing room, the owners of which she could not remember. This was a discussion among Ahearn, Butler, and Sean O'Malley. Raine got an eerie sense she'd drawn a scene equal to the one many saw when eminent Romans plotted to kill Caesar. She could not shake the foreboding.

The next sketch was the first drawing she had done of Gavin with his finger out pointing at Sean O'Malley in Hyde Park. Then the next was more detailed with a few other people standing by. Louise. Butler on the stump, hand up in full exclamation of some detail.

The next sketch was a finer one of Louise.

The next three were of the crowd. Curious faces. Angry ones.

The rest were all of Gavin.

Gavin with Sean and Louise.

Gavin walking away, murmuring to himself. His hands clenched. Striding past Ahearn and Healy.

Matthew Healy?

She flipped back to the three sketches of the crowd she had drawn. There he was.

She had forgotten he was there.

In the ensuing effort to put the scene on paper, she had forgotten her employer was present the day Gavin had argued in public with Sean O'Malley and Louise Stoddard.

Had Healy been interested in the Fenian cause that day?

She recalled his delight in her cartoon that Monday after the incident. How he enthused over it.

How he constantly monitored the demise of Gavin Sutherland's reputation after that. How he gloried in Gavin's resignation—and how he monitored Gavin's retirement to the country.

Thinking back on the months before she left the

Times-Daily, she remembered how Healy had never been so enthusiastic about any of her subsequent cartoons as he had been of the one of Gavin in Hyde Park.

She also recalled how he had encouraged her to take a holiday. He had chuckled one day as he noted how "Sutherland now advertises for a secretary. I doubt he'll get one, don't you?"

She stood.

Had Healy manipulated her? Used her to get at Gavin by encouraging her in her art?

She shrank back against the wall of her cottage, clutching her book, and closed her eyes in horror. If Healy had purposely done that, she had been his accomplice.

She did not know how long she stood there, fighting down the shame of that possibility. But suddenly, she was making her way back to the house. Mrs. McNally would wonder where she was, and she didn't want her to worry about such a small matter when they had so many big ones to ponder.

She ran back, closed the doors, and put her book down on Gavin's desk. She had to turn up the gas in three wall sconces because the office lay swathed in shadows.

She shivered and turned to view the night sky.

The moon was up. The sky soft black velvet. The wind picked up from the shore. It whistled through the rafters. She heard the hall clock chime half of the hour. Probably seven- or eight-thirty. Hours to wait yet to see if Gavin came on the next train.

She opened the book again, and this time she stood back to glare at another picture she'd created. A scene on a bright spring afternoon. Two men at luncheon in a cafe. One man with bright green eyes so verdant Raine wished for oils to paint them in. The other tall and dark, self-possessed, with the eyes of a predator.

A man she knew so well, a man who dined with politicians often because it was his job to know so much.

about government and issues. And controversies like the future of Ireland.

The memory of seeing Matthew Healy at luncheon should not make gooseflesh rise on her arms.

But it did.

Healy. Healy. Was he the center of this storm that had destroyed Gavin—and her?

The clock struck eight.

A clatter in the kitchen and a thump had Raine frowning. That sound was more than a pot falling to the kitchen floor.

"Mrs. McNally?" she called out before she pushed open the kitchen door and saw the woman's body sprawled across the tiles.

Raine cursed in French at the tall gangly man who stood before her. His dark eyes devoured her, reminding her of a scavenger. His looks, she thought for the first time, matched his professional standards. Of which, she now knew, there were none.

"Hello, Matthew." She glanced down to see his gun was calmly pointed at her.

"Tsk, tsk, my dear, no great joy to see me?"

Raine bent to the housekeeper. "You didn't have to hit her over the head."

"One must do that to some people who won't cooperate. I had to show her a bit of my power, didn't I?"

"She's bleeding," Raine damned him.

"She'll recover. Now if you'll oblige me and get me a length of rope, you can tie her up for me."

"Why?"

Healy chuckled. "Because you are going to help me and as you go about it, I want no interference from her."

"I don't know what you want, but I won't assist you. You have done enough to hurt us all."

"Your sentiments, my dear, are a little late and rather misplaced." He stepped forward and hovered above her. "Would you rather I shoot her?"

Raine rose, wiping the blood from Mrs. McNally's wound on her skirts. "No. There is a length of rope in the shed."

He followed her out, the gun firmly pointed at her back, while Raine tried to imagine how she might escape him.

When they returned, he ordered her to wrap Mrs. McNally's ankles in the rope and then her hands. Nonchalant, he said, "You are not surprised I am here."

"I expected you to come."

"How astute of you, my dear. But you have done nothing with the knowledge. Too bad your timing is so poor."

"You cannot escape detection," Raine warned him.

"I have so far."

"Neither will your friends," she added with great relish.

"Figured that out, have you?"

"Yes, I think I understand it. All of you conspired to create such havoc in the government that there'd be a crisis—"

"A war."

"That's not a solution. It's insanity."

"So that Ireland might be independent of Great Britain, anything is justifiable."

"You are pitiful," she challenged the man who had employed her and encouraged her to destroy an innocent man.

"Too bad you think so, Raynard. You may be smart, but alas," Matthew Healy feigned sorrow, "too late."

"I just want to know why Sean and Louise had to die."

"They did not wish to belong to our little group any longer. They wanted to run off and live a life of ease. Why should they have that privilege when so many of their countrymen wallow in poverty and hunger because of the damned English? Hurry up there. You're blasted slow." He poked the gun in her ribs.

She winced and made a show of tying the rope to the lion-footed leg of the stove. "Why were Sean's pockets turned out?"

"Hasn't Sutherland got a theory for that?"

She made a stab at the reason. "Sean took money that was not his."

"Wonderful, Raynard. You do exceed my expectations for perspicacity. I wish you'd not developed a conscience. You could have been on our side. It would have been more rewarding."

"To kill people? Slaughter them like animals?"

"One injustice deserves another."

"If you believe that, then your cause will truly fail," she said, sorry for him. "Where is your sense of right and wrong?"

"Gone. Destroyed by the British rule. Get up." He helped her to her feet and she shook off his assistance. "You will now show me around. I have a voyeur's need to see where the much maligned Lord Sutherland has spent his exile."

"What do you want?" she asked as if she could not predict his answer.

"The handkerchief, of course."

Chapter 15

"Everyone is a moon and has a dark side which he never shows to anybody."

—MARK TWAIN

RAINE HAD NEVER BEFORE BEEN IN GAVIN'S BEDROOM, but that was where Healy wanted to begin his search. The stark order of Gavin's private room personified the precise nature of the man she loved. Healy took glee in destroying it.

He swung open Gavin's armoire and riffled through the hanging shirts and chamois trousers. Dumped the contents of the drawers onto the carpet, so much tinder upon the fire of his rage. "Where the hell is it?" He rounded on her so often that she, without an answer, began to understand that if she had known where it was, she would have been dead before he and she had left the kitchen.

Healy was not to be outdone. "His dressing room, then?"

Raine did not bat a lash.

He came and struck her across the face. She swallowed her pain. Her ankles hobbled by a rope, her hands tied in more ways than one, she knew her chances for surviving this madman were slim. Somehow the resignation to it made her stronger. As if . . . as if her death did not matter as much as the fact that Gavin would survive. And she, sharp-witted even in this predicament, understood too how her parents and her brother had felt alone at the mercy of someone who would give none.

Healy tore Gavin's suits from their hangers, frockcoats and swallowtails piling high into evidence that he was failing.

"Has Sutherland got a safety box in the house?"

"No," she told Healy truthfully. "Not that I know of."

"I see. Come then." He yanked her by the arm and forced her back down the stairs into the office library. He pushed her into one of the leather chairs. The first place he destroyed was Gavin's desk. Papers flew into the air or slid in clumps to the marquetry floorboards. Pens, pencils joined them. A bottle of ink crashed and spilled.

His green eyes darted to the large cupboard.

No. Do not look there.

The conclusion that Gavin had hidden his handkerchief in that cupboard had long seemed the strongest possibility to Raine.

Healy tilted up his chin. "What does he use that for?" he asked rhetorically, all at once by the cupboard, trying to open little compartments. "Where's the key?" He rattled the main drawer.

"I repeat—" he lunged over at her and struck her across the other cheek, *"where?"*

"He carried it on him."

"How inconvenient." Healy pivoted and glanced about the room. Then he marched over to the fireplace and grabbed an andiron. He returned to smash the glass in the cupboard with such a ferocity that it showered over the room and Raine like prickly evil dust. She shut her eyes, ducked, but one piece struck her on her cheek and she tried to reach it with her shoulder but couldn't.

She had to get away from him. Had to at least try.

It was then she saw a movement at the garden doors. Brief. But it brought hope. When Healy struck the cupboard again and again, Raine saw Gavin slide into her view. His expression was dire. His chin jutted suddenly in the direction of the hall door. He wanted her to run for it. Lead Healy away from the garden doors. She wished she could make a dash for the door, but tied up as she was, the possibility of escaping was slim.

Still, a trickle of hope nourished her. But she balked. What chance of survival was there if Healy had a weapon and Gavin had none? She shook her head at him.

Anger flashed across his face. Sorrow, too. He motioned behind him and a wiry little man appeared, wearing the distinctive bowl-type hat of London bobbies. Gavin had brought help.

Slowly, she rose and began to inch her feet toward the hall. It took Healy a minute or more to notice. "Damn it, where are you going? Come back here." She didn't stop. "Come . . ."

She heard the sound of doors clattering to the walls, a gun blasted, glass shattered once again. Her leg burned with a hellish fire. Another shot rang out. And another.

Raine was losing her balance, her sight.

Then she heard some man yelling, "Get him fer Chrissakes! He's killed Sutherland."

Raine forced herself to turn. Her right leg was giving out. *"No!"* She was muttering in French. Stumbling to Gavin's body lying in a growing pool of blood upon the floor. Sinking down to lay beside him in an agony that she had not saved him at all, but led him to his death.

Ben had run to fetch the doctor from the next village north along the coast. The man arrived within the hour and put a tourniquet to Raine's leg wound, then ordered the policemen to move Gavin to his bedroom. Raine took a draught of morphine for her pain, but her wound was only the graze of flesh. She waited patiently for what seemed like forever, until he operated on Gavin, removed two bullets from his chest and shoulder, and assured her that he was breathing regularly.

"I think Lord Sutherland will recover with time and rest, Mrs. Jennings. You must let me tend you now."

Then the man who called himself Inspector Washburn echoed the doctor's sentiments. "Lord Sutherland will skin me alive, madam, when he comes to and realizes you are hurt. Have the courtesy to look repaired and in the pink, won't you?" He smiled with a stretch of his thin little lips, muscles which she thought he seldom used. "I was the one to reassure him we would be in time to save you from Healy. If you prove me wrong, I can never face your employer again."

As the doctor prepared to clean the scrape along her outer thigh, Raine was overjoyed to see a wobbly Mrs. McNally, with a patch on her noggin, come to hold her hand. "That's right, dear, you let this ol' sawbones do his duty. Then you'll be a-one, won't you?" She chuckled at her own joke. "His lordship'll need you to be better to help nurse him when he wakes up, won't he?"

Her wound drained her strength, however, and she couldn't walk around to tend Gavin very well. What she could do was sit by him, put cool cloths to his feverish forehead now and again, and chastise herself for the things she could have done to avoid bringing him to this pass.

Through Saturday and Sunday, he continued to be pale. Incoherent. Debilitated by the loss of blood and high doses of morphine to ease the pain. His condition, said the doctor, would improve. But the two bullets Healy had discharged hit Gavin very close to his heart. "Another inch to the left, and we would have lost his lordship instantly."

Raine had spoken at length Saturday about Matthew Healy with Inspector Washburn and the local constable. Gavin, Washburn, and a contingent of five bobbies from the London Metropolitan Police had traveled north from the capital city after they discovered that Matthew Healy had left on the afternoon train for Chipswell.

"Lord Sutherland had come to me Friday morning wit his publisher Ned Hollister to explain his actions over th last few months. He told me that he had decided to writ *The Accused* as true to life as possible. He said that h knew he must include the handkerchief because it was th only detail the murderer would know was real—and would make him or her commit some telling act. Aft Lord Sutherland and I saw each other Tuesday morning i his rooms at Brown's, I had revealed some facts tha allowed his lordship to put the puzzle together of wh killed Mr. O'Malley and Mrs. Stoddard."

"Can you tell me?" Raine asked. She saw no reaso why Washburn couldn't tell her because he had tele graphed his superior with the news of Healy's arre early this morning. At the same time, Washburn ha summoned reporters from many London and nation newspapers to recount the whole tale of conspiracy an murder. They had departed, chattering, eager to prin the story of how Gavin Sutherland had solved the crim of the century.

"I don't see why not," Washburn said. "The world wil soon know the details. Lord Sutherland cares for you ver much, Mrs. Jennings. He drove me and my two assistant mad to spur the horses and get here before Healy did. W failed you in that, of course, and I must apologize for th horrors he put you through." He indicated her bruise cheeks with a fingertip to his own. He glanced at her skirt and said, "I hope you will recover quickly. Lord Suther land sets great store by you."

"The feeling is mutual."

"So he said, Mrs. Jennings."

She comforted herself that Gavin was so protective o her that Gavin had not revealed her real name t Washburn. Gavin was also so confident of her regard fo him that he would declare his affection for her to a mar who was only an acquaintance. She sought to lea Washburn away from these personal issues, however

"How did Lord Sutherland learn that it was Matthew Healy who murdered those two people?"

"To put it short, he had his suspicions that O'Malley and Stoddard were in some sort of game they could not get out of. O'Malley's turned-out pockets gave him a clue, but he knew not what it meant. Neither did we. Then when Lord Sutherland came to London last week, he and I met. I told him a few facts he did not know." Washburn described a typewritten note to him exclaiming that Gavin had been at the Stoddard house the night of the murder. "I could not tell from his lordship's reaction to my revelation about the note if Lord Sutherland had been at the Stoddard house. But the note was unique in that it was typewritten—and so few people have the machines."

"Terrible contraptions," Raine muttered, telling him that Gavin had purchased one for her.

"Hate them, do you?"

"My fingers do not seem to work that way," she explained.

He smiled. "His lordship remembered the note was typewritten, a fact more important than I thought it to be. Anyway, after I left his lordship, one of my men followed him about the city."

"As protection?"

"No, ma'am. I did not fully believe Lord Sutherland innocent at the time. I put a man on him to see where he'd go and who he'd see. He saw a few men."

"Lord Falconer and his publisher."

"Yes. But between the two, he came across a hackney driver who led him to another man. This one told Lord Sutherland about two gentlemen who were constant visitors to Louise Stoddard. One was a member of the Atheneum club, another had business in Fleet Street. Lord Sutherland had a few other clues to the identity of the man in the publishing industry and went to Sir Edward Hollister to help him sort out his thinking. They came to me with their conclusions Friday morning."

"Which were?"

"Matthew Healy has often expressed his support o‍ Irish independence from Britain to Ned Hollister. A‍ long as Healy did not make it a major policy of h‍ newspaper, Hollister did not think much of Healy‍ position. But when Hollister also told Lord Sutherlan‍ that Healy was a close friend of Butler and O'Malle‍ Lord Sutherland thought it best to come to me with tha‍ I was able to put a few more facts together to conclud‍ Matthew Healy was a prime suspect. Healy has for man‍ years headed a ring of informants here in London for th‍ Fenians. With his interest in news, he kept his friends i‍ Ireland advised of the latest happenings in the goverr‍ ment. He insured his information was correct by payin‍ Louise Stoddard to regularly read her husband's paper‍ and pass on to her conspirators their contents abou‍ policy and funding for troops to be sent to Ireland."

"So when Louise finally fell in love with a man an‍ wanted to live a quiet life, she couldn't quit her espic‍ nage."

"Exactly, Mrs. Jennings. Healy nor his friends Rya‍ Ahearn and Timothy Butler wouldn't let her. Thei‍ arrangement had been too convenient and too produc‍ tive. When she refused sometime last June to give then‍ any more access to her husband's papers, they becam‍ furious. They told Healy. He followed them to Louise'‍ house the night Sean argued publicly with Lord Suther‍ land in Hyde Park. Healy wanted compliance or satisfac‍ tion, and when the two would not yield, he torture‍ them to prove his power. He had seen Lord Sutherlan‍ hand Louise his handkerchief in the park, and he stuffe‍ it into Sean's hand. There was blood on it and whe‍ Lord Sutherland found it that night in Sean's hand—"

Raine sucked in her breath.

"Oh, yes, Mrs. Jennings. Lord Sutherland told m‍ about its existence yesterday. I had suspected the hand‍ kerchief was real when I first read the description of th‍ murder scene in *The Accused*. All else about the scen‍

was so precise I had a feeling it had been in Sean O'Malley's hand, as Lord Sutherland had written that it was. When Lord Sutherland and I talked on Tuesday, I gave him to understand that if he were to find out the name of the murderer before I did, he must come and tell me. To his great credit, he did. He also told me how he had taken the handkerchief lest he be arrested for a crime he did not commit."

"And Healy?"

"I doubt he'll ever see the light from his prison cell, Mrs. Jennings. Treason is punishable by death. So is murder."

"And Ahearn and Butler?"

"They will suffer the same fate."

Raine sat by Gavin's bedside late that night and knew that a portion of her had died as well. Oh, yes, she rejoiced that Gavin was now free of the specter that had haunted him, washed clean by the arrest of the Fenian conspirators. But she knew too she had to leave Gavin quickly now more than ever.

Because if she might have harbored in her lonely heart the tiny possibility that she would reveal who she was and what she had done to him, she could not now.

She had been beguiled. Led by her own desire to be self-supporting, she had accepted Healy's offer of a promotion to editorial cartoonist. Healy must have seen her ambition. He certainly knew her interest in politics, encouraged her to attend sessions of Parliament and report back to him on debates. News was, after all, his stock in trade. And hers. Healy had only to cultivate her interests and reward her initiative by giving her the permanent job of cartoonist when her predecessor could not return to work. How fortuitous of the former cartoonist to become ill. How disastrous of her to accept the job, go at it with vigor—and lack of regard for an innocent man's reputation.

How naive of her.

Gavin could so easily wonder if she had drawn the cartoon because she was Healy's partner in crime.

Gavin might never ask. But she would always wonde if Gavin suppressed the question. In time, the silenc would drive a wedge between them.

No. She could never witness how she had kille Gavin's respect for her. She must go. On the first train t London Monday morning.

Chapter 16

"It is sweet to dance to violins
When Love and Life are fair . . ."

—OSCAR WILDE

GUS STOOD IN THE FOYER AT FORSYTHE HOUSE. "THIS MAKES no sense, Raine. You can't leave. Where will you go?"

"Any place where none of you can badger me about staying," Raine told her from the first landing.

The upstairs maid tucked her head down in an effort to pull a traditional servant's disappearing act. All the while she was recording the confrontation to repeat below stairs, Raine felt certain.

Bryce Falconer circled from behind his sister-in-law. He had arrived this afternoon to discuss with Gus plans for her parents' arrival in London and how they would handle the delicate issue of his and Colleen's divorce publicly and privately. When Bryce saw Raine had arrived home, he was stunned.

He exclaimed that he expected her to be in Chipswell with a recuperating Gavin. He waved a newspaper and said every city edition was sold out with the news of Healy's, Butler's, and Ahearn's arrest. All copies of *St.*

Andrew's with today's installment of *The Accused* ha
been sold since nine or ten o'clock. Bryce demanded t
know why she was here in London. Raine had told him
about how she had masqueraded as a widow to work fo
Gavin. She did not reveal why she had done it—or wh
she had left Gavin now.

"Raine, be sensible. The man is recovering from tw
bullet wounds. He will face a hail of police and politi
cians and reporters when he's up and about. He'll need
you. Gavin is a national hero for getting Healy to show
himself, and you helped to make him that. Yet you are
running from him? Don't you see that when Gavin
comes to his senses and finds you gone, he'll come here
looking for you?"

"Precisely why I'm leaving," Raine shot back, lifting
up her skirts. "You told him who I am, and he knows
where to find me."

"Of course, but I must tell you that Gavin needed little
help from me figuring out who you were, Raine."

"Bryce, I'm not accusing you of anything unethical. I
take all the blame for my lies on myself. And there is no
way to right the wrongs I've done Gavin."

"You could start by apologizing to him."

"Saying I'm sorry could never make up for my actions
No, Bryce, it is best that Gavin not see me again."

Bryce pounded the newel. "Dammit, Raine, the man
loves you! Whatever has kept you from him—"

"Is none of your business, Bryce."

"He is my friend, and he deserves a bit of happiness
after what he's been through."

"I cannot make him happy."

"Why not?"

"He is a politician, Bryce. He needs money to survive,
especially now that he will stand for a free borough.
Politicians in Britain need independent wealth. They often
acquire it from their fathers—or their wives. Gavin will
never go to the marquess again for money. Gavin will need
to find a sweet English girl to love and work with him."

"And support him?" Gus was amused at the very idea. Bryce laughed. "That'll be the day!"

"Both of you must listen to me." Raine was insistent. "I have nothing. Nothing but what I earn or what Uncle Skip gives me. We have all known it, but never had to discuss it. So let's not pretend I am like you, Gus, or Colleen or Ann. I am not."

Gus's petite frame shook with fire. "Raine, we have always agreed that money does not make a man or woman."

"We may have agreed, Gussie, but that didn't change the world. And this is England. We are not talking about America where circumstances of birth do not matter as much as what a person makes of oneself."

Raine shook off her tears. "Even if my parents had lived, I would never have been the heiress equal to the three of you. My father was a planter, a congressman—not a millionaire. And after the war . . . and all the destruction, I was needy of some family, some love. I came north with Uncle Skip. I lived in his house, ate his food, dressed in his clothes, went to the school he paid for. I was the poor relation. The orphan. I have worked. But we all know I wasn't earning my keep. When I went to work as an artist at *The Washington Star* and then here at the *Times-Daily,* I was investing in some self-respect. Then I threw it all away one day. . . ." She stopped, horrified at her outburst.

"Raine," Bryce pleaded, "I don't know what you're talking about but I do know Gavin has made his choice, and he wants you for his wife."

"Do discourage him from that, Bryce, I beg of you. I have hurt him enough."

"Gavin doesn't see it that way."

"Some conditions love cannot cure. You know this yourself, Bryce."

He looked as if she'd struck him.

"Oh, Bryce, I don't mean to hurt you."

"No, it's all right, Raine. I said the same thing to

Gavin last week. But he rejected the idea. Don't you se
why? He cares for you more than—"

"Not anymore, I'm sure."

"You can't know until you talk to him."

"But I don't want to know. Can't bear to find out—'
She'd lost him like so many others whom she had loved

Gus squeezed Bryce's arm. "Raine, there is a chanc
that you and Gavin are different from Colleen an
Bryce."

"We're not. Don't—" She took a step backward up th
stairs. "Please, don't continue this. Tell Gavin not to."

"What did he do to you, Raine?" Bryce was yelling
incredulous his friend could ever hurt her.

She was choking on the truth. "He loved me."

As Raine took the flight to her bedroom, she hear
Gus say to Bryce, "We must get Ann to come. She is th
only one left to talk some sense into Raine now."

Ann arrived within the hour from her home on th
Strand—and unfortunately before Raine's steame
trunk was full. Raine's cousin, younger by two years, ha
always been a person of strength and conviction. In th
last two years since she had married the love of her lif
and become his duchess and the mother of his heir, An
Brighton had transformed into an impressive force. I
she had been stubborn as a girl who had endured th
sufferings of a war-torn childhood, she was now a
businesswoman of great acumen and wealth. A woma
of logic and perception.

"Where will you go to escape yourself?" Ann aske
when no verbal greeting passed between them. Nor was i
necessary. Raine had known Gus and Bryce would di
vulge the argument they had had with her about leaving

Ann sat in a large wing chair near Raine's fireplace. Sh
arranged her turquoise silk skirts and removed her tid
matching hat. When Raine did not answer but went o
stuffing her gowns into the trunk, Ann sighed. "Th
newspapers this morning say that Gavin Sutherland con

tinues to recover from his gunshot wounds. He should be up and about in a week or two. Parliamentary sessions are filled with debate over the news that two of its members have committed high treason—and another died because he refused to continue to perform it. Gavin is heralded as the man of the hour. His heroic rescue of his housekeeper and his secretary add great drama to a tawdry story."

"I have read the papers, thank you, Ann."

"Well, then, let me tell you what is not printed there yet. Rhys has an interest in this mess because Timothy Butler sat in Rhys's borough in Dundalk."

Raine paused.

"Ned Hollister was just to see Rhys this morning. Rumors abound that the government will resign because treason and murder occurred on their watch."

Raine spun to face her cousin, joy arrowing through her. "Then there will be a general election?"

Ann nodded, her mahogany curls burnished like rich wine in the gaslight. Her voice was calm as she said, "Bryce has also told me and Rhys that Gavin wants to stand for Chipswell. That Mr. Pumphrey, the man who has represented the village for decades, may resign so that Gavin can run in this election."

"Oh," Raine clasped her hands together, "this is wonderful."

"Is it?"

Raine frowned. "What do you mean?"

"How can you care for a man and leave him when he is about to embark on reconstructing his entire life?"

Raine returned to her packing. "I cannot tell you."

"What are you afraid of, Raine?"

"I am not afraid. I confronted myself on this over a year ago and found my character wanting."

"Interesting. Did you note then that you are strong? You have been for all of us. Now you cannot be for yourself?"

"Strong is not the word I would use to describe myself. Reckless. Self-possessed. *Wrong.*"

"What did you do?"

"Ann, stop this."

"Did you stop when I would have married a man I didn't love?" Ann stoically prodded her. "Did you cease telling me what a mistake it would be if I didn't make peace with my father? Did you—"

Raine put a hand over her mouth. "I have lied."

"Raine, haven't we all?"

"I have done terrible things."

"How human of you."

"You don't understand, Ann."

"I think I do. You work for Matthew Healy's newspaper as an advertising artist. You earn a modest salary. One day you receive an increase in pay. I assume it is for work well done. Yet I do not see your art in the corset or the soap ads any longer. I see it elsewhere, under a pseudonym. Raynard the Fox."

Raine tried to keep a level head. "You knew from the beginning?"

"I have always known you had artistic talent. I understood you had ambition. You also had a desire to remain independent, in an effort I suppose to show my father and me that you had integrity. But sweetheart, you didn't have to demonstrate that. We knew. It was to be expected that when your talent was discovered and an opportunity given to you to make a career for yourself, you took it."

"And seized the first chance to create a scandal and ruin a man."

"You did it once, Raine."

"Once was more than enough. It implicated an innocent man in a crime he did not commit."

"The evidence against Gavin was circumstantial. Never enough to have the police arrest him, Raine."

"But he lost everything else because of my cartoon."

"Or did his opponents plan to hurt him for their own gain? Did other jackals rush to devour his career because of Gavin's own character faults? His anger, his impatience, his high sense of honor that demanded his party cohorts not desert him once they pledged their votes to him? Don't you see, Raine, Gavin contributed to his own undoing as much as your cartoon? Your drawing was the catalyst—"

"For his ruin."

"You put yourself on a rack ever since. Have you suffered enough?"

"No. My cartoon changed Gavin's life."

"So, I am told by Bryce, did your stay in Chipswell."

"What a joke on me. I try to correct the wrong I did, and I get caught in a bigger swamp. To think that I took so much time and care to tell you I wanted to go for a vacation to the sea, and you weren't fooled by my need for a different name."

"When I learned *where* you went, I knew *why.* Who was I to discourage you? You always stood by me when I felt compelled to do things that weren't exactly acceptable or logical."

"Have you told Rhys?"

"He is my husband, Raine. My other half. I do not keep secrets from the man I love beyond all others. You should not, either."

"I cannot make it up to Gavin for what I did."

"Didn't you try?"

"Yes, but any good I may have done was canceled by the fact it was my employer who was the murderer. Won't Gavin wonder for the rest of his life if I knew that—and cooperated with Healy to destroy him?"

"Can you live with yourself until you tell him you didn't?"

She did try.

Over the next two months, she really did try to tell herself that Gavin was better off not to see or talk with her again.

He was well. By the first of October, he had recovered physically enough to travel about to campaign. His schedule was printed in the newspapers in infinite detail and the crowds he drew numbered more than the inhabitants of Chipswell. Some editorials asked if Lord Sutherland were fated for more than merely a seat in the Commons. His speeches were reproduced verbatim.

The public could not get enough news of the man who had been resurrected from disgrace. They recounted how hale and hearty he appeared. How eloquent he was. How pursued he was by Chipswell and London hostesses. What an eligible bachelor he was, with a great future ahead of him.

And Raine had helped to make it so.

She took pride in that. And if there was jealousy that she had saved him for another woman to enjoy the benefits of her labors, she suppressed it in favor of a fine emotion.

She told herself she was glad for him.

But if that were so, why did she long for the sound of the sea as she remembered it from inside her little cottage while she was safe and warm in Gavin's embrace?

If she was so delighted for him, why did she curse herself that she could not share his happiness?

She was, in fact, quite miserable. Wanting once more what she could not have—Gavin, his love, and her own self-respect. Wanting what she would not take without confessing her wrong at the considerable cost of further damaging her self-esteem.

October drew to a cool end as it began to dawn on her that the damage to her character had already been done and could get no worse. She felt hollow, desiring little food, less company, and longing for sleep. And a raging need to see Gavin, face to face, happy at last. And inside her grew another need to tell him how sorry she was.

That same week in October and one week before the election, other news appeared that rocked Raine. William Pumphrey had died. Gavin attended the funeral in Chipswell village chapel. He called a moratorium on his campaigning in honor of the man who had endorsed him. Gavin's opponent—the man from Pumphrey's own party—could do nothing else but follow suit.

On election day, the voters of Great Britain gave Gavin's party the majority in the Commons. Among them was Gavin Sutherland, newly elected from Chipswell. The Queen would open Parliament next Tuesday by sending her usual speech, not her person.

Raine knew the time was right for her to see Gavin. She wanted him to begin his term with a clean slate, no hurts from the past to hinder him.

She wrote him a letter in Chipswell and asked him to meet her for tea Monday at a small tea shop in Bond Street.

He refused.

She was shaken. But she understood his reasoning. The day she had chosen was the one on which William Pumphrey's will was to be read in Chipswell. The man's solicitor had requested Gavin's presence, and Gavin could not refuse. Instead, Gavin politely wrote that he could see Raine the following week. She was to pick a time either Thursday or Friday afternoon, let him know what was convenient for her, and he would write again to inform her where to meet him.

His request sounded odd, but it was also definitely formal. A fact which pleased her because she could speak rationally to him if he had come to hate her. But a fact which tore her to pieces for the same reason.

Nonetheless, she jotted off an equally cool reply. Friday would be suitable.

The evening before, she received a letter which Gavin had penned and sent via messenger from Brown's. Evidently, he was staying at the hotel until he decided where his permanent lodgings would be. He told her to meet him at 14 Bedford Square at one o'clock and to be prompt. Insulted he should tell her to be punctual, and furious that he would think she could be so rude as to be late, she vowed to show up at half past twelve to be there when *he* arrived.

Jittery as a hummingbird, she alighted from her cab only to see his tall impressive form. His broad shoulders

stirred vibrant memories of him in her arms. His distinc
tive golden red hair sparked the recollection of wha
thick silk it was as it sifted through her fingers. But he
reverie was cut short by what she really did see here
Gavin was entering the house behind some woman.

The sight floored her. Why would he bring anothe
woman to this meeting? Had he taken up with some
one in the intervening weeks? Who was she? Wh
could she be? Probably some will-o'-the-wisp who sav
a good catch and snatched him up. An opportunis
who had invaded where Raine had left a vacancy
Anger and jealousy mixed with remorse in her chest
She marched to the Georgian brick house, up the ston
steps, and let the knocker drop with a bang. She woul
see who this woman was. Find out if she could possibl
love and care for Gavin with any—

"Mrs. McNally?"

"Hello, Miss Montand." She said it like any goo
Englishwoman should, *Mont-and*. Gavin must have tol
his housekeeper that his former secretary was a fev
things other than she appeared. Evidently, that sat al
right with the woman—and Raine was perplexed. In
trigued. "Come in, come in, 'is lordship and I arrived
bit ago. We thought you weren't coming for a while
'Ere—" She reached to pull on Raine's hand and get he
in the door. "Getting cool out there again, but oh, I d
love London. We've had such a go-round since you let
us, but it is wonderful to 'ave you 'ere."

"Thank you," Raine kept repeating, baffled as she'
never been before. The house was furnished to the gill
in true Victorian style, chock full of gleaming mahogan
and oppressive vermillion and forest green velvets. Th
circular stairs—broad, ivory marble—led up three sto
ries and were topped off by a glass-domed ceiling.

"Gorgeous, ain't it?" Mrs. McNally enthused as sh
followed Raine's gaze to the rafters. "I 'aven't seen th
like in all my years."

"Raine."

Gavin's voice came down to her as if he'd been watching her from heaven.

She scanned the banisters but did not find him until he stepped to the first landing. She had forgotten how formidable he could be. From this angle, he looked like the Viking marauder she'd compared him to that first day she had met him.

"Come up, Raine," he beckoned in a deep and emotionless voice.

She tried to keep from eating him alive with her eyes as she climbed the stairs. But her need betrayed her will.

He was beautiful, this man whom she had hurt. He was big and strong. He did not smile. He did not welcome her. He merely turned as she neared the top step and climbed the next flight of stairs. She followed, eager to see his face again, anxious to confirm for herself that he was recovered. But he wouldn't let her see his face. He kept it averted as she hastened her pace to come abreast of him on the steps.

When they made the second landing, he walked into a large sitting room through to a huge bedroom, past a water closet, and into an equally giant dressing room. Suits and men's attire jammed the racks. Men's shoes and boots were stacked in the shoe cubbies. Formal attire filled a third wall.

She heard the door latch click.

She turned and Gavin was pocketing the elaborate iron key.

"Why did you lock the door? Where are we and why are we here?"

"Sit down, Raine." Gavin indicated the only chair by men's black cutaways. He hitched his foot under a footstool and toed it under him. He put his foot on it and leaned over, one elbow to his thigh. His hands clenched and unclenched. He appraised her with narrowed gaze.

But he said, "You look well," as if he really didn't care.

His indifference made her eyes burn with tears. "Thank you," she managed. "You seem much improved—"

"From when you saw me last? Well, that is a matter of opinion, isn't it?"

"No." She did examine him. His color was better. He'd been out in the sun and the bronze of his straight bluntly cut hair was streaked with it. His skin shone with a tanned vigor. He made her mouth water with the desire to taste him on her lips.

Her eyes burned hotter.

She cleared her throat. "You do look healthy and . . ." *So mad at me.* She considered her gloves. "I won't take much of your time. I know you said to be prompt. You must be busy."

"Very."

At the gruff note of need, she looked up and his eyes were devouring her hair, her mouth, her breasts, her abdomen. But he stopped when her spine stiffened.

"I am damn glad you've gotten rid of the mourning clothes. I like this sapphire better." His words turned her mind into pudding. "It matches your eyes."

What was she supposed to say to that? "Congratulations on your election."

He stared at her.

"I am so sorry about Will Pumphrey."

He nodded, swallowed. That was the first sign of any emotion from him. Had he reverted to the brooding, hurt man she had met the day she applied to work for him?

If he had, all her hopes for him, all her love for him had gone for nothing. That slashed open her heart. But decorum had her saying ordinary things. "Mrs. McNall looks recovered from her . . ." Raine tore her gloves off, unbuttoned her suit jacket, rose, and had to step around him to reach the farthest point away from him. "I came to apologize." She faced him. "I came to explain."

"I often wondered if you could account for your lies."

"How does one ever do that?" she asked with an even tone that surprised her. "I want to try. I told you only one—and avoided telling others as much as possible."

"Finessed the words, did you?"

"Please, I—" She'd just get it over with. "I never was married to Winston. I thought saying that I was an attaché's widow would be a good way to explain why an American was in England and throw you off the scent of . . . who I really was." She squared a shoulder, but oh, how she wanted to run. "I could not bear to tell you I had drawn that cartoon, that I was Raynard. I was horrified at what I had done. Its implications and then I . . . I had to make it up to you."

His mouth softened. His dimple appeared. He looked as if he had a thousand things to say, but wouldn't. How well he had learned the art of patience.

"I know you must hate me. I wouldn't blame you. I—" She stuck a finger in her collar. "Why are we in this closet? It's very hot and I need—"

"I need to insure that you won't run away again."

"What?"

"I chose Will's dressing room because it is the farthest point from the front door."

"This is Will Pumphrey's house?" She should have known from the decor so similar to the man's home in Chipswell.

"Yes. Do you like it?"

"It's lovely."

"It's mine."

"But . . . how?"

"He gave it to me in his will. Said I had Chipswell, so I should also have what came with it. The means to do my work without fear of financial need." He walked away, leaned a shoulder against the wall, and crossed his arms. "You were saying . . . what?"

She could only think of that other house he had wanted to buy and share with her. "What have you done about the Parker house?"

"I bought it."

"Oh."

"With my royalties from *The Accused*. Ned tells me there'll be more as the series continues, and then there

will be quite a bundle when he prints it in book form
For now, I have invested in a cruise line company tha
brings in about twenty percent growth profits per year.

She laughed at the network of friends who had helpe
to restore Gavin to his rightful station. "The Guardia
Shipping Line?" Her Uncle Skip's and Bryce's venture

"Bryce advised me it was a solid means to make a
annual income."

"I see. Well, you should do very well then." He ha
more than she ever expected him to regain. As sh
examined him, she realized he was amazed himself.

"I have two houses, where I need them. I have a job t
do which I love. I have a regular income from inves
ments earned on a writing project that brought m
fortune and fame—and freedom. In fact, I am so sati
fied," he told her with assurance, "I wonder what else
could want in this world."

"I am happy for you," she told him in a whisper.

"I am so very glad one of us is." His anger flamed.
Blasted her open.

"Oh, Gavin, I acted irresponsibly for my own purpose
Foolishly. For my own self-serving ends. I was an artist a
Healy's paper. I drew ads for soap and stockings an
corsets. I made a little money and I wanted *more.* I wante
to be free from my uncle's generosity. After years of livin
with him and Ann, I felt it was charity and I dreamed o
living on my own, supporting myself. But I never mad
enough money to do that. Not unless I left Forsythe Hous
and went to live in a terrible part of the city. And I wa
weak, afraid to do that, afraid to live without people whos
company I enjoyed and loved and needed. . . ." She woul
not cry now, but apologize and leave.

"Our arrangement seemed so acceptable," she said on
ragged breath. "I was an unmarried woman after all. A
American girl, brash and expected to do different thing
from the English ladies. I was no American heiress but
was fortunate to be surrounded by family and friends. W
all seemed to have a secret pact, Uncle Skip and Ann

Colleen and Gus and I. We silently ignored the fact that I was different from Ann and Colleen and Gus."

"Society dubbed you one of the American Beauties."

"Wit." She said it ruefully.

"So I have heard from others."

His emphasis on the last word made her ashamed of her lies to him again. But then he said, "They were not wrong in their assessment, Raine," and she took the compliment as balm for a wound so wide she wondered if she'd ever find a cure.

She glanced at him. He wasn't smiling, but he appeared to be more inclined to listen to her with some equanimity.

She hurried to tell him all and leave.

"One day Healy came to me in the artists' pool and asked if I would substitute for the newspaper's cartoonist. The man was sick, and Healy needed to fill a gap on the editorial page. I jumped at the chance. Healy liked my work. Asked for another and another. When the cartoonist became more ill and couldn't return to work, Healy offered me the job permanently. I was overjoyed. Here was the opportunity to become self-supporting. I took it."

"As anyone would."

"Yes," she said with disgust. "And what did I do with my precious opportunity? I tried to make a name for myself."

"Doesn't everyone who ever takes a job?"

"They do it ethically."

"*Do* they?" He was sarcastic now.

"They try."

"Raine, I cannot believe you didn't."

"Worse, I thought I did. I used to go to the visitors' gallery in the Commons to listen to the debates. I'd frequent Lotham's cafe where gossip came with the menu, and politicians dined with their friends and foes. I strolled in Hyde Park. One afternoon in June I saw a man who was an MP arguing with a colleague and that man's mistress. I recognized all three. I went to my office, drew the scene, took it to my publisher, and I wanted to print it. In the days between me drawing the cartoon and taking it to my employer, the two in the park had been murdered. The cartoon, I knew, would establish a confrontation between the men. Little did I know that they might actually suspect the angry man of murdering the two only hours later. But it did—"

"Because there were things you did not know about that argument."

"Oh, of course," she waved a hand in sarcasm, "let's dismiss it with that. My cartoon contributed to the public's knowledge, didn't it? I was performing a public service, wasn't I?"

"Yes, you were."

"That does not justify what I did."

"You and how many others, Raine?"

"They don't matter to me, Gavin." She put a fist to her chest. "I take responsibility for what I did. I was the first to expose you to ridicule and accusations. After me, the reporters came like a pack of dogs. The police came to ask you questions. I created a public outcry for your statement, your resignation. Your family deserted you."

"My father turned me out. I have since learned that a loss I can bear, Raine. Perhaps, in time, he'll come to me. Ask for forgiveness or understanding. But then what will it profit him? Our relationship is forever altered. When I needed him, he was not there to support me. He will live with that."

"So will you."

"If it was not the false accusation of murder to bring my father to that point, don't you realize it would have been some other cause? Some other event would have shown me what was most important to him? Don't you see that he and I would have parted over some point in the future? We would have, Raine. Like you, I am not a person who takes charity for long without seeing the toll it takes on my integrity."

"You had great integrity before this happened."

"So did you, Raine."

She shut her eyes.

"Look at me." He waited patiently until she could. He looked awfully blurred through the tears that brimmed along her lashes. "You still do."

"How can you say that?"

"Because I saw what courage it took to come to me and apply for the position I had. A woman for a man's job. A woman alone, doing what she felt compelled to do for so many good reasons. I see that same courage now."

"I am here only to tell you firsthand how I hurt you, destroyed you. I didn't come here to show you my courage or anything else."

"You're so noble, darling. And you show me the real you. Finally."

"Mon Dieu, Gavin. Don't uphold me. Can't you see, I am trying to tell you how sorry I am. How wrong I was."

"I hear you. I accept your apology. I hope you're going to try to never hurt me again."

"Oh, God, no. I *love* you. How could I ever—?" She froze with what she'd said.

He went to stone.

She sank against the wall. It was the only solid substance in a world convulsed by the horror that she had now declared the very emotion that would do neither of them any good. "That was the one thing I did right," she told him with conviction.

"Is it also right to go on punishing yourself?"

"I never thought," she said slowly, "I did that."

"Perhaps not. I think you developed a stern sense of justice because you have lived with the injustice of war and the loss of your family. Whatever the cause," he took a step nearer, "you have suffered enough. It's time to stop."

"I can never go back—"

"Thank God."

"Never change what I did."

"You did something much better, darling."

"I—"

"You saved me."

"Gavin, you had the idea to write the novel. To duplicat[e] the murder. You thought to bring the criminal out. Yo[u] saved the inquest notes and the newspaper clippings."

"And you put them all together for me. Made order o[f] the chaos of my mind." His hands were pulling he[r] forward. "Like one of your recipes, you put them al[l] together and added the right pinch of ingredient[s.] Things I needed, Raine. You gave me help, laughter[,] insight. Hope."

She would have objected again when he caught he[r] shoulders. "Will you make us both unhappy for the res[t] of our lives because of one mistake you made a year an[d] a half ago?"

He brushed a tear from her cheek. "I have everythin[g] today I wanted in this world before the day you saw m[e] in Hyde Park. I have position, my own money, influenc[e,] recognition. But I don't have the one ingredient to mak[e] the dish divine. I don't have you, Raine."

"You still want me?" It wasn't even so much a questio[n] as a startling vindication. As if Gavin had brought her i[n] from a storm into a house with the promise of sunshine[.] She threw her arms around his neck.

"Need you. Have to have you. Won't find much joy i[n] my good fortune without you." He cupped her face[.] "Marry me."

She kissed him for an answer.

He took her lips again and again as if to brand her wit[h] his ardor. His arms clamped around her as if to prove t[o] them both she could not fly off. "Promise me you won'[t] ever keep secrets from me or leave me alone."

"Never again."

"Oh, *mon coeur*," he crooned into her ear, "I love you.["]

Epilogue

"How happy we are here!"

—QUEEN VICTORIA OF BALMORAL

December 1879
London, England

GAVIN LET HIMSELF IN THE FRONT DOOR, HUNG HIS HAT AND coat in the hall closet, and took the marble stairs two at a time. He'd come home later than expected—two hours later—and he expected his wife to be in bed.

Precisely where he wanted her, God knew. But not exhausted—and his supper party at Brooks's with Bryce and Ned and two of the party organizers had gone on much longer than Gavin predicted.

Just when he wanted to be home with her, he was called away. Repeatedly. It was the price of his public service.

Raine never minded. She had her own occupations. "I use my time alone," she had told him soon after they had married in December of '77, "to do what I need for myself."

Bearing two children in two years, she had her hands full. They employed a nurse for Marie, who was fourteen

months old, and William, who was two months toda
But Raine was an attentive mother, singing to ther
taking them out for daily strolls in the new doub
carriage. He chuckled. Last week he came upon h
waltzing with Marie in her arms in the upstairs nurser
Raine even insisted on breast-feeding her children,
terribly unfashionable endeavor for most women of the
class.

But Gavin encouraged her, applauded her, adored he
And with two pregnancies in a short time, he had ver
few chances recently to demonstrate his devotion phys
cally. They often laughed together that they had mac
love often before they were married, but no seed ha
ever come of their union. Not until after they were we
They agreed it must be marriage which, like the or
ingredient that makes an entrée a pièce de résistanc
ensured they had two priceless proofs of how well the
were matched.

This morning, before he left for his office, Raine ha
hooked her arms around his neck and urged him back
bed. "I think I am recovered enough that we can b
lovers again." They had had three months of abstinenc
and the renewal of their physical union had made toda
a joy. Created a rash he needed to cure again with th
sweet balm of her body.

This woman who was his wife was so many things t
him. His hostess, his campaign manager, his confidante
had also transformed into a hot enchantress in his bec
To have her once was to plant the desire to enjoy he
again. This morning, starved as he had been for so lon
while she gave birth and recovered, he had made lon
gentle love to his wife. When he left her in their bed, h
was sated—and not.

She had known, smart woman. "When you com
home tonight," she had winked at him before he lef
their suite, "I think we must meet like this again."

He took his shoes off at the top landing and tiptoe

down the hall. If she were asleep, he didn't want to wake her. He felt great disappointment that she would be.

Until he opened the door. Dropped his shoes. Removed his coat.

He could not stop his grin from spreading at the sight of her.

"Hello." She peered at him over her new little reading glasses. They were, he noted with instant sexual arousal, the most substantial thing the lady wore. She had donned the diaphanous lingerie set he had insisted on buying her in Florence on their wedding trip. The damn things were sky blue, trimmed with cream lace, and beautifully translucent.

She cocked her head to one side, removed her glasses, and put aside her sketchbook. "I've finally revised the drawings for my children's story. If I tell the tale with each of them as animals, it's more amusing."

"I'm pleased you've found your medium. Ned said tonight he wants to see it when you're done."

"But he doesn't publish children's books."

Gavin worked at the buttons of his waistcoat. "He says he made so much money from one Sutherland author, he'd try another."

"Why doesn't that famous author come over here," she crooked a finger, "and give me a kiss?"

He never refused such an invitation.

"Mmm," she licked her lips, eyes closed, "absinthe."

He sat on the arm of her chaise longue and gave her another sample. "Champagne, too."

"No pipes?" she asked, her fingers diving into his hair.

"I think I'll quit. Don't like the taste anymore."

"Good," she oozed in that sultry voice which never failed to start an erotic melody in his blood. "I have a few other ideas about what you can do with your mouth." She cupped his face and graced him with a thorough example.

"I'm so glad you're awake," he told her as he slid the

peignoir and gown off one shoulder to nuzzle her fra
grant skin.

She purred deep in her throat. "I couldn't think c
sleeping. I thought of you all day."

"How convenient." He stood and pulled her up int
his arms. "Coincidental, too."

"Really?" She was shivering charmingly as he pushe
her ensemble down her curves to fall to the floor.

"I didn't get much done today. I should have com
home to work on a project I have in mind." He put a
arm behind her back and caught her up so that he coul
relish her breast. The smoothness of her satin nipple wa
complemented tonight as it had been this morning b
the warm candy of her milk.

Her nails dug into his shoulders. Her head was flun
back, her moonlight hair rivering to the carpet. God
how he loved the sight of her enraptured with him
She made him feel strong, noble, proud, hungry
"What . . ." she tried for breath, "is your project?"

"Loving you until we can't talk or walk."

"I always did like your policies," she crooned as h
took her other breast in his mouth. "I have a few plan
I'd like to implement myself."

"Whatever you want . . ." He was losing track o
conversation as she undid his cravat and began takin
out his shirt studs. "Tell me."

She kissed his dimple. "I'd like your tongue."

His eyes drifted open.

Hers were hard with need.

"Where?" he asked, thinking how cool he sounde
when his skin was on fire everywhere her fingers went.

She grasped his hand. "Here," she put his palm to he
throat, "and here," her firm thigh, "and here." Her we
womanhood.

"Why, Mrs. Sutherland, you astound me. You are
becoming quite a tart." His fingers sluiced her and
anticipated how savory the cuisine was going to be.

"Well then, sugar, you better come have a taste."

He hooted, reveling in his good fortune.

She led him by the end of his cravat to their bed. She had, sometime earlier, turned down the counterpane and plumped up the pillows. She gave herself over to helping him undress. "You are quite a treat yourself, you realize," she said, concentrating, her tongue darting to the corner of her lips.

"Darling, I'm only—"

"English meat and potatoes? Much more. You've got these nice arms." She ran her splayed fingers up his biceps. "A bit of ham. Always good for a politician."

He snorted as her hands yanked out his shirt from his trousers and her mouth skimmed his torso. "A wonderful rack of ribs."

"Raine—" He was going to lose control any second and not be able to treat her tenderly if she didn't hurry. "Can you step this up a bit, *cherie?* I'm not—"

"Simmering a bit is good preparation."

"Roasting is more like it."

She slid her hands inside his trousers, let them fall to the floor, then flicked off his small clothes. She pressed herself against him and ran her hands down his back to squeeze his buttocks. "Hard buns." She tilted her head, mischievous brat, and rubbed her breasts against him as she whispered, "Want to know what I love most?"

"Do tell me quickly, madam, so that I—"

The air whooshed from his body as she wrapped her hand around the part of him that craved her most and said, "Your banger."

He had her on her back before she could tempt him speechless. "You're a witch."

She grinned and undulated beneath him. Her hands in his hair, her legs around his hips, her succulent body opening for him, taking him, welcoming him.

"Raine." He got lost in her, said a dozen spontaneous things that made so much sense, and drove her to loud moans of delight. And in the mating, as he always did, he found intricate meanings of his love for her.

Much later, he told her, "I think we need to do this again so that you get what you want."

She languished against the pillows, his naked siren with the voluptuous contours of a young mother. She ran a fingertip up his chest. "But I did."

"You needed to go slowly."

She arched a wicked brow. "I needed you any way I could have you. Besides, if you don't think you got it just right, you can try again."

"Give me a few minutes and I will."

"Tell me about what happened at supper."

"Ned has sold *The Accused* to French and German presses. The first American printing has sold out. I can safely say that you and I are going to be rather well-set financially, no matter if the Guardian Shipping Line sank tomorrow."

She beamed. Gave him a big smacker on the lips. Flung an arm over her head and wormed her way back into the pillows. "And your speaking tour of New York and Washington?"

"Plans are firming up for the summer, instead of spring." At first she hadn't wanted him to go, but when he said he'd never go anywhere without her, she had rejoiced at the idea of visiting the two American cities she had lived in. She had balked at the prospect of leaving the children in England, however. "I think we can afford to take Marie and William now. And the nurse." He was not interested in taking his two sweet babies on a transatlantic trip if he and Raine didn't have help.

She sat up. "I'm glad we'll be home for Uncle Skip's ball in honor of Gus. She needs our moral support. She's so nervous about who might snub her because of Colleen and Bryce's divorce."

"I know you want to stay for it. That's one of the reasons I told Ned we couldn't go until June." He dropped a kiss to her shoulder. "Another is that my father came to see me this afternoon."

Raine stared at him, openmouthed.

"He took a while to get to it, but he apologized. His months without Mama have taken their toll. He wishes us to come to Cranborne Manor for the christening party of Derek and Darcy's baby."

"He spoke to you only once at Derek's funeral last autumn. If your mother hadn't invited us and stood her ground when we arrived, he might have asked us to leave."

"But he didn't, did he? In the last few months, he has changed even more, I think. But I gave him no answer about visiting. I told him I would consult with you and write to let him know."

"Do you want to go?"

"I do. He is much changed. The fact that I have been successful and our marriage is much praised in society as a grand alliance has affected him in a positive way."

"Despite his dislike of Darcy's American boldness?"

"My father resented her honesty to tell him she had never loved Derek." Gavin's oldest brother had married his American beauty for her money—and discovered that for all Darcy Warfield's charm and fortune, he did not love her. They had endured a brief six-month marriage, in which Derek had taken an old flame as a mistress—while he had impregnated his wife with his heir. Then, to make the muddle worse, Derek had died in a riding accident, leaving Darcy about to give birth to the future marquess of Cranborne—and desperately in love with her brother-in-law, Reginald, Gavin's younger brother by five years.

"Now he resents her turning to Reggie for comfort."

"And blames Darcy for turning Reggie's head. Sad and true. But Darcy and Derek's unhappy marriage showed my father that he cannot control everything. Now that Darcy and Reggie admit they have fallen in love, my father realizes he controls so very little about any of us." Gavin sighed. "It is so odd to see my father with the wind gone from his sails, but he has become mellow. I am certain my mother's new assertiveness has much to do with that, too. So to answer your question, yes, I want to go to the christening. But only if you come with me."

"And Marie and William. I want your father to meet his grandchildren. It will do him good."

How many ways did this woman satisfy him? In the thousand ways he never even knew he needed—until she gratified him with her perceptions and her sweetness. He touched her cheek. "I would like to go as a family, yes."

She scrambled up on her knees, her hands clasped demurely between her parted legs. He shifted, his desire for her humming in his ears, as she said, "What about Bryce? How is he?"

"Fine physically. But harried as usual. He's darting between London and Aldersworth once or twice a week to keep his business appointments here and make certain Ford is happy at home. Bryce looks like he hasn't slept in months. He had the eye patch on again tonight."

"His old fencing wound bothers him when he's over-worked."

"When he heard we are going to America, he said he's considering going himself this summer and taking Ford, too."

"Why would he go to America?"

"To inspect his cattle ranches in Texas and Kansas. He hasn't been back since he bought into them with Skip in '73. Besides, I think he wants to escape the brouhaha here."

"About Colleen?" she asked.

"Yes. He has learned she has a new lover."

"Any ideas who it is this time?" Raine wondered.

"I doubt we want to know." Gavin put his hands to Raine's waist and led her to straddle him. His friend's loneliness and frustrations as a single parent only under-scored how fortunate Gavin was to have the love of his life in his bed in his home, with his children well cared for by her. He weighed her breasts in his hands. "I feel so

rry for him." He thumbed her nipples and the dia-
onds he produced made him suppress a groan.
cannot think how I would carry on if I ever lost
u. . . ."

She brushed his lips with hers. "You can't."

He explored her mouth with delicate thoroughness.

She caressed his torso down to his thighs and found
hat she wanted, then positioned herself over him.
And what news of the state of the union, hmmm?"

"That depends on precisely which union, darling, you
ave in mind."

"Why Britain, of course," she purred, teasing him
ith a lengthy kiss. "What did Richard and Albert have
say tonight about the party's chances in the next
ection?"

"It's ours." It was the last thought that made any sense
she took him inside her.

She arched, as incapable of speech as he. The affairs of
ritain would have to wait while he insured his own with
s wife.

Afterward, she sank against him and said the words
at gave his life untold worth. "I love you, Gavin
itherland."

He smiled, content. It had been so simple to love this
oman from the start.

Author's Notes

So many of you have written to me over the years, delighting in the many historical details I work into my novels. In the American Beauties series there are so many, I've created a newsletter to try to give you more pleasure in them all.

Three of the interesting tidbits in *Never Again* are:

Members of Parliament did not earn a salary for their public service until 1911. A man did need to have private income from his family, wife, friends, patron, or his political party in order to stand for office—and then to keep it.

Grebes—these funny little birds who carry their chicks on their backs—really were almost extinct in the latter half of the nineteenth century. Organizations did form to persuade the government to protect the wildlife from the demands of the millinery trade.

Newspapers in England did report everything and anything they could get their hands on. Inquest notes, autopsy reports . . . not much was sacred. Journalism was not regulated. The voraciousness of tabloids was born in this era—and we see its legacy today.

What did *not* happen—what is my fiction here—was the general election of 1877 caused by a scandal of murder, treason, and corruption. I have taken the background of what was becoming a terrible problem—the inability of the British Government and the Irish citizenry to find a peaceful solution to the need for equality of the Irish before the law. Happily, both countries seem to

have come to a solution more than one hundred and
twenty years later.

I hope you'll join me for *Never Say Never,* the third
novel in the American Beauties series, when Gus
launches into the whirl of another London season. She is
sought after by many a beau, but can't seem to fall in
love with any of them. Her sister Colleen continues to
overshadow Gussie's happiness with her scandalous
behavior. Then Colleen commits a heinous crime—and
Bryce seeks out the only person who can help him. Gus

Please write to me, send a legal-size self-addressed
envelope, and I will gladly send you the latest issue of my
American Beauties Newsletter—"Never-Neverland."
Then you'll receive it regularly. In it, you'll find more
delicious little facts about "those American gels" who
enchanted European men with their humor and spunk.

My address is:

4319 Medical Drive, #131–298
San Antonio, Texas 78229–3325

Also visit me on line at:

jpoweron@aol. com

For a look at my other novels and excerpts from them,
visit my website at

www.romanceweb.com/joannpower.htm

or

www.tlt.com/authors/jpower.htm

Happy Reading!

February 1880
London, England

I'll abduct her.

If she won't help me, I'll force her.

Committing such a violent act made Bryce Falconer smile sardonically. But the injustice of kidnapping this innocent woman made him curse.

He flipped up the collar of his greatcoat against the sleet that had dogged him south from his home for the past three hours. He could have arrived in London before this damned dinner party started if it hadn't been for the storm.

Yet now that he had arrived at Forsythe House, he froze in place. An ice man, standing in a barren garden, staring at the only person in the world who could help him.

And what was Augusta VanderHorn doing as his world was battered by a crime as ugly as this storm?

Bryce rubbed a gloved finger beneath his eye patch and studied her.

Gussie was doing what she usually did. Chuckling.

Tonight she did it with her friends—and his—Ann and Rhys Kendall and Raine and Gavin Sutherland. Gussie was bubbling over some matter. Typical of her to do that, creating a life—and an identity distinct from her sister, Colleen. Dodging the demands of her mama to marry as nobly as her notorious sibling. Living down the scandals Colleen created and tarred her with. Joking often. As she was now and charming the suspenders off one more English man.

The trilling sound of her voice permeated the panes of glass in the garden doors. The delicacy of it rushed through Bryce, warming like brandy. Boiling his blood.

Damn Colleen. She destroyed his enjoyment of everyone. With her new outrage, she could ruin the best friendship he'd ever enjoyed with a woman. Despite the fact that the very female was his former sister-in-law.

Bryce marched toward the kitchen entrance. He hoped to God none of the servants was using the back stairs. He'd scare the hell out of them, breaking in like a thief.

He'd do it anyway. He did not want to go in the front doors and confront the Kendalls and the Sutherlands with their questions. He needed to talk only to Gussie. Alone.

He pushed in the door and stood a moment inside the threshold. Shivering as the heat of the house chafed his face, he listened for sounds. No servants were on the stairs. No music came from the drawing room. Doors slid open. Voices drifted as people bid each other good night.

Bryce took the stairs two at a time up to the second story. He knew where Gussie's bedroom was. He had been there before when the suite had belonged to

Colleen, before she and he were married . . . and his life became a nightmare.

Five years ago, he had entered this way three times. Colleen would ensure the lock was off this same door, and he would enter at precisely one o'clock, stealthy as a tomcat, up the curving staircase to her suite on the second floor. There on her divan, she allowed him liberties that whetted his appetite for all of her. By his third visit, he had put her to her bed and satisfied himself—and her, too, he believed—planting the seed for his son and heir Bradford. Establishing the need for their hasty marriage. Inviting a she-devil into his heart and home only to make a mockery of love and marriage and now, even motherhood.

Tonight, Bryce had come intending to enter through the front door of Forsythe House. He'd wanted to be polite, to ask to see Gussie, to be rational about this matter. Skip Brighton, who rented the house and who was Gussie's guardian in England, would let him in. Skip and Bryce had been friends and business partners for seven years.

But when Bryce's coachman had stopped before 15 Belgrave Square, Bryce had peered through the tall drawing room windows and had not seen Skip among the six who laughed together. Nor did Bryce find Ellen Newton, the duenna whom Skip had hired to chaperone Gussie. Bryce had seen only Gussie with the Kendalls and the Sutherlands. Bryce also noticed the other man. The one Gussie flirted with. The one whose hand lingered so long at the small of her back.

Who was he? Why did the man merit an invitation to a little dinner with Gussie's friends?

Bryce let himself inside her bedroom and paused in the gaslight, shrouded in a fresh misery. Was she finally interested enough in some man to ask him to small at-home?

The picture of Augusta VanderHorn naked across some man's bed flashed into his head. It startled him.

Even more surprising, it saddened him.

Hell, what was wrong with him? He always knew the day would come when she would marry and become less available to him. Less inclined to see him on a minute's notice.

No matter. She would see him tonight.

He swept off his top hat, upending it on her cluttered reading table. He tugged off his gloves and dropped them in his hat. Removing his greatcoat, he spread it over the wing chair before her fire. Gussie appreciated warmth and always requested strong fires to receive her.

But the flames that began to heat his body were doused by the chill of what he saw on her mantel.

A dozen or more photographs of Ford graced the ochre-veined marble. In gilt frames or silver, square or oval, big or small, stood the cherubic face and form of his darling boy. Some of these pictures Bryce had himself. Gussie had given duplicates to him as soon as she took one which passed her standards for excellence. But her collection included the ones which were too under- or over-exposed. The ones which were blurred with the movement of a child who could not sit still to wait upon the foibles of a camera.

Tears at Ford's loss choked him. He clamped his eyes shut. He could not gaze at these!

He spied a chair in Gussie's bedroom beyond the sitting room. He would wait there. Where he could not see the photographs of his son. Where he could see the bed in which his boy was conceived—and where he himself had lost his mind and his soul to a woman who was not worthy of any sacrifice. It was hell's own irony.

that he would sit here tonight, where he could gird himself to view Augusta VanderHorn, not as his friend, not as his confidante, not as his ex–sister-in-law, but as the only person who knew where Colleen had taken the one person he loved in this world.

His son.

Gus cocked a brow at Ann Kendall and Raine Sutherland. They were donning their coats to go to their respective homes with their husbands. The two men stood by the front door, debating a topic of their own. "I can't wait until lunch tomorrow. Tell me now what you think of Lionel."

Ann's expression went deadpan. "Do I detect anxiety?"

Raine went wide-eyed. "That sound we hear of drilling in the floor? She's tappin' her foot, sugar."

"Let's leave before the floor caves in."

Gus was grinding her teeth. "If you don't tell me right now what you think of Lionel Eldridge, I will spit."

Ann feigned shock and looked at her cousin Raine. "Thank God there are no reporters here to put that in the gossip columns, Raine. Why, we'd be lambasted again as those gauche American 'gels' who—"

"Ann," Gus was insisting, "be quick about this."

Ann glanced at Raine, her tone matching her imposing title of the Duchess of Carlton and Dundalk. "Darling, were we cold?"

Raine flattened a palm to her chest. "Why, I do declare, warm as butter over flapjacks."

"I'm going to warm your ears in a minute, if you don't tell me—"

Ann grinned. "He's certainly qualified to become the husband of the most eligible American heiress in London this season."

"*Comme ci, comme ça,*" Raine reflected. "He's g[o]
nice ears, sweet chocolate eyes, and—"

"Raine."

"A few other assets." Raine checked Ann's gaz[e]
"Shall we?"

"First," Ann raised her hand and one finger, "an[d]
most important to your mama—"

Gus relaxed. This was their routine the three o[f]
them called the "Tally," their analysis of all potenti[al]
suitors who crossed their paths. Ann, Raine, and Gu[s]
had perfected the repertoire for Gus. Heaven knew
Gus had been approached by many an eager bachelo[r]
from the Isle of Wight to the tip of the Highland[s]
since she'd debuted here in London two years ago
She had no illusions about her appeal. Her looks wer[e]
more perky than pretty. Her dowry, more allurin[g]
than the infamy by which her sister shamed her
Augusta Roberta VanderHorn was the last of the fou[r]
famed American Beauties yet to be married. Ann
Brighton had married Rhys Kendall, the sixteent[h]
Duke of Carlton and Dundalk. Raine had found th[e]
love of her life in famed novelist and member o[f]
Parliament Gavin Sutherland. Gus's sister, Colleen
had married the twelfth earl of Aldersworth, Bryc[e]
Edward Falconer, borne his son, and then was di[-]
vorced by him for adultery.

Raine nodded. "Lionel has a grand title."

Ann elaborated, "The Viscount Gormsley."

"Second, he is heir to his daddy's marquessate.'
Raine stuck up a second finger. "Your mama likes lot[s]
of land."

"Third," Ann said, "there is the matter of his
money."

"Of which," Gus declared, "there is a goodl[y]
amount."

Ann arranged her hood over her rosewood curls. "So we can assume Lionel is not pursuing you for your fortune."

Raine's sapphire eyes flashed with the perceptiveness which made her invaluable to her husband's political career. "Honey, we can safely say after looking at Lionel tonight that he sees beyond the blinding light of the five hundred thousand greenbacks Gus's papa has set aside for her groom."

"Imagine," Ann urged, "how much the interest alone is."

"Do you think," Gus insisted, "he cares for *me* alone?"

Ann's hazel eyes shimmered with concern. "What does your instinct say, honey?"

"I think Lionel is right for me, more so than any of the others I've liked."

"Of which," Raine made a circle with her thumb and forefinger, "there have been none."

Rhys and Gavin approached, and each claimed his wife.

"Are we done with the Tally?" Rhys asked, turning his wife in his arms and securing her cape around her throat.

"You knew about the Tally?" Gus was laughing.

Gavin draped an arm around Raine and hugged her to his side. "Sweetie, we've been in this family too long not to notice." That Gavin used the term *family* had them each grinning at all the others. Gavin continued, "So? What's the analysis? Does Lionel win the day—and the lovely damsel?"

Raine kissed her husband on his cheek. "He gets a high score. What do you and Rhys think? Shall we allow the man inside the gates?"

Rhys gazed down at his wife. "Your father lik
him. Gives him a sound financial rating."

"We know," Gus added, "he'll tell that to Daddy.
do want to marry a man both he and I like."

"We'll talk more tomorrow over luncheon abo
that," Ann promised. "Come early and we'll take t
afternoon to dissect Lionel's character completely."

"And exhume any Eldridge family skeletons
Raine added.

"Yes. Before Mama arrives in May," Gus vowe
"I've got to be ready for her. This year, she'll launch
full-scale attack to get me off the market."

When Veronica VanderHorn had arrived in Londc
last May to open her younger daughter's secon
season, the woman had insisted that Gus accept
man's proposal before June was out. Gus, she d
clared, was becoming more than a spinster. She w
becoming a subject of speculation. Therefore, sl
must marry soon to show that she had none of tl
deleterious qualities her sister Colleen exhibited.

Gus had obliged her mother by promptly receivir
two proposals of marriage. She accepted neither. H
mother had sailed for New York on July 1 in a hu
threatening to cut Gus's allowance, confiscate h
shares in her father's companies, and make her retur
to New York. Gus's father had saved the day b
refusing to follow his wife's edicts. He did, howeve
notify Gus that she was to fiancée herself to someor
this spring—or find her mother in permanent res
dence in London until she did take a husband. Th
possibility that Gus might have to endure living wit
her mother day in and out motivated Gus to find
least one suitable candidate for wedded bliss. Onl
Lionel Eldridge had emerged from the pack with h
ever-ready smile as his drawing card.

"Don't worry, honey," Raine soothed her, "we're going to help you."

Gus puckered her lips. *If you really want to do that, you could help me remain single.*

"Unfortunately," Ann said as if she had read Gus's mind, "opening your own fencing academy—"

"Or photography studio—" Raine interjected.

"Is not on your mama's list of acceptable pastimes," Ann concluded, as she tugged on her gloves. "Come tomorrow with your own list of reasons why Lionel is the right man."

"And that list," Raine continued, "should be short."

"Very," Ann insisted. "There is one reason only to marry him."

Do you love him?

Gus could. If she put her mind to it. She would begin tonight, before Ann and Raine raided it tomorrow.

She shooed them toward the door. "Go home, the four of you." She kissed them each good-night. Simpson, the butler, who had stood by during all this like a wooden statue, forbore Gus's intrusion on his duties. He locked the doors with a snick of rods and a flick of the key.

By the time Gus heard the clink as he deposited it in the silver bowl atop the reception table, she was climbing the stairs. She had enjoyed the evening, but she had fretted the entire time. A week ago, Colleen had promised to come here to see her tomorrow morning to visit. But a note from her, delivered by regular post in this afternoon's delivery, said she wouldn't arrive. Changes in plans were a normal occurrence for Gus's sister. Especially when Colleen was in the throes of an affair with a man.

Gus thrust open her door and sighed, sinking

against it as it clicked in the lock. She removed he
earbobs and reached around to undo two of th
covered buttons of her dinner gown. The silk sli
through her fingers like water, and the bodice gaped
She needed to be able to breathe when she rerea
Coll's letter. She must think clearly, because whateve
her sister planned, particularly with a lover, mear
Gus would deal with the dust Coll kicked up.

Gus didn't want Colleen to ruin her prospects wit
Lionel Eldridge. Lionel was the only eligible bachelc
who could make Gus's heart pound with his littl
jokes and his endearing blue-eyed winks. His kisse
accomplished something more extraordinary. The
made her want him physically. The way she ha
yearned for only one other man, who was forbidde
to her. Forbidden by law, custom—and a bitter pas
that Colleen had created without remorse.

She would not think of him. Lionel was the one sh
would concentrate on. She smiled.

She tossed her jewelry in the air, grabbed it, an
decided against pulling the bell rope for her maid. Sh
didn't want to talk with anyone. She needed to com
to terms with the fact that she had to marry thi
season. Or never.

She strode toward her fire and halted.

The sight of a man's greatcoat draped over he
chairs like a raven's wing startled her. But her recogni
tion of the initials tooled into the leather glove
calmed her.

Bryce. Her heartbeat picked up a faster tempo.

Bryce was here. But why was he in her bedroom
He had never acted rudely to anyone, including her

She was gazing into the flames, but she could swea
she felt his breathing. Inside her. Where she neve

wanted him to be. Where she had shut him out for five long years.

Why had he come here? In the middle of the night?

The voice of experience announced the cause.

Colleen. Of course.

What had her sister done now?

Gus turned about slowly. In the umber shadows cast by the gas lamps, she could detect his long legs in dark trousers. His hand, broad but finely boned, lay along the armrest. His gold signet ring hung heavy on his smallest finger. In this pose, he appeared the lord of all he surveyed. The twelfth earl of Aldersworth whom her sister Colleen had loved, married, and cuckolded as viciously as any shrew would gut a foe.

Gus walked toward him. Her heart banging against her ribs, she watched his breath expand his chest like bellows. She knew well this sign of his anger. "Bryce." She knelt before him. Took his hand. For a man who was hot-blooded, his skin was as cold as a dead man's. "Did Simpson let you in? He didn't tell us."

"I came in the servants' entrance."

"But why? Ann and Raine were here for dinner with Rhys and Gavin, and you could have joined . . ." He shifted, and she suddenly saw his face. ". . . us."

My God. In the past five years, she had seen Bryce Falconer happy, thoughtful, sad, enraged, but never like this. Never desolate.

"What's wrong?" she whispered, but didn't want to know. She recoiled at the horror she predicted was coming. What had happened? She pressed her palm to his cheek. He stopped breathing. "Oh, Bryce. What's the matter?"

In the crystal blue of his one good eye, insanity glittered. "Where's Colleen?"

"What?"

"You heard me."

Gus drew back. Bryce Falconer had never spoken t
her with animosity. "I don't think I—"

When she took her hand from his face, he seize
her wrist, and forced it to his thigh. Beneath h
flesh, she felt the corded tension of his. She ha
fantasized for months after she first met him
touching him so intimately, tracing his contours wit
her fingers . . . and her lips. But she had put tho
daydreams away when Colleen married him. Gu
told herself she thought of Bryce now exactly as h
did of her. As a friend.

"Don't pretend you don't know, Gussie."

She pulled farther away. "I'm not."

He dragged her forward, between his legs. "She tel
you everything." He was seething.

Her breasts, bare in the low-cut gown and barer sti
because she had loosened her bodice, rubbed acro
his smooth wool frockcoat. He caught her around th
waist and crushed her closer. Her skin slid along th
pebbly damask of his waistcoat and her sense of sme
roused to the enticing aroma of his sandalwoo
cologne. What frightened her was the way her bod
reacted to his—the way it always did.

He cupped her chin. "You know where she is. I ca
see it in your eyes." His own misted.

Her anger melted, but not her resolve to maintai
her role as friend to both her sister and her forme
brother-in-law. "Bryce, I've worked too long at carv
ing an impartial position for myself to give it up now
I don't know why you want to know where Colleen i
but you must realize that you cannot force the infor
mation out of me."

He cut her a look that warned she could try him to

far. But he swallowed hard and reconsidered as his gaze dropped to her mouth. His grip on her convulsed. Then it changed nature entirely, drifting from force to embrace. He brought her nearer and put his lips to her hairline. "God, I'm sorry, Gussie." He kissed her temple, and her eyes closed. She couldn't help herself as she nestled closer, her hands free and climbing around his shoulders.

You cannot do this. She pushed back. There was a limited amount of Bryce Falconer she could enjoy and remain sane. That meant staying out of his arms.

She rose to her feet. She headed into her sitting room and without asking, poured both of them a draught of cognac.

He had his head in his hands when she returned. She knelt again before him. When he did not move, she combed her fingers through his straight blond hair. "Drink this."

He raised his face and inspected hers. "How can the two of you be related?"

"We have qualities in common." She wrapped his fingers around the delicate glass.

He snorted. "Like what?"

We both adore you. "For every trait I'd list, you'd only refute me. Take a few sips of that. Come into the sitting room and get warm by the fire."

"I can't."

"Why not? You mustn't sit here. You're still frozen." He tried the Napoleon and shook his head no. She did not want to argue with him, but help him, whatever his troubles. "Did you come all the way from Aldersworth tonight?" She understood from Colleen that Bryce had taken Ford to his country estate before Christmas and had expected to remain in Northamptonshire until spring.

"Yes. I came as fast as I could." He took another sip.

"By train?"

"My coach."

"In this storm? The train would have been safer."

"It wasn't running. The rails were iced over. I had to see you tonight. My man made good time."

"Did you bring Ford?" She panicked. It wasn't like him to travel without his three-and-a-half-year-old son.

"No," he said above a hush. "I need your help Gussie."

Bryce was the only one who still called her Gussie. She bristled at the name which made her sound like the dart in a garment. "I will do whatever I can for you, Bryce. What has Colleen done?"

Gus knew some of Colleen's news from her note. Colleen had taken up with another rogue. An Irish poet. But that wouldn't send Bryce into such an agony. He was inured to Colleen taking lovers.

Bryce put his glass down. He laced his fingers together and slowly squeezed. His knuckles whitened as if in his viselike grip, he was strangling her sister.

He stared at Gus. "Colleen has kidnapped Ford, and she wants two million pounds sterling for his ransom."

Look for
Never Say Never
Wherever Paperback Books
Are Sold
Coming Soon from
Pocket Books